TABLE
For Two

TABLE
For Two

By
Sheryl C. S. Johnson

Covenant Communications, Inc.

Cover image: *Place Setting* © Cybernesco, courtesy iStockphoto.com.
Cover design copyright © 2012 by Covenant Communications, Inc.

Published by Covenant Communications, Inc.
American Fork, Utah

Copyright © 2012 by Sheryl C. S. Johnson
All rights reserved. No part of this book may be reproduced in any format or in any medium without the written permission of the publisher, Covenant Communications, Inc., P.O. Box 416, American Fork, UT 84003. This work is not an official publication of The Church of Jesus Christ of Latter-day Saints. The views expressed within this work are the sole responsibility of the author and do not necessarily reflect the position of The Church of Jesus Christ of Latter-day Saints, Covenant Communications, Inc., or any other entity.

This is a work of fiction. The characters, names, incidents, places, and dialogue are either products of the author's imagination, and are not to be construed as real, or are used fictitiously.

Printed in the United States of America
First Printing: July 2012

18 17 16 15 14 13 12   10 9 8 7 6 5 4 3 2 1

ISBN-13: 978-1-59811-979-4

BEFORE I WAS MARRIED, I dated my future husband in the temple every week. Each month we'd attend a sealing session, where I could be part of families being sealed together forever. Because my parents were divorced and at that time were not active in the church, I began worrying about my own eternity. How could I be sealed to a forever family? Even in my own genealogy, I was having problems reconciling families with divorces and remarriages. How did this all fit together? How could I ever fit into any kind of eternity if I couldn't be sealed to my own parents?

One month, as I was feeling particularly depressed about the problem, the temple sealer stopped his work, looked pointedly at me (though I hadn't said a word) and taught us about the family of God. I felt and knew that I was a daughter of God, He loved me, and I was part of *His* forever family. Suddenly, the problems I was having with my own genealogy dissolved. I realized I wasn't sealing together my family at all. It was *His* family.

I dedicate this book to my children and father so they will always know they are beloved spirit sons and daughters of a heavenly King who very much wants them sealed to Him for time and all eternity.

ACKNOWLEDGMENTS

I give special thanks to Brother Beckstead, Holly Johnson, Nancy Morrill, Lisa Owen, Samantha Van Walraven, and my own forever family. I thank my mother-in-law and father-in-law, Bryan and Judy, for teaching me about the love of family and fathers. I owe my mother, Carol, a special debt of gratitude for teaching me how God loves His children and for keeping my children alive while I've been absorbed in writing. I especially thank my husband, Benjamin, whom I love so much that I wonder if time and all eternity could ever be long enough.

TABLE OF CONTENTS

Chapter 1—*Fruit Punch*.................................... 1
Chapter 2—*A New Home*................................ 21
Chapter 3—*Let's Get to Work* 29
Chapter 4—*Ambush*.. 41
Chapter 5—*Sobering Valley*............................ 71
Chapter 6—*Fish*.. 91
Chapter 7—*Waiting*.. 99
Chapter 8—*The Right Pond* 107
Chapter 9—*Stolen Glory*............................... 109
Chapter 10—*Purple Sanctuary* 123
Chapter 11—*Leisurely Stroll*......................... 135
Chapter 12—*Gopher* 149
Chapter 13—*Ledgers and Raindrops* 153
Chapter 14—*Change of Scenery* 165
Chapter 15—*Boundaries*............................... 177
Chapter 16—*Zorro* 185
Chapter 17—*Cowbells* 205
Chapter 18—*Fish Bait* 211
Chapter 19—*Two Nuts*.................................. 227
Chapter 20—*Turkey Roast* 247
Chapter 21—*About Time*.............................. 255
Chapter 22—*Thornless Roses*....................... 259

CHAPTER 1
Fruit Punch

I WANDERED OUTSIDE TO WAIT for my ride. My car would be ready in two days—two sweet days and I'd be free of needing rides from Brad. I sighed and tucked an errant strand of blonde hair behind my ear. I wanted to feel more for him. After seeing so many of my friends get married, it felt like it was time for me to get married, even though I was only twenty-four. I pictured Brad's handsome face. I doubted myself and was beginning to think I had been holding my expectations too high. In recent weeks, I'd found myself imagining us married with children, because in my daydreams, the gnawing feeling that he just wasn't right for me was completely gone.

A hand on my shoulder brought me out of my frustrating meditation. Brad smiled at me. I wouldn't have been surprised if the clouds had broken open so a ray of sun could illuminate him with a heavenly glow. He *was* tall, dark, and handsome. That wasn't the problem.

"Jana, you okay? You look glum."

Just thinking about you, is what I wanted to say, but I still needed a ride, so I checked my tongue. "I had a hard day."

"Every day is a hard day here. You should quit."

I knew the rest of what he *wanted* to say. He'd actually said it a few times. He'd said it when college was hard. He'd said it when I was looking for a job. He wanted to say, "You should quit, marry me, stay home, have children, and live happily ever after." At least three times last week he'd told me how much his annual income was, no doubt trying to help me come to the conclusion that he was more than ready to financially support a family.

On the twenty-minute drive home, I pretended to be asleep so I wouldn't have to talk to him. The feeling of dissatisfaction was a thick fog in my head. I was coming home from a job I hated with a man I didn't really desire. The longer I dated Brad, the more controlling he became. We'd met in college after my mission. In the beginning, I was flattered that someone so unbelievably attractive would want me. I thought all my dreams had come true. He had a flare and style I had never known could exist: flowers, notes on my windshield in the mornings, phone calls every night. Baubles were strewn across my shelves. I was absolutely spoiled.

To a point, I'd accelerated with him, responding to the attention in the way he'd hoped. My heart had raced when he'd appeared at my door and each time he'd reached for my hand. But I'd hit my crescendo about the time he should have been proposing. The glitter of shiny things and the scent of roses grew commonplace. Our conversations felt more and more contrived as time went on. I began to back out of the relationship, realizing if I didn't, he'd pull another shiny thing out of his pocket—for my finger this time.

I blamed it on graduation. We both graduated at the same time, though his law degree made my bachelor's look like a plaything. I told him I needed space and began to take people up on offers to date their brothers and grandsons. My mother was mortified. To her, Brad was everything a young man should be and more.

He continued to ask me out once a week, keeping gifts to special occasions. For a while, I continued to accept his invitations for my mother's sake. Then I started earnestly trying to sever all contact with him. He talked himself out of all of the conversations so that at the end of each one, I felt like I was the Wicked Witch of the West and he was Dorothy. He'd argue his case until I actually left feeling a debt of gratitude toward him. It would take a few hours to wear off, and I'd realize I'd been bewitched by his cunning arguments again. That's what I got for dating someone who cross-examined people for a living.

I opened one eye and watched him drive. *Would it be so bad?* I bit my bottom lip. *Yes.* It *would* be that bad. I might fool myself into being happy for a while, but I would find a day when I discovered I'd cheated myself. Only this time, it would have eternal consequences.

* * *

"He called again." My mother greeted me at the door.

"Who called again?" I watched Brad walk down to the curb to pick up the newspaper.

"The long-distance mystery man. He left a number, just the same as yesterday. He said it was very important and begged me not to forget to give you the message." She swiped her dishcloth over the counter. Her short, grayish brown curls shook loosely as she concentrated on scrubbing a particular spot. "Why don't you call him and put me out of my misery. I'm dying to know who he is. The area code is out of town."

"It's probably a telemarketer."

"Just call him. If it is a telemarketer, tell him you're not interested." She triumphed over the spot she was scrubbing and looked up at me, her pale blue eyes pleading.

I picked an apple from the fruit bowl and studied the scrap of paper with the phone number on it. My mother had underlined the word *important* three times. With the apple crunching in my mouth, I drearily dialed the number. Mom was an irresistible entity. I knew she'd wear me down and I'd eventually end up calling anyway. It was easier not to resist her. My father often likened her to a tornado when she wanted something, no matter how small. She was persistent in her goals.

A sonorous voice answered. "Hello, Alex here." I could actually hear him smiling.

"Hello, this is Jana Barrowman. I received a message to call you."

"Miss Barrowman, thank you for returning my call. I am contacting you in response to a résumé we received awhile back. I would like to interview you for a position."

"I haven't sent out résumés for over a year." After graduation, I'd tried to find work in the art field, but I'd sent out so many résumés to so many places that I drew a blank on the two-oh-six area code.

"I need a creative consultant. Your résumé is at the top of our list."

"I actually have a job as a legal assistant now. I'm not a creative consultant anymore." I cringed to hear myself say it. My consulting career consisted of six blissful months at a décor store downtown. His list must have been pretty short if that had put me at the top. The doorbell rang, and my mother showed Brad to the kitchen. I exhaled, feeling the fog of dissatisfaction settling in on me again, weighing down my shoulders. "Where are you located?" I asked the stranger on the phone.

"I'm in Seattle. I know it seems far, but you were willing to come when you sent the résumé. I'm ready to set up an interview if you'll make the trip."

I was surprised. "I don't know if I'm in a position to travel that far for an interview right now."

"I'll fly you out here, pay for a rental car. I'll provide everything you need."

I heard a weird rustling sound on the phone and noticed my mother was gone.

I found her in the family room eavesdropping on the other line. When she noticed she was caught, she mouthed the words, "Do it."

"Mr.—uh, I didn't catch your name."

My mother was bouncing with impatience to hear me say yes.

"Alex Steadman."

"Mr. Steadman, can you hold for just a moment?"

"Take as long as you need."

Putting my hand over the phone, I pointed for my mother to set the other phone down on the receiver. "I don't want to go to Washington," I told her.

"Tell him you're coming, and I'll go. I haven't seen my cousin April in ages."

"I'm not lying to him. I don't even know how to do the job he has for me." I picked up the phone she had been using, gave Brad the just-a-minute sign as I walked by him, and took both phones to my bedroom.

"Mr. Steadman, are you there?"

"I'm here." He was laughing with a child in the background.

"Mr. Steadman, I'll be honest with you. I wasn't in the creative line of work for very long. It may not be worth the money to fly me out there."

"It's money I'm willing to spend." There was a short pause. "I need someone like you. My wife was starting a business a few years ago. That was her line of work. She started businesses and then sold them. She was starting a gift boutique when she was called away. I have all of her notes. She kept books full of pictures and plans. I have it all on paper. I just need someone to make it happen. I was looking through her things, and she had your résumé, your name circled. You are the one she wanted."

"Oh, I don't think I could start a whole business. That sounds like a big job. I know you probably want to surprise your wife, but I don't know if I can live up to her expectations. But if she wants to file a judgment, I'm her girl."

"Let me read this to you." He was *stubborn*. "Your résumé says, and I quote, 'If you have a vision, I have the talent to bring your vision to fruition. I can create what I can see.' Miss Barrowman, can you still do that?"

"Honestly, I don't know. I haven't tried in a long time." A pang of longing filled my breast. I could remember when I was that confident. Memories of creating made me hungry for it again.

"Could you do it before? When you wrote this? Could you do it?"

"I could have. I wouldn't have written it if I couldn't."

"All I'm asking is for you to take a little vacation to look at what we have. I can do the interview over a weekend."

I'd been thinking of polite ways to get off the phone when he said the word *vacation*. I *could* use a vacation. It wouldn't hurt anything for me to take a weekend to get out of town. The attorneys left at noon on Fridays anyway.

"I'll tell you what, I don't mean to be difficult, but if you give me two airline tickets so I can bring a family member, I'll meet with you." My mother would be beside herself with glee.

"Thank you, Jana Barrowman!" He said it as though I'd been called to the stage on *The Price Is Right*. I could hear the child in the background cheering. "If you're still on Bridgette Lane, I'll mail a packet out today. Is this weekend too soon?"

"No." I was surprised that he'd agreed. Maybe I should have pushed for a few tickets to Disneyland too.

* * *

I couldn't sleep after a long day at work and another torturous date with Brad. I swung my legs over the side of the bed and decided I could sleep on the plane. My sweet tooth wanted ice cream.

The kitchen light was on. My father sat at the table, reading the paper. He looked over his glasses at me. "Honey!" He held his arms out to me. "Where's my hug?" My dad, Stanford Barrowman, stood six feet tall exactly. He had a thick mane of silver hair and was fit for his age. At five-foot-six, I felt dwarfed by my father as I disappeared into his hug. I had been a surprise baby for my then-forty-year-old parents, who were now sixty-four years old. I was the youngest of five children. My parents loved having me home, but they were anxious to have me married so I could know the happiness they had. They would tell me this every Monday night as they bore their testimonies at family home evening. I felt like a failure every time they mentioned it.

"How was your date? Did anything special happen?"

"Yeah, I ordered dessert."

"That wasn't what I expected you to say." My father looked concerned. "I thought he might ask you something special tonight."

I drizzled chocolate syrup over my ice cream before fishing in the drawer for a spoon. "I'm glad he didn't. I wouldn't have said yes. Besides, you know I don't feel like Brad's the one for me."

"Who is for you, Jana?" He put down the newspaper and gave me his full attention. It was going to be one of *those* talks.

I sighed heavily and sank into a chair across from him. "I don't know. Maybe there's no one. Maybe I'm just one of those girls who isn't meant to get married." Why he was disappointed was beyond me. I knew full well he didn't care for Brad.

"I've been thinking about this. I don't want to pry too much, but I do want to tell you what I told the young ladies when I was bishop." He leaned back in his chair, taking a paper and pen from the counter. At the top he wrote, "What Jana wants." "Now, pumpkin, if you don't know what you want, you're never going to find the right man. You need to decide what you want before God will send him to you. So you write down here what you want."

I took the pen and wrote, "My dad."

He smiled. "Let's be more specific. You want someone like me? I'm flattered. What do you like about me?"

"Well, you honor your priesthood . . . You're not ornery . . . You're honest . . . You are willing to give service . . . You work hard . . . I have fun with you . . . You treat me with respect . . . Never condescending." I wrote as I spoke. "You served a mission . . . I just know you'll do what's right whatever happens . . . I like to talk to you . . . You're the perfect height for hugging . . . You keep the commandments, even the small ones . . . You follow the prophet." I flipped the paper over. "I like the way you dress . . . I like how you call Mom when you're away from home . . . You've always shared your popcorn with me when mine runs out."

My father put his hand down on the paper. "I see why you're not married. I'm too perfect." He laughed.

He looked tired. He'd gotten home late from the temple again, and I said, "Let me ask you this: if the temple is full of sweet old people like you, why do they keep it open so late? Don't they know you need your rest?"

"There are more important things than rest going on there, and you know it. I spent a half hour on the lawn today talking a sweet eighty-year-old sister into being sealed to her deceased husband so she could be sealed to her children. 'No one told me I had to be sealed to my husband to get my kids. I spent enough time with him here. Why would I want him for all eternity?' She finally did it for her kids. She wanted her kids forever. But I tell you, I laughed all the way home. You should have seen the look of shock on her face when she realized she'd be sealed to him."

"Well, he must not have been much of a husband if she didn't miss him."

"Can't say. Maybe he was, and she was just used to being alone. Never know what people have been through. Can't tell."

It was just like my dad to refuse to judge anyone. I pulled the paper toward me and wrote as I said, "Nonjudgmental."

* * *

The plane trembled from turbulence. I looked out the window but could only see clouds where the pilot said Seattle was. In just a few minutes we'd be able to stretch our legs and move around again. I was stiff and sore from sleeping upright on the two-hour flight from Salt Lake City. I held the manila envelope with the maps and gift certificates. This Alex Steadman must have really wanted my services. There was a two hundred and fifty dollar gift certificate to a restaurant named Shallots, another certificate for a day spa, and BMW rental car information.

My mother stretched beside me and pushed her book into her bag. "I say we pick up April and take her to lunch. She says she's been dying to go to Shallots but couldn't because it was too expensive. Well, now she can afford it because it's on us."

"Who knows, maybe it's so expensive that two hundred fifty is only enough for soup and salad," I said.

We both laughed.

* * *

I looked around to see if we were disturbing anyone with our loud laughter. The lunch crowd was thin at Shallots. I liked my cousin April. She was a year younger than my mother but as hip as any sixty-three-year-old woman could be. When she grinned, her cheeks gathered up into girlish flesh under eyes that sparkled in mischievous merriment. I usually only saw her at funerals in Utah. This was a treat.

I hadn't been excited about Seattle or the boutique until April was. She was contagious. Her dyed, reddish-blonde hair turned gray about three inches from the roots. It came to her shoulders in a course, bumpy perm. She was wearing a bright floral shirt and fuchsia pants. Her clothing was the brightest thing in the restaurant. Shallots was trimmed with dark woods and jewel-toned fabrics.

Before my mother could stop laughing at yet another humorous story, April pointed a finger adorned with a chunky ring at me. "When are you going to settle down? You can't play the field forever. The worst day married is better than the best day single. That's what my Frank always said."

Frank had died five years ago. I searched her face for grief but didn't see any. My mother's lips were set tightly against her teeth as her eyes narrowed to look at me accusingly. She knew Brad was ready to marry me as soon as I said go.

"I'm just waiting for Mister Right. If you see him, send him my way." I tried to laugh, but the strangled sound that escaped my throat wreaked of desperation to turn to another topic.

April sensed my paranoia and broke into another humorous story about a man named Harlow who her father wouldn't let her marry because he wore his hair too slick. Soon my mother was laughing again. It was easy to see why she and April got along so well. Though my mother lacked April's enthusiasm, they both had a childlike joy to them. They had the same twinkle in their eye that said they knew some special, wonderful secret that lit them up. My mother seemed ten years younger when she was with April. Before we were finished with our salads, my face hurt from smiling so much.

April ordered roast duck and shallots. My mother ordered the veal. I wanted something unlike anything I'd had before. For these prices, I'd better get it. I ordered butternut raviolis in cream sauce. The food was not disappointing. We all shared bites, and I found myself wishing I'd ordered the duck. It practically melted in my mouth.

Before we left, a young man with dark hair and an apron approached us. He pulled a chair over from a nearby table and straddled it, facing us. "How was your food tonight, ladies?" The hair on top of his head had a slight curl to it and threatened to hang over his eyes; the rest of it was shorter, though still a little shaggy. His apron and the disarray of his hair expressed that he'd been working hard in the kitchen.

April spoke up, stammering, "It . . . it's . . . it's you. I didn't know you'd actually be here. Oh, you look just like your picture."

The man nodded modestly, keeping his eyes calm. He was used to being recognized.

April picked up her napkin and motioned to him. "He, he writes. He writes the column. Oh, the best recipes. I haven't cried when I've cut an onion in months. He's wonderful. He knows everything." Then, turning to the chef, she asked, "Could you . . . would it be wrong for me to ask for a recipe?" She was bouncing a little with excitement.

"It depends on the recipe. I share some. Which did you want?"

"The butternut cream sauce. Could you? I understand if it's too much." By now April was like a school girl, all a titter.

The chef pulled a dessert menu out of a passing waiter's apron pocket and took the pen April had waiting. He scrawled the recipe out in the margin.

"Sign it," she commanded then, catching herself, added, "I mean, could you please autograph it? It is so good to meet you," she gushed.

He smiled. "It's good to meet you too. I'm happy you enjoyed your meal." He stood, making a special point of shaking my mother's hand warmly, eliciting a flicker of jealousy on April's face. He started to walk away then stopped and turned back, fixing me with a searching gaze. I shifted in my seat and awkwardly studied my glass. When I hazarded a glance up, he'd disappeared.

The whole trip was worth it just to see April so happy about meeting the "Master Chef," as she called him. I'd have to thank Mr. Steadman.

"Oh, look at that," April whined. "You're not going to have time to drop me off now and make it to your meeting."

"We'll take you with us," my mother assured April, putting an arm around her cousin. "We can go to the spa while Jana's at her interview." She fished in her purse and pulled out the gift certificates to wave in front of April's face.

April's eyes lit up with greedy delight. I was jealous as I calculated how much time an interview would take and when the flight home would leave. I wouldn't be going to the spa anytime soon. I sighed and said, "I hope this interview is worth it."

"I thought you didn't want this job." April eyed me suspiciously.

"Maybe I do. I won't know until I see what he needs." It was amazing what a good lunch with a positive energy like April's could do for a person's outlook.

* * *

A block away from our destination, I noticed a black Honda following us. When I parked in front of a two-story home, the black car parked behind me, and the chef got out. I automatically checked for my purse, thinking he must have chased us to give us something we'd left at the restaurant. Maybe our gift card wasn't good after all.

April piped up. "Alex, what are you doing here?" She bounded out of the car, her face alight.

"Alex?" I asked, shutting the car door.

"I have a meeting with Mrs. Barrowman," the chef said, motioning toward my mother.

My mother nodded toward me. "You have a meeting with my daughter, Jana."

"Ah, Jana." He looked at me appraisingly. "You are younger than I imagined. Let's make introductions and clear up this confusion." He extended a hand. "Hello, Jana Barrowman, *I* am Alex Steadman." His focused regard for my mother in the restaurant now fell entirely to me.

His handshake was firm but not painful. I looked at him carefully for the first time. He hadn't been important to me at the restaurant, but he was now. He had hazel eyes, a wide jaw, and a dimple on his right cheek when he smiled. He looked a little less overworked without his apron, and he was about as tall as my father. He could have been April's son for all the happy mischief I saw in his eyes at the moment.

I tried to match his gaze with as much humor in my eyes. "This is my mother, Abigail, and you've met my cousin April." At the end of the introduction, I hoped he hadn't thought I was staring him down, but he so obviously wouldn't blink or look away from my eyes that I didn't want him to think I would shy away from a challenge.

"It is good to meet all of you. This is going to take a few hours. Shall we?" He motioned to his front door, finally shifting his gaze.

I looked at my mother and April, imagining them blissfully fanning themselves with umbrella-garnished lemonades while someone filed their toenails. "I'll be up in a moment," I told Alex. I turned to my companions and hugged each of them. "I'm a little jealous. Have some fun for me. I'll call you when we're done here."

"I wish you could go too," my mother said.

"When I get out of this meeting, it will be time to go back to Shallots, and I probably won't feel like going to the spa after dinner. I'll be full and sleepy. Use the certificates so they don't go to waste."

I watched them drive away then turned to look down the street. All of the homes were attractive. The smell of ocean air wafted from behind the houses. I walked up the steps and rang the doorbell.

Alex answered. "I *am* sorry about that," he said. "I assumed it was your mother I was meeting with. I had no idea . . ." He trailed off. His eyes were still laughing, and it bothered me.

"My mother will tease me about that when we get home."

"Come in and have a seat. I'll get the papers."

I sat down on a brown leather sofa. The room was mismatched, as though no one had gotten around to decorating it. Boxes sealed with tape were stacked in the corner. A large bay window let in ample light and a view of the enormous trees outside.

A little girl with long brown hair came shyly into the room. She clung to the doorway and stared at me. "Well, hello there." I smiled brightly. "What's your name?"

"Elise."

"Hi, Elise. How old are you?"

"I'm six." She smiled shyly. "Did my daddy bring you here? Are you Jana?"

"I am."

"Can you really build Mommy's store?"

"I don't know. That's why I'm here. We're going to find out if I can."

"If you can, can I work there?"

I laughed. "I don't know. We'll have to see. Besides, that would be your mommy and daddy's choice, not mine." I didn't want Elise to think I was making any promises.

"My mommy would let me."

"That is good to hear. What's your favorite color?"

Elise was listing all of her favorite colors when Mr. Steadman returned with his arms full of scrapbooks.

"Here it is. I need you to sift through these and tell me what you think. I have the building. It's just next door. We bought the two houses together so she could work close to home." The humor was gone from his eyes, and he seemed all business.

He set the enormous scrapbooks on the coffee table. I flipped the first one open. It was a picture of a house. Under it was a sketch of the same house with a sign over the door and a larger sign on the front lawn. The name of the store was Sheer Pleasures.

I excused myself to stand outside with the scrapbook so I could look at the store from the front. I really didn't think I could build a business, but I thought I'd better give him my honest opinion after he'd flown me all the way out here. To my surprise, he followed and stood behind me silently while I compared the scrapbook with reality. I sat down on the grass, facing the house. The sketches were better than real life. Mrs. Steadman had put shutters and gingerbread work on the outside of the house. There were flower beds in her sketch and a driveway with a More Parking in Back sign.

"I can't do some of these things."

"What can't you do?" The way he said it sounded as though he thought I was capable of anything.

"I would need contractors to put in the driveway, parking, and woodwork. I could make the sign. I would need someone to cement it in. Then the flower beds, I *could* do that. Do you want me to *make this* make this? Do you want me planting flowers?"

"I can get contractors for you. You just tell me what you need."

"These are costly additions. Are you willing to spend the money?"

"Money isn't a problem. Can you do it?"

"I can do the outside. How long do we have before your wife gets back?"

"Vanessa died a year ago."

I turned to look at him. "I'm sorry."

He didn't show any emotion. "You would be working with these." He pointed to the scrapbooks. "They are full of her ideas for the business. She was getting ready to build it when we discovered the cancer. She kept working on it, hoping she would be here to finish it. She never believed she wouldn't make it, until the end when she posted the job notice with the employment agency." His eyes were far away.

I didn't know what to say. I wanted to look closer at everything now. It seemed nobler to do something for a woman who had died than it did for a living soul. "Why are you finishing the business now? Are you going to sell it?"

"Elise. I want Elise to know something more of her mother." Now a hint of emotion played across his face. "I want Vanessa to feel closer for Elise, for both of us." He looked at me with a soft expression.

"Can I see inside?" I gathered the scrapbook.

"Yes." He pulled keys out of his pocket. "And that's another thing. When you decide to take the job, there is an apartment upstairs so you won't have to commute."

When I decided to take the job? He was pretty confident.

"I had the building zoned commercial. That was a headache, but everyone knew Vanessa, and they knew about the cancer. I know they wouldn't have done it otherwise. There are other businesses north of here on this same road, and the residents aren't happy about the traffic. Any road like this that goes anywhere is going to have traffic. It's the only way to the beach." A digital tune came from his pocket, and he pulled out a cell phone. Holding up a finger to me, he said, "I'm sorry. I have to take this one." He handed me the keys and walked to the street to talk.

The house was a quaint, two-story structure. The wallpaper was peeling. At first I noticed the shaggy old carpet and dings in the walls, but then I started thinking about changing it into a shop. How could I do that? I thought of the different things I could put in it but had the feeling that my ideas weren't for this house. I walked upstairs to see the three-bedroom apartment. There was a kitchenette and modest bathroom with a claw-foot tub. It smelled like an antique shop. I wrinkled my nose, hoping I could get used to it. I went downstairs and sat on the living room floor, facing away from the bay window. I opened the scrapbook. The main floor was small, with a counter separating the kitchen from the living room. The scrapbook showed a cash register on the counter and the kitchen as a storage area.

Vanessa's ideas were better than mine. As I turned the pages and studied the pictures I found myself nodding my head in agreement. There were several sketches that had been crossed out. They were wrong for the house. I felt it instinctively. Page after page had me thinking, *I could do this. I know how to make that. This is a piece of this and an edge of that.* Vanessa had abundant pictures of the shop's inventory. Almost all of it was like what I'd seen in Utah craft shops. There had to be people who would buy these products. Sheer Pleasures was a store I would have wandered into for ideas. And usually, if I wandered into a store for ideas, I'd inevitably wander out with a bagful of those ideas.

Footsteps in the kitchen startled me. Elise peeked around the corner. "Hi. You gonna do it?"

"I still don't know. How did you get in here?"

"I come here all the time. Come see."

I left the scrapbook on the floor with my purse and followed Elise to the kitchen. She opened the back door. We walked no more than fifteen steps into the backyard before I found myself standing in the Steadman's kitchen. "Wow," was all I could say. The houses were closer together than I'd thought.

"Isn't it great? And when it rains, you hardly have to get wet. But I like to get wet in the rain." Elise lifted her head to face the ceiling, as though ready for raindrops on her face.

The kitchen was gigantic. The dark granite countertops were higher than normal. I felt miniature next to them. Dark oak cupboards towered over me. I'd never be able to reach the top shelf or the second to top or the third, for that matter.

"There you are." Alex's voice startled both of us. He was carrying my purse and the scrapbook. "I thought you'd vanished like a ghost. I see Elise got ahold of you." He put the items on the counter and offered me a stool. "What do you think?"

"It's the most beautiful kitchen I've ever been in."

"Thank you, but what do you think about the shop?" His dimple deepened. His gaze swept the room, looking down at the floor before thick lashes carried his eyes back to mine. "Can you do it?" The humor was back in his face.

"It isn't a matter of whether or not I can do it. I know I could. I would have to make a lot of life changes to be available for the project. That's my only reservation. If this were in Utah, it would be a different story."

Alex checked his watch. "It's almost time for dinner. Why don't I cook us something here."

"We're going to Shallots to eat dinner."

"That dump?" He laughed. "I can do better than that. I hear the owner is a real cad."

I had to admit, April would be overjoyed to eat at the Master Chef's table. "That sounds nice. Thank you." Elise bounced off down the hallway. The echo of a video game wasn't far behind her. "Do you own Shallots?" I smiled. "Are you the cad?"

"I don't really think I'm a cad, no. But I guess it depends on who you listen to or what paper you read. The public thinks what it wants to, despite reality."

"Are you the owner?"

He swept a hand towel over the counter. "That, I am."

I traced my finger over the specks in the countertop as he chopped vegetables for lasagna. Watching his hands fly with the knife made me nervous, so I stopped watching them. I had the overwhelming desire to take the knife away from him before he chopped off a digit. I glanced at his face as he worked. It was serene. I grimaced when I asked, "Is there anything I can help with?"

He must have heard the hope that there wasn't because he declined with a shrug. "It's faster if I do it myself. It won't take long." I felt like the five-year-old who wanted to hold the hand mixer when her mother made cookies. He was right. It was faster his way. I looked down at his hands and then quickly away. He noticed and talked to me without watching the knife. "It bothers you?" He raised an eyebrow. I held my breath, waiting for him to look at his moving hands.

I bit my bottom lip. "It's a little disconcerting. Do you ever miss?"

He looked at his hands again, and I couldn't help sighing with relief. "Don't you trust me?" he asked.

"I don't know you. How can I trust you?" I laughed. The corner of his mouth turned up in silent amusement. I wished I could read his mind. What could anyone be that constantly amused about?

He didn't answer my question. He turned to slide minced onions and garlic into a sauce pan. I was sure if I measured the tiny cubes they'd be nearly uniform in size. My eyes watered slightly. He pulled a bag of tomatoes toward him. "You laugh a lot. It sounds like wind chimes," he told me.

"What would make you say that?"

He shrugged. The knife was flying over the tomatoes, and I realized I'd never had lasagna made with fresh tomatoes before. No can of tomato paste here. "I watched you at the restaurant," he admitted.

"You knew who we were? Why didn't you tell us you were Mr. Steadman?"

"*Mr. Steadman* is my father. I wish you'd stop that. My name is Alex. I thought you knew who I was. Your aunt knew me."

"She's my cousin. She said you were the *Master Chef*." I studied the granite again. "I don't usually laugh so hard. April is . . . entertaining."

He set down the knife and studied my face. His eyes were full of mirth again. The kitchen was quiet, and I felt like running away. "I thought it was your mother. I waited all afternoon. I suppose it was just a lucky guess that I found your table. I was sure I was talking to the right lady."

I blinked and looked away to hide my smile. "Anytime someone can confuse me with my mother, I'm flattered. She's quite a woman."

"I'm sure she is." He picked up the knife and busied himself by scraping escaping pieces of onion into the sink. "What do you think? Will you take the job?"

"I don't know." I was worried because building Sheer Pleasures was a big job. I didn't know anything about running a business, but I was confident that I could copy Vanessa's ideas.

I would miss my father. If I was being completely honest with myself, that was the only thing that would hold me in Utah. The choice was between telling Alex no, after all he'd done to get me out there, or turning my life upside down to take a chance. This would change everything. No law office day in and day out. I smiled and pulled a receipt and a pen out of my purse to start writing a pros and cons list. It was one of my father's favorite ways to make hard choices. I drew a minus as I lamented being away from him.

Alex pulled a pad of paper out of a drawer and handed it to me. "You don't have to write on that. Here, take this."

I took the pad and looked at the blank page. "Mr. Steadman—"

"Alex," he corrected.

"Alex, if you can make a restaurant like Shallots, why would you need someone to tell you how to build another business?"

"Did you see my wife's notes? I don't know the first thing about fluffy female shops. I know food. I studied food. I can sell food. I'd be lost picking out doilies and flowers. This just isn't down my alley. I need help." He started pulling cooking utensils out of a drawer. He snipped some leaves from a plant on the windowsill. "I have a great collection of wine. Does your aunt prefer any certain kind?"

"She's my cousin, and no wine. She's a Mormon. We're all Mormons."

He set down a cutting board and looked at me as though he were seeing an animal he'd never come across before. It was a long awkward moment before he said anything. "Right. I see. Utah. Mormons. I get it. You're really Mormons? I've never met a Mormon."

"Have you been to Utah?"

"I ski in Utah, in Park City."

"Then you've probably met lots of Mormons and just didn't know it."

"So if Mormons don't drink wine, what do they drink?"

"Anything but alcohol, coffee, and tea." I watched him smile at the hard lasagna noodles in his hand. Before he could say anything I continued. "We do drink just about everything else—juice, soda, and herbal teas."

"Are you vegetarians?"

"No, just no alcohol, coffee, and tea. Are you sure you don't want us to just go to Shallots?"

"No. Stay. I want to cook for you and your family here. Your cousin likes me, remember?"

"I'm surprised you noticed." I raised my eyebrows in innocent sarcasm. "April said you write for the paper?"

"I write a cuisine column, a few recipes and techniques every week. I guess she's a fan."

He let me sketch out my pros and cons list in silence for a while. Every now and then he'd look over my shoulder, so I began to write in code. By the time I pushed the paper away, the kitchen smelled like basil and oregano. "Am I the first one you've interviewed?" I asked.

"The very first."

"Doesn't that bother you? I mean, there may be dozens of people more qualified than I am to do the job."

"Vanessa wanted you. I want you." He looked up from the sauce he was stirring when he said it.

"I must have sent out some fantastic résumé."

"Not as good as the real thing, I'm sure." His look was admiring.

I tried to study the walls as I pushed down a blush. No, I definitely couldn't work for him. Suddenly, I wanted to run, screaming, back to my boss at the law firm. Nice, safe, old, married, fatherly Larry.

When Alex announced that dinner was ready and we sat down to eat, I decided he must have been a waiter in a previous life because no cup was left empty for more than a second. Luckily, he had some fruit punch on hand that Elise claimed was hers. I was sure it was the first time the Master Chef had ever served adults fruit punch with dinner. I considered myself a connoisseur of lasagna because it was the food of choice for every family party, and this lasagna was the best I'd ever had.

During dinner, April grew friendly with Alex. She regaled him with her stories, and he laughed in all the right places. I tried not to laugh. I wasn't sure if the sound of wind chimes was a good thing. April drilled him about cooking. My mother and I were content to watch her on what seemed like Christmas Day for a child. This was better than any stocking stuffer, anything we could have wrapped for her.

I was impressed with Alex. He was very good to her. Maybe he thought that was how he could win me over. Even as I sat sipping fruit punch, I knew I couldn't leave Utah. I loved my family. I wasn't ready to be that far away from my father. I made my choice as I speared a piece of lettuce in my salad bowl. Yes, I *could* do this, and no, I wasn't going to. Now I just had to tell the chef.

I helped him clear the table while Elise showed my mother and April the apartment next door. "Mr. Steadman," I began, not knowing what I'd say next. "Thank you for . . ."

"Alex. My name is Alex." He turned away from the sink and smiled warmly at me. "My father's name is Mr. Steadman," he reminded me again. Drying his hands, he asked, "Now, can you do it? Can you create Sheer Pleasures?"

"After looking at everything, the question is not *can I do it*. Of course I can do it. It would be hard to leave my family. This is so far away." He stared at me, and it felt like his eyes pierced me. My stomach became queasy. He was handsome in a different way from Brad. He had a natural attractiveness that wasn't contrived. I wished I wasn't noticing it at the moment.

"You want to," he said. "You want to do this. You aren't happy as a legal assistant. No one who can do what you say you can do would be happy filing papers all day. You *will* be happy here. And it wouldn't be forever, just until the business is going. However, I do need an answer." He walked over to me. "Jana Barrowman, will you try? Will you make it happen?"

I wasn't going to turn my life upside down to do favors for some complete stranger in a different state. It was too much to ask, even if his wife was dead. It would feel wonderful to be able to create, but I had a career to think of. If I took this job, I would have to start all over in the real world when I was done. His eyes held mine again, and I tried not to flinch. I formed a solid, strong, and unwavering no in my mind before I said it. I was surprised to hear "I'll do it" come out of my mouth.

He was smiling before I realized the words had been my own. The sound of footsteps was getting closer as the others came up the walk. He plucked up Elise when she returned. "She's going to do it."

"Hurray!" Elise was bouncing in her father's arms. "I knew she would. I knew she would."

My mind raced. How was I going to tell him now with everyone watching? I opened my mouth to speak but closed it, not trusting it after its recent betrayal.

April spoke up. "That's right, girl. Why don't you stay awhile? You can't get better than working for the Master Chef. I'll help you get settled."

My mother looked at me with obvious astonishment.

Alex was full of gratitude. He and April talked about me getting settled. I sat down heavily at the table, and Elise flung herself onto my lap, chattering about paper birds she knew how to make. I put my arms around her waist and tried to think of some way to get out of this. Alex watched me from the corner of his eye while he talked with April and my mother.

We stayed for another half hour, arranging details until it was time to drive April home. Alex helped me into the car and whispered, "You won't be sorry. Don't worry about it. Easy as one, two, three."

I repeated the words in my head. *One, two, three.* It was like he knew I hadn't meant to take the job. His eyes weren't mirthful anymore. He looked tired.

I smiled nervously. "Sure."

* * *

On the way to April's house in Bellevue, I told them what had happened and how terrible I felt.

April looked back at me. "Now, girl, sometimes God helps us say things we can't say ourselves. You're supposed to be here. That's the Holy Ghost working. Who knows but this little family needs someone like you to help them out of a bad spot." And then, as though she hadn't said anything to me at all, she went back to telling stories to my mother.

I knew God was better than that. He wouldn't have to go digging three states away to find someone to help a family. I bit my lip. Maybe I *was* supposed to be in Washington. I had to admit that something had intervened. I had not been in control of my mouth when I'd said I'd do it. Hadn't someone else's words slipped through my lips? Maybe the words my father whispered to me the first night I came home from my mission were true. *A mission never ends.*

CHAPTER 2
A New Home

Brad returned from carrying another suitcase out to the car. He sat down on the couch. "You must have cement in those bags. I feel sorry for you when you have to get them out to the taxi."

"Mr. Steadman is picking me up. I'm sure he'll help." I had to smile. He was right; the luggage was heavy. My mother had packed several of the suitcases. I wasn't even sure what was in them.

Mom hefted a duffle onto the table. "Why don't you just put your purse in here?"

As I put my purse in the bag, I couldn't help wishing Brad would disappear so I could say a private good-bye to my mother. As if on cue, he volunteered to shift the luggage around in the car to make more room for the duffle.

"I always knew I'd see you leaving here with that boy someday," my mother quipped.

"Very funny. Leaving with Brad, and off I go to another man." I hadn't meant it to sound like anything other than a joke, but she latched on to it right away. When she raised her eyebrows and stared, I added, "You know I'm kidding. I'm going to miss everyone. It won't feel like I have a family. It's too far away."

"We'll e-mail. You can make a new family." After a hug, she coaxed me toward the door.

"Mom, I'm going to work, not to get married."

"He's handsome, that chef. You could do worse."

"He's not Mormon."

"How do you know? He looks like he could be."

"I know he looks like it, but he's not. I'm not interested anyway. Besides, he didn't show any interest." I pointed at her. "Not that it would matter if he had."

My mother wouldn't be deterred. "Well, it's a whole new ward, isn't it? New men. Maybe you'll find one you like."

I felt a little disconcerted about being booted out the door with so little feeling. "Maybe I would if I were shopping for a man. I'm going there to work, not shop. Call me if anything happens. I wish Dad could have been here. When he gets home, give him this for me." I hugged and kissed her.

"Call us when you get settled."

Brad had the car idling. He talked nonstop about work for a half hour while we were stuck in traffic. He surprised me by saying, "You know, I might have actually missed you if we'd been spending more time together."

I didn't know what to make of his comment and decided to just nod my head like I'd taken it in good humor.

"I've wanted to talk to you for a while. I need to tell you that while you're gone, I'm going to date other women." He paused—a little too dramatically—and waited for me to say something. When I didn't, he went on. "Are you not attracted to me? Don't you find me attractive?" His voice was filled with frustration.

"You're attractive. I mean, you're handsome, a good-looking guy."

He nodded his head. He had known he was handsome. "Am I boring?"

"No. You're very interesting."

"I don't know what it is about you. You drive me crazy. But it has to stop. Right now is perfect because you're leaving anyway." He paused for a moment. "Jana, I've been chasing you . . ." Assuming I was surprised at his words, he went on without looking at me. "Yes, I said *chasing you*, for a year. That means you're running from me. I don't know why. Maybe you're not ready to commit. I'm not sure. But I have got to get on with life. I thought we could have something great, you know, but you're just not showing up for this relationship."

I wanted to say, "*Oh really?*" in mock surprise but decided to keep my mouth shut.

"I'm ready. You can quit working. I'll support you. We can start a family. I'm ready, but I'm not even going to ask you. Even now I feel like I might as well be alone."

This was a very calculated talk, considering it was weighing the importance of my romantic future. But I noticed it was missing important elements, such as the word *love*. And I noticed what was there, such as the word *crazy*. I drove him crazy. Somehow, I'd never dreamed of driving a man crazy. Sarcastically, I wondered what woman would want a man to *love* her when she could have one who was *crazy* about her. Did crazy last as long as love?

He parked the car at the airport. I cocked my head and looked at him thoughtfully. He pulled me close and kissed me like he never had before. My eyes widened in surprise, then I closed them and, for the first time that day, focused all of my attention on him. It was, after all, most likely our last kiss. His lips were warm, and I was suddenly dizzy.

He stroked my cheek with his thumb and looked deep into my eyes. "Now take that with you to Seattle and know if you decide you're ready to show up for it, it will be waiting here for you—but not for long." He didn't say much more as he helped me load luggage onto a cart and wheel it into the airport. I watched him curiously and tried again to remember that he was a manipulative Jim Dandy. The kiss kept pressing in on my mind. It had left a mixed feeling of euphoria and assault. As I watched him walk out of the airport, I noticed several female heads turn his direction. However sorry he was to lose me, he wouldn't have to be sorry for long.

* * *

"I bet you're hungry." Alex was a complete gentleman when he met me at the gate. He paid an attendant to load my luggage into the car. I was grateful because by the time I landed in Seattle, I had a hideous headache. Massaging the bridge of my nose didn't alleviate the pressure but I couldn't help myself.

"I don't think I could eat. I have this headache . . ."

"Headache? I do headaches. I can fix that." He pulled out his wallet and left me standing by the curb, watching the man arrange luggage in the trunk. I didn't care where Alex went. The headache was throbbing and making me nauseous. I sat down on a nearby bench.

He returned with a can of soda. He produced a bottle of ibuprofen from the glove box. Shaking out a few pills, he said, "Take all of these and drink most of this, and we'll have you up and about in thirty minutes."

"Thank you." The world was swimming in front of me. Within a few short moments, my stomach calmed. Soda was the last thing in the world I would have taken when I felt so bad, but it worked. Soon I was asleep in the car as he drove.

When I opened my eyes, we were parked in front of the Sheer Pleasures house, and Alex had his hand on my wrist. I blinked, willing my body to wake up. "I'm sorry. I must have drifted off. I don't remember driving here. I don't remember leaving the airport." I imagined my head lolling off to one side, mouth open, a snore escaping, and wondered what Alex had seen.

"How's the headache?"

It was almost gone. "Wow, a bottle of pop and a few pills. Who would have known? I feel a lot better."

"Do you get headaches a lot?"

"No, almost never. I used to get them when I had finals in college, but that's about it."

"So it's stress related. It is stressful to pack up life and move, especially with a family as close as yours." The reminder that I was leaving my family stung. I nodded, avoiding his eyes. I pulled a duffle from the backseat and walked past him to wait at the door.

He met me with luggage in both arms. He set the luggage down, fished in his pocket, and handed me a key ring with three keys on it. "I need you to fill out some paperwork so I can pay your taxes and have you on record as an employee, unless you want to be an independent contractor."

"I can fill out the paperwork today."

He set the last of the luggage down in the living room and left to check on Elise. I found the upstairs apartment furnished and ready to live in. The furniture was new. The mattress on the bed was still covered in plastic, and a package of sheets was sitting on the edge. I could smell the new furniture and the old house at the same time. I'd have to buy a scented candle soon.

The doorbell rang, and I hustled downstairs to answer it. Alex stood on the doorstep holding a large shopping bag. "I didn't know what you'd like, but I thought you'd need a blanket. We're having dinner at six if you're hungry by then. I have to run to the restaurant to finish up some things. If you need anything, here's my cell number."

The house was eerily silent when I closed the door. His business card had a little whisk printed on it. I leaned against the door and stared at the empty living room. I closed my eyes and visualized Mrs. Steadman's shop—Vanessa's shop—Sheer Pleasures. I could see the counters, shelves, and displays. Every nook and cranny would be stuffed with treasures. It was simple in my mind, but when I opened my eyes, the task of creating it felt enormous.

* * *

I opened the comforter set Alex had bought me. It wasn't the blanket I'd expected. The burgundy jacquard fabric with satin rope trim warmed the white room. After making the bed, I lay down on it to make a list of things I needed to begin transforming the house tomorrow. I fell asleep with the notebook on my stomach.

Even though I could hear the muffled ringing, it took a few moments to remember the phone was in my pocket. "Hello."

"Jana, it's Rachel. How's Washington?" Rachel was my next oldest sibling. We'd always been close, despite the five-year gap between us. Rachel had been so excited to have a baby sister that she had coddled over me most of my young life.

"Wet." I tried to command the grogginess out of my voice. "Green."

"And how's the handsome chef?"

"Oh, the old widower? He's not too ornery." My mother had told everyone about the *handsome chef*. I didn't want anyone to think I was in Washington to chase him.

"Old widower, my foot! I Googled him. Have you Googled him? He's hot."

I thought of Alex, with his messy mop of hair and apron. Somehow, even though he was handsome, *hot* was not the word that came to mind. "He's just a nice man with a nice job for me to do. It's not like what you're thinking. He's got a kid. He's married."

"He's widowed. You didn't tell me he was young or widowed or . . . or famous."

"He's not," I protested. "He's old . . . well, older than me, and he's not famous beyond his own city."

"Seattle's a big city. You should Google him. He's probably more than you think. I wouldn't discount him just yet. How's the apartment?"

"Hey, really, don't get any ideas about this guy. He's not even LDS. The apartment smells like Grandma Jenkins's house."

"Oh, I'm sorry. Maybe some air freshener?"

"Maybe if I paint it. If people are going to shop here, I don't want them to have to hold their noses. How's the baby?"

"Which one?"

"The one in your belly. Amanda isn't really a baby anymore, is she?"

"If it's in a diaper, it's a baby." Rachel sighed. "I'm fat, fat, fat. Every day I think this is it, this is as fat as I'm going to get, and the next day *Shazam!* I'm an inch bigger."

"You should stop measuring. Besides, it isn't you; it's the baby. *You* are perfect. Just five more weeks. Hang in there."

"Yeah, I'm hangin'. So Dad was pretty upset that he didn't see you before you left. Mom says he's been moping around all day. You should give him a call."

The picture of my father moping pained me. I coddled him like Rachel coddled me. "I'll call him tonight after dinner." I looked at the clock and realized I was five minutes late for dinner. "Hey, I'm going to dinner next door. I forgot. I'm late. Got to go. I love you."

"Love you too. E-mail me and tell me how he cooks. Bye."

I told her to Google it, but she'd hung up before she heard.

* * *

Standing on the Steadman's doorstep with empty hands felt unnatural. I should have had some token of gratitude for the invitation to dinner, the furnishings in the apartment, the help at the airport, and the cure for the headache.

Elise opened the door. She yelled, "Told you so," over her shoulder. The aroma was heavenly. I suddenly discovered I was hungrier than I knew.

When I saw Alex, I said, "Thank you so much for inviting me. I fell asleep. The phone woke me." I self-consciously ran my fingers through my hair, wondering what I looked like. "I still have to go to the store and stock the fridge and get a few other things." *Like toilet paper.* Luckily I had those napkins in my purse.

"You can take the Honda. I'll drive the Beemer while you're here. I should drive it more."

He pulled a chair out for me. The thought occurred to me that I wouldn't even be able to find myself on a map right now, let alone a grocery store. "Where do you shop? How do I get there?"

Carrying over a platter of French fries, he said, "You know, maybe I can drive you there tonight. I mean, it's going to be dark soon, and I don't know if I would describe it right. It's Stewart's down on Third. To tell you the truth, I haven't shopped around here for a very long time. Gretchen does my shopping. I just leave it on the magic list, and it pops up in my magic fridge."

"I've got to get myself a list like that. She sounds great."

"She's a lifesaver. I hope you like fish because we're having broiled salmon."

Elise chimed in with a sad face, "With soggy broccoli."

Alex corrected. "Steamed broccoli. It's good for you."

"I hate broccoli," she pouted.

"Five bites," he said.

"Two," she countered.

"Six."

"Okay, five." She stuck her bottom lip out in another round of pouting.

I stifled a laugh. Elise was a beautiful little girl, and her pouty face was irresistible. Alex was unaffected by it though.

Dinner was simple and delicious. I helped clear the table, then he drove us to the grocery store. I talked to Elise about her school. Before I knew it, we were at the store and I'd missed how we had gotten there.

Alex insisted on pushing the cart. I felt self-conscious buying toilet paper, but it was nothing compared to how I felt when he took the boxes of food I'd chosen and read down the labels, pointing out sodium and triglycerides. Never again, I decided, would I take him grocery shopping. It was bad enough to be shopping with a complete stranger, in a strange state, let alone having to hear a critique on my every food choice. He insisted I stock up on produce, so I tossed a few bags of salad and some fruit into the cart. He scoffed at the bagged salad, but I was a bagged salad sort of girl. Washing, drying, and tearing lettuce just wasn't my idea of fun. I was relieved when he left me alone so he could find some salad dressing. He had offered to make his special variety, but by that time, I didn't want anything else from him. While he was gone, Elise and I chose a few boxes of cookies that were full of saturated fats. I chuckled wickedly as I displayed them at the top of the groceries in the cart.

A few people in the store recognized Alex and greeted him with friendly hellos.

He was kind to each of them and returned their greeting with a genuine smile and hello of his own. I was happy to see he wasn't full of himself but wasn't ready to forget his criticism of my food. It was dark on the way home, so there was no hope of memorizing the route to the store.

Alex and Elise helped carry food inside, but they left quickly so Elise could go to bed.

I'd bought more food than I could eat in a month. As I shifted it around in the refrigerator, I realized for the first time that it was a new fridge. Alex must have spent a ton of money furnishing the apartment.

I stayed up late, looking through Vanessa's scrapbooks. The bottom scrapbook had a thin journal stuffed between the pages. I wondered if Alex knew it was there. I opened it, deciding if I knew Vanessa better, perhaps it would be easier to capture her vision for the store.

> *I watched Elise play in the sand for hours. She would build her castles and squat, waiting for the tide to wash them away. She wouldn't wait long. Soon she'd haul water, bucket by bucket, and dump it on the castle until it was destroyed.*
>
> *Al met us when he was done with his meeting. He chased Elise up and down the shore, and then they looked for seashells. I still wasn't feeling good, but I did take off my shoes and comb the shore for shells. Al would pick up my shells so I didn't have to bend. There was a moment just at sunset when I looked at the horizon with orange clouds hovering over the water and I thought I had never seen anything more beautiful. Then I looked over at my family. Elise was on Al's shoulders. The sun shone on her hair until it looked like morning sunshine glowing in the breeze. Her peach skin was kissed with the sunset's orange glow. Al's hair was like shining raven feathers. He was smiling and dancing with her in the waves. And suddenly, the sunset was nothing to me because I knew I was looking at the most beautiful thing I would ever see in my entire life. My family. Mine.*

I closed the journal, feeling like an evil trespasser. This was obviously too personal for me to use. I could see Elise with sunshine hair, but I couldn't picture "Al" with his raven feathers. I wondered what it would be like where Vanessa was, not able to touch her family anymore. My father told me that when we die, we are greeted on the other side by those we love and by those we've forgotten because of the veil that comes over us when we are born. Would that be enough to console Vanessa? I looked at my hands, grateful for my own body. I thought of those I loved and thought of hugging them. It was past ten, but I called my father anyway.

CHAPTER 3
Let's Get to Work

THE SHOWER PIPES KNOCKED AND clanged. There was warm water, but the pressure was dismal. Perhaps I would be taking baths for a few months.

At nine, the doorbell chimed before a loud knock. Alex was waiting for me, holding two mugs of something hot. I could smell the coffee. He handed me a mug. "I don't drink coffee. But thank you."

"This one isn't coffee. It's hot chocolate. I didn't know what you like to wake up with."

"Thank you." The first few sips of chocolate didn't taste good with the residue of toothpaste still in my mouth, but I drank it anyway to be polite.

"So what do you have planned today? How are you going to start?" he asked.

I had stayed up late looking at Vanessa's scrapbooks and making to-do lists. "I need to buy a few things, then I can pick a corner and start painting."

"That's a productive day. Where do we begin?"

"*We*? Don't you have to go to work or something?"

"I don't *hav*e to go to work. Not every day, or every week, but it helps if I show up from time to time. And I have other things I work on."

"Then what do you do all day, every day?"

He looked down at the floor and smirked. "I go to work." He looked up guiltily and smiled. I noticed he hadn't shaved. "But today I thought I'd work here with you. I'm sure you could use some help. I know my way around. You don't."

"You're the boss. But I have to warn you. This isn't real machismo stuff we're doing here. It's pretty girly. I think you'll get bored soon." He looked undeterred. "Hey, if you want to help, be my guest." I surprised him by grabbing a clipboard and my purse. "Let's go."

I started with the stores that were closest, letting Alex drive. This time I watched the roads so I could find the way again. Seattle was beautiful, with ivy adorning most street corners. I rolled down my window and let the moist air gust over my face.

Alex pushed shopping carts, following me while I filled them. He talked the whole time, telling stories about the places we passed. While we were shopping, he told me stories about his brother and his parents. By the time we parked at the hardware store, I felt comfortable around him. I'd never been with a man who talked more than Alex. He made Brad seem shy in comparison. His natural, contagious enthusiasm for everything he talked about made it easy to see why he was a local celebrity.

On the way home, Alex said, "You know, you don't talk very much."

"I usually do. I've just been listening. A person can't talk and listen at the same time, can they?"

"Good point. It's your turn."

"I like Seattle," I quietly said after we'd driven a block in silence.

"That tells me a lot about you. I'm glad we could have this discussion."

Alex helped unload the car. When all the bags were inside, we both sat down on opposite sofas. I figured I had two hours left of an eight-hour day. I ticked off projects in my head, trying to think of one I could complete in two hours with Alex leaning over my shoulder.

The doorbell rang, and Alex raised his eyebrows at me. I shrugged and jumped up to get the door. A beautiful, black-haired woman stood there. She wore a tight business suit that boosted her tanned cleavage into view. Her perfume wafted through the door to assault my nose. She looked me up and down like I was a piece of trash. I felt suddenly self-conscious of my worn jeans and tennis shoes.

"Is Alex over here?" she asked with a haughty toss of her hair.

In an instant, Alex was standing behind me. "Kristen, what are you doing here?" He sounded guilty.

Kristen's eyes blazed over to him then back to me. "I thought we were having lunch today. Where have you been? You haven't been answering your phone."

I had seen him pull his phone out of his pocket several times at lunch then put it back after checking the number.

"I said if I had time, I'd stop by. I've been with Jana all day. I couldn't fit it in." I looked at him. He was all innocence. Just then, a curl flopped forward on his forehead, and he could have been ten years old with his hand in the cookie jar. I took a step away from him to distance myself from whatever Kristen must be thinking. Alex took a step closer to me and gave me a pleading sideways glance.

I spoke up, looking at him with the most adoring look I could muster. "Thank you for your help today. I don't think I could have gotten so much done without you." I stopped short of batting my eyes. Obviously Alex needed me to say more, but I didn't know what. Was Kristen a business acquaintance, a fan, a girlfriend?

Kristen looked at her shiny, black, stiletto heels. "What about tonight? Are you still going to the banquet? Can we go together?"

"I already asked Jana to go with me. I didn't know you went to things like that."

"If you're there, I go to things like that, Alex." Her annoyance was plain. "Listen, could I talk to you outside for just a minute?" She looked at me. "In private," she snarled. He followed her down the walk.

I quietly closed the door then shuddered, squeaking, "Ew, my boss." I was hoping beyond hope that he was just conveniently using me to get rid of Kristen for the moment. If he thought for a second that I'd really go out with him, my life would suddenly be very complicated. I was stuck here in Washington. What would I say after he had paid so much money to set up an apartment and job for me? The truth. I didn't want to date him. He wasn't Mormon. That made me feel much better. I only dated Mormons. I had a built-in excuse. I twisted the gold CTR ring on my finger and took a deep breath.

I heard an angry squeal of tires when Alex opened the door to come in. "I'm so sorry about that. Eek. Mad woman." He laughed.

I creased my forehead and looked away awkwardly.

He crossed the room to me. "Thank you for helping me out."

I couldn't honestly say he was welcome, so I looked away, silent.

"Now, hey there. I'm not like that. She's my mortgage lady, and she's been on my tail for months. It won't hurt anything if she thinks I'm moving on. She's just a little overconfident. Surely you've known someone like that before."

Brad. "What's she going to say when you go alone tonight? She'll know you lied."

"You could come to dinner. I'm taking Elise."

"I can't go." I peeled the price tag off the glue gun.

"You have plans? You haven't been here two days. What kind of plans could you have?"

"I don't have plans." I looked down at the scrapbooks and started to flip pages. "Look, I'll fix up this corner over here." I pointed to the sketches then the wall. "We'll just start with the paint."

"You don't want a night out? Didn't bring the right clothes? Turn into a pumpkin after eight? What?"

"No. I just . . . Well, you're my boss. I don't want to blur any lines." What happened to the part where he wasn't Mormon?

"I could fire you and hire you back tomorrow."

"No."

"I could pay you. You'd be on the clock."

I rolled my eyes and glided into the kitchen, calling over my shoulder, "Pay an escort if you're that desperate." My heart was beating hard, and I could feel the color in my cheeks. I poured myself a cup of water and started gulping it down, hoping it would cool the fire in my face.

"You sure you won't go? It's just a business banquet. You know, a small group of businesses around Main. They figure the restaurant brings them customers and wanted to say thank you."

"So it's no big deal, then. It sounds small. You can brave it by yourself."

He moaned. "Yes, small and well-covered by the local press. I sneeze, and it's in the paper." He'd followed me into the kitchen and was leaning against the counter. He puffed his cheeks and exhaled heavily. "I wish I didn't have to go at all, to tell you the truth."

"Call in sick."

"I don't get sick." He shrugged.

I met his gaze and studied the color of his eyes, keeping my legal face in place. I'd never seen eyes like his before. The dark hazel green was flecked with gold. They were beautiful, and I wondered why I'd never noticed before.

When his face lit up with a bright smile, I thought he knew what I was thinking. Tiny crow's feet stretched out from the corners of his eyes, making them even more beautiful. I was relieved when he said, "You're right. Why not call in sick? I am *sick* of going to these. I don't want to be rude though. I don't want to burn any bridges."

"Send a representative, someone from the restaurant," I suggested.

He smiled again, jumping up. "That's a great idea." He rushed to the door without looking back. "Gotta make some calls."

The door slamming echoed through the room. I locked it behind him. He was an instant friend. He didn't seem to notice we hadn't known each other since childhood. All day he talked like we'd never been apart. The silence rang in my ears compared to the last six hours of constant chatter. I was fine with a new friend, but I would have to keep the line at friendship. I hadn't seen anything that told me he was thinking of more than friendship. Then again, hadn't he just asked me out? No. Not really. He just needed help out of a bind. It didn't matter anyway. I only dated LDS men.

* * *

While Alex was skipping the banquet, I ate dinner with him and Elise again. I should have declined the offer, but Elise brought a bite of swordfish for me to try when she invited me. I couldn't help myself. I decided it was the last time I'd eat dinner with the Steadmans. How long could I eat with them without being absorbed into their family? At dinner I caught myself tucking Elise's hair behind her ear and laughing too often. Alex was more intent on pulling stories out of me. As soon as I would answer his question, which always had to be answered with a story, he'd ask me another. He walked me to the shop after dinner, and my palms were actually sweating in anticipation of a doorstep scene. He walked away as soon as my key was in the door though. I sighed in relief once I was inside.

I went to bed at a decent hour, only to wake up at midnight to the sound of something sliding around in the attic. I sat bolt upright in bed and strained my ears to decipher the sound. I stood under the attic door, but when I turned on the hall light, the noise ceased. It took me a long time to get back to sleep. I finally fixed myself some chamomile tea and said a prayer. I dreamed about living in a haunted house. I probably was. In my dream, cupboards opened and slammed and hairbrushes hurtled through the air at my head.

In the morning, I woke to rhythmic banging downstairs. I rolled over, chagrined to see I'd overslept. I stretched, listening to the tempo of whatever Alex was doing. I should have showered, but I called Rachel instead, sure she was up after getting her kids to school. "My house is haunted," I announced. The banging had stopped, replaced by a scraping sound.

"Cool."

"That is just like you. I'll never sleep," I said then told her about the mysterious sliding object in the attic.

"Maybe the chef will let you stay next door with him."

I pictured her bobbed brown hair jiggling as she laughed. "Wouldn't that be nice? Maybe I'll ask," I said dryly.

"So what's he like so far?"

"Don't you mean to ask, what's the *job* like so far?"

"No. I'm more interested in the chef."

"He's old, married, and uninterested."

She laughed so hard that I thought I heard her set the phone down until she could gain control. Finally, with a few snorts escaping, she asked, "Don't you have the Internet?"

"No. Rachel, I'm calling so you can help me feel better about the house haunting."

"Give me some dirt, and I'll make you feel better."

I sighed. "You're in the enemy camp. How can I be sure you won't say anything to mom?" I was my father's baby, and Rachel was my mother's. I'd swear they shared thoughts by telepathy.

"On my honor, if I tell her, you can tell Dad about the time I took the car at midnight and knocked Sister Turner's mailbox over."

"I'll hold you to that, though I don't know what he'd do about it now."

"Maybe I'd get the cold shoulder for a month. He wouldn't just gloss over it. He was furious about the mysterious dent."

"Okay, Alex is a good cook—too good." I told her about Kristen and the awards banquet he asked me to.

"Duh, Jana. When someone that hot asks you out, you say yes!"

"This isn't making me feel better. I'll never date him. He's not . . ."

"LDS, I know."

"And he only asked because he was in a bind, so it isn't what you're thinking."

"Well, call me back and tell me what's for dinner tonight," she said sarcastically.

"I can tell you what. Peanut butter and jelly from my cupboard. Now, can we get back to why I called?"

"You did dish. Okay, go look in the attic."

"Eek, what if it's a rat?"

There was a soft tap on the apartment door. I left my room and padded across the front room to answer it. Alex was wearing a ball cap, blue jeans, and a white T-shirt. He looked at my pajamas and smiled, crow's feet growing by his eyes. I turned away from him and plopped down on the couch cross-legged.

Rachel blew a soft raspberry. "If it's a rat, kill it."

"I called for this?" I asked her. Alex sat down at the other end of the couch, and I cringed.

"Call Ghostbusters? I don't know, Jana. I've seen some pretty freaky movies. To be honest, if it were me, I'd move."

I looked at Alex and kept my voice level. "Next door?" I asked her. He waited patiently for me.

"You know me so well." She chuckled.

"Alex just knocked on my door, so I've got to get going."

"Are you going to work with him every day?"

"I hope not," I answered. He'd taken his hat off and was brushing white dust off of it onto the hunter green couch. He noticed. When he started to dust the white speckles off, he left a white handprint. I reached over and put my hand on his to stop him. I shook my head at him.

"Well, if you need anything else, call," Rachel offered.

"Yeah, you've been a big help." I rolled my eyes, even though she couldn't see it.

I closed the phone and told Alex I was sorry for sleeping in. I realized my hand was still on his, and I jerked it away.

He laughed. "Did you sleep well?" he asked.

"Not really. I'll have to be careful about setting the alarm. I usually wake up at six thirty on my own."

"Come see what I started."

"I'll get dressed and be right down." I wouldn't have time to shower. I realized I didn't know what I looked like and hoped it wasn't horrible. *No.* I didn't care, because it was just Alex. I sat a little taller and pursed my lips. It didn't matter what I looked like for *him*.

"What's that?" he asked.

"What's what?"

He sat up taller and mimicked my lip pursing. I laughed. When I tried to speak, I laughed harder. He started laughing too, but I wasn't sure what about. Our laughter mingled like musical notes in the room. After too long, we quieted down. Tears were starting in my eyes from laughing too hard.

I stood up and walked to the door, holding it open for him.

"You're not going to tell me are you?" he asked.

I laughed again. The door shut slowly, scooting him out as it closed. There was a residue of white dust on my hand from touching him. A sudden wave of panic hit me as I wondered what he'd been doing to make such a mess. I yanked on a pair of shorts and pulled a buttoned short sleeve shirt over my head. I had my hand on the doorknob when I decided to check the mirror. My hair was too fluffy. I pulled it back and twisted a pencil through it. Some rebel tendrils escaped. I pulled them behind my ear. It wasn't permanent, but it would do. I reached for my purse to apply some makeup. I had to stop and remind myself it was just Alex. I didn't need to look good for him. He was just my boss.

When I opened the door, he was still standing on the landing. It bothered me to think of him waiting there. "Let's see your little project." I led the way down the stairs. I felt a twinge of regret for the condescension in my voice until I saw the project.

In the living room, an A-frame ladder was butted against the wall, and a large section of plaster had been knocked out, exposing thin board slats with dried mud between them.

"Alex, this isn't going to help. It's going to take longer. That was the corner I was starting in."

"I know. There was some water damage. We'll have to remud it. I had the roof done last year, but I want to replace that section. Didn't you notice the stain?"

I leaned against the wall. "No. You're right. It's the best thing to do."

"I thought you'd like to learn how to mud."

"Fun." I smiled. "Are you sure they don't need you at Shallots?"

"Are you trying to get rid of me?"

"Not exactly. I need you to mud the wall first, then I'll try to get rid of you."

He ran his white hand through his hair, leaving a dusty trail in the loose curls. "If we work on the shop together, it will get done that much faster."

My fear was confirmed. I was standing next to my constant nine-to-five companion. "I don't know. I can't see you tying satin ribbons and fluffing dried florals."

"You want me to stay. Trust me."

I blinked at him and narrowed my eyes. "Whatever you say. You're the boss." His smile was brilliant. "But I don't want to mud. You can do it yourself or hire it out. I'll start sponging somewhere else."

"Suit yourself." He climbed up the ladder and began scraping.

I was almost done taping plastic sheeting to the floor when the doorbell rang. I stood up stiffly. "If no one usually lives here, why does the doorbell ring so often?" I opened it, expecting Kristen.

Her exact opposite stood before me. He was six foot something with bright blue eyes and smooth blond hair. His cologne, like Kristen's perfume, drifted into the room, only instead of an assault to my nose, it caressed me and made my knees weak. He wore an expression of dawned understanding then looked past me to Alex. "You dog," the man accused. Alex looked guilty. The visitor laughed loudly and shook his head.

"Scott, this is Jana. Jana, Scott." Alex made the introduction but didn't seem pleased to be doing it.

Scott took my hand gently and smiled. "Jana, it's good to meet you." He held my hand too long.

I looked at Alex in panic. He leapt off the ladder and made it over to us in three long strides. He stepped between Scott and me, making it necessary for Scott to release my hand. "And you need what?" he demanded in a harsh voice.

Scott craned his neck to look behind Alex at me. His handsome face beamed, and he winked at me. I looked away. He let out a low whistle and smacked Alex's shoulder. "I'd stay home for that too, buddy. I need you to sign for these." He handed Alex a clipboard.

I thought I could hear Alex's teeth grind. I picked up the masking tape and sat down on the floor to finish the last edge of sheeting. I could feel Scott's eyes watching me. I kept my face down, keenly aware of the makeup I wasn't wearing.

"Good-bye, Ja—" The door slammed on him before he could finish saying my name.

I smirked at the floor. Alex sat by me. "Awkward," he said.

"Mmm." I continued staring at my work.

"I just want you to know that—"

I held my hand up to stop him. "Some conversations are better left unhad." I flashed an amused smile at him and went back to work.

Alex blew out a long breath. "Did you eat?"

"I forgot."

"I'll fix you breakfast." He opened the antique fridge, realized it was empty, and bounded up the stairs to my apartment. I started to get up but decided to let him go. So what if he saw my laundry on the bathroom floor? It was just Alex. *Just Alex*, I repeated to myself. He would be like a brother, only more cheerful. I sponged light cream paint onto butcher paper to make sure the texture was right. I pressed the sponge to the corner and began texturing the wall.

Breakfast was an omelet with bell peppers. Alex said he'd already eaten. "This is so good." I looked up at him. "You must be tired of hearing that."

"Not from you."

"I can understand why your cooking made you famous. I bet you get sick of cooking though."

"I don't mind." He climbed the ladder, and the sound of the trowel scraping filled the room. "We could have something basic tonight, like dumplings."

"I can't come to dinner tonight." I focused on the wall.

"Why?" It sounded like he already knew because he inflected the last of the word in a higher pitch.

"It's complicated."

He stepped down the ladder and stood by me, focusing on the wall and my work. "We're friends, right?" he asked.

"I guess."

"And Elise is there, right?"

"She is."

"And you have to eat anyway, right?"

"Alex," I whined. He raised an eyebrow at me when I looked at him. "I can't just keep coming to your house for dinner every night. What will people think?"

"Who are you going to tell? And what does it matter what anyone thinks as long as we know we're friends and it's just a bit of shoveling chow into your gut."

Shoveling chow into my gut sounded as uncomplicated as he intended it to. I bit my lip. "I don't know."

"Just going to eat here alone?"

"Maybe."

"I don't bite. I'm just your boss."

I narrowed my eyes, trying to picture Larry asking me to come to dinner with his family. "Okay, but just tonight."

"Sure." He smiled, and I saw a certainty in his eyes that told me he expected me every night.

He sat down and watched me sponge. The corner he had just repaired was drying a different shade from the rest of the wall, but it looked good.

After a half hour, I decided he was being too quiet. "Aren't you bored?" I called over my shoulder. He didn't answer. I turned around to find him asleep on the couch we'd pushed against the wall. I had planned to finish only one wall, but since he was asleep, I started the next. I was finishing a fourth wall when he finally stirred.

"Hey, Sleeping Beauty, have any good dreams?"

He rubbed his eyes and yawned. He looked at his watch. "Oh, I've got to get to Shallots, or Scott's going to kill me."

"Is he your boss?"

"No, he's my right hand. I don't want to push my luck. If I leave a note for Elise, can she come over here and stay with you?" I nodded. He was nearly out the door when he asked, "Six o'clock okay for dinner?"

I sighed. "It's fine, thank you."

He winked at me and shut the door.

CHAPTER 4
Ambush

I SMACKED THE ALARM CLOCK Sunday morning. For three weeks, Alex had been my constant companion eight hours a day and usually two more for dinner. I knew I should refuse dinner, but his cooking was divine, and I was lonely when he was gone. He was so cheerful and funny that I had a hard time thinking up reasons to stay away from him. He hadn't said anything else about dating me since asking me to the awards banquet my first day. As far as I could tell, it was just his nature to be friendly. A cooking, dimpled, happy man was hard to resist.

I hoped I'd get a break from him today. I was surprised when Alex wanted to work Saturday, but other than unpack a little, I had nothing else to do. He painted the downstairs kitchen. Elise had "helped" too. Watching Alex slow down all progress to kneel beside his daughter to help her slowly help him was heartwarming. He had no end of patience for Elise. She could interrupt any conversation, and he would answer her question then remind her not to interrupt. Each day when she got home from school, Elise would come over to the shop to "help." It slowed me down when I had to stop to show her how to string beads or clip the thorns off of the fresh roses, but Alex didn't mind.

I'd spent the previous two Sundays with April in her ward, but it was time to brave my own ward. I had toyed with the idea of attending a singles ward, but I wanted to feel anchored. I wanted something to feel familiar. It was hard enough living in a strange state by myself. I just didn't feel like putting forth the effort to be social. I felt like I could blend into the background in a family ward. Surely they wouldn't have as many social events. Besides, I wanted a break from dating after Brad. Not that I was getting the break I had expected. He had called a few times to see how I was adjusting. He kept his tone upbeat. I asked if he'd been dating. He said he had but they weren't like me and he wanted me to come home. That's where the conversations got awkward and I found reasons to end the phone call. The last three times he'd called, I'd let it go to voice mail.

I already knew my church house address, the name of my bishop, and the time of the meeting. I pulled on my sweats and sank to my knees by the bed for my morning prayer. I rummaged through some suitcases and pulled out my khaki skirt and turquoise shirt. I was shocked to see how wrinkled they were. I should have pulled them out yesterday. Now it was seven in the morning, and I had no iron. I decided to hang them in the bathroom while I showered. Perhaps the steam would straighten them out. I stumbled into the bathroom and pulled the curtain around the old claw-foot tub. The pipes clanked and rattled. A dismal stream of water trickled out of the shower head then stopped. I looked skyward and asked, "What? Don't you want me to go to church today?" I turned the water off and tried again, this time not even getting a drizzle. *Life is a test, my own little test.* Looking up again, I promised, "And I'll pass this one."

I checked the faucets all over the house and discovered I had no water. I went back to the bathroom to see how much repair work I could do with no water. Bed head. Bad bed head. And a case of pillow face to boot. I pulled at my hair and finally gave up. I picked up the phone and dialed Alex's cell phone.

"You've reached the Master Chef. I'll return your call when I can."

"Alex, my water isn't running, and I have an early appointment this morning at nine. I wondered if I could use your shower today. Give me a call."

Within twenty seconds, my phone rang. "You called?"

"Did you get my message?"

"Nope. Just found the phone." He sounded sleepy.

"Well, my water isn't working, and I have an appointment this morning. I need to shower. May I use your bathroom?"

"Oh, uh, yeah. Come right over, through the back. I'll meet you."

I quickly dumped out a suitcase and packed it with toiletries and clothes.

Alex was waiting, shirtless, with the kitchen door open.

"Thank you so much," I squeaked out, trying to ignore his state of undress. I was suddenly self-conscious of my hair and pillow face. I reminded myself we were just friends anyway and it didn't matter. He might as well be one of my brothers. He still looked half asleep and probably wouldn't notice how I looked.

He padded over to the fridge and pulled out a jug of orange juice. "It's up the stairs and to your left."

"I'll be about thirty minutes. Is that okay? I thought I'd just get ready here too." I didn't even look at him.

"I've never seen a woman get ready in less than two hours. However, *you* are painfully honest. I'm intrigued. Knock yourself out."

I was dismayed to find that the shower he had directed me to was the master bathroom. I tried not to look at the crumpled sheets on the bed. The bathroom smelled faintly of shampoo and aftershave. Like everywhere else in the house, it had never been decorated. The green tile floor had a manly look to it. I started to peel off my socks when a knock at the door made me jump. I caught my balance on the counter.

"Fresh towels?"

I opened the door, grateful he had remembered. I hadn't thought of that. I looked at the towel hanging over the shower and realized it was no doubt the one he'd used to dry his body yesterday. My stomach rolled. I reached out for the towels. "I forgot to ask. I need to beg you for an iron. Do you have one?"

"Yeah, I don't know where, but Gretchen will know. I'll give her a call."

"No, don't wake her up. I'll make due."

"It's not a bother. She's on her way here. I have an early morning appointment too, and she's going to watch Elise."

"Do you need the shower? I'm so sorry."

"I've got it covered." He was laughing, clearly amused at the whole turn of the morning.

"Thanks again," I said as the door closed.

"It's seven thirty-nine. I'll see you at . . . buh-buh-buh—looks like eight-oh-nine," Alex teased through the door.

The *William Tell Overture* sounded in my mind, and I commenced the fastest shower I'd ever taken. The strong water pressure was a treat after the dismal squirt I still hadn't gotten used to at home. It was sheer willpower that kept me from standing under the showerhead to enjoy the moment. I forced my hand to turn the water off.

I half dried my hair and ran some mousse through the top layer. I applied some light makeup and shrugged back into my sweats. It was nice to let the steam out of the bathroom and breathe the comparatively cold, dry air. Seven fifty-eight. I had eleven minutes to keep my honor intact.

I smiled when I noticed the ironing board set up in the corner of the room with the iron plugged in and hot. Three minutes later, I was back in the bathroom buttoning my blouse. Alex was thankfully absent when I emerged, and I didn't see him until I was in the kitchen with my suitcase in one hand and nylons in the other.

"Two minutes early. I am more than impressed." His eyes looked me over. "Come eat." Alex's hair was glistening with moisture, and he was fully dressed in Dockers and a polo shirt. He must have taken a shower in another bathroom in the house. A house this size should have three, I thought. I wished I could have showered somewhere other than his room.

"I don't know if I have time to eat."

"Where are you going?"

"Seventeenth East and Waterford Drive."

"That's three blocks away." He waved a plate with an omelet on it under my nose. The smell was intoxicating.

"Okay, but I'm getting fat. I've got to start eating at home."

He sat down with me and paused quietly while I blessed the food.

"Eating in that ramshackle house of yours? How can you cook without water? You should call the landlord and complain about the squalor you have to live in."

"I don't want him to kick me out for nitpicking. All alone in a strange state, you know."

"With an appointment. Where are you going in a strange state so early in the morning?"

"Church."

"Going with April again?"

"Today I'm going to meet my own ward. Oh, Alex. Mmm! This is amazing. You should open a restaurant or something."

"Nah, too much trouble."

I checked my watch and decided not to eat the last third of the omelet for the sake of my waistline. I looked at his still-wet hair; he looked nice. He was ready to leave, but I decided to ask even though I already knew the answer. "Do you want to come with me?"

"What, to church?"

I nodded.

He smiled, looking amused. "No, but thanks for asking."

"You're always welcome to come. I'd love the company." He didn't say anything. "I have to find my shoes. Thank you so much for the shower and breakfast. You're wonderful."

"I know." He smiled smugly. "Hey, I'll call a plumber. Maybe the water will be back on when you get home."

"No, don't. It's Sunday. Call tomorrow."

"That's inconvenient, isn't it? What kind of a landlord would I be?"

"I hope the kind that will share his water for a day and let some poor plumber have his Sunday off. See you."

I could hear him call after me, "Plumbers aren't poor. Have you seen their bills?"

* * *

Sitting through sacrament meeting made me feel closer to my family. They weren't as far away when we were all doing the same thing. The biggest difference between being at home and here was the bald brother behind the organ. He played the songs fast. I loved it, but I felt sorry for the young men preparing the sacrament. They were scrambling to break the bread before the hymn ended.

Sister Anderson befriended me right after sacrament meeting. She was thin, with brown hair that she wore in a sweeping, feathered 1970s style. Big brown eyes stared through large, round, owlish glasses. "Time for Gospel Doctrine, then we have combined Priesthood and Relief Society today. We're holding class in the cultural hall. You know who you want to meet is the Taylors. You say you're up here alone?"

"Yes. I came up for a job."

"The Taylors have some kids about your age. Of course, Jonathan is on his mission."

I blanched at the words *kids about your age*. Sister Anderson walked with me to the cultural hall and introduced me to the Taylors. They all had the same shade of sandy hair. Brother Taylor shook my hand firmly. After class he invited me to dinner and drew a map of where they lived on the back of an elders quorum social invitation. Wanting to fit into the ward as soon as possible, I eagerly accepted the invitation. It would be good to skip dinner with Alex for a night. He didn't complain about having me over every night, but I was sure I must be hampering his social life. I'd even eaten at his house the last two Sundays with April in tow. I smiled, thinking of how hard she'd made us laugh.

My first reservation came when Sister Taylor walked me to the foyer after Relief Society and a serene-looking, tall young man with flawless skin greeted her and took her bags.

Please, not a son. I could have stayed in Utah for this. How many awkward "You're going to love our son" dinners did one person have to go through in a lifetime?

He leaned down so Sister Taylor could whisper something to him, then he zeroed in on me with a large, dawning smile. I had to steel all the muscles in my face to keep my eyes from rolling. I smiled tightly at him, hoping to convey a silent message of *don't get your hopes up*. Before the Taylors could introduce me, I stepped quickly into a crowd going the opposite way and ducked out another door. I had to walk around the church to find my car, but it was worth it.

* * *

I must have pulled up right after Alex because he was hefting a bag of golf clubs out of his trunk. He looked up, set them down, and ran over to open my door. "How was your first day?"

"Great. They're good people."

"So I was going to whip up a lunch for us and Gretchen too. Don't you want to meet her? She's dying to meet you."

Thinking of my tight waistband, I sighed in surrender. "I'd love to meet Gretchen." Then I looked at him hopefully. "Hey, you don't want to go to dinner at a friend's house tonight, do you?"

He raised his eyebrows. "Are you asking your boss out?"

"No. It isn't like that. It would just help me out of a spot."

"A spot?"

"I've been invited to eat dinner with some new friends. They're very nice."

"You're shy, and you need a good conversationalist?"

I looked sideways. "Uh, yeah."

"Or maybe you have a reason to want to look like you're *with* someone." Looking at my guilty face, he continued. "They have a Kristen, maybe?" I looked down and he bent to look into my eyes from an odd angle. "A Kristenopher?"

I laughed at that. "Maybe." My face flushed.

In a mock female voice, he said, "Now, I would, but I don't want to blur any lines here."

"I could fire you and start again tomorrow."

"First, you can't fire your boss. Second, I wouldn't have said no three weeks ago, but now I know you better, like we're friends. I'm more comfortable telling you no. But I'd love to take you out to a movie, dinner, anything *real* date-ish. If you won't fake date me, I won't fake date you."

I stood there with my mouth open. Alex was heading for his golf bag. He turned around. "Well, c'mon; let's eat. You'll love Gretchen."

* * *

Gretchen was a beautiful, middle-aged redhead. She was roundish with porcelain white skin and a short crop of hair. Alex treated her with near reverence.

I wasn't very talkative because I was still digesting Alex's fake date remark. Was he holding a grudge because I didn't save him from Kristen? He was right. It wasn't fair to ask him to the Taylor's dinner tonight. But it would have been nice. I liked that he'd said we were friends. There was the line, and he'd drawn it himself. I could honestly say he was my best friend in Washington. I was spending almost every spare minute with him, and I didn't know anyone else. He wasn't that bad for a guy. I'd never had a male friend this close before. Was it wrong? I thought about it as I pushed the food around on my plate.

When I looked up, I was alone at the table with Gretchen. "Huh? Oh, where did they go?"

Gretchen smiled. "They're starting the movies. Every Sunday they watch the movies. That kid's always tired Monday for school. I try to talk some sense into him, but he won't stop."

I suddenly felt guilty for not talking through lunch. "So, he's pretty dependent on you." I started helping Gretchen clear the table. "I think he'd be lost without you."

"If I thought he could handle it, I would have retired months ago. He's just not there yet, you know? He's been much better since you've been here though."

That piqued my interest. "Really?"

"I haven't seen him sullen since you said you'd take the job. Since you've been here, he's almost buoyant." She filled the sink with water and dish soap. "I didn't think he would ever start dating again."

"Oh, no, no. It's not like that. We're not like that. I'm just putting the shop together, that's all."

"I thought you were dating . . . I'm sorry. I never guessed . . . He's been so happy."

"Maybe he just needed a friend." I shrugged.

"Well, you must be a good friend for him. No one's been able to snap him out of this gloom. Not that he doesn't have a reason for the depression after Vanessa's cancer. He's always been bright around Elise, but the minute she's not in the room, you'd swear he has nothing to live for."

"They've been helping me every day. Maybe he's so excited about bringing Vanessa's shop to life that it's just invigorating him."

"I don't know. I think he'll sell the shop. I can't see him staying here and running it. He's not like that. Now if it were food or a restaurant, you could get him to care about that. Even when Vanessa was here, he was just humoring her. He had another place picked out, but she didn't want it. She never was one to just settle down. She had to be accomplishing great things. A busybody who loved success."

"So were you their . . . did you help around here when Vanessa was here?"

"I started working for Al after Joe sold him the restaurant. I was the head waitress. Soon I was keeping the books too. Then Vanessa got sick, and I was helping over here. When Vanessa died, he asked me to do a few more things, and I put my foot down. I made him hire three people to replace me at work and pay me a full-time salary to keep this up for him." She sloshed a dishcloth out of the water to motion around the room. "But I still keep the books."

"Wow, you've done a lot."

"Don't say it like I'm kind and charitable. He pays well. The thing with him is he doesn't trust anyone. So he will find someone he does trust, and he'll lean on them like crazy. That's why I thought you were dating him. He never leaves the restaurant. He never trusts anyone to take care of it. All of a sudden, Scott's in charge and they've seen Al once all week. Would've been good for him to date again. He hasn't dated at all since the funeral."

"Oh." I didn't know what to think. I was sure he wasn't missing work because of me. I hadn't seen any sign that he was interested in me in any way other than a friend. I'd had enough admirers that I would recognize the look in their eye, their body language, the dawning grin of young Brother Taylor, Scott's lingering handshake. Alex wasn't like that. He treated me almost like a sister.

"He says you're a Mormon."

"I am."

"My cousin's a Mormon. I was baptized a Mormon when I was about twelve, but I never went to church. No one to go with. I don't even remember what they told me to get me into the water."

"You can go with me. I don't have anyone to go with."

"No, I'm a firm agnostic now. But thank you for the invitation."

"Why aren't we using the dishwasher?" I asked as I dried dishes.

"He won't put them away. He used to. He used to keep the whole house before she got sick. Some days I'm proud that he's even gotten out of bed. I know it's been hard for him. Anyway, they'll just use them out of the dishwasher. So if it's a day when I'm going away sooner, I do it by hand. I don't usually come out on Sunday, but he wanted to golf this morning. He hasn't been golfing since before she died. I had to find the clubs. He'd lose his head if it wasn't screwed on."

I wiped down the table. I'd rather help Gretchen clean up here than wait for the dinner hour alone at home.

"I almost forgot. I put old pop bottles full of water in your bathroom so you can flush your toilet. He says you don't want a plumber until tomorrow."

"Thank you. I didn't think of that."

"Well, that's it." She dried her hands. "Should be good enough. I spend Sundays with my mother at the home. Maybe I'll see you tomorrow. He does keep you to himself, doesn't he? Maybe I won't see you for another week. He and Elise have been a lot easier to take care of since they're usually with you." She headed for the living room.

I sat down at the table, not excited about going home and not excited about dinner at the Taylors.

Alex broke into my thoughts. "You're awake!"

"I'm sorry about lunch. My head's been somewhere else today. I don't know what's wrong with me. I visited with Gretchen for a long time to make up for it so she didn't think I was a mute or something."

"You're not mad at me for not going tonight, are you?"

"No. It was wrong of me to ask. I didn't want to do it for you. I can see how you don't want to do it for me."

"I'll tell you the truth. I just don't want to be ambushed by a bunch of religious people. If it were something else, I *would* fake date you. I'm guessing you met your friends at church today."

"They probably would ambush you. I'm being ambushed. I didn't even see it coming."

"He's probably not that bad. So what did you and Gretchen talk about?"

"The only thing we have in common."

"Me." He smiled and sat down at the table.

"So now I know all your dirty secrets, the way you like your socks folded, the aversion to emptying clean dishes out of the dishwasher."

"She say anything embarrassing?"

"What? Like things that would make you cringe if you heard her telling me? Those things?" He nodded. "Yes, all of those things. I know it all. Everything, every detail. Anything that the last fifteen minutes could afford. You have no secrets from me now, Alex Steadman." I laughed maniacally.

"You're sassy when you're depressed."

"I guess I do *sass* a little when I'm stressed." I laid my head down on the table. "I'm sorry. I don't mean to pick on you. I'm just not looking forward to tonight, and this is a good diversion." I realized this was a familiar feeling. I felt cornered. Would a whole ward expect me to date their sons? My Salt Lake ward had expected it. I was as noncommittal as possible on every blind date, at every dinner, and at every young adult activity. Even so, the ward had dug up more nephews, sons, and grandsons. People just couldn't stand to see me single. At least Brad's presence seemed to lessen the abundant dating opportunities.

"Daaaaad!" Elise called from the other room.

"Popcorn, honey! Just a minute." He looked at me. "You have time to watch one movie, or at least the last of this one. It's my favorite. Godzilla and Rodan work together at the end to defeat Monster Zero."

"You're making Elise watch old Godzilla movies?"

"No. She always chooses the movie. This is the sixth week of this one. I don't need the subtitles anymore. I can do the voiceover myself."

"As fun as that sounds . . . I think I might take a nap."

Before I could open the door, he asked, "Is it just because I'm your boss?"

"Is what because you're my boss?"

"That you won't date me?"

I couldn't see any fondness for me in his eyes, just a blank look. I wondered why he was asking. His face was devoid of interest. "The truth is I only date Mormon men. I would never date someone outside of my religion."

"Never? That's a little strong. There are good people outside of your religion."

"I know that. There are tons of good people out there. It's a common-goal type of thing. It's better in the long run."

"So I don't smell bad? It isn't the way I look?"

"Alex, half of Seattle is after you because of the way you look. And I've never been close enough to you to know how you smell." He looked a little sad. "But you're a really good boss, a nice guy, and the best cook in the world," I said, trying to make him feel better.

He smiled his boyish grin. "Yeah, I am."

* * *

The Taylors had a large, two-story home, similar to my home in Utah. Though I'd helped my father plant trees years ago, they weren't as gargantuan as the Taylors' trees. Good old Washington rain.

I held a bowl of prepackaged pasta salad as I stood on the doorstep. I had laughed wickedly while making it, knowing how mortified Alex would have been to read the label. The list was full of preservatives I couldn't even pronounce.

Sister Taylor greeted me at the door. To my relief, the house was full of Taylors I hadn't met. There were little girl Taylors, gawky teenage boy Taylors, and Grandma and Grandpa Taylor. At least I wouldn't have to be alone with Ambush Taylor.

As I helped Sister Taylor, who I was now demanded to call Karen, set the table, I asked, "So how many children do you have?"

"Seven. One's on a mission. One's married. The brunette over there, she's an import, my new daughter-in-law, Sarah. Jared will be here soon. He had to work. Can you believe it? On a Sunday? Had to cover a shift. How many kids do your parents have?"

"Five." I was talking loudly now because of the chattering around us. "I'm the youngest. The house is empty most of the time."

"Well, out here, people think we're nuts for having so many kids. I try to make it look good, as good as you can with seven."

A high, comical voice behind us broke in. "And if you don't behave, the world will see you and never have any children of their own because of your terrifying example." Laughing, Mr. Ambush walked off to pull Grandma's chair out for her.

After we were seated at the table, Mr. Ambush said the prayer. I was relieved that he was seated across from me and not beside me. The table was huge, like our table at home. There was plenty of room for the banquet in front of us. Before we could start passing food, Brother Taylor stood up to introduce me, then he went down the table and introduced everyone else. I immediately forgot all the names except one. Mr. Ambush, Jeffrey, (who, from the cringe at his name, most likely preferred to be called Jeff), smiled at me when he was introduced.

After introductions, the chatter started up immediately. Jeff wasted no time in starting an interview. I wasn't as annoyed as I usually was. Perhaps it was because I was with a large family again. Maybe I was desperate for that feeling of home.

"Why are you in Washington?" His sandy blond hair sported a missionary cut. He had sky blue eyes that were too bright to be allowed and a square jaw.

"It's a sad story really. There is this nice, old widower who wanted to finish making a business his wife had started. I guess before she died she had my application in all of her papers. So he called to see if I'd come out and finish what she started." *Old widower?* Well, when they found out it was Alex Steadman, I doubted they'd put the word *old* on him. But it sounded better than saying, "This handsome, young celebrity shacked me up next door and feeds me every night while I spend my days with him making craft bunnies."

"Wow, you make businesses. That must be pretty fun. What kind do you make?"

"I'm usually a legal assistant. This is the first time I've ever done anything like this. It's more fun than printing judgments. They're holding my job for me back home, but I don't know how long they'll hold it. I don't know how long this will take."

"Do you like it here? Would you consider staying?"

"I don't know. I haven't thought about it." I looked down and started cutting the chicken on my plate with intense interest.

I had to give him some credit when he took the hint and didn't speak for several minutes. I also had to admit that he wasn't bad looking at all. I might have found myself staring at him in a crowded room. I certainly didn't feel as annoyed with him as I generally did with most of the men I'd been set up on dates with. Maybe I could make my father happy and be a good sport for once. I looked up and found him studying his own chicken. "So do you like it here? Has your family always lived in Washington?"

He looked up at me, surprised. "It's great. It's so green here. I love it. We lived in Arizona all my life, so this deciduous forest thing is amazing. I got off my mission and came home to a whole new house and state."

"Arizona? Wow, I have an uncle who lives there. Where did you used to live?"

He smiled, looking a little relieved. "Right there in Tucson. Did you ever go there?"

"I spent three summers there. When I came home, it was ninety degrees outside and my family was boiling. My blood was so thin that I thought it was chilly."

"Yeah, I'll never forget shopping for my first coat. That was just weird. I went to Brazil on my mission. It's not cold very often down there either. I had a suntan line around my tie because the sun would get me right through my shirt and garments, but it couldn't get through the tie."

The rest of dinner went the same way. I had a lot in common with Jeff. He was also twenty-four, but I was three months older than he was. He had me laughing a lot with stories about his siblings.

The Taylors' house was situated on a half acre. Jeff offered to show me the yard when the chatter was so loud we had to shout to hear each other. Outside, the rustle of the leaves was like a whisper.

"I have to tell you, you're not all that bad." Jeff plucked a tiny leaf off of a blackberry hedge.

"All that bad? Why would you have thought I was *all that bad*? What do you mean?"

"My mom has brought home three girls for dinner this year. The others were *that bad*."

"They weren't *that bad*. They were just *special spirits*."

He laughed. "Special spirits are hefty. These girls were . . . well, they didn't look so bad. One was an avid rock climber, and that was the only language she spoke, and the others didn't speak at all." He stopped and looked down at me, a little depressed. "If I go back in there without having asked you out, I'll get the silent treatment and cold dinner for two weeks."

"She wouldn't do that."

"She would, and she has. Not to mention everywhere we go and everyone we meet she points to me and announces my bachelorhood then takes off on a long, lamenting oration of having a single son as old as me. I'm only twenty-four. You'd think I was thirty."

"How old was your brother when he got married?"

"Twenty-six. He just got married last month. He loves watching me take the heat now, and I get twice as much. So," he glanced toward the house, "Jana, will you go out with me?"

"To save you from your harmless mother? I'm so flattered that you'd choose me. I'll tell you what. I'm stuck in Washington with nothing else to do, so," I sighed and faked boredom, "I might as well."

"Well, that wasn't flattering either. But I guess I could have done a better job at asking you out." He glanced at the window, and this time I saw the shadow of someone looking back. "Here, let's do this up right, and maybe I'll get cake for breakfast." He dropped to one knee and took my hand. "Jana, can I take you to a movie and dinner Thursday night? Will you grace me with your stunning beauty for one glorious evening?" I pulled my hand back, laughing. He said, "Uh-uh. I need the hand for the cake. Give me the hand." I wasn't going to. "The beautiful hand of a maiden so fair? I'll save you a piece of the cake."

I gave in and flopped my hand back into his. "Will you get up already? I think they're gone."

He stood up, looking like he didn't care about the conversation anymore. "So will ya go?"

"Thursday? That sounds good."

"I'll pick you up at six."

"Oh, pick me up? Maybe I could just come here."

"No. I'd get in trouble for that one. I've been in training for this date half my life. There are rules."

"Your mother isn't stable, is she?"

"She's just goal oriented. Don't want me to see your house?"

"Well, it's my boss. He's just a bit . . . fatherly. I don't know how he'd take it."

"You live with your boss?"

"No. I live next door to my boss, and he's a little nosy. Maybe I can meet you at a restaurant." I didn't know if Alex *was* nosey, but I could imagine him charming Jeff into staying for dinner. Wouldn't that be nice to sit between them while Jeff summed up how old Alex was?

"I'm good with people. Don't worry about it."

He found a little bucket, and we picked blackberries until my fingers were stained. "I wish we had blackberries at home. These are wonderful."

"These are nothing. You should taste Mom's blackberry pie . . . blackberry jam . . . blackberry syrup . . . blackberry pickles."

"So you're a little sick of blackberries?"

"The novelty of it wears off after awhile. It doesn't wear off of my mother, but the rest of us are pretty much blackberried out. She'll be thrilled to hear you like blackberries."

"Maybe she'll make you a blackberry cake."

"No. It'll be carrot cake. We should pull some carrots."

"You really think you'll have a cake in the morning?"

"She really likes you. I'm sure you're worth a cake. Food talks at our house."

"Yeah, my house too." I was thinking of Alex when I said it.

* * *

I pulled into the driveway just after eleven. Jeff had kept me late, drilling me with questions until I finally told him I had to work early the next morning.

I screamed when I opened the door.

Alex was standing there in a T-shirt and pajama pants. "I'm sorry. I didn't mean to frighten you."

I had to sit on the sofa and breathe for a minute. "What are you doing in here?"

"I thought you could sleep at my house tonight, and I could sleep here. Then you'd have water."

"Thank you, but I think I'd be more comfortable here."

"I've already got it set up. You can sleep in Gretchen's bed. Of course, I'll just sleep here on the couch."

I noticed there was a sleeping bag under me. It was a good thing I wasn't a privacy freak, or I would have killed him by now. Why did he think having a key meant he could use it? This was supposed to be my space . . . *and his shop*, I realized. There were a lot of blurred lines after all. Maybe we needed a little meeting in the morning about employee relations issues.

"Elise will be at home with you though. Then you'll know she won't be getting into things here."

"I'm really fine here."

"You'd be better off there. I've already set it up. Water. Think water."

I did love his shower, but it wasn't tempting enough. "It's just better if I stay here."

"Gretchen put new sheets and pillow cases on the bed. It's just waiting for you."

"I don't think so."

"Whaat?" It was a two-syllable whine. "Now, Jana, grow up and go to bed. I've got to get to work early, and you're home late keeping me up." He had an irritated, commanding look in his eyes.

"Alex, you should've asked me. I would have told you not to bother."

"I guess someone doesn't use her cell phone on Sunday." He leaned on the wall. "I can see I've caught you off guard." He put his arm around my shoulder and started to walk me toward the kitchen. He opened the back door. "It looks like you have two choices. You can go over to my house and explain to Elise that you're not having a sleepover after all, or you can get me to sleep earlier by being a grateful renter and saying, 'Oh, Alex, you're so thoughtful. Thank you for all the trouble you went to in making me comfortable. I appreciate being able to sleep in the most comfortable bed in your house while my water is out.'"

I bit my lip. "When do you have to wake up?"

"Four. I have to get my orders in early, drive around the city, pick up fish and produce from my suppliers. I can't just go to the Quickie Mart for Shallots' food."

"Oh. That fresh, huh?"

"Just on Mondays, Wednesdays, and Fridays. Don't tell anyone. Business will drop on *T* days." He ran his fingers through his hair. "I'm sorry. I didn't know this would upset you. It must be a woman thing I'm just not in tune with. But the damage is done now. Gretchen's bed is great. You'll love it. I just got it three months ago. There isn't even a dent where she sleeps yet." His voice was tired. He looked older. "Course, she hardly ever sleeps there."

"I don't want to be ungrateful." I decided it wasn't a big deal if I didn't make it a big deal. Not this once anyway. "I'll sleep over there tonight, but tomorrow you're giving me the key, or we can put a different lock on the upstairs apartment or something. You're creeping me out with your good intentions."

"Okay." He was heading for the couch. "Go be *creeped* out. I get home about seven or so. Don't let me scare you again. I can't stand to hear you scream."

"Hey, speaking of creeped out, this house is haunted. But don't let it bother you." I headed upstairs to get my suitcase.

From the couch, he called. "Speaking of *creeped out*, how was dinner?"

"Good. Not as good as yours, but it was good. They're a nice family. I like them a lot."

"No ambush?"

"Oh, there was an ambush. But it wasn't so bad. Good night."

"Mm-hmm." He sounded half asleep already.

His house was silent. Gretchen was in the kitchen, writing in a ledger. When she saw me, she closed it and stood, picking up her purse to go. "Where have you been?"

"I was at a friend's house. I hope you didn't have to stay late on my account."

She shook her head. "I can't get that girl to calm down. Alex shouldn't have told her you were sleeping here. Now she's too wound up. Every time I think she's asleep, I check on her and the light's on again."

After I locked the door behind Gretchen, I crept upstairs and down the hall to look for Elise. She was sitting up with her lamp on. "Hey, kiddo, I get to sleep at your house tonight. Is that okay?"

"Yeah! It will be fun. Wanna sleep in my bed?" She had a queen-size bed.

"You know, I sleep sprawled out with my legs everywhere. I'd just kick you in the bum. I snore too. Probably best I just sleep down the hall. Whatcha got there?"

Elise had a scrapbook on her lap. "It's how I say good night to Mom." There were pictures of Vanessa, Elise, and Alex together. They were taped on cardstock in page protectors. The pages had been very loved. Elise was about five years old in the pictures. Vanessa looked pale and sickly. "I wish I had new pictures, but we can't take pictures of her when she doesn't have a body."

I thought that was very insightful for a small child. I looked around the room at the bare walls. "Hey, we could make some pictures of you and your mom for your walls. Would you like that?"

"In purple frames? I want a purple room. My friend Karma has a purple room. It's the best."

"I bet we could put all the things you love in it."

"She has a disco ball too."

"I don't know about a disco ball. But we can make some great pictures of you and your mom and dad. And I know where we can get a good price on purple paint. You can help. You know how to paint now. We can make some curtains."

"I saw curtains with lots of beads in a magazine. Lots and lots and lots of beads. I love beads."

"Well, I can sew, but I'm not spending an eternity stringing beads. You can make as many bead strands as you want for it, and I'll help you tack them to it before we hang them up."

Elise stood up on her bed and started to jump excitedly. "And we could put a slide in it."

"Nope. I don't know how to make a slide."

"My own purple room; I can't wait. When can we do it? Can we start tomorrow?" She was jumping higher and higher.

Recognizing too much before-bed energy at such a late hour, I tried to calm her down. "We'd better get to sleep now. Say your prayers and get into bed." After I said it, I wondered if Elise was used to praying before bed. I had taken it for granted that my family prayed before bed but had to remind myself the rest of the world wasn't like my family. However, Elise must have been used to praying at night because she bounced through a very heartfelt prayer, asking God to kiss her mom. Obviously, she wasn't new to praying. I wondered if Alex prayed with her at night. Elise was still wiggling when I tucked the covers around her. "Maybe I could read you a story."

"The journal. Read me the journal!"

"What journal?"

"My mom's journal. It's red and gold, and my dad keeps it next to his bed."

"Oh, you know, that journal is in my apartment. Maybe I could read you something else. Do you have any other stories you want to hear?"

Elise calmed down immediately. "No, I guess not." She rolled onto her side and was still.

The ticking of the clock was suddenly loud. "I'll see if I can find it."

"Thanks, Jana." Elise yawned.

I put my suitcase in a room with a lilac bedspread. It reminded me of Gretchen. The room was decorated meticulously, unlike the rest of the house.

I screamed again when I found Alex in the kitchen, drinking from a carton of milk.

"Wish you'd stop screaming," he said sheepishly.

"I thought you were asleep at my place."

"Your house is haunted."

"What did you hear?" I laughed.

"What do you think I heard?" he asked, looking at me suspiciously.

"Something like a box sliding across the floor of the attic."

"That *is* what I heard. How did you know?"

"I sleep there more than you do. Want to change your mind? I bet this house isn't haunted."

"Where are you running to?" he asked.

"Elise wants me to read to her from the journal. It's on my desk with the scrapbooks."

"You'd do that? You're pretty great. Sometimes she needs a little extra something to calm her down. I'll go get it for you."

I'd wanted to know for weeks. "Isn't it private? I feel like I'd be trespassing to read it."

"I gave it to you so you *could* read it. I thought if you knew Vanessa better, it would help you build the shop. She does say I'm a mean, ornery ogre though; don't believe that part. She always did exaggerate. Does it bother you too much?"

"No. I just didn't want to invade her privacy." Surely Vanessa would be nearby watching me read the journal.

He must have sprinted because he was back before I was finished pouring my own glass of milk out of the new carton. He handed me the journal. When I went to take it, he didn't let go, so we both held it for a few seconds while he looked at me, obviously wondering something. "What is it?" I asked.

He blinked, as though he were just waking up. "Oh, uh . . . how do you sleep through the ghosts? Does it stop or go all night? I can't believe you didn't say anything. Aren't you scared there at night?"

"What's to be scared of? A ghost? And I'm not saying that's what it is because it could be any number of things. But if it doesn't have a body, it can't hurt me. Annoy me? Yes. Hurt me? No. I'm not easily spooked."

"I don't believe that for a minute. I've heard you scream twice just tonight."

"Okay, *you* are unbelievably spooky. But for normal things, like sliding boxes, I handle them fine." I thought of Rachel laughing at me because she knew what a sissy I really was. "I actually listen to classical music and play it on repeat all night. I don't have to have it turned up too high to cover the attic noise."

Alex left the room. I passed him a minute later on my way up the stairs. He had a handful of CDs and a boom box.

"G'night," he called over his shoulder.

I opened the door to Elise's room and found her fast asleep with her blankets off. I set the journal on the nightstand, pulled the blankets onto the sleeping angel, and crept out of the room.

In Gretchen's room, I pulled out my Book of Mormon and climbed under the covers. I hadn't read in three days. It felt good to get back to the scriptures.

After I changed into my pajamas, I turned out the lights and looked through the window at the trees swaying in the wind. After saying my prayers, I snuggled into the bed, trying to forget that I was sleeping in Alex's house. I tossed and turned. Finally, I got out of bed and said another prayer, asking Heavenly Father to help me forget where I was. It was five minutes to midnight. When I ended the prayer, my cell phone rang. I leaped to answer it before it woke Elise.

"Hiya, pumpkin." My father.

"Dad! You're the answer to a prayer."

"No kidding? How's that?"

"I couldn't sleep, so I prayed that I'd be able to soon, and you called."

"I'm that boring, am I?"

"Is everything okay? Why are you calling so late? Is everyone okay?"

"Well, I was sitting here eating my ice cream, and I was thinking about how we haven't talked in a while, and a little voice in my head said, 'She's still up.' So I called you. Don't tell Mom. I'll get in trouble for calling so late."

"I am still up."

"What's keeping you awake?"

"I'll tell if you tell."

He cleared his throat. "I'm awake because I was lying in bed and I remembered seeing your mom come in with a lot of grocery bags this afternoon. Well, I started thinking about that and I thought, *You know, Stan, that woman loves you so much that I bet she got some burnt almond fudge ice cream.*"

"Did she?"

"No. It's Twilight Mint. But it isn't half bad. Perfect for Christmas."

"I wish I were there with you."

"You'd just get in trouble too. Better that I take the heat alone. The carton is half gone. I'm going to have to jog for a day to make up for this."

"I should start jogging again too. My boss is a really good cook."

"I read all about him. Rachel showed me how to Google."

"You're on a computer? I'm so proud of you."

"Don't jump to conclusions. I can look things up, that's all. It's like a whole library in my own house. The pipes under the kitchen sink were dripping again. I found a website that has step-by-step be-your-own-plumber pictures. I fixed it. *I* fixed it. Your mom stood there the whole time, wagging her finger, saying I couldn't, but it's dry as a bone now."

"That proves her wrong. I get a plumber at my place tomorrow." I explained about having no water then told him about my day, ending with my current location and why I couldn't sleep.

"So do you like this Jeff more than Alex?"

"Dad, Alex isn't Mormon. I'm not even considering him. I like Jeff more than Brad."

"You like chickenpox more than Brad, honey. What does Jeff do for a living?"

"I never asked him. It didn't come up. He went to Brazil on his mission."

"I can't wait to meet him. I don't like not knowing where you are."

"I'm in Washington."

"But I can't see it. I don't know what it looks like. I know where everyone else is, but you're just dangling out there in the middle of nowhere. My little baby off on her own."

I rolled my eyes. "I'm not a baby. I'll take some pictures and send them to you."

"E-mail them."

"You have your own account? Wow, Rachel really got to you, didn't she?"

"Papa Barrowman at Lock Heaven dot com."

"You're using Troy's site?" Lock Heaven was my brother-in-law's company.

"It's free. Oops. I hear your mother," he whispered. "Better to get caught with a bowl of ice cream than a bowl of ice cream and a phone. Love you, honey."

He hung up before I could say good-bye. I shut the phone and crawled back into bed. I fell asleep quickly but dreamed of Brad chasing me. I was in a flouncy wedding dress and had kicked my high heels off so I could run faster. He was yelling behind me, "I can take you to the temple. He can't . . . He can't . . . He can't." He was suddenly holding me with his face inches away from mine. "Show up for this." Thankfully I was able to pull myself awake before the kiss.

Stripes of sunlight were shining through the blinds. Gretchen's clock radio showed seven forty. I blinked a few times and realized I hadn't taken off my makeup before bed.

"Wow," a tiny voice interrupted my thoughts. "I think you had a bad dream, Jana."

I sat up. Elise was sitting on the floor just inside the bedroom. Her hair was braided with ribbons, and she was wearing a blue-and-white-striped shirt. "What makes you think that?"

"You said, 'I won't, I won't,' and you were kicking."

"How long have you been watching me?"

Elise shrugged. "Gretchen said I could come be with you after my cereal was gone."

"Gretchen's here?"

In answer, Gretchen called from downstairs, "Elise, time to go."

"I have to go to school. Can we paint my room tonight?"

I rubbed my face. "We have to ask your dad."

"He's asleep downstairs. I'll go ask him."

"No. Don't wake him up. He's more likely to say yes if we let him rest first, okay?"

"Okay. Bye, Jana."

When she left, I reached over and picked up my phone. I called my voice mail and erased all of Brad's messages without listening to them. I opened my text messages menu and scrolled through the fourteen texts he had left me. Without opening them, I could only see the short first line of each one as I erased them. "Gone 2 long, miss u, time 2 come home . . ." caught my eye as I pressed Erase. However, the one he had sent earlier in the afternoon said, "Coming 2 take u home." I opened it and read, "Coming 2 take u home. Sick of waiting. Why aren't u calling me back?"

I replied to this one. "I am happy here. Don't come. I'm not coming home. We're done dating." I smiled, thinking how much easier this was than having a long conversation with him where I'd end up dating him at the end anyway. "How do you like them apples?" I said to the phone as I flipped it closed. It buzzed immediately. I opened it and read the message. "It's the chef, isn't it? Your mother told me." I snapped the phone closed with too much force. What was my mother doing talking to Brad? I thought about calling her but decided it wouldn't be wise until I'd calmed down. I stuffed my phone into my purse.

I took a long shower in a hall bathroom, letting the water beat down on my shoulders. I skipped drying my hair but redid my makeup. I put on a pair of old jeans and a sweatshirt then tiptoed down the stairs to peek in on Alex. He was out cold, with his feet hanging over one end of the couch and one hand touching the floor. He was wearing tan slacks with a blue shirt and burgundy tie. I felt a pang of guilt for sleeping so much. I stood over him, debating waking him so he could go up to bed. He rolled over and smiled. If he was having a good dream, I wasn't going to wake him. At least someone had a good dream to go with their sleep.

I found a basic ladder suspended on a wall in Alex's garage. As carefully as possible, I hefted it to the apartment. The call of mysterious attic boxes couldn't be ignored any longer. I had talked myself into believing my imagination was running away with me. Knowing Alex had heard it too, I was now driven by a strong curiosity. If it wasn't a ghost moving boxes, maybe it *was* just a nest of rats. I shivered at the thought and stopped for a moment at the top of the stairs to rethink my bravery.

I shook my head to clear it before I pushed the ladder up through the door in the ceiling. The ladder was barely long enough to rest on the edge of the opening, but it was enough. I took my first step onto the bottom rung and bounced to make sure it was safe. Plaster dust drifted down like snow. Taking a deep breath, I climbed up.

The attic had a makeshift floor of wooden slats lying across the ceiling joists. There were at least a dozen cardboard boxes and an old steamer trunk. The air was thick and dusty, well lit by the light from a round window at the end of the room.

As I was lifting myself into the attic, the plaster the ladder was leaning against cracked, and the ladder pushed forward like it was slicing through chalk. Before I knew it, there was nothing under my feet, and I was listening to the echoes of the ladder clanking on the wood floor below. I was leaning into the attic from the waist up, my legs dangling. I tried to pull myself all the way into the attic, but I couldn't get a good grip. Every time I moved, I slipped down a little.

"What's up there?" I could actually hear him smiling, but I didn't care. I was glad to hear his voice. I wasn't going to break any bones today.

"A ditzy blonde lady who thinks she's more athletic than she really is. Why do you ask?"

"Up you go." He pushed on the bottom of my feet, making it possible for me to shimmy onto the floorboards.

I turned to look down at him from the hole. "Thanks." I smiled at him.

"I'm not going to ask you what you were thinking because obviously you weren't." He bent over the ladder. "You didn't adjust the ladder. It needs to be taller for that. See here." He pulled on the top half of the ladder, and it caught three rungs higher. He started to lift it up to the hole.

"No, don't. There's nowhere to rest it. It just cut through the plaster here."

"Look around the hole. There's got to be a joist or something."

Opposite of where I'd put the ladder, a wood beam ran along the hole. I grabbed the top of the ladder and swung it around to rest on the wood. Alex stepped onto the bottom rung. More plaster dust drifted down and landed in stark contrast on his raven hair.

"Okay, it's safe," he called. Come on down."

"I just got here. Come on up."

"Are you kidding? It's haunted up there."

I folded my arms and frowned at him. He shook his head and started loosening his tie. After he draped it over the banister, he started climbing. He got high enough that his head and shoulders were in the attic before he looked around and said, "Wow, dust. That's neat, Jana. Let's get some breakfast."

"Look, it's the boxes." I crawled to the steamer trunk. "And look here; you can see the marks where they've been dragging through the dust."

He was suddenly interested and climbed farther through the hole. "Any footprints?"

"Not even a mouse. Will you help me get them downstairs?"

He rolled his eyes and looked at the ceiling. "Jana."

"Please. I'll do it without you, and you know I'll get hurt." I hated to do it, but I turned my most affectionate eyes on him.

"Women can be so evil," he said. "Let me change my clothes."

I was so excited I almost clapped. "I'll wait here." I started unstacking the boxes. I couldn't open the steamer trunk and was looking around for a key to it when Alex came back.

"Okay, how heavy are they? We're going to have to make some kind of sling." He slapped a roll of duct tape on the floor and sat next to me in blue jeans and a black T-shirt.

I smiled at him and realized he didn't seem quite awake yet. "Oh, you look so tired." Pity pulled at my conscience. "I guess we could wait until later. Maybe you should take another nap."

"I look like death warmed over. I can hear it in your voice."

"No, you look a little tired, that's all." The attic was silent. A stream of light from the window lit the dust particles between us. I realized I'd been looking at him too long when I felt a few butterflies in my stomach. He hadn't looked all that handsome to me when I'd first met him, but after the last few weeks, I looked at him with different eyes. He wasn't the same kind of handsome as Brad. He was more rugged with a broad jaw. His lips were smooth. The bottom edge of his lower lip pouted out ever so slightly. Looking into his hazel eyes, I realized why he was the most hunted bachelor in Seattle. It was like seeing him for the first time. He was gorgeous—more than gorgeous. Stunning. My face flushed involuntarily, and I could feel my ears burning.

He looked at the ceiling and smiled, making the dimple in his left cheek the most pronounced I'd ever seen it. He coughed and looked past me. "Would you look at that? An old boat trunk." He stood up, almost bumping his head on the ceiling. He tried to open it like I had. "Guess what?" He was looking a little too happy and suddenly awake. I looked down to study the dust on the floor, certain his transformation had had nothing to do with the trunk. "I think the key to this might be on an old key ring I got with the house. It's a spooky little barbed thing. I always wondered what it went to." He looked back to study me. His eyes moved across my face. It looked like he was carefully calculating the color of my burning ears. Keenly aware of my sudden attraction for him, I felt heat as my blush deepened. At the exact moment I was sure my face couldn't get any hotter, his face lit up with pleasure.

I studied the cobwebs in the rafters. He knew what I'd been thinking. I saw it as plain as day on his face, probably as plainly as he'd been able to read mine. My mouth dropped open, and my heart quickened. It didn't matter, I told myself. Nothing had changed. So he was gorgeous, at that moment, the most beautiful man I'd ever seen. He was still my un-Mormon boss. That's all that mattered. I looked up and found him narrowing his eyes as he continued to study me. My ears continued to burn. He raised an eyebrow, sitting in front of me. I looked down and rubbed the dust between my fingers.

"Jana." He lifted my chin and leaned toward me. His hand smelled like soap. A satisfied smile had reached his eyes. "Your ears are red."

I looked down again. "It's hot."

He stroked my cheek with his thumb. A current of electricity ran through his hand until it reached my toes with a shock. "Your cheek is warm."

I wondered if he could see the vein on my neck pulse with my heart. I opened my mouth and tried to breathe slowly to calm my heart. I heard a faint ringing in my ears. Then it stopped then started again. I furrowed my brow, trying to clear my head. It stopped. When it started again, I realized my phone was ringing. I sighed, relieved to have a reason to get away from him.

"I've got to get that." I scrambled down the ladder, deciding to change the ring on my cell phone to a musical tone. "Hullo?" I was holding the bridge of my nose between my fingers, still trying to clear my head.

"Hey there." It was Rachel. "Hope I didn't wake you up."

"Oh no. I'm up." Though, feeling mortified, I wished I'd been dreaming.

"How's it going? You got a minute?"

I walked into my apartment, locked the door, and sat down on the couch. "Right now, I've got all the time in the world." I'd have given anything to not have to open that door again.

"Well, I've got some good news, some medium news, and some bad news. What do you want first?"

Sudden anxiety about my family cleared my head. "The bad news."

"Dad went in for his colonoscopy Tuesday, and the doctors found a polyp about the size of an olive."

"Medium news?"

"After a biopsy, they decided it has to come out. It's nothing they can't remove quickly, but it's cancerous. They're going to take out a small part of his intestine too, just to be safe. He'll be up and around in two weeks."

"What's the good news?"

"We're going to California next month."

"That's great. Back to Dad here, okay? When does he go in for surgery?"

"Sometime this week, probably tomorrow. I didn't think he'd tell you because he wouldn't want you to come home. So I called Mom to make sure they called you. She said exactly what I thought she would. Didn't want to worry you when you were so far away. So then I started thinking I'd want to know about it. And let's face it. I love him, we all do, but you're a lot closer to Dad than anyone else. I couldn't live with myself if I didn't tattle. And I know you'd kill me later anyway if I didn't call you."

"Is Mom taking it okay?"

"She says she fasted and prayed about it, and she knows it will be okay. But I think she's still pretty worried." Rachel paused while I let everything sink in. "So?"

"So what?"

"Are you coming home?"

"I'm already there. See you tonight."

"Wait! Don't hang up. Did you look in the attic?"

"I did."

"How was it?"

"Terrifying." I shut the phone and stared around the room. Tears pressed against my eyes, threatening to spill over. I commanded myself to get a grip. Then I slipped to the floor and prayed for help. I'd need help getting home quickly, help comforting my mother, and help being strong myself. Most of all, I prayed for my father, reasoning with God that he was needed here on earth so he could keep doing temple work, keep being an example to his children, and keep being an anchor in my life. The last and hardest thing I said before ending the prayer was, "Thy will be done in all things."

I rushed out of the room and down the stairs to find Alex. "Alex," I called, trying to keep the panic out of my voice but failing when I called too loudly and my voice cracked.

He was at the bottom of the stairs. "What is it?"

"I need to get home. We have a family emergency. Do you have the Internet?"

"Follow me." Without asking why, he quickly led the way back to his house. I followed him upstairs to an office where a closed laptop sat on a desk. He opened it and had the Internet running in seconds.

He pulled a chair out for me, and I sat down. I stared at the screen, trying to remember what airline I'd flown in on.

"I think you're a little upset. Let me help you."

"I need to get home."

"You're going home? You're leaving?" I could have smacked him and expected to see the same look on his face.

"I'll come back," I promised. "It's my Dad. I need to get home. Fast."

"We'll just call Gretchen."

"This is faster." I motioned to the computer.

"You don't know Gretchen. She can move planets. I'll give her a call. We'll get you on the next flight out." He was leaving the room when he turned around to ask, "And you said you're coming back, right?"

"Yes." I couldn't help sounding angry. I followed him down to the kitchen.

He was already on the phone. "Two tickets. You can pick up Elise, can't you?" He pulled out a chair and motioned for me to sit then grabbed two bowls with his free hand. He handed the phone to me.

"Hello?" No one answered.

"You're on hold." He sat down with a box of cereal, jug of milk, and two spoons. He poured the cereal and milk then held his hand out for the phone.

I stared into the bowl. Why was I still sitting here? I should be packing.

"Eat. You look like you need it."

"Why do you say that?"

"I think it's the vacant, comatose stare."

"I've really got to go pack. I need to get gas."

"You need to get airline tickets," he said in a bored tone, finishing my list. "I don't think you should drive. You're spacey." He pushed the bowl toward me.

"I can handle it. I have to get going."

He shifted the phone to his other ear and looked at me pointedly. "And the airport is where, Jana?"

I thought for a moment then smiled sheepishly. "In Seattle."

"Bingo. I'm driving. Eat your breakfast." He used the same look he used with Elise. "Then you can go pack, and I'll grab you in fifteen minutes to take you to the airport, where we will probably have to wait anyway."

He left his cereal at the table. "I'm going to change my clothes—again." I heard him on the phone as he went upstairs, ". . . her father. I don't know, maybe a day or two, three tops . . . We'll just have to get those when it's time . . . Uh-huh, Scott can take care of it . . . I don't know, we'll just pay him more. He went with me last week. He knows the routine . . ." His voice faded. "I'll call Elise at school to let her know."

I obediently took three bites of cereal before I took the bowl to the sink and rinsed the rest down the disposal. Alex was probably right. I felt like I was walking around in a fog. I wouldn't be able to find the airport on the best day, let alone when I was upset. I was grateful that he was helping me, but at the same time, I felt a tremendous irritation toward him. The all-knowing smile he'd flashed me in the attic was too much. I wasn't going to be attracted to him. It wasn't an option. He knew it wasn't an option. The problem was, he'd caught me. Would he just forget that he'd seen me blushing, that he had read my mind? I certainly wasn't going to bring it up. I thought of what I'd seen. The look on his face was now seared into my memory, burned into place by the blush that had given me away.

Nice, real nice. I pushed it out of my mind. Now I had more important things to think about. He was behaving like a complete gentleman, albeit a bit fatherly and overbearing. I wasn't going to decide there was a problem where there wasn't one. I rushed home to pack.

CHAPTER 5
Sobering Valley

GRETCHEN *could* MOVE PLANETS. ALEX herded me to a counter and through security to a terminal. The flight was boarding as we walked up. The more I thought about my father, the more I felt immersed in fog. It wasn't until Alex handed the terminal clerk two tickets that I realized something was wrong. I had been in such a daze, worried about my father, that I hadn't noticed what Alex was doing. But I suddenly realized he had helped me through security instead of staying on the other side of the gates, and a flash of "Scott can take care of it . . . he knows the routine," jumped into my mind. I grabbed his sleeve. "Whoa, where do you think you're going?"

He pulled me through the line and alongside him into the walkway. "I'm just making sure you get home safely." I struggled against him. He firmly took my hand, ignoring my resistance. "Let's get you on the plane."

"You don't have to go with me. I'm fine now. I'm here. I know my way around Salt Lake. I'll get a cab." I dug in my heels. People were backing up behind us.

He looked at me like I was deranged. "Jana, I've been lucky that you've had one foot in front of the other the whole time we've been here. I've kept you from smacking into at least eight people and some very obvious walls. Come on, people are waiting." He leaned in closer. "They're watching us. They're watching me."

His warm breath on my ear made my stomach tremble. A quick flash of light made me look behind us. I was surprised to see a crowd of curious people. One had a camera. There was another flash of light. I walked quickly down the walkway behind Alex, letting him guide me.

He was still holding my hand five minutes later when the stewardess asked if we wanted anything. Realizing that it looked like we were together, I shook my hand loose. Alex laughed and ordered a soda for me. I sat up taller and looked around. The last hour and a half was disjointed in my memory, with large chunks missing. I couldn't remember the drive to the airport. I could remember part of walking through the airport and the crowd of people looking at me, at Alex.

"You're flying us first class?"

"All they had this fast."

"I'll pay you back for the tickets. Thank you so much. You're right. I'm a little spacey right now."

"A little?"

"That bad, huh? I just feel . . . foggy. I can't think straight. I'm so worried about my dad. I can't believe they weren't going to tell me."

"So now that we're on the plane to Salt Lake, do you want to tell me what's going on?"

"That's right. I didn't tell you. You did all this for me, and you didn't know why. I'll pay you back. How much do I owe you?"

"Business expense. It's nothing."

"How can it just be nothing?"

"I am a corporation. It would be more bother than it's worth for you to pay it back. Besides, it's just a drop in the bucket compared to our other expenses. I'll scout out suppliers while I'm there."

"You're a corporation?"

"Steadman Corp."

"What does it do? I mean, is it the restaurant?"

"It's all under a corporate umbrella. It protects profits. Take, for example, my board of directors. They have four meetings a year, and we fly them out to Disneyland for those meetings."

"Disneyland? For a corporate meeting?"

"Elise and I are on the board, and she always gets to pick."

"Oh." I had never been to Disneyland in my life and couldn't imagine going four times a year. "Well, thank you. I am still in your debt. I really appreciate this. I think it's a waste for you to have to go too though."

"I wouldn't be able to sleep tonight if I didn't know I'd seen you safely home. What's up with your dad?"

"He's having a little surgery tomorrow to take some cancer out of his colon."

"How little is the surgery? Is it outpatient?"

I laughed. "Yes, it probably is. I guess it looks silly for me to be this worried. They caught it early. It shouldn't be a problem. The hardest part of being in Washington is being away from my dad. I can't think of him going through this and me not being there. It's making me a little crazy."

"Well, you'll be there. Don't worry." He shifted in his seat, picked up a magazine, flipped it open, then put it back. "You've got two hours to entertain me. Tell me more about your family."

"Entertain you? I'm not as interesting as you. I'm afraid you're out of luck."

He shrugged and motioned for me to get on with it.

"You asked for it. I know you think you want to know all this, but when I'm done, you'll be terrified and sorry you ever asked."

"Like I said, we've got time."

"Okay, I'm one of five children."

He let out a low whistle.

"I'm the baby. My parents were forty when I surprised them." I told him about my brothers and sisters, ending with my favorite. "And then there's Rachel. She's my favorite. She married Troy. They have three and a half kids."

"Were you spoiled?"

"Not necessarily." I looked at him. "There wasn't enough room or money to be spoiled. But I am the closest to my father out of any of them. You can probably imagine they all wanted out of the crowded house pretty fast. In that, I was spoiled. I had space. I always had my own bedroom so I don't know what it's like to share a room with three other kids. I spent most of my life in the new house. I don't remember much about the two-bedroom house in Magna." After a short silence I asked, "So are you frightened?"

"That anyone could live through that many children is amazing. Your parents must be quite something."

"My mom is organized. I never got to see how she did it, but I remember a lot of kids borrowing the car. Vacations were crazy. But we all got along pretty well. The Taylors I went to dinner with last night have seven children."

"Wow. Which one did they choose for you?"

"Second born."

"Are all of your siblings Mormon?"

"Yes. They all made it."

"Made it where?"

"Well, you always wonder how your kids will turn out. You hope they'll stick to the gospel and do what's right. We always had family scripture study.

My dad would wake us up at six every morning before he left so we could have family prayer and a little devotional. I guess it worked because other than a few bumps along the way, we all stayed in the Church." I wanted to paint a wider gap between us to show him how important my religion was to me, just in case he felt like reciprocating any of the attraction I'd discovered in the attic. "It probably sounds pretty fanatical to you, doesn't it?"

"No. Just amazing, that's all." He looked at me. "It helps a little, you know, for me to understand why you'd only date a Mormon. It's all you've known. It's probably what you've been taught since you were born."

I nodded.

"But it's wrong," he said and completely surprised me. "There are a lot of good men who aren't Mormon. You're selecting fish from a very shallow pool."

"Huh." I scoffed. "Maybe you don't know much about fishing. I'll be selecting fish from the best pool in the world, with the clearest water and the healthiest fish."

"I bet these *fish* are jumping into your net and you keep turning them back. If they're so great, why haven't you kept any? You know, take one home and fry it up."

"I'm just waiting for the right fish."

"What if he's waiting for you but he's swimming in a different pond?"

"Alex, you're being obtuse. Think about it. If I marry a Mormon, a returned missionary, I know he can budget money, sew on his own buttons, obey the Lord, sustain a testimony, and take me to the temple, a place where our family will be sealed together forever. I know he will help me rear my children in the Church. They'll have both parents to show them the gospel is true."

"I'm just saying you should at least try fishing in different ponds so you can see if yours is really the best."

"If you know you'd never take it home and fry it up, why bother fishing for it in the first place? If you knew from the beginning you'd never marry it, why date it?"

"I see you don't understand the true joy of fishing. I should teach you how to fish." He smiled.

I laughed. "*You're* going to teach me to fish? You haven't been fishing since Vanessa died. Gretchen told me." My eyes grew wide. I wondered if I'd hit a nerve. I didn't know how sensitive he was about being alone without his wife. "Oh, I'm sorry. I didn't mean . . . It must be hard. I just got carried away."

"It's okay. I'm fine with it." He looked thoughtful, suddenly grown-up. He rested his head against the back of his chair. "But I think I'll still teach you to fish." He turned his head toward me, looking tired, like he had in the attic that morning. "There are some great places in Utah. We can go up Bear River. You'll like it."

"Exactly how long do you think you're staying in Utah?"

"Exactly how long are you staying in Utah?" He raised an eyebrow. "That reminds me. I was going to compliment you. I've never seen a woman pack so light." He yawned. "One carry-on. It must be another amazing Barrowman talent." He closed his eyes and shifted in his seat.

"You'd think so, but my closet at home is full of clothes. I didn't need to pack much."

He was quiet after that. I leaned back in my seat and wondered what I'd do with him while I was home. At least Rachel could meet him. I thought about what Gretchen had told me. He didn't trust anyone. It must be a big sacrifice for him to drop everything for me. He'd have to trust a lot of people in Washington to leave everything in their hands, especially his daughter. He didn't treat it like it was out of the ordinary to drop everything and fly to a different state for an employee.

I watched him sleep. He looked so peaceful. His skin was slightly suntanned. His head crept closer to his shoulder as his neck relaxed. I knew it must have cost him a lot of money to fly both of us to Salt Lake first class at the last minute and wondered why he was doing it. He was right. I would have smacked into heaven knows how many walls and people. The fog was gone now as I puzzled over him. I wondered what he thought of how crazy I could be when I worried about my dad. I *was* crazy about my father. It was sickening to think of him in surgery, passed out on a gurney, with green clad men standing over him, ready to cut him open. I didn't care how standard the procedure was.

Alex was crazy to fly all the way to Salt Lake though. He could have booted me onto the plane. I would have made it home. His chest gently rose and fell. I had to admit that it was nice not being alone. And I hated to admit that I wanted to spend more time with him. Ever since I'd seen him in the attic earlier, my heart raced if I looked at him too long. It was nice to have him sleeping so I could look as long as I wanted without him knowing. There he was, my forbidden fruit. Surely it was wrong to indulge in my study of him, especially since I knew I'd never take him home and "fry him up." I shook my head so I could start thinking straight again. I leaned on my armrest and looked across the aisle at a chunky redheaded man. He reminded me of an attorney I knew.

I did like my new job, though my fingertips were calloused from burning myself with the glue gun every day. I looked at my nails. They still had cream paint spattered across them from Saturday. Out of curiosity, I looked at Alex's hands. He was wearing his wedding band. A lot of good that did him. He was still being chased by hungry wolves like Kristen.

I wondered if he really meant to stay in Salt Lake as long as I did. Maybe he was afraid I wouldn't come back and finish the shop. It was unfathomable to me that he would even consider staying a day. I decided to try to talk him into going home when we got off the plane. He wouldn't. I knew he wouldn't. Even if I showed him I was sane, he wouldn't budge. I imagined showing up on our doorstep, Alex standing beside me, my mother beside herself jumping to all the wrong conclusions. Why didn't it bother anyone that he wasn't LDS? Rachel didn't care. Mom didn't care.

I *did* care. I didn't even know if he believed in God. I remembered Elise praying. Someone must have taught her, perhaps her mother. I realized I was probably flattering myself that Alex was even interested. He could have any one of hundreds of women to choose from. I probably looked like a country bumpkin to him. He'd only ever seen me in my holey jeans, except when I went to church. Maybe he *was* a cad and just got a kick out of how women felt when he stopped their hearts. It could have been he did want me but only because I said he couldn't have me. Maybe I was just a game to him. No. I was sure I wasn't. He wasn't shallow. He was a deep soul. He was incredibly tenderhearted despite his celebrity status. I would have expected him to be more emotionally hardened because of Vanessa's death. Maybe fathering Elise had kept him genuine.

I wondered what my father would think of him. What was I thinking? It didn't matter what my father thought of him because he wasn't a keeper. He was just my boss. I sat up taller in my seat and folded my arms. I was not going to fall for the great Alex Steadman, chef divine. I stared at the seat in front of me.

I had made the decision not to drink alcohol or take drugs when I was ten. I had made the decision once. I made the decision to go to the temple. I had made the decision once, and years later, I went to the temple. I didn't rethink it time and again, making the choice anew at each temptation. So here I was with Mr. Temptation, who probably wasn't interested anyway. I didn't have to make my choice again. I was going to marry a Latter-day Saint man. I didn't need to "fish" in other ponds. Luckily the laugh that escaped my lips wasn't very loud. I wasn't about to trifle with eternity. The idea was suddenly ludicrous to me. Everything became very simple in my mind. I wanted my husband and my children, whoever they were, to be mine forever. I wouldn't risk that for anything. I leaned back and rolled my head to face him. He was more beautiful than ever. I closed my eyes to take my own nap, with my last thoughts tainted by his handsome face.

* * *

"You look like you're doing much better. I haven't had to save one pedestrian since we got here," Alex commented on the way to the rental car counter.

"It's Salt Lake. It's a very sobering valley. Can I talk to you for a minute?" I had to try to reason with him. "Come, sit down."

We found a bench nearby. "Alex, I think it's all right for you to go home now. I'm fine." I held up my hands to show him I was working now. "Look, I know how hard it is for you to be away from the restaurant and everything at home. Gretchen told me that you don't like to . . ." I was hoping I wasn't betraying Gretchen's confidence, "leave things to other people. You like to take care of things yourself. You look like it isn't bothering you a fig, but I'm sure it's harder than you're letting on to just drop everything and fly away." He stared at me with an unreadable expression. "It's not that I'm not grateful. I am. I think you're wonderful for bringing me out here. It's probably the nicest thing anyone has ever done for me. It's above and beyond the call of a good boss. But I don't want to be a hardship on your business and family."

He clapped silently. "Bravo. Let me see if I can counter that performance."

I looked at him crossly, folding my arms. "It wasn't a performance."

"I'm sure in the past, what Gretchen said would have been true, but I'm, for lack of better words, growing up now. I feel fine about leaving for a few days. In fact, I've been so annoyed at work lately that I was excited to leave. This is different from a sick day. They can't get me here. I'm free. Perhaps it's just for a few days, but I'm free just the same." He looked truly excited. "And if you will let me escort you home, I'll spend some free time in Park City. I promise I won't be sorry for it later."

"What's in Park City?"

"Haven't you ever been there?" he asked incredulously.

"Of course I've been there. I was just wondering what you thought you were going to be doing up there."

"I have a condo. I think I'll take a long bath, rent some movies, and take myself to dinner . . . You know, have a little vacation."

I looked at him, deciding it probably wasn't likely that I'd actually be able to persuade him to go home. I couldn't call him obstinate. He just knew what he wanted. He didn't make his choices more than once either. We had a lot in common. I sighed. At least he'd be spending the time in Park City. "C'mon. I'll drive."

When I saw my house, I started to undo my seat belt. I pulled into the driveway and yanked the key out of the ignition. When I reached for the door handle, he said, "Let me get your door. What will your father think?"

"He doesn't know I'm here, and he'll think you're from the wrong pond anyway, so it doesn't matter." I opened the door, but he was on the other side of it, offering me his hand before I could blink.

"Does your father fish?"

I took his unnecessary hand for the smallest moment to be polite then skirted around him. Running to the door, I managed to call behind me, "Does a bird fly?" The door was locked, so I pressed the doorbell half a dozen times, hoping it would hurry my mother to answer. She didn't disappoint.

"Jana, what are you doing—? Alex!" I tried not to resent that she had a warm smile for him and not for me. You would have thought I brought Santa Claus.

I squirmed around my mother and darted through the entry, calling for my father. I found him at the kitchen table, reading the paper. I stopped and plopped into a chair as casually as possible, trying to hide my ragged breathing. He looked up over the edge of his glasses at me and raised an eyebrow. "What took you so long?"

"Mom didn't call. I had to hear it through the grapevine."

"I knew you'd be here. It's all for nothing though. I'm fine."

Tears threatened to spill over. He looked so good. It was heaven being close to him again. "You'd better be." I didn't want him to see me cry. My mother's laughter drifted into the kitchen.

"What's she going on about?" He listened intently. Alex's voice drifted into the kitchen. "You brought a man?"

"A man brought me. It's just my boss. He wanted a little vacation."

"A man brought you? The chef?" He was standing up, clearly amused. "I know all about your chef."

I lowered my voice, not sure if they were heading for the kitchen. "He's not *my* chef, and I don't know what you think you know, but you don't know anything if you heard it from Rachel."

"She helped me Google him. Remember?"

"Good grief," I said loudly. "What would this world do without Google?"

"Google?" Alex entered the room, extending his hand to my dad. "Mr. Barrowman, I am Alex Steadman."

I felt a little betrayed at how happy my father looked to see him. Did nobody notice he wasn't a fish from the right pond? Were my parents so desperate to get rid of me that they'd settle for anything? Surely their standards must be higher than a floppy-haired, non-Mormon chef. I turned to see if I could discern what they saw when they looked at him. His hair wasn't tousled at all. He looked almost professional. I'd spent hours with him and hadn't noticed. When I looked at him, I could only see the best of him. He was radiant. No doubt the same radiance that had Seattle falling for him. The longer I watched him talk to my father, the more silent my world became. I could see lips moving, but I couldn't hear their words. Alex was a little too perfect. He stood straighter. He dimpled deeper when he smiled. His voice was steadier. He was *schmoozing* my parents. He was using whatever had made him the celebrity he was. I had never seen him like this, but I recognized it from Brad. My eyes narrowed, and the silence broke when he looked my way. The sound of the dishwasher rang in my ears. I don't know if he saw the suspicion dawning on my face, but he winked at me, accentuating the light crow's feet around his smiling eyes. I focused on the conversation, hoping to undo some of the damage.

"We could leave in the morning. I could be here around nine. Is that too early?"

My dad scratched the stubble on his chin. "You say you'll bring the poles?"

I stood up. They weren't going to pal around together on my watch. I had visions of my whole family extolling the benefits of other ponds. I stood between Alex and my father. "He can't go. He has surgery tomorrow, remember?"

My mother corrected. "Oh, sweetie, you came so fast we couldn't tell you it was postponed a day." She hadn't called me sweetie since I'd graduated from college. It was a term she saved for those times when I was especially pleasing her.

My heart started to thump a little faster. "He has cancer. He should be in bed, not fishing."

"Nonsense," my father boomed. "I don't have cancer. I have a polyp, a little olive in my gut. I'm fine."

"A polyp in your gut is called cancer, Dad." I said it a little too condescendingly and felt immediately repentant.

"Honey, I had it a week ago, a month ago. I've been playing basketball, golfing, planting trees. I haven't keeled over yet. It is nothing to worry about. I've always wanted to learn fly fishing . . ."

"Fly fishing?" I turned on Alex. "You're going to take my dad to stand in the middle of some raging river when he's in this condition? You have got to be kidding."

"I said I'd teach you to fish. I'd love to bring him along."

"I don't want to fish." I hissed it, barely moving my lips.

"We'll miss you." Alex's smile was kind, but I could see a cunning hunter in his eyes. He knew he was gaining a point I didn't want him to have.

My mother moved in. "It does seem like a bit much, Stan. Maybe you could take Jana along just to make sure you're okay."

"Honey?" My father looked at me.

"You could sit on the shore and watch," Alex suggested. "You don't have to go in, but I have some waders if you change your mind."

My mother was looking at me like I was retarded. *She* would probably put waders on for the Master Chef. "I'm not a doctor. How do I make sure he's okay? I think you should take it easy, Dad."

"Well, we will miss you." I was surprised to see the same cunning look in his eyes that Alex had. He knew I wasn't going to let them go off on their own together. I wished I'd been listening to the first half of their conversation so I could tell how Alex had bamboozled my father so quickly.

When situations became too hard for me, I generally stopped talking and took a break. Maybe that's why I could never gain a conclusion with Brad. He would talk me into a corner, and I'd give up until another day. I didn't want to commit to going fishing, but I could already see myself sitting on the shore, flinching every time my father stumbled on a rock in the current. "I'm going to unpack."

"I'll get your bag." Alex left the room, and my mother followed him like a seagull waiting for bread crumbs.

"Dad," I whined.

"You're acting like I'm making friendly with the enemy. Is he a bad guy?"

"No. He's fine. You should just take it easy." I started pushing the chairs in around the table.

"Jana, what's wrong? I haven't seen you hang your head like that in a long time."

I looked at my dad, my best friend, the one with the olive in his gut. "Everyone likes him," I said in a disappointed tone.

"What's not to like?"

"I just . . . I just hope you all realize he's not a Latter-day Saint, and there's nothing between us. There never could be. Just tell me you know that, and I'll be okay."

"He's LDS. He just doesn't know it yet."

"Dad," I whined again.

"He's not what you want, and there's nothing between you," he said in a monotone voice.

"Can't you just say he's not Mormon."

"Everyone's Mormon; some people just don't know it yet." He kissed me on the forehead and left the room.

That was just like my father. I wished I were more like him. He'd make his final points then leave. I wanted to learn to make my final points. I thought of Brad. Brad always made his final points. I was spineless.

Alex was waiting in my bedroom.

"You know, I've never had a guy in my room before. This is weird," I said when I walked in.

"Is it bad? That I'm in here?"

"If we were teenagers, my mother would be in here with a shotgun."

"Your *mother* has a shotgun?"

I didn't answer. He studied the pictures on my walls. "This room is like you." He turned to look at me, his eyes roving over my face.

"How so?"

"It's constant, the same themes and colors everywhere. It knows what it is, comfort in every corner . . . It smells like you."

"I smell?"

"Yeah." He smiled wider.

The butterflies in my stomach began to flit around. I had to dredge up my annoyance to stamp them back down. "You know you aren't running for president here. You don't have to bamboozle my parents. They would have liked you plain."

"I didn't *bamboozle* anyone. I just asked if he'd like to go fishing."

"You know what I mean. You turned the ol' Steadman charm on them."

He laughed. "I think that's a compliment. You just called me charming."

"You know what I mean," I said again. "You're not like that usually."

"Not like what? You *don't* think I'm charming?"

I rolled my eyes at him. I postured to show him. "The straight back, the smooth voice, the dimple."

He laughed some more, a little louder this time. "I have a dimple?"

I picked up a pillow and threw it at him, glaring. "You know you have a dimple."

He picked the pillow up off the floor and said, "I'm glad we've progressed in our relationship to the point where you're comfortable throwing pillows at me." He smelled it and tossed it on the bed. "It smells like you too."

I growled.

"Okay," he said, "when you're nervous, you annunciate your consonants sharply."

"Huh?" What that had to do with the price of rice in China I couldn't figure out.

"So when I'm nervous, I guess I command an air of, well, I'm . . . I don't know . . . I go into this mode, my people mode. And when the people go away, I go out of it."

"Am I not a *people*, because I've never seen this *mode* before?"

"No. You're better than a people. You're real." He walked to the window and looked down on the backyard. "Wow. That's some yard."

"We went a little nuts with the garden rooms. If you want to plant a tree, I'm your girl."

He turned his head to look at me so swiftly that I wished I could take back the last sentence. "I've got to go. I promised your mother I'd help with dinner."

"Oh no. I'm sorry, Alex. You come all the way here and you have to cook. Why don't you take a night off? I'll explain it to her."

"I offered." He shrugged. "It was my idea."

"Now listen," the breath coming from my nose was hot with irritation, "you can't do this. You can't make them like you like this. It's going to make my life very difficult if they think there is a chance we'd date. They'll be on me night and day." I remembered that I was assuming a lot to think he might be interested in me at all. "Not that you think of me as anything more than an employee . . ." I trailed off weakly, realizing how foolish I was sounding.

"No . . . I can't have you misled." He stepped closer, and his eyes weren't moving from mine. "You have me pegged." The expression on his face softened. "I'm sure whatever your worst fears are—and I can't think that they're that bad because I've never seen anything so wholesome in my life—but whatever they are, I'm sure they're true."

I stepped backward and bumped into the nightstand. "You can't. We . . . nothing could be there."

He nodded. "Nothing." He took two crystal cat figurines Brad had given me off of a nearby shelf and set them on the windowsill facing each other. He sat down on the edge of my bed and said, "Look here. Say this is me and this one is you." He set them farther apart. He looked around the room until he picked up a pen that was sitting on my vanity. He set it between the cats. "And this is the divide, your religion. You see, it's impossible for us to be together. I can see that too, from your eyes." He understood this better than I thought. "What you don't realize is," he lifted his cat over the divide and set it next to mine, "it's too late. I'm already there." He smiled triumphantly.

"You cocky weasel."

He had the audacity to smile at me. "Yes, dear." Then he left me standing there, appropriately backed into the corner of my room, spineless and not gaining the last point.

* * *

Having my fears confirmed didn't help my disposition. Through dinner, I had to make a heroic effort to look as though I was being polite to him. Watching him act honey sweet toward my parents and knowing he was doing it on purpose to build an army against my resolve made it harder for me to force pleasantries.

Rachel had come to dinner with her family. Alex had captivated the whole of her attention, leaving Troy to watch the children and make sure they ate. Troy finally gave up and sent them to play. I could tell he didn't like Alex, or, at least, he didn't like that Rachel liked Alex. With the children gone, Alex quickly recognized Troy was annoyed. Like a pro, he started a conversation that hit on at least six subjects they had deeply in common. I wasn't surprised. With Troy's attention completely occupied, Rachel tugged me into the dark family room and sat me down at the computer.

"I don't think you totally value this guy." She flipped on the screen.

"I value him," I said with no emotion. "I just don't want to value him."

I let Rachel lean over me and pull up the Google search. Ten pages of related links came into view, with an arrow hinting that there were more pages unnumbered. I didn't move. He was here, but I didn't have to bask in his glory. That would just add steam to his engine. Rachel prattled on about "had to see this . . . wouldn't believe it." I sat, looking at my hands in my lap, waiting for her to get the hint that I didn't care what was beyond the links in front of me. A myriad of professional pictures flashed before my eyes. I tried not to notice his airbrushed perfection. There was one in particular of him on a beach with Vanessa that made my mouth drop open for the slightest moment. I snapped it shut quickly, but not before Rachel noticed and smirked.

All through dinner I'd been thinking about staying in Utah, telling him I couldn't finish the shop. That would be best. I felt something for him that I shouldn't, and the best thing to do would be to get away from him. He was like booze, and I was like an alcoholic. The smart thing to do would be to remove the booze from the house. Finally, Rachel gave up and left me there in the dark family room, the glow of the screen illuminating my hands. I heard soft footsteps on the carpet. I knew it was him because I could feel what I didn't want to feel whenever he was within three yards of me.

"Hey."

"Hey."

"What are you doing here in the dark?"

"Thinking about how you're so much like booze."

"At least you're thinking about me." He sat down on the arm of the couch behind me. "You Googled me?"

"Rachel Googled you. She wants me to read it."

He stood and leaned over my shoulder to open the first link. It was the website for his restaurant. He closed it and moved down. The next page was an article on one of his books. He scanned through it. "I've never done this. It might be fun to see who I am to other people."

He scanned the pages quickly. His chest pressed on my back, and his head was too close to mine. I could smell his aftershave. My stomach swam, and my neck burned hot. He was clicking through pages too fast for me to catch anything.

I hadn't noticed my father until he opened the blinds. I jumped when he did it, but Alex didn't move at all, like he'd known my father had been there all along. Dusky sunlight flooded the room. "You want page six. There's one of you and Jana."

I slid my hand under Alex's and took control of the mouse. "Which one?"

"Sandlebark, saddlebark . . . I don't remember exactly."

"Saddlewood." Under a short gossip article about the governor of Washington was another little article about Alex. And there was a small two-inch-by-two-inch picture of us at the airport. Wow, the media was fast. In the picture, Alex had his arm around my waist, and he was leaning in, speaking to me. I remembered the flashes on the walkway only hours ago.

I took my time reading the article, but before I was a few sentences into it, Alex tried to pry the mouse from my hand. I smacked his hand and continued reading. "Master Chef, Alex Steadman, was seen at the airport this morning with a mysterious blonde. They left on the 10:15 to Salt Lake. Sources close to Alex tell us he hasn't been coming into work lately. 'I don't think much of it. He gets like that when he's working on a book or something. He's very private.' The two were purportedly holding hands. Could it be that our Master Bachelor is looking to settle down? He has been widowed for nearly two years. His wife, Vanessa, died of cervical cancer, leaving behind their daughter, Elise. Is he ready to take the plunge into deeper waters?"

I clicked the page closed, and he said, "I told you they were watching."

"But that isn't true. How can they just throw it up on the Internet like it's true?"

"Since when do we trust what's on the Internet? Besides, it is true. I left on the ten fifteen this morning with a beautiful blonde, and I had to hold her hand to tug her down the walkway. You get used to it. If I sneeze, it's somewhere in the media. It might be buried at the back of the paper, but it's somewhere. I'm only a local. Can you imagine what it would be like to be really famous? You wouldn't be able to go anywhere or do anything. It's crazy."

A movement outside the window caught my eye. A familiar silver Honda pulled into the driveway behind Rachel's car. I looked at my dad and back to Brad, who was shutting his car door. "Hide me," I squeaked. Brad was too fast. I knew my father wouldn't hide me anyway. He was too honest. My mother had Brad in the entryway before I had a chance to dart down the hall. When I knew I had failed in my escape, I turned to face him.

"You're home, and you didn't call," he accused.

"I just got home a few hours ago. I'm only staying awhile. I just wanted to check on my dad, then I have to get back to work."

Alex stood inconspicuously behind my father.

Brad was hurt. "You were going to *pop* in and not call me?"

This was a nice display in front of my mother, sister, father, brother-in-law, and not totally disinterested boss. "If I had time to . . ." I looked around at our audience, avoiding Alex's eyes. I smiled kindly at Brad, trying to keep my composure. "Would you like a drink?"

He looked around at the crowd, seeming to realize for the first time that we weren't alone. His eyes lingered a little too long on Alex, who matched his gaze with a good-natured façade. "Yes, thank you."

After we had settled on the stools at the kitchen counter and he had silently drained his glass, he said, "I can't believe you weren't going to call."

"I thought we were done dating."

"I just stopped because I noticed so many cars here. I would have missed you completely."

"This is a dead-end road. Why would you be driving by?"

"I drive by often, hoping to see you. You don't call."

"I texted. We're not dating." I tried to sound commanding.

He put his elbows on the counter and rested his forehead in his hands. "Look, I'm not stupid. I know I care about you more than you care about me. Have you even thought about showing up, like we talked about when you were leaving?"

I didn't try to hide my surprise. "You were going to date other women. There was nothing to think about."

He leaned into his hands, clearly frustrated as he pressed his thumbs to his temples. "Listen, while you're off living your little dreams, racing from flower shop to flower shop, could you stop sometimes and take a moment to realize there is a man back home whose every day, every thought, every breath, is waiting on you." I just stared at him, not knowing what I wanted to say or feel, trying to remember why I didn't want him. He'd turned on the persuasion. I could feel myself being pulled in by the sincerity of his voice and the beauty of his face. In the back of my mind, I was hoping this wouldn't be one of the longer conversations. Laughter from the hallway drifted into the kitchen. He continued. "You torment me. You absolutely torment me. I'm only half a man when you're gone." He stepped toward me and kissed me like he had at the airport. I stiffened and pushed away, staring at him. His heart was beating fast and hard under my hand.

I closed my eyes in frustration when his gaze became too intense. "Why are you not getting this?" I asked. Why couldn't he just let me go? The laughter sounded louder. It was Rachel.

He shoved his hands deep into his pockets. "I love you. No matter what, I love you." He picked up his glass, looked into it, then set it down forcefully. He left through the kitchen door, not looking back.

I listened for the sound of his car leaving, then I went into the backyard. I sat down on the bench swing by the pond. I touched my lips and shuddered. Brad's kisses before the airport were like pumpkin pie to me. The best pumpkin pie I'd had wasn't much better than the worst. But these stolen kisses were a whole different dessert. I wasn't sure what I thought of them. They temporarily made me the stupidest creature on the planet, but after them, I couldn't help feeling assaulted. Staring at the goldfish in the pond, I had to admit I didn't ever want another one. Since I had such a hard time making my points with him in person, I decided before I went to bed that I'd use the pen on my windowsill to write them down and then I'd send the letter certified. I couldn't talk to him. He could talk his way out of anything I could try to talk him into. I had to accept that there would never be a day when he would agree that I wasn't going to feel the same way he did about me. I pulled my knees close to my chest and rested my head on them. There was a strong possibility that a letter wouldn't be good enough for him. I was trying to figure out what, if anything, would help me get the message through to him when I heard whistling in the garden.

"Hello, Alex."

"I can't sneak up on you, can I?" He sat down on the swing at the farthest spot away from me. After a long silence, he said, "I didn't know there were other fish." He tossed a small pebble into the pond.

"There are millions of other fish."

"You're quite a woman. It makes sense that there would be other fish."

"It's good to hear you humble." I spoke into my knees.

"Oh, I'm not humble, not about this anyway." We swung in silence for a while. "Jana, look at me."

I did, but at that moment, whatever evil female hormones Brad had stirred up made my eyes fill with tears, and I involuntarily trembled. Alex slid toward me and wrapped his arm around my shoulders. He wisely didn't say anything while I silently let the tears fall. I was crying because, however dizzying the trip to the moon Brad's kiss had caused was, I still felt assaulted. I was crying because my father had an olive in his gut. I was crying because I was having the best moment of my life crying in the arms of the man I wanted and wouldn't ever let myself have.

We swung until my tears dried in place on my cheeks. Alex stopped the swing, speaking into my hair. "I don't like him. He makes you cry."

"You make me cry."

"I *have* been a cad. I am sorry. Your family is in love with me now though; it's too late." The hinges on the swing began to squeak. "I like them too. I never knew you could use canned soup in so many recipes."

"You know what I think? I think you don't even like to cook." I still didn't look at him.

"Really? Why do you say that?"

"Just a hunch. It doesn't seem like something you'd like."

He laughed hard and long. "It is kind of a pansy occupation, isn't it?" His torso was still having spasms from the laughter.

"I didn't say that."

"I'm good at it. It just makes sense to make money at something you're good at. It's true though, that I never dreamed of being a chef. I wanted to be an architect."

I looked up at him. "Why aren't you?"

"The math, the building codes. Somewhere along the way it occurred to me that if I drew a line wrong, hundreds of people could die in a fire or earthquake. There are a lot of codes. I was never great with math. I gave it up."

"What would you do now if you could do anything?"

He was smiling down at me when he answered. "I think I'd like a little country place, a few more kids. You know, retire but work around the house, get a barn, have some horses."

"Gretchen would never believe that."

"No, she wouldn't." He pulled his arm away from me and stood up. "I've got to get driving if I'm coming early in the morning. I'll need the rest." He held out his hand to help me up. "After tomorrow, I'll fight fair, I promise. I like your dad. He's going to love fly fishing. I'll leave you alone after that, and you can call when you're ready for me to take you home."

"You don't have to wait that long. You could go home without me. I'm sure Elise will miss you." We began walking toward the house. "Besides, I was thinking about not going back." I said it quickly so I couldn't change my mind.

He didn't even miss a step. "I know. But you'll come back. You have a job to finish."

"How can you know?"

"A few more days of Mr. Uptight and your mother, and you'll be back soon enough." I assumed he was talking about Brad. He surprised me when he said, "Take a few days or a week. You'll come back. I can wait. I might fly Elise out, but I can wait." He didn't say it with any arrogance, just with a calm knowing.

We stopped at the door. I looked up at him and had to admit, "You're probably right."

He leaned down and kissed my forehead. "Get some sleep. We're leaving early."

"I'm not coming."

"Uh-huh. Right. I'll see you in the morning." He rolled his eyes and walked away.

CHAPTER 6
Fish

At seven in the morning, Alex opened my blinds. "Rise and shine."

I pulled the covers over my head and mumbled, "You said nine."

"I said early. We decided on nine, then your father said eight thirty. I countered with eight, and he petered me down to seven thirty. I thought, with you being a female, you'd like the extra half hour to spruce up for the fish."

I rolled over and covered my head with the pillow. "I'm not going."

"Just your father and me, alone for hours on end, nothing to talk about except you. You're right. I'll probably learn more if you stay home. See you."

He closed the door. I threw the pillow at it. He opened the door and threw the pillow back at me. "This pillow tossing really is a milestone in our relationship. Nice pajamas." He closed the door again.

"We don't have a relationship," I mumbled to empty air.

I was in the kitchen within five minutes, wearing my favorite ball cap and almost no makeup. Alex handed me a rose and a card. "You really can get ready fast when you want to."

"Of course I can. I don't have any fish to impress today." I meant so many things by that, and I hoped he had caught at least one of them. I looked down at the rose. "Thanks. Do you give roses to all of the girls you take fishing?"

"It was with the paper when I came in. I guess Mr. Uptight had an early morning too."

"His name is Brad Monson." I opened the card. "*7:30. Dress for Buena Zifta.* I wonder what Buena Zifta is."

"That's a restaurant downtown. Aren't you from here? I know Salt Lake better than you do. I know Park City better than you do. I wonder if you're telling me the truth about having lived here all these years."

"How do I dress for it? What do you wear?"

"You like him less than chickenpox and you're considering dinner? I'm wounded."

"You've been talking to my father."

"I saw some pretty great pictures of you with spaghetti in your hair last night."

"I'm glad the two of you are getting along so well. If you went to this restaurant, what would you wear?"

"My best pearls, some nice heels." He posed in a feminine stance.

I rolled my eyes. "You'd look stunning."

"You think so? My legs look thinner when I wear black."

"Okay, now you're being ridiculous." I plopped down into a chair.

"C'mon, what does this guy have on me that you'd go to dinner with him when he makes your stomach turn?"

"I need to explain some things to him . . . *again*. It's a good opportunity." I plucked a petal off of the rose. Alex sat across from me. He held his hand out for the rose.

"What does *Brad* do for a living?" He picked a petal off of the rose too, tossed it to the middle of the table, and handed the rose back to me.

I plucked off a petal and tossed it. "He works in the district attorney's office in Salt Lake."

He held out his hand for the rose again and plucked another petal. "Is he an attorney?" He handed the rose to me.

"Yes." I plucked a petal and handed the rose back automatically.

"He's a young attorney." The petals were making an impressive pile in the center of the table.

"He's ambitious and driven. He has political aspirations." I peeled a thorn off of the stem.

"I see. Why don't you like him?" Alex peeled another thorn off of the stem.

"He's too ambitious and driven to listen to me." Another petal fell.

We continued passing the rose back and forth in silence. Finally he held it up with one last petal. He plucked it and said, "She loves me." He tossed the stem into the pile and walked out of the room.

* * *

I was glad I'd brought a book. I wished I had a pillow. My father had excellent balance in the river. He and Alex stood side by side, laughing and talking. I knew whenever I saw the Provo River again I'd see them there in my head. They were two peas in a pod. Alex was that way though. He could bend to find whatever it was he had in common with anybody. My father's fishing line didn't land in the water as gracefully as Alex's, but he was improving every moment. I lay back with my arms behind my head and studied the clouds. There was a hoot and holler as my father caught his first fly-fishing prize. They set it free and started again. I closed my eyes against the bright sunshine and breathed in the fresh air. I drifted off to sleep easily with the sound of the river trickling by.

I woke up to Alex propped on his elbow beside me. "How long have you been there?" I asked.

"Don't know." He had a small pile of grass blades next to him.

I sat up to see my father still in the river. His casting was now almost as graceful as Alex's. He was smiling ear to ear.

Alex nodded toward him. "Two fish so far; that's fantastic, especially for a first-timer."

"He's always fished, just not like this."

"Sure you don't want to try it?"

"I'm sure." Watching my father, I felt a swelling gratitude. "Thank you for teaching him. He loves it. I see hundreds of dollars' worth of fly fishing purchases in his future. My mother should appreciate that."

"I want to teach you to fish."

"Are we talking metaphors and similes or real fishing?" I knew the conversation was too good to be true.

"All of it."

"I already know how." I lay down again and stared at the clouds.

He lay down too and stared into the sky. "Remember when I came into the attic, the second time?"

"There are certain things I choose not to remember, and that's pretty high on my list." In my mind, I imagined him shutting up and just lying there, not ruining my moment.

"What were you thinking when you looked at me like that? When you blushed?"

"I was thinking how wonderful it was that you thought of bringing a roll of duct tape." I looked the opposite direction so he couldn't see me smile.

"Duct tape? I say to myself, 'Alex, don't ask,' and yet I do it anyway."

I was too curious. "What do you want me to say?"

"The truth."

"The truth is I wouldn't have thought of bringing duct tape to make a sling to lower boxes. It was ingenious."

He was ever patient. "Let me ask again. What were you thinking when you looked at me like that?"

"Like what?"

"So that's how it is?" I didn't answer him. "I'll show you *like what*. Look at me now."

"Not for all the fish in the world." I rolled onto my stomach and started laughing, the scarlet hue of my face burning. "Why don't you go stand in a river or something?" My words were muffled in the blanket.

He stood up. "Coward."

* * *

I hung up the phone and rubbed my temples. Brad hadn't taken the news that I wasn't coming to dinner as well as I'd hoped he would. This time he accused me of leading him on for a year just to get my kicks. I felt like the Wicked Witch of the West, but it wasn't nearly as bad as his usual manipulation in person.

My father walked into the room and pulled ice cream out of the freezer. He was supposed to be fasting for the surgery in the morning. I took it from him and put it back in the freezer.

"I broke up with Brad again . . . I think." I sighed and sank against the kitchen counter. "You never did like him. Why does Mom like him so much?"

"That boy's too smooth. 'Taint natural. I think your mom likes him because he has a heartbeat and you've dated him more than twice. 'Course all she likes now is Alex."

"Alex is just my boss. When she finally figures that out, she's in for a heap of disappointment."

A musical tone emanated from my father's pocket. I smiled. "You have a cell phone?"

"The cook left it in my car." He fished it out of his pocket and tossed it to me.

I answered. "Mr. Steadman's phone."

Alex sighed. "How many times do I have to tell you *Mr. Steadman* is my father?"

"Hmmm, you without your cell phone. That's kind of like a king locked out of his kingdom, isn't it?"

"I thought it was at the bottom of the river. I'm so glad you have it. I'll come get it."

I thought for a moment about my recent conversation with Brad and began to calculate how long I had before he came to the house to educate me on the ills of single life and the horrors of living out of state. "Why don't I bring it up?"

"I don't want you driving the canyon in the dark. We could meet halfway."

"Sure, we can meet at Jack's up on Twenty-First." I borrowed the car keys from my dad.

I convinced myself as I drove that I didn't want to see Alex. I was just doing him a favor—and getting out of the house.

Alex pulled up beside me. Jack's was my favorite dive of a burger joint. The hamburgers were still a dollar, and the fries had the skin on them. I'd been watching the customers inside, coveting their greasy dinners, when Alex rapped on my window. My heart leaped in a surprise rush of adrenaline. "Shoot."

He was laughing when I got out of the car. He held out his hand for the phone. I gave it to him. "A little underdressed for Buena Zifta, aren't we?" He looked at his watch. "Where you should have been arriving a half hour ago."

"I called him." I shrugged.

Alex pointed at Jack's. "Hungry?"

I grimaced. "That's like a date."

"It's a corporate meeting. We'll talk about the shop. I'll write it off."

"Underneath it all, it's a date."

"Underneath it all, it's two friends getting a bite to eat. I'll let you buy, and I won't enjoy a minute of it." I looked at him sternly. "I promise," he said.

My mouth watered for the skin-on French fries inside. "Okay, but you can buy. I didn't bring my purse."

Inside, Alex pointed a fry at me. "How were you going to eat without any money?"

"I was going to grab something at home." I took a long sip of soda.

"This burger tastes like they melted a bar of butter into it. I'm going to die of a heart attack." He pretended to silently choke.

"Hey, insult my burger joint, and you insult me."

He took a sip of the milkshake we were sharing. "If I pay for it, it's a date. This is our first date."

I didn't say anything. If he wanted to feel like he had triumphed and gotten a date out of me, I'd let him. *I* wasn't on a date. *I* was just eating dinner with one of my best friends. It wasn't my fault he was male. It wasn't my fault he was attracted to me. And it wasn't my fault he was hopelessly handsome.

He pointed another fry at me. "Now, be honest. Not dating me has been better than dating any Mormon guy you've ever dated. I'm better than all of them. You like me more."

"Stop pointing fries at me. I don't know what you're talking about. You're not making sense."

He set the fry down. "Right now, this minute, sitting here, you're not dating me. Doesn't it feel better than any date you've had with a fish in your pond?"

I took a long sip of milkshake until I got brain freeze.

"I've delivered you to Utah. You owe me. Just yes or no."

He was right. I wouldn't be here for my father's surgery if it weren't for him. "You can't get a big head about it or rub it in my face later."

"I won't."

"Okay, right now, this minute, sitting here, not dating you feels better than any date I've had with any fish in my pond." Now I pointed my fry at him. "Don't push your luck. I'm done talking about this."

"Why? It's just talking."

"No, Alex. It's talking in circles. It always comes back to the same things. It doesn't change anything. It just fills the world with a little more hot air, that's all. And what's more, it's a bit excruciating, like hitting yourself in the head with a brick repeatedly."

"It's only excruciating for you because you're going against what's right." He smiled smugly.

I should have just dropped the subject. I don't know why I pressed on. "It's wrong, and you know it. I can't go down this road. I won't. Imagine if I did have certain *feelings* for you, feelings I was not supposed to be having. They would torment me. And every time we talked about it like this, it would be flaunted in front of my eyes that I couldn't have what I wanted. It's like eating a candy bar in front of a hungry man. It's mean, and I don't want to talk about it anymore."

We ate in silence for a while, and then he said, "What if I were Mormon?"

I looked up at him. "Do you want me to call the missionaries? Do you really want to know?" I didn't feel any hope, but I had to ask, just in case.

"I'd only do it for you."

"Well, if you ever *really* want to know, to know for yourself, just tell me." I started piling napkins and wrappers onto the tray.

"You are so brainwashed." He wadded a napkin and tossed it onto the tray.

"And yet you still want me. Who has the addled brain here?"

"Think about it, Jana. Christ lived over two thousand years ago. Scribes wrote down His words from dictation. How many mistakes could be made there? Churches changed. Everything that is here now is just an interpretation of men. He's gone. Maybe He was that great when He was here. He's gone now, and all that's left is a bunch of men scrambling to put logic to why they exist. All you've got is some man calling himself a prophet. You follow him, and you brainwash your children to follow him."

I had tears welling up in my eyes. I wasn't mad at him. I could feel my testimony swell deep inside me. I smiled warmly at him and even took his hand across the table. A tear spilled down my cheek. He looked sorry. "It must be terrible to feel that way, to feel like you're only following men. I'll tell you what, Alex, every other religion on this planet has a man behind it telling you what to believe. The Church of Jesus Christ of Latter-day Saints is the only church on the earth that tells you to find out for yourself. You read the Book of Mormon, and there's a promise that God will witness the truth of it to you. It's not that some man will tell you it's true, but that *you* will receive an undeniable witness from *God* that it is true. We're the only church with a guarantee to be true." I smiled again. "I *was* taught the gospel from my birth, but I have tested that guarantee. I have received a witness that I cannot deny. It wasn't from my parents or any other man on earth. It was from God. That is the void between us. I would never step over it, and you could never pretend to."

He stared at me for a long time then wiped the trail from the tear off of my cheek. "I didn't mean to be insensitive."

"You haven't been. I might cry when I talk about it, but I'm not sensitive about it at all."

"I think you're a fanatic, but I still want you. In everything except this, you're the most grounded, sane person I've ever met. You are absolutely magical. And you're almost as good looking as me."

I threw a handful of wadded napkins at him. "You're a dork. And you need a haircut."

He threw some fries across the table. "There's nothing wrong with my hair."

"No, of course not, Flopsy Mopsy; it's very roguish. It matches your dimple." I wondered what he'd look like with his hair trimmed short on top in a missionary style.

He took the lid off of the milkshake and loaded some onto a spoon. He held it in launch position. "Say you like my hair."

Very slowly, I said, "You . . . need . . . a . . . hair . . . cut." Before he could launch it, we were startled by a flash of light followed by a jingle from the door closing.

"Utah has discovered I'm here."

"I'm sure Utah doesn't care." I took the plastic spoon out of his hand and tossed it onto the tray. "You're just full of yourself."

"We'll see about that one. You just wait. Headline: Master Chef eats junk food and is berated by mysterious beauty." He leaned back and grimaced, "I think you're killing me. After that butter burger, I'm not feeling so hot."

I slugged him lightly in the arm. He had just called me a brainwashed fanatic, insulted my favorite burger, and pointed sharp fries at me. And I liked him more than ever.

CHAPTER 7
Waiting

I SET DOWN THE MAGAZINE and watched my mother pace. She had straightened her cardigan five times in two minutes. She was chanting something under her breath. Even though we had gathered for a priesthood blessing before we left and she had borne her testimony that she felt everything would be all right, she didn't look like she believed it now.

I put my arm around her. "Mom, why don't we get a bite to eat?"

"Bring me some fries; the baby ate my breakfast," Rachel called out, patting her stomach.

We had the waiting room to ourselves. My other siblings figured the surgery was so small that they didn't need to come to the hospital at all. "Really, Jana," Jacob had said, "it's outpatient. How bad could it be?" I had come to the conclusion that it wasn't the big deal I thought it would be either, but sitting in the waiting room with my mother, I was glad I had come. She was beside herself. I had never seen anything like the way she was pacing now. She turned to me. "You know when they put him under they get him as close to dead as they can so he won't feel anything past the anesthesia."

"Mom, stop it. He's fine. They do this hundreds of times a day all around the country. It's standard."

"They don't do it hundreds of times on my husband. I doubt they have any inkling of an idea what a great man he is." She spat the words.

"They will do their best. Why don't we go down and get Rachel some food. We don't want her blood sugar to drop. You know how ornery a pregnant, hungry woman can get."

"You go get it. I'm staying here just in case."

"In case what? Mom, they aren't coming out until it's time for us to go up to his room. Nothing is going to go wrong."

She ignored me and started pacing again. I sighed and headed for the cafeteria. If any of us ever needed surgery again, I was going to arrange for a sedative for her. This was much harder on her than I'd expected it to be. During the blessing, I'd felt the quiet calm of the Holy Ghost telling me he'd be fine. I thought she'd felt it too.

The cafeteria didn't serve fries, so I bought Rachel a turkey sandwich and chocolate milk. When I approached the waiting room, I heard my mother giggle. I rounded the corner to find Alex standing with her. "Alex, how nice of you to come all the way out here for this." I smiled tightly at him.

He pointed to my mother. "I'm here on demand. She called this morning. I'm sorry I'm late." He had the audacity to kiss her on the cheek, and she beamed.

"Mom," I growled.

"Jana, after flying you out here, he's a part of this family too. Where are your manners, your gratitude?"

Alex nodded his head and stepped behind my mother. I glared at him. That would feed the monster within. Now he was an official part of my family. Within five minutes, I begrudgingly admitted to myself that I was glad he was there. He was doing a better job at getting my mom's mind off of what they were doing to my dad. They talked about cooking, my mother's shotgun, the time Alex's brother accidentally shot his dad in the leg, and the coast, and I unfortunately heard my name mentioned more than once. I could only catch snippets of their conversation. They spoke in softer tones when they were talking about me.

I sat across the room with Rachel. She put her arm around me. "I like him more than ever now. I don't know what's wrong with you."

"I like him, just as a friend, that's all." I could tell from the look on Rachel's face that she was using her super sister powers to see through my lie. She sat back and clucked her tongue at me. "What is it with all of you? You expect me to suddenly change my standards for some guy?"

"Who says you have to change your standards?"

"I know it would make all of you happy to see me just jump on this ship and let it take me off to happily ever after. What you're forgetting is it isn't going to the same place I want to go to. There's no happily ever after at the end of this cruise for me."

"Jana, I love you. Just remember I'm saying this out of love; don't get all defensive on me. I just want you to listen. No one is saying you need to change. No one has said anything about you changing. We're not even holding pompoms and cheering on the sidelines; well, maybe I am. But no one else is. It sounds like it's *you* you're trying to convince, not me."

I silently ran Rachel's words through my mind. I already knew there wasn't a chance. I didn't need to convince myself. I looked at Alex across the room and the distance between us seemed to swell. It was a mistake for us to have eaten dinner together last night. It was a mistake for me to have taken a job that so intimately involved him. It was a mistake for me to have eaten dinner with him every night in Washington. Every time I felt a little more comfortable around him I was pulled deeper into a danger zone. I was *falling* for him. When he wasn't with me, I was thinking about him or trying not to think about him. His laughter rang from across the room. I looked up, and he winked at me. I could feel some invisible rope tying us together, even though he was half a dozen yards away. I imagined a celestial ax from heaven dropping from the ceiling to sever the rope, but it just bounced away leaving the rope unharmed.

I looked at Rachel. "I love you too. You're a good sister. I think I'll go for a little walk, stretch my legs."

I wandered aimlessly through the halls. Even then, when I should have been thinking of my father, I was only thinking of Alex. I took an elevator up three flights and found a glass-wall corridor that looked out over the valley. I watched the tiny cars on the tiny roads. I told myself I wasn't returning to Washington, but even as I said it, I knew it was a lie. I would go wherever he was. At that moment, it felt like I would go wherever he was for the rest of my life. Perhaps someday he would find someone special and get married again. Then maybe I could tear myself away and eke out some lonely existence without him.

What was I thinking? I wasn't in love with him. He wasn't *that* great. Well, he was pretty wonderful. But was I so pathetic that I'd hang my entire existence on another person? I physically shook myself. I was a confident, able woman. I could do a little job in Washington, come home, marry a great not-Alex guy, and be happy for time and all eternity. My thoughts rang of a lie again, but I shoved the bells to the back of my mind and decided I could handle Washington. My heart felt heavy as it beat slowly in my chest. *It will all turn out right. It will all turn out right. This is just a bump in eternity. I don't want him. I don't want him. I don't want him . . .*

As if he were magically summoned to me, I heard his voice. "You look like an angel when the sunlight touches you like that. You look peaceful."

I guffawed at the word *peaceful*. I turned my head to him. "How did you find me?" I'd meandered aimlessly for more than a half hour to purposely get myself lost.

"I could just feel where to go. It was the weirdest thing. Like a little voice: turn left, go up, turn right. And here you are."

"Weird." It smacked of the Holy Ghost. I looked heavenward and silently asked God, *And you too?*

I looked forward again, though I wondered how *he* looked when the sun lit him up. I studied the tiny cars with more interest. I searched out the temple steeples. He stepped closer. I concentrated on the pigeons pecking on the lawn below. *I feel nothing. I feel nothing.* He put his hand on my shoulder. I felt a current surge through my body and warm my feet. *I didn't feel that. Not a thing.*

"Listen, Jana, he's going to be okay. This is just a routine surgery. Hundreds of people have it every day. They wake up, go home, and live happy, healthy lives."

He was right. I should have been thinking about my father. I felt evil. I wasn't worried about my dad at all. I felt confident he'd be playing golf by next week. My eyes started to warm with tears. Alex turned me to him. I looked in his eyes and repeated *I don't love you* to myself. He gave me a boyish grin. Suddenly, I could see myself with him and Elise in a park, floppy haired mini Alexes and curly Janas jumping around us. My tears spilled over, and I thanked God that I'd worn waterproof mascara.

"C'mon." He pulled me into a hug. "Who do you cry on when I'm not around?"

I sobbed harder. *I'm not loving this. I'm not loving this.* It felt wonderful to hug him. I felt truly evil. Not only was I not thinking of my poor father stretched out under a surgeon's knife, but I was also thinking of the unthinkable. I was thinking about committing treason against myself, my future children, and my God. I couldn't stand myself. I pushed away. "Thanks," I said in a monotone, "for being there when I cry." A fog of self-loathing settled over me. I turned away from him and headed for the elevator.

We passed the doctor on his way out of the waiting room. Rachel was straightening magazines. "He's ready for us to go into the recovery room. Dad's waking up."

Alex hugged my mother. "Well, my work here is done. Call me if you need anything. And I mean *anything*. You have my number."

"I'll see you in a few days," he said to me as he walked out of the room. As we followed Mom to the recovery room, Rachel looked me over and said, "I hope you didn't do anything stupid. He didn't look upset or anything, but you sure do."

"Whatever I do concerning Alex is always stupid, Rachel," I muttered.

My father felt cold and rubbery from the anesthetic when I hugged him. I tried to hide the fog that had settled on me. Either he didn't notice I was exuding a whole different energy or he chose not to ask me about it around my mom. I tried to make up for not worrying about him by becoming Nurse Jana. I ordered warmed blankets, got his water, and fluffed his pillow. I overcompensated in every way I could imagine.

At home I made sure he had every creature comfort available within arm's reach. I put so many blankets on his bed that he begged my mother to take half of them off. I was clearly annoying my mother. I knew I was diverting my thoughts to something more worthy, but I was suffocating my father with love in the process. I went to my room to lie down. I didn't sleep. I just lay there dressed, studying the ceiling. My mother came in.

"Thank you for your help. It's been wonderful having you around."

The dismissal speech. "It's been wonderful having me around, *but* I'm mother-henning him and driving you both crazy."

"No. I didn't say that."

"You don't have to." I laughed. "I'm driving myself crazy. I don't see how I could do anything less to you." I sat up to face her. "It's probably okay for me to go home now, isn't it?" I said it so she wouldn't have to.

"He'll be fine. I take good care of my man. But you're welcome to come home anytime. You know that."

"I know it."

"You make sure to tell Alex thank you. I don't think you show him enough gratitude."

"You're probably right." I wasn't about to start showing him an abundance of gratitude anytime soon. I just wanted to survive my little temporary job and get away with my heart intact. "I'll call Alex tonight. I bet we can leave in the morning." My mother looked tired to the bone. "I love you, Mom."

"Are you okay? You're so worried about your father."

"I know he'll be fine. Girl hormones. You know how I get."

"Well, I'll go get you a B vitamin."

"I'm coming down in a while. I'll get one. Thanks for thinking of it. That's a great idea." My mother came from the generation where a vitamin could fix anything. I needed a great big vitamin or a handful of whatever cured an overdose of Alex.

* * *

Alex tousled my hair and stole one of my peanuts. "I think we'll call it Zombie Jana."

I leaned forward, trying to get comfortable in my seat. First class was much better than coach. I missed the space. "Zombie Jana?" I asked. "What are you talking about?"

"The coming and going Jana who bumps into walls and passes out on car rides. We'll call her Zombie Jana, and then the normal you that I expect to see when we get home, we'll call her Jana Jana. I can't call both of you the same name because I'd swear you're not the same person. Have you been seen for a bipolar disorder?"

"Oh . . . am I acting different?"

"Different? It's like someone sucked the light right out of you. You're deflated. Are you taking medication I should know about? Or is there medication you *should* be taking and aren't that I should know about?"

I leaned my head back and rubbed my forehead. "I just have a bit of a headache."

"I can fix that." I was expecting pain pills and Coke. He surprised me by taking my hand. He opened my palm and began tracing the lines with his finger. His hands were warm. Mine were cold. "There's a pressure point right here." He pressed down, and I stifled a yelp. It worked. How could I possibly dwell on the pain in my head when I had shards of pain emanating from my hand? "Sorry. I guess that was too hard." He began tracing lines again. "Your hands are cold." He put my hand to his mouth and breathed warm air on my knuckles.

"S . . . stop." I couldn't feel my headache anymore. He breathed again. My stomach gave a happy turn. "Please," I said weakly.

"Is it the candy bar in front of the hungry man?"

"If it *were* something like that, I'm sure I wouldn't admit it to *you*."

"How's your headache?"

"Gone for now."

"I'm glad you're coming home tonight. Let's celebrate. I'll cook a special dinner."

"I have a date tonight."

"Bring him to dinner." Alex was smiling.

"He's really nice. You'd like him." I was thinking, *Give him ten minutes and he'd join your fan club too. I'm sure you have loads in common that I never dreamed of.*

"I like him already, except the part where you're going on a date with him. Is he like Brad?"

"Not at all."

"Is he like me?"

"Not at all."

"I cook better."

We both laughed.

I looked down at my hand in his and sighed. When I started to pull it away, he said, "Just an hour, like it's normal."

"It would be a lie."

"Would it?"

I left my hand there, and we didn't speak for a minute. Then I said, "It doesn't mean anything."

He closed his eyes and leaned his head back. "Of course it doesn't." But he didn't let go.

CHAPTER 8
The Right Pond

I PULLED INTO THE RESTAURANT parking lot five minutes late. Jeff was waiting at the door. "Next time, I pick you up at your house. Your boss can't be all that bad."

I rolled my eyes. "If you only knew." Jeff looked handsome in a hunter-green sweater and khaki pants. I smiled. "Sorry I'm late. I still don't know my way around. I passed Vermont Avenue twice before I realized the sign was behind a tree branch."

"My lady." He held out his hand for me. "You're going to love this place. They have the best calamari."

"What's calamari?"

"If you don't know, it's probably better if I don't tell you until after you try it."

We sat down and ordered our drinks. I told him all about going to Utah, leaving out Alex. He told me about his boring job at a mortgage office. "Sometimes I go in early just to rubber band the receptionist's drawers closed. She gets so ticked."

When the waiter came back, he said, "You look familiar. You look like that woma—"

"I have a generic face like that." I gave him my best end-of-conversation look. I wondered if it was possible that people actually still read newspapers. Since Jeff knew the restaurant, I let him order for me. I pushed the ice cubes around in my glass while he talked about Brazil.

When the waiter brought the calamari, he tried again. "I'm sure I've seen you—"

"You have." I smiled and again tried to convey my coldest end-of-conversation stare. Perhaps being away from the law offices had made me soft because he wasn't deterred.

"Really? Wow, so are you . . ."

"No. Could you excuse us?" This time I tried a patronizing look.

He left the table. Jeff leaned over. "What was that about?"

I looked at Jeff and decided I'd never been a good liar anyway. "Promise to still like me if I have a big, hairy secret?"

"Cross my heart."

"And I'd appreciate it if you don't tell anyone at church, though after that display, I don't see how it would stay a secret long anyway."

"On my honor." He gave me the Boy Scout sign.

"My boss is Alex Steadman."

"Who?"

"You don't know him?" I sighed with relief. "He gets a little attention because of a business he owns. There are some pictures in the newspaper of us."

"Wow, what are you doing in the pictures?"

"Nothing," I growled. "People take his picture like crazy, and I just happen to be in there too, that's all." I stabbed a piece of calamari.

"I guess you don't like having your picture in the paper, then."

"I don't like the press right now." The calamari was wonderful. "I officially declare to you that I like whatever this is. Tell me what it is."

"*My* big, hairy secret is that you're eating squid tentacles."

"Your secret is much worse than mine." I popped another piece into my mouth. "That is so gross. I wonder how they make it taste so good."

Somewhere in the middle of dinner, he said, "You know, Jana, it feels like I've known you for a lot longer than I have. This doesn't feel like a first date at all."

"You're right. This isn't as bad as a first date should be. How can we make it worse?"

"Do you want to go out for ice cream?"

"Ha, ha. I'm stuffed. I won't have to eat for a week. Do you want to go to a movie? My treat."

"Chivalry isn't dead yet. I'll buy."

CHAPTER 9
Stolen Glory

THE DOORBELL WOKE ME AT eight thirty. Luckily, the only one who ever came over in the morning was Alex. I shrugged into my bathrobe and was halfway down the hall before I decided to walk back and look in the mirror. I told myself I didn't care what Alex thought. I just wanted to be presentable. The doorbell rang again. I hurried to the door, trying to smooth my pillow-induced cowlicks.

It *was* Alex. He was standing there with two plates balanced in one hand and a jug of juice in another.

"Crepes?"

I had fallen asleep thinking of all the ways I could distance myself from him. I willed myself to decline breakfast but heard myself saying, "Yes, they look delicious."

We ate in silence until he looked at me with penetrating eyes. "I think it's because you just woke up . . . You actually looked happy to see me. You look great in that shirt."

I picked up our plates and walked to the kitchen. "I'm always happy to see you," I said honestly.

"I thought so."

"Well, it's time for us to *stop thinking* now. If we think too hard, we might hurt ourselves. Let's get to work." I rinsed the dishes.

"I just complimented your shirt. Aren't you going to respond in kind?" He handed me a dish towel.

"I like your white cable-knit sweater."

"Really? I hate that sweater."

"Then why do you wear it? You should do women everywhere a service and toss it out. It's inhumane to look that good."

"You *are* attracted to me," he accused.

I defiantly looked him in the eye. "I am, but that doesn't mean I'm going to do anything about it." Before he could say anything else, I added, "I'm attracted to Alaska, but I don't want to live there."

"Ouch . . . Good fishing in Alaska. I should take you."

I rolled my eyes and kicked off my slippers. "I have to get dressed. Oh, I have bad news. I think I'm out of man work for you. You might have to get a real job." I headed upstairs.

He called up after me, "Hey, let's get out today. I want to show you something."

I looked down at him. I didn't really feel like working, but it seemed foolish to spend a day with him for no reason at all when he was such a temptation for me. "You'd have to give me the day off, no pay."

"Would you take a day off without pay to be with me?"

"No."

"If I said please?"

His dimpled smile was too hard to resist. I sighed in defeat. "I guess it couldn't hurt."

* * *

We drove for a long time in silence, and then he said, "It's nice having a day off like this."

I closed my eyes and leaned my head back. "We should be working. I've got so much to do. When I say *we*, I guess I mean *me*. I really have run out of manly jobs for you. I can't see you pressing flowers and tying ribbons."

"Neither can I, but I'd sit and watch you."

"That's just wrong. I can't work with someone watching. I'll screw up."

"I used to think the same thing, but I do it all the time now." He turned the radio to lilting classical music, and we drove in companionable silence for a long time.

My phone rang. It was Jeff. "Did you get home okay? I'm going to drive next time, especially since I know who your boss is now."

"Why would that make a difference?"

"Little old widower, Jana? C'mon."

"You looked him up."

"I looked him up, all right. I got ten pages of web links. You're right, your picture's all over."

"If you had to look it up, at least you could have had the decency to not open the pages."

"So I had fun last night. Thursday's a good night for me. We can go to another movie or something."

"A movie sounds fun." I looked at Alex, who didn't seem to be listening.

"I'll pick you up at seven next Thursday. See you Sunday. I saved you some carrot cake. It's in the freezer. Man, it was the best yet. She must really like you."

"I'm glad. I can't wait to try it."

I hung up the phone and watched the grass bend in the field as we passed. I wasn't sure how long we'd been driving. The landscape was completely different. Meadows rolled out on either side of the road. A sliver of ocean was visible to the west. To the east of the meadows a trimmed forest stretched out for miles. A shabby red barn sat on a hill in the distance. Occasionally we'd pass a house or grazing horses.

"Alex, I can honestly say that I don't think I've been anywhere so beautiful in my entire life. Where are we?"

He was smiling, satisfied that I approved of the drive. "The country, of course."

"Well, I'd take a day off without pay for this anytime. Wow."

He turned onto a poorly paved road that led to a two-story, white house with a wraparound porch.

We parked in front. Alex opened my door and helped me out. We walked onto the porch. The breeze smelled like freshly cut pine needles. I waited for him to knock. "Who lives here?"

"No one."

I sat on a porch swing and closed my eyes. "Could you imagine just sitting here at night? This is fabulous." I jumped up and walked all around the porch. "The views are to die for."

I followed Alex to the backyard. A gigantic apple tree had fallen over but was still alive. Grape vines crawled over it. The apples were plump and red. I had to be careful not to step on the old fruit. He handed me an apple he'd picked from the tree. A pine tree towered nearby with a tire swing hanging from it.

"Oh, poor old pine tree." I walked to it and pushed the swing.

"Why is it a poor old pine tree?"

"Well, someone has snatched its glory. See, a pine has a beautiful gown that reaches all the way to the ground. Someone has trimmed this one's skirts, and its ankles are showing. It's always sad to see a pine cut up like this."

"If it weren't cut, you couldn't hang the swing. The branches would use up twenty feet of yard. This way you can sit under it and enjoy the shade."

"Well, a pine isn't a proper shade tree," I continued pushing the empty swing. A sparrow landed in some nearby bushes. We stood, listening to leaves rustle in the breeze.

Alex hadn't spoken for so long that I jumped when he said, "There are berries. The garden is in shambles, but someone could do something great with it." He showed me the garden and a small greenhouse that was in slight disrepair.

"Alex, what is this place to you? Why did you bring me here?"

"I watch it for a friend. I've always wanted it. He just hasn't been willing to let me have it yet. I wanted to see what you'd think of it."

"Maybe he'll sell it to you someday."

"Things are changing in his life right now. I'm confident he'd let me have it."

"Can you afford it?"

He looked at me like I should know better. "It's a funny time in life when you finally have enough. Enough money, enough fame, enough friends. You find yourself sitting around alone one day thinking, *Well, now that I have the world at my feet, what do I really want?* It's a harder question than you'd think it would be." He pulled a needle off a pine tree and spun it in his fingers. "I had this hole in me when Vanessa died. When I'm here, especially right now, the hole is gone. Not that I could replace what Vanessa was to me, but I feel complete here." He looked at me. "Right now."

I looked away, afraid I was the part of the "right now" that made him complete. I felt color creep up my cheeks, and my heart beat faster. Changing the subject I asked, "What's it like inside?"

He pulled keys out of his pocket. "Let's go see."

"Haven't you seen it before?"

"I want to see it through your eyes today."

The entryway had a dusty hardwood floor. The main level had a sitting room and a small office. The kitchen was tucked into the back of the house. It wasn't nearly as glorious as Alex's kitchen. "Could you settle for a kitchen this small?" I asked.

"Could you?"

"I'm not the chef." I tried to sneak the unavoidable in before he started dreaming things up that weren't possible. "And I'll never live here." He didn't even flinch. "The important thing is, could the chef settle for it?"

"You could see yourself living here."

"I thought we were going to have a nice afternoon together."

He clenched his jaw, and his eyes flashed hot anger. He looked down for a moment. When he looked up, he had a pleasant, calm look on his face. "I've heard it said that your soul mate is the one who can infuriate you the most. You're just about there for me, Jana."

"What charming criteria for a soul mate," I said sweetly. "Yes, that sounds just like what I'd want to spend the rest of my life with, the most infuriating person I could find."

"You are being obstinate and pigheaded. There is something here between us, and you know it just as well as I do." His phone rang. He answered it with an angry hello and walked upstairs.

I opened cupboards. The kitchen was as big as the one I'd grown up with. It was a good size for *normal* people who didn't care if the only cheese they had in the fridge was cheddar. I opened the oven and inspected the racks, trying to notice things I didn't care to see. In the back of my mind I chanted, *Alex is just my boss. Eternity is worth it. I love my future family* . . . over and over again. It was my fault for coming. I looked out the window. I couldn't be entirely sorry that I'd come. It was true that I had never seen anyplace so beautiful. I closed my eyes and opened them again. I imagined my hands in a sink full of soapy warm water, running a cloth over dishes. I looked out the window and imagined Elise on the swing. I imagined Alex coming up behind me and putting his arms around me. A tear rolled down my cheek. Now I was just torturing myself.

Near to where he was in my imagination, I heard, "Hey." I turned. He was right behind me. "Oh, don't cry. I'm an idiot. I shouldn't push you." He wiped my tear away with his thumb.

I just frowned at him, not daring to say anything.

"I'm sorry, Jana. Will you forgive me?"

"What's the use? You'll just bring it up again and again."

"I won't, unless you do first. I promise to be a normal, boring employer from this day forward. I don't want to hurt you anymore. I care about you too much to keep hurting you." He looked out the window. "You are a beautiful, wonderful woman. You deserve everything you want, even if it's a Mormon you don't like as much as me."

"You are a cocky . . . a cocky . . ." I wasn't used to insulting people and couldn't think of what else I wanted to say.

"I'm not cocky. I know what I see in your eyes. It will help me sleep at night knowing you're making yourself as miserable as you're making me."

I glared at him.

"I was planning a nice little picnic lunch, since we were enjoying each other's company so much. But now we might as well get going. We can eat in the car. I have a boring business proposition for you."

I didn't feel like eating. I didn't feel like leaving. I wanted to stay all afternoon. I wanted to stay with Alex. I wanted to *hit* myself. I chided myself for letting myself wish. I was in charge of my thinking. I could easily think up a better place to be. I thought for a moment as I stood on the front porch staring out over the meadows. I was right where I wanted to be with the person I wanted to be with, and I hated myself for it. While he locked up, he asked, "Do you like it here?"

"I love it here," I said in barely a whisper. I knew he heard it.

He opened my car door then tossed a plastic bag on my lap. "Voilà, lunch."

"Mmm, granola bars and Gatorade, my favorite."

We drove in silence past the meadows. When we turned onto the freeway, he said, "All right, then. I need some help with Gretchen. She's overwhelmed and has had just about as much as she can take. She's threatening to quit unless I get some help."

"What would I be doing?"

"Mostly administrative things. Not what you hired on for, but it would just be for a short time. You'd see less of me." He looked at me and smiled like that would be a good thing.

"What about the shop?"

"Eight-hour days, you could do a little here, a little there in the extra hours. I'm in no hurry about that."

A dull voice in the back of my mind said it would be a good thing to see less of him.

"When do I start?"

"Better make it tonight. Why don't you come into the office with me? I'll let Gretchen show you where to start."

"Okay, but if the three of us are at Shallots, what are we going to do with Elise?"

"The Chadwicks are watching her tonight."

I nodded and looked out the window. I hoped I wasn't making a mistake. The biggest mistake I could see so far was not staying in Utah. Everything else was just snowballing from there.

* * *

I dressed in my legal clothes and pulled my hair up. Though Alex didn't mind being in the limelight, I did. If I had to be gawked at, I'd make sure I looked as though I didn't care.

I was slipping on my heels when he knocked on the door.

"Wow. You look different."

"Severe? Scary? Administrative?"

"I'd tell you what I think you look like, but I made a promise I intend to keep."

We walked out to the car in silence.

"I'm nervous about seeing all of these people who have seen my picture," I told him once we were driving.

"Don't be. They're good people. Besides, you'll mostly be with Gretchen."

I followed Alex through the restaurant. We walked through the front doors, past a crowd of people waiting for their tables. I heard a whispered "That's her" and held my head a little higher.

"Gretchen's in my office. It's back here." Before he opened the door, he said, "She's in a bit of a foul mood. My fault. You can handle her though."

I followed him through the door. He walked to his desk and discreetly tipped a frame face down. The office had pictures of various Italian scenes, mostly vineyards and bottles of old wine. A brown leather couch ran along one wall. Dark wood shelves lined the wall behind his desk.

Gretchen was sitting in his chair with a calculator. She looked up at him with great distain. "Really, Alex, what were you thinking? It has never, never been this bad before. Couldn't you lift a finger? Do you need a babysitter?" He inched behind me as though I'd protect him. "Jana, I see he roped you into this. We'd better roll up our sleeves." She glared at Alex.

"I'm going. I'm going." He backed out of the room, closing the door softly.

"Has he been out gallivanting all day while I do his dirty work?"

I sat down across from her. "Yes."

"I thought so. I've been here since noon. It would serve him right if I quit today. Look at this. Just look at it."

"What is it?"

"This pile here," she pointed to a mound of receipts on the table, "is the receipts from his food purchases. This pile," a flatter pile with larger receipts, "is his sales. This one is not related to the restaurant but is related to other parts of his corporation. This one is for his personal expenditures, and I don't know why he bothered saving them other than to cause me more headache sorting them out. And this," she kicked a large cardboard box out from under the desk, "is full of the ones I haven't sorted yet." Receipts fluttered out of the box. "You mark my words, he did this on purpose. In five years, he's never done anything like this. Look. Look." She pulled out a plastic file box from a bottom shelf behind her. Inside were tidy files of receipts. "I've never had to file for him before. He's gone and lost his head. He wasn't even this bad when Vanessa died."

I looked at my shoes, hoping his antifiling behavior wasn't my fault. Reading my mind, Gretchen promised, "There's more here than he could do since you came. He's behind the whole year. It's like he gave it up in April." She ran her fingers through her short red hair. "Well, at least he had the decency to toss them in a box. Let's get moving. I have third-quarter paperwork to get ready for."

I knelt down by the box on the floor and took a small handful of receipts. It was easy to tell the sales receipts, but I had a hard time with the rest. Turning one over in my hand, I asked, "How late do you think we'll be?"

Gretchen moaned softly. "I honestly don't see an end to it anytime soon. We'll be late."

"I hope the Chadwicks are okay watching Elise that long."

Gretchen didn't look up from filing. "Sleepover."

"On a school night?"

Gretchen chuckled. "Can't reason with him . . . no use. He's no respecter of school nights."

Noticing what an inept helper I was, Gretchen suggested I put the receipts that were already sorted in order by date. After an hour of putting them in order, I could tell which ones were which and moved on to help sort them from the large box. After two hours, Gretchen pushed her chair away from the desk. The box was only half empty.

She stood tall and stretched. "So what have you two been doing today?"

"He took me out to a house in the country."

"The old Steadman place?"

"You've seen it? Isn't it beautiful?"

"I just saw it once when he bought it. Vanessa was livid. He finally gave in and bought her this house here in town, but she always hated that he had the other two. Said he was going to run off and sleep in the other houses when he got mad at her. But he never did. The cancer hit so fast. They stopped fighting each other and started fighting it."

"He told me he was *thinking* about buying it. He didn't mention that he already owned it."

"Maybe he's thinking about moving." She lay down on the couch. "Are you dating him yet?"

"Yet? I'm never going to date him. We don't have enough in common . . . and he can't file."

"Did you tell him?"

"Everything except the filing."

"It's getting late. Can you go back to the kitchen and get us something to eat? I'm not picky. I'll just close my eyes for a minute."

I think she was asleep before I left the office. I followed a waiter to the kitchen. The lights were much brighter than the dining area and Alex's office. I looked for Alex. There were about ten people in the kitchen. I tried to hug a wall so I didn't get in anyone's way. The smells were heavenly. The pots clattered, and the cooks joked loudly. I couldn't see Alex. A woman saw me. "Jana." She said it loud enough that everyone looked at me. Suddenly, the only sound was the bubbling of something in a skillet nearby.

"Hi." I gave a meek little wave. "Gretchen wanted me to come in and get her some dinner. Where can I find that?"

I recognized Scott, who set down a saucepan and looked truly happy to see me. "What kind of dinner do you want?"

"Gretchen said she isn't picky."

Everyone laughed. Scott shook his head. "Well, that's a lie, but you wouldn't know that. We know what to get for Gretchen. What do you want to eat?"

They had all stopped working to watch the exchange. I shrugged. "Some bread would be fine." They all laughed again. I wanted to run and hide.

Just then Alex walked through the swinging doors wearing a clean apron. "What's so funny? I've got four orders pushing late and no fettuccine on table five. Get to it, people."

Scott nodded toward me. Alex turned my way. His whole demeanor changed. His face softened. Everyone laughed again. He looked at his employees. "I don't know what you're all laughing at. She stopped you dead in your tracks too. I want to see pasta, fast!" The sound of metal clanging filled the room again, accompanied with loud laughter and talking. He walked over and leaned down to my ear. Speaking close enough that I could feel his breath along my neck, he asked, "Were they picking on you?"

"No. Gretchen's hungry."

He pulled a stool up to a counter and patted it. "Just a minute."

I watched everyone work. They were fast. I would have cut off all my fingers trying to wield a knife like that. I silently thanked Heavenly Father for food processors. It was eight o'clock when a waiter came in to report there was still a line at the door. Alex told him to close the door for admittance at nine and take everyone who was in line by then. The cooks groaned.

Alex handed me a plate of salmon in white sauce, and he held a plate of naked noodles with a lemon wedge and fresh parmesan on top. "For Gretchen. Let's go." We were almost to his office door when he asked, "Is she still mad?"

"I think she's asleep. She told me you already own the *Steadman place*." I raised my eyebrows at him.

He smiled his deep-dimpled grin. "Sorry, this is one of those things I promised not to talk about."

"I thought you promised not to talk about other things, not why you didn't tell me you already own the house."

"If it's all tied together in my complicated little brain, then it's covered in said promise."

I rolled my eyes.

He motioned to the door. "Shall we?"

Gretchen was still asleep on the couch. Alex set her plate on the desk and squatted down next to her. He shook her shoulder gently. "Gretch, Gretch, wake up. I brought dinner."

She blinked her eyes then sat up slowly. "Where's the avocado?"

"I'm out."

Gretchen yawned. "I want a day off, two days off. I could throttle you."

"I *am* sorry. You can take as much time as you want. All paid. I owe you. I should have kept up."

"I can finish up here tonight, Gretchen," I offered. "I've got the hang of it now."

"And that one there," Gretchen nodded to me, "doesn't want you, so you can just stop playing around and get back to work."

Like I wasn't there at all he said, "Oh, she wants me. Won't have me, but she wants me. World of difference there."

She looked at me for a rebuttal, but I wasn't going to lie, so I didn't say anything.

Gretchen started laughing. "Fine boat the two of you have gotten yourselves into. I'm going home." She picked up her plate and left the room.

Alex stared after her. "You know, she never brings the plates back. I'm going to start buying china just for her."

"I'll finish up in here."

"I'm going to be late. You heard about the big crowd tonight. Why don't I take you home now?"

"No, there's a lot of work here, thanks to Mr. Won't File Anything. I think I'll stay and make a dent in it. If I get tired, I'll sleep."

"There's a blanket in the cupboard and a pillow in the closet."

Before he left, I asked, "Alex, why didn't you file this year?"

"If I tell you, you have to swear to secrecy, as a friend, not an employee."

"I swear."

"By now, I wasn't going to own it. I was trying to sell it all, retire."

"Why didn't you?"

"See, you're the only one who doesn't look at me like it's a sin to sell it. I had a lot of buyers, but I wanted to find a buyer who would look out for the people here. I just couldn't find anyone right. I was gone all the time. Finally, I just gave up."

"What does Gretchen think about you selling it?"

"I can't sell it fast enough for her. She's done with me. I know she loves me, but I've worked her to death."

I sat down behind the desk. "You could have started filing when you decided to keep it."

"By then, you were here. I had better things to do."

I lifted up the frame he had placed facedown hours ago. It was a pixilated picture of us in Utah at the burger joint. I put it face down again. Pretending I didn't see it, I asked, "So what do you have to do to sell it?"

"I need the records up to date. I need to travel around. I was talking to this franchise guru out in New York who said he could franchise it and manage it. All I'd have to do is pose for pictures and pick up my checks."

"That sounds good."

"No, it doesn't. What if he starts doing things I don't want my name on? I'd be helpless to stop him. If I pull out, I want to take my name with me. Then I can still sell my books and do my television gigs."

"Television gigs?"

"You don't watch me?"

"I didn't know. I shouldn't be watching you anyway."

There was a sharp rap on the door, and Scott poked his head in. "Alex, I've got the mayor out here for you."

"Time for more song and dance. Holler if you want me to take you home."

I put the picture up on the desk again. I remembered the argument we were having when it was taken. We were both smiling. His hair *was* too long. I looked heavenward and wished I didn't care about him. I got up and locked the door. Then I knelt down to pray. Even though I knew He was watching every part of my little soap opera, I told God all about it. When I was finished, I asked Him what I should do. I waited for an answer. Without receiving one, I closed my prayer. The blanket in the cupboard was a thick quilt made of denim squares. I grabbed the pillow and lay down.

* * *

I woke to the rustling of paper. Alex sat at his desk, working under the light of a lamp. "You should have woken me up."

"And miss watching you sleep? Not on your life." He shuffled the papers into a tidy pile.

"What time is it?"

"Almost midnight. I'm just about done here."

"Almost midnight? What about Elise? We've got to go."

"You must be tired. She's at Missy Chadwick's house, remember. They walked home together. It's a sleepover."

"Ah, that's right. Gretchen mentioned the sleepover. But on a weeknight? Alex, she's going to be exhausted for school."

"They do it all the time. Sometimes it's our turn; sometimes it's theirs. Missy snores. Her parents went on a cruise for a week last year. Longest week of my life. I was a prime candidate for sleep deprivation studies."

"Close the door. You won't hear it."

"Missy didn't keep me awake. When Elise couldn't sleep, she came to my bed. She's made of elbows and knees." He stapled some papers and filed some receipts then changed the subject. "I had to use a credit card to get in. Why'd you lock the door?"

"For privacy. You could have knocked."

"I did. I was really worried."

"Well, I'm fine." I stood up and started to fold the blanket. "Where did you get this blanket? It smells like cinnamon."

"My mother made it. You like it?"

"It's great, a bit heavy but warm and soft. I've never seen one like it."

"When you meet her, tell her you like the blanket. That will win her over."

"Don't you like it?"

"Oh, I like it fine. Vanessa hated it; wouldn't have it in the house. It's been exiled here for at least five years. Take it."

"Doesn't it mean anything to you?"

"Sure, it means something. It will always be the blanket I watched you sleep under."

"I would think since it is from your mother it would mean something more to you." I put the blanket back in the cupboard then followed him into the dark restaurant. "Wow, it's so quiet compared to before."

"Amazing, isn't it? It can buzz like a beehive or sleep like a cemetery. I used to love it here."

He stopped at the front door and turned to look at me. "You're beautiful in the dark."

"That's like saying *you look best when I'm blind*. Besides, you're done saying things like that, remember?"

"I'm done talking about anything that has anything to do with any relationship we are or are not having. I can still shell out a compliment, albeit a bad one." He stepped too close to me and put his hand under my chin to tilt my head up.

"Alex." I tried to make it sound like a warning. He traced his thumb over my lips. Chills ran down my spine. "Don't." He leaned close. My heart was trying to escape from my chest. My ears burned.

"Please," he whispered.

"No," I whispered back, trying to bolster my waning willpower.

He held perfectly still. I could smell his sweet breath, spicy aftershave, and hint of woodsy smoke. He stared into my eyes. I tried not to blink first, but I did. He pulled away. "Sometimes I wonder if you're not the one waving the candy bar," he complained as he unlocked the door.

CHAPTER 10
Purple Sanctuary

A GLOB OF LAVENDER PAINT dripped down my thumb. Painting Elise's room was easier than painting the shop. The lavender was a compromise between the neon purple Elise had chosen and the barely tinted purple I wanted. I placated Elise with a little paintbrush and bowl of white paint. She painted several frames on top of a canvas tarp near her bed.

"Why can't the frames be purple?"

"They won't show up on the purple wall. You want to see them, don't you?"

"What are you going to put in them?"

"I thought we could find some things that would make you happy. You know, pictures of you, your mom, dad, friends . . . favorite places, flowers, pets . . . This should be a place you can dream in, the happiest place you could be because you'll be here so much."

"Can you decorate my new room too?"

"New room?" I asked, worried that I'd just painted the whole room for nothing. "Where's the new room?"

"At the country house. Mine's upstairs with the biggest window. I can see the water from my window."

I put down the roller. "When are you going to live there?"

"When you come with us."

"Elise, did your daddy tell you I'm going to live there?"

"He said someday, but he didn't know how long. He says you're slow."

Not too slow to clobber him when I get a chance. "Well, I don't know that I'll ever live there. I bet you and your dad will though."

"Jana, do you love me?"

"What makes you ask something like that? Everyone who knows you loves you. You're a very lovable little girl." I sat down beside her.

"Go like this," she said and held her hand up with her fingers splayed. I did, and she pressed her hand up to mine. She had a sad, faraway look in her eyes. "My mom used to see if I was as big as her yet. You're smaller than her, so I guess I'm not as big as her yet. See, my fingers aren't as long as yours." She dropped her hand to her lap.

"You miss her."

Elise sniffed. "I think about her a lot every day. I don't remember so much what she looked like. Well, I sort of do. But I don't want to forget. When we go to Grandma's house, Grandma's eyes are just like hers. It's almost like she's here again."

"Don't you feel your mother close sometimes? I can't imagine her staying too far away from you."

Elise looked up at me cautiously. "I feel her sometimes. I feel her a lot of times. I know she's not far away because sometimes I hear her voice too. Like the other day I was stepping into the crosswalk, and she said, 'Leesie, go back.' I did, and a car came zooming right where I would have been."

"Wow. See, she's not far away. Did you write that in your journal? It's a pretty special experience."

"I don't have a journal."

"We're going to have to get you a journal. The twenty-five-year-old Elise will thank you for that memory. You can write everything you remember about your mom in it before you forget. Then you can just open it up to remember again."

"Where do you think my mom is now?"

"I *know* where she is. She's with Heavenly Father and Jesus, watching over you and your dad." The room was quiet for a moment. "People think the spirit world is so far away, but it isn't. The spirit world is right here with us. We just can't see the people who have passed on because they're made of finer matter, more see-through stuff, than we are. And your mom doesn't have her body so she isn't in any pain anymore. But someday she'll be resurrected, like Jesus was, and so will you. She'll have her body again. You'll be able to hug her. She'll tell you how proud she is of you. You'll be together with your mom and dad forever." It was a painfully simplified version of the plan of salvation, but I figured I'd covered most of it.

"You really think so?"

"I know so." I took her into my arms and smoothed her hair. I wondered how long it had been since a woman had held her. I sang "Families Can Be Together Forever."

When I finished the song, she said, "You have a pretty voice. Sing it again."

"I know more songs." She snuggled in closer to me. Alex was right; she was made of knees and elbows. I started into "I Lived in Heaven."

When I finished the song, she wiped her eyes and sat up. Her face was creased from being pressed against the folds of my shirt. "Can we put pictures of my mom in these?" She put her hand on the frame, forgetting it was wet.

"Yes. And I know how to take a brand-new picture of you and an older picture of your mom and put them together. We can make a picture of you at the beach, on an airplane, in a parachute, or riding horses."

"You can do that?"

"I can. And I can take a picture of Godzilla and put your dad's head on it." The thought made me smile. How dare he misinform Elise when he knew how I felt?

Elise laughed.

"I have the software too. Why don't we go ask your dad if we can load it onto his computer now? I need a break from the purple pandemonium that will be your sanctuary."

"What?"

"C'mon. You ask your dad. I'll go home and get the disk."

* * *

"How much longer are you going to be?" Alex folded the newspaper and tossed it onto the coffee table. He was letting me use his laptop. Luckily he had pictures of Vanessa on disks so I didn't have to scan them in.

"I'm sorry. I start having fun with this and I forget the time. How late is it?"

"Almost five. What do you want for dinner?"

"I think I'll run down and grab a salad."

"A salad?" He snorted. "That's not dinner. That's predinner."

"Truth is, you're making me fat. I either need a salad or a new wardrobe. The salad is less expensive."

He sat on the couch next to me. "Hey, is that Godzilla?"

"Yes, it's for Elise." I used the mouse to move Alex's head on top of Godzilla. I pixilated the fringes so the image morphed naturally into the alligator skin.

"That's pretty good. Are you mad at me?"

"Yes, why do you ask?" I said in a sweet tone.

"I don't know if you view this as an improvement." He casually put his arm around me. Feeling sixteen again, I pretended not to notice.

"Look at these. I'm making them for Elise's wall." I pulled up a slideshow of Elise and her mother, the three of them together, and my favorite of them standing on the beach. They were silhouetted against a sunset that kissed the tops of the waves. I pulled up a picture of their wedding day and paused the slide show. "She was beautiful, wasn't she?" I asked. Vanessa's eyes glowed with joy. Her skin looked flawlessly airbrushed. Dark curls cascaded over her shoulders. Alex looked like a lucky teenager, far out of his league.

Alex smiled sadly. "She was."

I cocked my head to the side. "But Elise looks like you."

"She's stunning," he said defensively.

"She's the most beautiful little girl I've ever seen," I said to soothe his defenses.

"So if she looks like me, you're saying I'm beautiful?" He leaned in close.

"No," I laughed, "you just look like a little girl. It's the long hair."

He growled and lunged at me. I tossed the computer onto his lap and leapt up.

He pressed play on the slide show. "I like this one. I want a copy for my office and my wallet."

I sat on the couch a little farther away from him so I could see the picture. "No. That's not real; I couldn't . . ." It was a picture I had scrapped together. Alex and Elise were alone, and I wanted one of them with Vanessa so I pasted a picture of me and put her head over mine. The picture Alex was looking at was the version before I'd pasted his wife in.

"Let's get a real one. I know this woman who does great work."

"Alex, that's hardly appropriate."

"I thought you were gathering pictures for Elise's walls?"

"I am. I want her to see her family close around her. I'm not family. I don't belong on her walls."

He stared at me without speaking. After a long, uncomfortable silence, with my ears burning, he leaned closer. I caught myself leaning forward. His lips barely grazed mine before I jerked back and looked away.

I coughed into my fist. "I'm going to get that salad now." I stood up and started to jog to the door.

He shut the computer and stood up. "I'll drive."

I could hear the keys. I felt foolish running away, but that's exactly what I wanted to do. I turned around so fast that he nearly ran into me. I put my hand firmly on his chest to stop his forward momentum. "That's okay. I can drive myself."

He put his hand over mine. "Jana, I want to . . ." His eyes scanned the floor. "If we could just . . ." He stopped himself again. He took my hand and traced the lines on my palm with his thumb. He sighed deeply and said simply, "You infuriate me."

I pulled my hand away and flexed my fingers. "I know the feeling. I'll see you later."

* * *

I drove past four fast food restaurants on the way to April's. Again and again I finished the laptop scene in my head. Each time, I leaned in and kissed Alex at the end. By the time I pulled into April's driveway, I had the radio blaring to drill the scene out of my head. It wasn't working. A tubby man in a blue jumpsuit was leaving when I walked in. "April, it's me. Where are you?" I called.

"In the kitchen. Watch your step." A thin layer of water covered her kitchen floor. "Are you okay?" she asked. "You look out of sorts."

"Am I okay? You're standing in a lake, and you're thinking about me?"

"This is nothing. We'll have it up in a minute. Harvey's taking care of it."

"What happened?"

"A little leak." April looked guilty, so I raised a questioning eyebrow. "I started the sink going so the dishes could soak, and I left it on while I took a bath."

"Oh."

"Don't tell my kids. They'll pack me off to the geriatric castle."

"Your secret's safe with me. Can I help?"

"No. Harvey's got it." On cue he came in, pulling a Shop-Vac. "Come, sit down. It will be good to forget about this for a minute. What's got you in a bunch?"

"Nothing. Just wanted to visit, that's all."

"Your ears are still red. I've been alive a long time. You can't hide it from me."

"As bad as hiding a lake in the kitchen, huh?"

April nodded. "So what's wrong?"

I shrugged.

"Does it have anything to do with a Bachelor of the Year who's madly in love with you?"

"He's not. But you're right; it is about him. I don't know what to do. I can't keep this job. The line between the job, my life . . . everything is so confusing. I am going crazy." I started to cry. Harvey came in to talk to April but wisely sloshed back into the kitchen when he saw me crying. She pulled me into a hug.

"Now, now. There, there." The vacuum hummed in the background. I cried until it shut off.

"I feel so stupid. I'm sorry," I said, wiping the tears with the back of my hand.

"Did Alex say something to upset you?"

"No. He didn't say anything."

"Has he been mean?"

"No. He's been very nice."

"Well then, you'd better start at the beginning."

I told her about the box in the attic, the trip to the country house, and the growing tension between Alex and me.

"Jana, you are making your own problem here. He's not off-limits."

"He *is* off-limits. He's married. He isn't a Latter-day Saint. He isn't right for me. It hurts to even look at him right now, and he's always there, every day, every time I turn around. And if he isn't there, then I'm thinking about him anyway so he might as well be there."

"Slow down, honey. What makes you think he's married?"

"We'll he is, isn't he? I just spent all day scrapbooking pictures of him and his wife for Elise's wall."

"'Til death do us part,' April said. "That's what he said when he got married. She's dead. They parted."

I looked at her, unimpressed. "Families are forever," I said simply.

"Was he married in the temple?"

"No, of course not. But if he knew . . . if he really understood what's important. If he understood the gospel and how Elise could be his forever . . . how Vanessa could be his forever, well, it wouldn't take much for him to want to be sealed to Vanessa. No more 'til death do them part.'"

April sat back and folded her arms. "Think this through. First of all, just because he was married doesn't mean he can't be again. He deserves every happiness. If you married and died young, would you want your husband to languish on earth without a companion?"

"Yes," I said spontaneously. April gave me a reproachful look. "Well, I wouldn't want to share him. I can't see myself dancing for joy in the streets of heaven because my husband remarried."

"I think if you examined your heart, you would find that you would love your husband enough to want him to be happy, not lonely, for the rest of his life on earth. If you had a child, wouldn't you want your husband to remarry to give her a mother? If you could choose someone for them, wouldn't you choose someone like you?"

"Humph." I folded my arms. "You've got a bigger heart than I do, April."

"Think about it. Put it to prayer. See if you change your mind."

"Okay, I'll put it to prayer." I had come expecting sympathy, not a reprisal.

"And about his religion—I know a lot of women who married good men who weren't members of the Church."

"Yes, but did their children make it?"

"What do you mean?"

"Did their children grow up in the gospel? Did they gain testimonies? Did they get married in the temple? Are their children happy today?"

"Many of them are."

"*Many* isn't enough. I want my children to know the joy of living the gospel. I don't want them to look at golfing on Sunday as an alternative to eternal life."

April looked sourly at me. "What about Lehi and Sariah? They were good parents, weren't they? And they had two sons go bad on them. What happens, happens. You just do your best along the way."

"My best would be to marry a member of the Church."

"Well then, child, make him a member of the Church."

"You don't know Alex. He wouldn't. Well, not for real. And I wouldn't want him if it weren't for real, if he didn't really have a testimony."

"Stay here," April commanded. She came back with a large bucket of chocolate ice cream, some bowls, and some spoons.

"What's this?" I asked.

"Burnt almond fudge." She pried the lid off the bucket. "We're going to have to agree to disagree. You're just like your mother. I can't reason with you. Put it to prayer. No one on earth has a claim on that man, except possibly you. Ask God if you're wrong. You are, of course. For now, we feast." She pushed a bowl toward me. It wasn't exactly the salad I had planned on.

After my first bite of ice cream, I asked, "Do you want to go shopping?"

"Chocolate and shopping are the best medication for the blues. I'm on. But I've got to blow dry the floorboards first."

"I'll help."

* * *

Feeling more levelheaded, I balanced bags from various department stores while I unlocked my front door. I dropped one, and several blouses spilled onto the doorstep.

"Jana." Alex was walking across the front lawn. "That must have been one huge salad. You've been gone forever."

"I had a little shopping to do." My little bit of shopping had used all the money I was saving to fly home for the holidays. I'd have to start saving it again.

He scooped the blouses into the bag and opened the door. "A *little* shopping?" he asked skeptically, hefting the bag.

"New wardrobe, remember?"

"Ah, I see." He followed me inside. "I just wanted to make sure you weren't mad at me."

I looked up at him. "Why would I be? You haven't done anything."

He nodded. "You're right, I haven't."

I stared at him a moment, then I stepped closer to him, dropping the bags. "Well," I said breathlessly, trying for a hint of coy, "there is something."

Suspicious, he stepped away. "What's that?"

I put my hands flat on his chest and stood on my tiptoes a little to make sure he could feel my breath on his face. I hoped I didn't smell like rancid ice cream. "Chemistry abuse."

His eyes grew wide, and he stuttered, "Ch-Chemistry abuse?"

"What's wrong, Alex? Is your heart beating a little faster?"

He stepped back again, and I countered by stepping closer and leaning my face toward his. "Are you on something?" he asked.

I dropped the act. "No. I just wanted to make sure you knew what chemistry abuse was. So stop it. We need to have boundaries." I turned my back and started to carefully pull slacks and blouses out of the bags.

"You are scary, woman."

I turned around. "I am serious, Alex. It is chemistry abuse. It would make my life a lot less complicated if you'd just stop getting so close to me."

"If you're talking about earlier with the pictures, *you* leaned in," he accused.

"You leaned in first. You are an incorrigible tease. Have a heart."

"The exact point is that there *is* chemistry. You're missing it."

"I am not missing it," I growled. "I *want* to be missing it, and I can't *miss* it if you keep pulling it out and using it against my will."

He lay down on the couch and rubbed his eyes.

"Make yourself comfortable," I said dryly.

"Someday you will thank me for my incredible capacity to hold my tongue. You will also praise me for my patience. It would all be easier if I thought you didn't feel anything." He sat up partway. "Lie to me, Jana."

I sat on the edge of the couch and stroked a curl away from his forehead. "I can't stand you, I hate being around you, and you're no fun to talk to," I said kindly.

"Thank you." He collapsed back onto the couch. "Now I can be free from your siren's call."

"I'm glad I could help." He was most irresistible when he was boyish. Thoughts of hugging him and running my fingers through his curls reminded me of my earlier resolve. "Probably time for you to go."

"First I have to talk to you."

"You *have* to talk to me? Are you sure you aren't just stalling?"

He sat up and draped his arm over the back of the couch. "I'm serious. These are important things. I need to change your job a little and tell you about horses."

"Okay, I'm all ears. Tell me about horses."

"This one starts with a promotion."

"What kind of a promotion?"

"Doing a lot of Gretchen's job, and I need a sort of nanny."

I wrinkled my forehead. "I'm not so sure *nanny* is a promotion."

"There would be bookkeeping too."

"I don't understand."

"I'm going to try to retire again." He leaned forward with his elbows on his knees. "If I sell things off just right, or even open up some contracts with reputable businessmen, I can have nearly the same income I have now. I'll be able to live in the house I took you to, ride horses, and be free. I'd like to help build a few children's hospitals, you know, still work, only work doing what I want."

I sat there, trying to hold my mouth closed.

"Aren't you going to say anything?"

"This is a really big step for you." I looked around, wondering how Sheer Pleasures was going to fit into his new plans.

"That's all you can say?"

"What do you want me to say? Have you ever taken care of a horse?" I asked him.

"No. It just seems like the thing to do."

"Oh."

"Jana, talk to me. You're my best friend. I was hoping the conversation would be a little longer than this."

"I'm your best friend?"

"You are."

"I don't suppose you'll be keeping Sheer Pleasures?"

"I found what I was looking for when I started it. I don't need to finish it."

"Then my job is basically gone?"

"Unless you're leaving, then I'll keep it to keep you here."

"To keep me here?" I asked.

"To keep you here . . . I'll be flying in and out of town for a while to look at buyers. Right now, I really need a Gretchen instead of a creative consultant. She's still mad at me, and she's been spending a lot of time with her mother. "

My head was spinning. He was saying too many things between the words. "What if I just go home now?" I asked.

He quietly examined the floor then looked up and said, "Please . . . don't."

"You want me to stay because you need me to help take care of Elise?" I nodded at him so he would know "yes" was the right answer.

"I've been forbidden to tell you *why* I want you to stay. It would be convenient if you could watch Elise and do some bookkeeping."

I felt suddenly ashamed. I wanted him to say he needed me to stay because he loved me. It was a rotten thing to expect since I would never reward that love. I yearned to hear it just the same.

He stood up and walked to the front window. He parted the blinds. "Fred Harrobuck across the street came over to tell me that a silver car parks in front of his house every night. He thought I should know. I called my friend Trisha at the Division of Motor Vehicles with the license plate number. I want to know who it is because it might be a stalker. I figure Fred has a right to know who's parking in front of his place every night, at any rate."

"Okay, I'll watch for a crazy woman. I'll call before she breaks in and steals any recipes. You can catch her at the door."

Alex didn't laugh. "Jana, is Brad still in Utah?"

I sat a little straighter. "How would I know?"

"How can I find out?" he asked.

"Why would you need to know?"

"Is he what you would call *mentally sound*?"

"Well, he's a little dense when it comes to me, but other than that, he's brilliant. He's a smart guy."

"Who you like less than chickenpox," he reminded me.

"So he has his obvious flaws. What does any of this have to do with Brad?"

"That car I just told you about is registered to him. It was purchased two weeks ago in Utah but registered here last week."

A chill went up my spine. My stomach churned from more than hunger. "I'm sure it's fine. He's just being a little weird, that's all. Are you positive the car comes every night?"

"Every night."

I shifted uneasily in my chair. "I see." I felt in my pocket for my cell phone, thinking of the more than ten texts and four voice mails from Brad that I hadn't answered in the last five days. I shuddered, realizing ignoring the problem wasn't working.

"Bet you don't want me to leave now."

"You've got me there." I tried not to look worried.

He tightened the blinds. "Think about my offer. You'll have to tell me within a week or so. I need to get moving on this. Let's take you home and get you a proper dinner. Ice cream won't cut it."

"How did you know I had ice cream for dinner?"

"When you were gone so long, I called April."

"You checked up on me? You could have called my cell."

"I thought you were mad at me. Anyway, I had things to talk to you about. Dinner is getting cold."

"What's for dinner?"

"Peanut butter and jelly sandwiches, your favorite."

I raised my eyebrows, "You've been talking to Rachel."

He shrugged. "She e-mails."

CHAPTER 11
Leisurely Stroll

THE RINGING PULLED ME OUT of a dream. I reached for the phone, registering that the digital display on my clock showed three twenty in the morning. "Hello?" I didn't try to hide my groggy voice. Before I heard an answer, I sat up, suddenly worried that something had happened to my father.

"Jana?" Rachel's voice sounded tired.

My heart stopped beating. "It's me. Rachel, is everything okay?"

"I lost some weight today." She sounded happy.

I looked at the clock again. "That's great." I toppled back on my bed. I heard beeping in the background. "Where are you?"

"I lost a lot of weight today. Six pounds, twelve ounces, to be exact."

I screamed. "She's here?"

"Okay, I should have shielded my ear for that. I know how you are when you're excited."

"And . . . ten toes? Ten fingers? Hair? Eyes? Tell Aunt Jana about it."

"Yes, she has all of those." Rachel laughed.

"C'mon already. Tell me all of it."

Rachel told me everything about baby Anna, including her delivery and what the other children said when they met her. I walked around with my phone and finally settled at the kitchen table with a bowl and some fat-free ice cream. An hour later, I flipped the phone closed and plugged it in to charge. I walked to the front window and parted the blinds. Alex was pulling out of his garage. I stretched and turned off the lights. When I was in bed, nearly asleep again, the phone rang.

"I know you're up. I saw your light on when I left. Everything okay?" Alex didn't sound tired.

"Other than I was almost asleep again, it's great. Rachel had her baby this morning."

"Fantastic! We'll send some flowers. I thought you were up thinking about me."

"No. That would put me to sleep," I lied. His chipper tone grated on my fatigued ears.

"Not sitting there with a mile-long pros and cons list about taking Gretchen's job?"

"Yeah, well, as interesting as this conversation is, I'm going back to sleep now."

"You'll be thinking about me. You won't be able to sleep."

"Alex," I said in exasperation.

He laughed. "Okay, try to sleep."

I flipped the phone closed and punched my pillow. I never did get back to sleep because I was thinking about the chef.

* * *

As the next few weeks wore on, Alex took my chemistry abuse plea to heart. For the most part, he stopped flirting with me and became ultraprofessional. He still stayed with me most of the time when I was working on the shop. He didn't try to kiss me again or get close to me. It stung my pride a little. Now everything was just as it should be, though I still ate at his house every night. Alex really was just my boss. Even Rachel had stopped calling because I didn't have any dirt to dish.

I tried to fight my deserved depression by rejoicing in the shop. Alex had built shelves, and they were nearly full with merchandise, looking exactly as Vanessa had drawn them. The fridge and cupboards downstairs were finally useful, full of stock. A cash register sat on the counter. The downstairs smelled like potpourri. The sound system played light classical music while we worked and laughed. We laughed a lot. Instead of creating distance between us, his lack of romantic interest seemed to break down barriers. We were even at the point where we were finishing each other's sentences.

Fred Harrobuck had called to let Alex know the silver car had stopped parking in front of his house. I had texted Brad, afraid to call him, lest he use his persuasion skills on me. I demanded to know what he'd been doing in Washington. He replied that he hadn't been in Washington and I was paranoid. I *was* paranoid too, until my mother called to tell me he had stopped by her house in Salt Lake to see how everyone was doing. That made me feel better.

Jeff filled up my Thursday nights. Alex was never around when Jeff came. I hoped that was his sense of common decency or at least his sense of self-preservation because I would have pummeled him if he dared to intrude on one of my dates.

Jeff and I had run out of non-R-rated movies to see, so tonight we were going to the mall. In the car, he said, "I've been reading lots about you."

Rain blanketed the windshield. He hadn't set the wipers fast enough for my liking. "I thought I told you to stop looking at that stuff. It's garbage."

"Then you don't want to know what it says?"

"No."

"It says that you won't have him. He chases you and chases you, but you won't give him the time of day."

"Well, there you go right there. He doesn't chase me at all. He's a very busy man." Alex wasn't exactly chasing me. He wasn't even pursuing me at a leisurely stroll anymore.

"Reportedly, he's spending all of his time with you."

"The key word there is *reportedly*, isn't it?" I looked at him. "Are you jealous?"

"No. But my mother's jealous for me. She isn't taking it very well."

"How are you taking it?" I asked.

"We're friends, right?"

"I like to think so."

"And you like hanging out with this *little old widower*?"

"It's a job."

"If you're okay with it, I'm okay with it. Everyone in the ward thinks I'm dating the girl who's dating the chef."

"I'm sorry."

"Jana, *you* are my social life."

We pulled into the mall parking lot. "What? Thursday is the only day you have a social life?"

"Aside from the people I work with, you are the only nonfamily member I talk to."

"Jeff, that's pathetic. I'm winning by default here. What about your friends?"

"They got married, or our schedules are too crazy."

"You need to get out and date more. You'll never get married at this rate."

He pulled the keys out of the ignition and tossed them in the air. "You sound just like my mom. Besides, who do you date besides me?"

"Oh, I date."

He gave me an incredulous grin.

"I do, every Thursday. Like clockwork. A real desperate guy with no social life. You'd love him."

"I thought so. What do we do after a year of Thursdays?" he asked.

"I don't know, maybe we can step it up and add Saturdays or something."

He laughed. "Help me pick out some shirts."

"Sure, that's easy. You look good in blue, green, gray . . ."

"Pink, pansy purple, sequined disco garb . . . Do you have anything you want to buy?"

"I just spent my life savings on a new wardrobe a few weeks ago. It was turbo shopping at its best. Quite something, really." As we walked into the mall, I couldn't help noticing how he only seemed as attached to me as I was to him. It was a lot like shopping with Rachel.

After an hour of hunting through racks and waiting while he tried shirts on, he took me to the food court. "They have the best Thai food here."

A beautiful, petite girl with waist-long, black, satin hair was washing tables nearby. "Melee, come meet Jana." She smiled a radiant smile for Jeff but scowled when she looked at me, flinging her towel over her shoulder. "This is my friend Jana Barrowman."

I held out my hand. She flopped her limp fingers into my palm. "Good to meet you."

"Did you read the book I gave you?" Jeff asked her.

"I'm reading it." She focused all of her attention on Jeff when she spoke.

In like fashion, I ceased to exist for him too. His eyes lit up attractively. He and Melee practically had sparks flying between them. If I'd liked him the way I should have, I would have been heartbroken. He'd definitely never looked at me that way before.

A short, balding man with the same bronze skin as Melee shouted her name from behind a counter. "I have to go. Good-bye, Jeff." She looked my way and turned her head so Jeff couldn't see her expression. With no life in her face at all, she gave a dismissive, "Jana," and walked demurely back to the counter.

"Wow, she's beautiful," I said, noticing Jeff had a dazed look in his eyes.

"Filipino. They are an attractive people, aren't they? I gave her a Book of Mormon a few weeks ago. Do you think she's really reading it?"

I leaned across the table and rested my chin on my hand. Batting my eyelashes, I said, "I think she'd read anything for you, Jeffrey."

"Ack. Don't call me that. Sounds like I'm ten."

"I'm pretty sure she's reading it," I said dryly.

"That would be so cool. I just got this feeling when I saw her."

Yeah, I bet you did, I thought but had the decency not to say aloud.

"You know, like she'd accept the gospel. I think her dad gives her a hard time though." Jeff was still watching her.

"I don't know what's good here. Why don't you order for me?" I said.

A familiar flash of light went off to my right. I turned. A man was trying to look as though he hadn't taken the picture. He had a professional camera hanging from a strap around his neck. Jeff turned to see him. "I hope you don't mind having your picture in the paper," I said. The photographer looked at me, and I waved.

"It would take some heat off me at home," Jeff said.

"Okay, if you're sure. Because we won't get any privacy here now."

"Well, if we're going to do this, let's do it up right." He stood up and walked over to the photographer. I followed.

"Can we get a copy of that? Was it any good?" Jeff asked.

The man looked at him suspiciously. He must have decided Jeff was trustworthy because he lifted the back of the camera so we could see it. It was an uninteresting profile shot. "Oh," Jeff said disappointedly. "That isn't very good. Do you think you could take another?"

Looking as though he couldn't believe his luck, the photographer said, "Sure, whatever you want." Then as an afterthought, he asked, "What's your name, son?"

Jeff told him his name and then went on to explain that we were out shopping for new shirts. I walked along beside them good-naturedly toward the nearest department store. We posed for him in front of the men's shirts. Jeff put his arm possessively around my shoulder. I stood closer to him than I usually did. In the distance, I could see Melee watching us with a clenched jaw. We smiled and posed for several pictures. The photographer followed us to get some "natural shots." Jeff asked him if he'd ever heard of The Church of Jesus Christ of Latter-day Saints.

Before I knew it, the three of us were standing in the dark by Jeff's car with the trunk open. Thankfully the rain had stopped. Jeff handed him a Book of Mormon. The photographer turned to me. "You are Jana Barrowman, aren't you?"

"That's me."

"You're dating Steadman."

"I can honestly say I've never dated Alex Steadman." A memory of sitting across from Alex over a tableful of greasy burgers and French fries flashed into my head. "But he did buy me dinner once."

I shivered. Jeff appeared behind me and put his arm around me. I stood closer to him to get warm.

"Well, you kids go get warm. Thanks again."

As we were driving away, Jeff proclaimed, "That went well. It's all about the energy you approach people with. That's what it is."

"You're right. I don't see how that could have gone better. I can't wait to see the pictures."

When we arrived at my house, a patrol car was parked behind a silver car across the street. Jeff walked me to my door as I tried to pretend nothing was wrong. My cell phone rang. It was Alex. "Having fun?"

"Yes. Yes, I am," I said crossly.

"Well, you don't want to go in just yet. Fred called the police to report that the suspicious car is back, and the officer just discovered it's empty. That means Prince Charming is creeping around somewhere. Right now, there are two cops in your—"

"Oh," I cut him off, looking up to the window, where I could see him watching us. Jeff followed my gaze, and Alex waved. There was a faint flicker of a flashlight coming from the shop window. I furrowed my brow. It had been three weeks since Fred had called Alex to tell him he hadn't seen Brad's car on the road. I was beginning to feel so safe that I'd forgotten what it was like to have the sickening plummet of my stomach when I thought about Brad. The reminder came, feeling familiar, and I couldn't help but shudder. "I understand. Can you call me when they're done?"

"Why don't you two come over for a drink or something? I have soda. I'll be nice."

"I'll see if he wants to." I hung up the phone. I looked at Jeff, who was looking particularly handsome in a burgundy sweater he'd just purchased. "So," I smiled at Jeff, "do you want to meet my boss?"

"No kidding? Ha. Sure." As we approached Alex's door, Jeff asked, "Won't he hate me? The paper said . . ."

"He's not like that. Before you know it, you'll be golfing together. You'll see."

"He's a golfer?"

"Yeah, c'mon."

I took Jeff's hand and led him across the lawn. Alex was waiting for us. "Alex, this is Jeff. Jeff, this is my boss, Alex Steadman."

Alex shook Jeff's hand. "Good to meet you."

"You're taller than I thought you would be," Jeff said.

"I don't get that one much." Alex motioned us into the kitchen. He made a shush motion and pointed upstairs, indicating that Elise was in bed. He took some cups from the cupboard. "So Thursday's a good movie night. What did you see?"

I shot a warning look at Alex.

Jeff popped open a can of soda. "Nothing good out tonight. We went shopping. Jana helped me pick out some clothes. We even got our picture taken."

Alex's good-natured façade faltered. "Why?"

Now it was my turn to smile. I hoped he thought they were engagement pictures.

"It's my turn to be in the papers with her." Jeff laughed. Turning to me, he winked. "You just come with more and more perks, don't you?" He tousled my hair in a brotherly way. Alex noticed and gave me a satisfied smile. I stepped purposefully closer to Jeff while I stared Alex down, daring him to say anything.

Alex laced his fingers. "Speaking of perks, when the police found the empty car, Fred sent them over here. I told them what I knew, and they wanted to make sure he wasn't inside your house. The doorbell keeps ringing, and I'm trying to get Elise to stay in bed."

Jeff turned to me. "Who's the *he* they're looking for in your house?"

"It's this guy from Utah I used to date. He was parking across the street every night a few weeks ago. I guess he came back. He hasn't told me he's here or anything. The neighbor noticed the car so Alex started checking it out."

"Excuse me a moment." Alex returned in seconds. "Now there are two more patrol cars. I bet you had a guest. They have a dog."

I couldn't imagine Brad sneaking around outside, being chased by a dog. "I really didn't think he was like this. It's so weird. This is, well, beneath him. He's usually such a classy guy." I thought of Brad sneaking through my house. It wasn't possible.

I went to the front room to peek out of the blinds. Alex and Jeff must have shared a funny joke because they were suddenly laughing hard. Five patrol cars were parked out front now. An officer was approaching the door. I threw it open before he rang the doorbell.

"Miss Barrowman?" I nodded. "Can you ID this guy for us?" He pulled out a pencil and small pad of paper. "He's cooperating. We just need to tie things up."

"Where did you find him?"

"He was jumping over a side fence when Pylon got him. That's going to hurt for a few days. Looks like he entered through a back window and exited through a bedroom window."

I made a sour face. "Can I get a restraining order or something?"

"You can now, sure. You should have been doing that a few weeks ago though. We could have booked him on heavier charges. Mr. Steadman confirmed a pattern of stalking."

Alex and Jeff followed me out to a patrol car. The officer pointed to a back window that was rolled down. I knew I wouldn't see Brad there. There had to be a mistake. The backseat was shadowed. I bent down close to the window. "Hello?"

The man looked up. It *was* Brad. He was clean shaven and wearing an expensive silk shirt. Blood was smeared across his right cheekbone. He still looked handsome. "Jana, tell them you know me!"

"What were you doing in my house, Brad?" I tried not to sound panicked. The officer had his back turned to the car, but I could see he was taking notes.

"I came to talk. I was going to surprise you. I was just leaving some flowers."

"Oh . . . Even so, this doesn't look too good. I don't think there's anything I can do to help you." I didn't want to seem like the bad guy. If Brad was crazy, and it was looking more probable by the moment, I didn't want him to aim any revenge at me.

His anger flashed. "*Doesn't look too good?* Jana, stop messing around and tell them who I am."

"They know who you are," I hissed. "You didn't have permission to break into my house."

"Break into your house? Jana, it's me. Look at me. You really think I'm some thug who goes around breaking into houses? Tell them who I am so I can get out of this blasted car and talk to you."

Alex took me by the elbow. I jumped. He whispered into my ear. "This is just going in circles. It's time to say good-bye. He has an appointment to keep." It was the closest he'd been to me in weeks, and I couldn't help the happy chills that ran down my spine.

Brad glared at Alex, who smiled kindly back at him.

"Good luck." It was all I could think of to say to Brad. Suddenly, he was shouting words I had never heard him use before. A power window was sliding up past his face, and the officers' radios and a barking dog drowned out the sound. I looked around in a daze.

An officer with a large black dog approached me. "You have verified the identity of the suspect. I need to ask you some questions, then we're done here." He wrote down my information and asked me a few questions about my relationship with Brad. "Crime lab will be about another five minutes, then it'll be safe to go home."

"Thank you." I reached down to pet the dog. "Is this Pylon?"

"Yeah, he's our best. Going to retire next year though."

"Did you really catch Brad climbing a fence?" I thought of Brad in his white tennis clothes, balancing a racquet in one hand. He was athletic enough to jump a fence, but I just couldn't mesh the two images together in my brain.

"Pylon got him in the calf. The wound is deep. The suspect will be transported to the hospital for a few stitches before we take him in."

Alex took my elbow again and guided me inside. "See there. Nothing to it. It's all over now." He led me to the couch.

Jeff was there too. "Jana, are you going to be all right? You're white as a ghost."

"Huh?" I looked up at him. "Yes. Thanks. I'll be fine. It's just a little disconcerting. I'll get over it."

"Give her a couple of hours," Alex said. "She's in shock. She'll snap out of it." Alex had seen me like this before.

They talked companionably for a while. I lay down on the couch. Alex draped a throw over me but kept talking to Jeff. I knew they would get along. I couldn't imagine anyone not getting along with Alex. Of course, Brad didn't look very fond of him. I yawned and tried to listen to the conversation. Pictures of Brad getting stitches at the hospital and fingerprinted at a jail kept popping into my head. It just didn't fit. I wavered between wanting to drive down to save him and wanting to shoot him. I wasn't sure how scared I should feel. If his kiss at the airport had made me feel violated, this was at least a thousand times worse. Even if I had walked into my house and he had been standing there holding flowers, I wouldn't have been happy to see him. Breaking and entering just wasn't a good way to say hello.

I exhaled deeply, sat up, stretched, and forced Brad out of my mind. The first-meeting feeling was gone from the room. Alex had worked his magic. Though I was completely out of the conversation, I enjoyed watching Jeff talk animatedly to Alex about baseball. Luckily, they liked the same teams. Alex really was the perfect people person. As I studied his face, I couldn't see any hint that he wasn't as excited to be talking to Jeff as he seemed to be. He was completely genuine. That's why people loved him so much. He was genuine. He was truly excited to be talking to whoever it was he was engaged in conversation with. Alex laughed at something Jeff had said, and the tiny crow's feet appeared around his eyes. I loved those lines. I loved to see Alex happy, and if those lines were there, I knew he was happy. Unfortunately, I was caught in that thought, with a dopey lopsided grin, when their conversation lulled and Jeff said something to me. I looked up a little dazed. "Huh?"

Jeff tousled my hair again. "It's late. I should get you home. I have to work in the morning."

Alex set his glass down. "Oh, morning. That reminds me, Jana, Gretchen isn't sure she's going to make it in the morning. Can you come over and get Elise ready and to school if necessary? I've got to pick up some orders."

"Sure." I wish he could have asked it at a different time. I didn't want it to sound like . . . *like what*? Like I was as close to Alex and Elise as I actually was? I studied Alex's coffee table as I thought about that and they said good-bye.

Jeff walked me back across the lawn. "You know, he's really nice."

The night was quiet again, though the silver car was still parked across the street as a reminder. "Yeah," I admitted, lost in thought.

"And youngish."

"Uh-huh." I absently fished for the keys in my pocket.

"There was this look you had on your face right at the end there when you were staring at him . . ."

My head shot up. "What look?"

He blossomed his hands out in front of me. "Your eyes all lit up, mirroring back his face, admiration dripping like caramel off a hot apple."

"Jeff, stop it. It's bad enough I have to put up with the press. I don't need you teasing me."

"I'm just saying . . ." he left off dramatically.

I poked him in the chest. "No. You're not *saying*."

"Okay, I'm not saying. I'm not saying. Sheesh." He tilted my chin up so I had to look him in the eyes. "You still good for next Thursday? Opening day for the new *Brandish* movie. I'm sure it will be crowded."

"I'm good for it if you are."

He touched my nose playfully and let his hand fall. "See you Thursday, then." He was walking away when he turned around. "And, uh, Jana, bring that look." He winked and watched me disappear inside the house. I grimaced on the other side of the door.

I sat down on a Victorian chair we'd found for the shop the day before and stared around the dark room. I tried to picture Brad alone in the dark doing . . . what? What would he have been doing? The doorbell rang. I looked through the peephole. It was just Alex. I let him in.

"Not even going to turn on a light?"

"I was getting to it. What are you here for?"

"Thought you'd like me to check for the boogie man. I noticed Jeff neglected that little detail."

I lowered my head. If he'd been watching, he probably noticed other details, like the absent kiss. "I'm a grown-up. I don't check under the bed anymore."

"Well, obviously you *should* be checking under your bed." He flipped the light on. I had to shield my eyes. The shop looked the same. I followed Alex through the house. True to his word, Brad had left a vase of daisies on my dresser. "Maybe you should sleep at April's tonight."

"I'm not worried. I'm pretty sure Brad's busy doing other things right now."

"We need to get you another place."

"Alex, let's not blow this out of proportion."

"No, let's. This is serious, Jana. What could have happened to you? How cracked in the head is this guy?"

"It's just Brad."

"Yeah, well *just Brad* crept up to your window and jimmied it open. *Just Brad* was waiting in here to surprise you when you got home. *Just Brad* . . ." Alex's voice was becoming more heated.

"Okay, okay. Calm down." I folded my arms and faced the wall.

"I swear if I see *just Brad* again, I'm going to . . ."

"You're going to calm down," I admonished.

Alex walked out to the landing and sat down on the first step. "You're getting new windows in the morning; new dead bolts, the works." He put his head in his hands.

I put my hand on his shoulder. "If that makes you feel better, then do it."

"The crazy thing is, you don't look as worried as you should be."

I sat down beside him. It felt too close because the stairs were narrow. "I'm still processing it. I'll probably look worried in the morning. I've had a long day." I thought about Melee, the photographer, and the car window sliding past Brad's face. "You should be home with Elise. Tonight, we don't have anything to worry about. We can worry in the morning."

I stood up and started pulling him down the stairs.

"I don't know if the antique wiring in this place can support an alarm system, but we'll figure something out."

"Uh-huh." At the door, I said, "Thank you for looking under my bed. I appreciate it."

Alex looked at me quizzically then opened the door. He turned sharply before he left. Pointing at me, he said, "You call me if you hear anything. Keep your phone by your bed. Lock every door."

I smiled and nodded. I left the shop lights on and went upstairs to call my dad. He was boiling mad, demanding that I come home. My mother took the phone from him and told me it couldn't have been Brad. She'd seen him just last week. I promised her it was. After spending a half hour reassuring them that I was fine, I repented the phone call. Perhaps it would have been better if I'd never told them. I hung up, fixed myself some peppermint tea, and watched television until my eyes were too tired. After I prayed, I lay awake in bed another hour, staring into the darkness, trying to figure out what Brad had been thinking.

* * *

I was planning on slipping silently into Alex's house in the morning, but a slamming cupboard startled me. The kitchen light was already on.

"Gretchen? I thought you weren't going to be here." She was fully dressed with perfect hair and makeup applied. Her eyebrows had been drawn in pencil and looked like they were arched in surprise.

"I get here at five. Since you're here now, why don't I start training you?"

"For what?" I asked, trying not to sound sleepy.

"My job. He said you'd be helping out."

"Well, I haven't decided yet." I had been gingerly avoiding the subject for weeks, afraid to commit to staying longer in Washington.

Gretchen's face contorted. "That spoiled rotten . . . He said you were on, that everything was good. He promised me. He's taking advantage of you now. Thinks he can tell the world to jump and they will. I don't know what he's up to nowadays, but I don't like it. It would serve him right if we both up and left him."

I thought about that for a moment. I tried to picture Alex without Gretchen and without me. It was easier to picture him without me. He needed Gretchen. "I didn't say I *wouldn't* do it." I was seized with a great sympathy for Alex and suddenly wanted to get him out of trouble. "I know he's been off lately, but he's just going through some changes. I'm sure he's talked to you about selling the restaurant. He's been really frustrated." He'd actually been buoyant with no trace of frustration, but that fact wouldn't help my argument.

Gretchen sat down. "He's been a self-absorbed pig."

"He just needs a little time to get back to normal."

"I don't have time. I've got to retire. I don't know how much longer I have with my mother. I can't keep spending this much time here. He promised he'd get help ages ago."

"I'll help."

Gretchen's face lit up. How bad could it be? He'd be at the restaurant most of the time anyway. She leaned forward. "Are you sure? Don't you go wasting your young life serving him. He gets charming you know. Quitting this job won't be as easy as you think it will be. Think long and hard about it. I thought you already had. He made me believe you were ready to take over any day."

"I'm sure he just has faith in me."

"He loves you. He won't let you go without a fight."

My eyes moistened. The core of my existence leapt forward and latched onto her words. "I know it," I lied, trying to look like she didn't surprise me. "I want to help. I can't imagine him leaving Elise with anyone else." April's voice came back to me. *If you could choose someone for them, wouldn't you choose someone like you?*

"You can't leave them any more than I can. You're already stuck." Gretchen shook her head in pity.

"Don't think of it like I'm stuck. This is just where I'm choosing to spend my time. I don't have anything better to do. I don't have a family of my own. I'm here by my own choice."

"If it would break your heart to leave it, you're stuck."

This was the point where April would pull out a bucket of ice cream. "We'll just have to agree to disagree." I smiled.

"Let's get to work." She pushed up her sleeves and walked to the sink.

A moment later, I was crossing the family room to put away some magazines. I looked up when I heard a stair creak. Alex was retreating to the upstairs hallway.

I climbed three stairs. "Were you eavesdropping?"

He had wet hair and a towel around his neck. I thought I saw a dab of shaving cream by his ear. The whole scene was adorable. I wished he were mine, and I hated the wish. "How can I be eavesdropping in my own home?"

"What did you hear?"

"Two women gabbing. Something about how I rank right up there with *nothing better to do*." He sounded hurt.

"Well, that's what you get for sneaking around."

He swept his hand in a grand motion. "My house." He walked down a few stairs to meet me halfway. "I am glad you're staying, even if it's only because you have *nothing better to do*."

"Have I wounded your ego?"

"I didn't know Gretchen felt trapped."

"She loves you and Elise. It's hard to leave someone you love. So in a way, she is trapped."

He had a distant look in his eyes. I backed down the stairs. As I entered the kitchen, I heard him say, "In any case, thank you for staying."

I hung my head out the door. "You betcha."

CHAPTER 12
Gopher

GRETCHEN'S JOB WAS INTENSE. SHE cleaned, shopped, pulled secretary duty, chauffeured Elise, and kept track of all of Alex's finances and bookkeeping. I mentally made notes of all of the things I wouldn't do. If Alex liked things a certain way, then he could do them himself. As far as I could see, I needed to make sure the shopping was done, Elise was cared for, and the books were kept. It was much simpler than the way Gretchen did things. If he thought I was going to mother him like Gretchen did, he had another thing coming. Gretchen was right. He was spoiled, but it was her fault for taking such complete care of him. I had no qualms about him using dishes right out of the dishwasher. Gretchen did many daily housekeeping chores. As I was mopping the already clean floor, I decided he could hire a housekeeping service once a week.

After a week of gradually letting me do parts of her job, Gretchen felt good enough about me to schedule a week with her mother. I sat in Alex's office. After hours of filing, his books were up to date and everything was in order. All I had to do was make day-to-day entries on the computer. He didn't have the software at home, so I traveled to his office to make the entries once a day. The bright afternoon sun striped the wall through the blinds. He burst into the office, laughing. To my surprise, Jeff was behind him.

Jeff was talking animatedly. "Then she looks around with this expression like a slack-jawed yokel and says, 'Where'd it go?'" They both started laughing again.

"Jana, I didn't know you were coming in today." Alex held his arms out like I'd run to him. I didn't.

Jeff sat on the edge of the desk. "Did you know he has a membership to the Tundra Golf Club? I've always wanted to play there."

I smiled at him. "Good. Two peas in a pod." Turning to Alex, I said, "Just remember what pond he comes from. You take good care of him."

Alex raised his eyebrows. "I don't see you admonishing him to take care of me."

"Jeff, he's a rascal. Watch yourself."

Alex scowled at me.

Alex opened the closet and hefted a golf bag onto the couch.

A pretty brunette waitress popped her head in. "Alex, what am I supposed to save out for the Berkshires tomorrow? We're out of everything."

"I'll take care of it. We'll just pick up some more supplies."

I saw Jeff appraising the waitress. When she left, he lifted Alex's clubs and said, "I'll just put these in the car." I was sure he was going to follow her.

Alex noticed too. When Jeff was out of earshot, he said, "I like that kid more every minute." I grunted and pretended to be absorbed in my work. "What I don't see," he continued, "is electricity. It's like neither of you has lit the match."

"I'm sure this is none of your business, but I find him very attractive, thank you." I spoke to the papers in front of me.

"Well, you've put me in my place, then." He pushed a golf ball around on the desk. "I do notice *he* doesn't mind fishing in other ponds."

I slapped my pen onto the desk and pushed the chair back. Alex could always tell what I was thinking before I thought it. I sighed and admitted, "I don't seem to be the catch of the day, do I?"

"You don't seem to be very upset about that."

"Well, at any rate, take care of him. He's a good guy."

"About the other pond thing—if he can do it, then . . ."

This was the first spark of interest he'd shown in me for weeks. "Okay, you want to play that game? I'll play it like he does. First, you have to read my book."

"What? The Book of Mormon?"

"That's what he does. He's still on his mission. I don't think he noticed that he ever came home. You watch. Leave him alone with your voluptuous waitress long enough and she'll have a book in her hand."

"Did he make *you* read the book?"

"I read it every night." I stacked some papers and pulled a file box into my lap. "I know you hate this conversation, but I dare you to read it. There's a promise that if you read it with the intent of finding out if it's true, you'll receive your own witness from the Holy Ghost when you pray and ask."

He got up and closed and locked the door. "What if it is true? If I had a *witness* and I knew it was true, then what about us?"

My heart did a little dance. He was still thinking about the possibility of us. Even though it should have been bad news, I couldn't keep the smile from my eyes.

"I guess we could see if there was really anything between us." I stapled some papers.

"I never have to read books to get dates with women. Usually they just—"

"Oh, I've seen them *just* all over you. I know how *hard* it is for you to get a date. Did you ever think of this? Maybe you only want me because I'm off-limits. Maybe I'm the only challenge you've had, so I intrigue you? Once I'm not a challenge, you won't want me anymore."

"Is that why you're playing hard to get?"

"I'm not playing anything."

There was a knock on the door. We stared at each other. Unsaid words hung in the air between us. The knock came again. I hated whoever was on the other side of the door because I didn't want to stop talking. "I think someone wants to talk to you."

"I don't want to read the book for nothing. I've got to know the carrot's at the end of the stick."

"Then you'd be reading it for the wrong reason, wouldn't you? You'd better go rescue your waitress from Jeff." He pointed at me, and before he could start, I said, "Infuriating. I know. Go. Golf. I'll see you tonight."

He opened the door. A fiery redhead squealed, "Alex! I was so excited to see you that I came here as soon as I got into town." He looked at me, pleading.

I sighed heavily, walked to his side, and slipped my hand into his. The contact was heavenly. I hated myself for liking it. "Channing, this is Jana Barrowman. Jana, this is *Mrs.* Channing Hansen." He was sure to annunciate the "Mrs."

"It is good to meet you." I held out my other hand. She shook it firmly, smiling widely.

She focused on Alex like I wasn't there. "I thought we could do lunch."

"Ah, you see, I have a golfing appointment today. I was just leaving." He leaned over and kissed me lightly on the lips. "See you tonight."

She followed him out. I could hear her. "That's a shame. I have so much to tell you."

I shut the door and locked it, a little disconcerted that the simple kiss didn't feel out of place.

I wanted him to read the Book of Mormon but for the right reasons. At least he was going golfing with the missionary who never returned. I was sure Jeff would talk to him about it. I started to tidy the desk so I could pick Elise up. As I worked, I had a disgruntled feeling that I was still working and he'd run off to play. That must be how Gretchen felt. Of course, I was getting paid to do the work. I shouldn't complain. It was like working for the attorneys. They took off when they wanted to. I couldn't. That was just my lot in life.

A rap on the window brought me out of my reflections. I pulled up the blinds. Alex was standing there. A breeze lifted his hair. I opened the window. "What's wrong with the door?" I asked.

"Channing is still in there having lunch. I need my gloves."

"Is she that bad?"

"No, but *Mr.* Hansen is. She won't leave me alone. Talk about a stalker. Maybe we could get her a cell next to Brad."

"Maybe you led her on."

"Would I do that? You know me better than that," he chided.

"No. You would never do that," I conceded.

"The gloves are in the left-hand drawer." He pushed on the screen frame until it popped into the room.

"Alex!"

"I'll fix it later."

I handed him the gloves.

"Lock up, okay?" He turned to leave then stopped. "Another kiss good-bye?"

I slid the window shut and pulled the blinds down.

CHAPTER 13
Ledgers and Raindrops

I WET TWO DISH TOWELS AND rang them out before spreading them on the floor. "This is what we're going to do. Take your shoes and socks off."

Alex wouldn't let me hire a housekeeper. He said it was too much of a risk because they stole property and sold secrets to the press. He had a point. He agreed that Elise could have a "job" and earn an allowance. The only housekeeping Gretchen did was in the kitchen and living room. "Now stand on your towel and scoot around like this. Mopping at its best."

"We have a mop," Elise said as she stepped gingerly onto the towel.

"That's no fun." I put on some bee-bop music.

Alex came home a half hour later, catching us in bare feet, singing into wooden spoons, and wiggling to the beat. The floor was clean by then.

"Don't say a thing about it, Alex Steadman. I'm getting paid for this, and I know you don't like your job half as much." I tossed my spoon into the sink.

"As long as you're happy. I wasn't going to say anything." He looked tired and worn out.

"Hard day golfing?"

"No. Just politics at work. Nothing to worry about."

I dried my feet and followed him into the living room. "Want to talk about it?"

He plopped down on the couch, kicked his feet onto the coffee table, and turned the television on. "How can you tell there's anything *to* talk about? Am I wearing a sign or something? I've got to work on my poker face."

"You usually have a natural buoyancy, and it's gone. Your shoulders look weighed down with worry. Your crow's feet are smooth, and you sucked the happiness out of the room like a vacuum."

Strains of Elise's song swelled over the sound of the television. Alex turned the TV off. "Channing is Mr. Hansen's wife."

"I knew that part."

"Theodore Hansen holds a controlling interest in the company I want to sell Shallots to."

"Mr. Hansen doesn't like you?" He just raised his eyebrows at me. "Channing likes you too much?" He nodded and pinched the bridge of his nose. "What are you going to do?"

"I'll have to find another company. I thought this one was perfect. I knew they'd take good care of my people. That's what Channing came to tell me today. He's not going to allow them to consider the sale. My head cook overheard and offered to buy it. I know he can't afford it. I didn't want anyone to know I was selling it. It will just make it harder to work with them. Now they probably all know."

"Which one was the head cook?"

"Scott."

"He's hot. He could probably pull it off."

"This isn't improving my mood. I spent two hours with your boyfriend telling me I didn't stand a chance. Katherine has a Book of Mormon, and . . ." he fished in the leather satchel at his feet, "now I have one too." He smacked the book on the coffee table. "Plus, now I find out you have a thing for my head cook."

I had to laugh. He didn't seem to appreciate it, so I covered my mouth. "I don't have a thing for your head cook. I'm just saying he could probably do what you do."

"What do I do?"

"The morning shows, you know, stirring up female interest. What if you just sold him half of the restaurant?" His eyes looked more tired than ever. He stared at me mutely. "Okay. I see. You're going to be like this, huh?" I took his heavy hand and led him up the stairs. I gave him a little push into his bedroom. "Why don't you lie down until you feel better? I'll take Elise out to pick up pizza. If you feel better by then, you can come down and eat with us."

He collapsed backward onto his bed and pulled a pillow over his face. "I don't like mushrooms."

"Jes, Meeser Steadman, I know what chew like on jor pizza."

I heard the pillow hit the door after I shut it.

* * *

The next day I ran errands then worked in the shop for a few hours. For lunch, I slapped some turkey on bread and added a skiff of fat-free mayonnaise. I was balancing the plate on my lap, holding the sandwich in one hand, and drinking milk when the doorbell rang. My mouth was full, but I tried to say, "Just a minute." Chewing fast, I set the milk on a shelf and answered the door, still holding my sandwich.

"Ah, lunch. Great." Alex was wearing a T-shirt, shorts, and tennis shoes. He looked like he'd been running.

"If you're coming here for lunch, you must have hit bottom. I don't even have pickles."

"Whatever you're having is fine."

"How 'bout the fussy chef makes his own sandwich with whatever he can find in my kitchen."

Ten minutes later, he bounded down the stairs with a sandwich that made mine look pathetic. My mouth salivated just looking at it. "I can fix yours up too," he offered.

"No." I held up my sandwich with three bites left. "*This* is fat free. *That* will go right to my hips. Besides, I like cardboard. It's an undervalued food group." I sat down on the couch across from him.

Alex studied the ceiling, "So, you notice anything different about the shop since you got back today?"

I stopped chewing and looked around, suspicious. I stood up excitedly when I noticed the old steamer trunk from the attic sitting by the door. The shop was such a great collection of vintage-looking hats, florals, and jewelry that the trunk had blended right in. I hadn't even noticed it when I answered the door for Alex. "When did you do that?"

"When did I *pay* someone to do that? I gave Fred and his son thirty bucks to bring it down. They made it look easy. I can't believe you didn't notice."

Alex walked over to the trunk. "Don't you want to look in it after all the fuss you made to get it down?"

"What about the key?"

"I've got it. I put it in my wallet a long time ago. Look at this." He fished it out and handed me the small skeleton key.

"Oh, it's so Victorian. I love it. I hope it fits." I turned it in the keyhole, and the lock clicked. "Voilà! Stuff that's probably none of our business."

Alex swallowed a large bite. "I bought this 'none of our business' when I bought the house. It's my business, then, isn't it?" We knelt in front of the trunk and lifted the lid together.

"Awesome." Alex pulled out an old wool army uniform. "Look at these." Various medals hung from the coat.

Underneath an embroidered tablecloth was a ledger. I opened it and gasped. It was full of family names and birth, marriage, and death dates. "Hollander family genealogy. This is priceless. I can't wait to find them. They'll be so excited."

"About *genealogy*?"

I clutched the book to my chest and hustled to the couch to settle in. "Amanda Sarvant Smith. She must have died right after she gave birth to Chester. Yep, his birthday is the same day she died. Oh, that's so sad. She had one, two, three, four, five children. Only three were living then. Can you imagine having so many children just to have them die? I'm so glad we live now. Eighteen eighty-nine would have been such a sad time to live. But her husband got remarried in a year and had four more children. Only one of those died. Then he died before his new wife. The kids were pretty old by then though."

"Fascinating," he said in a bored tone.

"It is, actually. These people were really here. They're waiting right now. They have been counting on someone to find this so they'll be remembered." I ran my fingers over the yellowed pages. The ledger must have had twenty pages nearly bursting with names, and I had a sudden thought. "I think this is why I'm here. This is why I came to Washington. I was so confused. At first I thought I came for you and Elise, but that was all wrong. I'm supposed to find this. I'm supposed to find these Hollander people. I know it."

"If you don't mind, I'll choose to think you came for me. It strokes my ego better than thinking you came to dig up dead people."

I looked at him. "Alex, I know you'll never understand this, but now they can be forever families. They'll go through the temple and be sealed. I'm so excited. I have to find the Hollanders. I've got to call my dad. I have to call Rachel. This is so cool."

He studied my face. "I'm free all day. Let's find them today."

"Why do you want to do something that is so obviously boring to you? What are you up to?"

"Are you refusing my help? I know my way around. I even know a private investigator."

"I repeat: what are you up to?"

"I just want to spend some time with you. I've never seen you so excited about anything."

I didn't want to "just spend time" with him. But he seemed so harmless today. I bit my lip, debating.

He upped the bounty. "You can take me for a haircut too. You choose."

"For a man with a public image to uphold, that's a pretty risky offer, isn't it? Why don't you take me to Disneyland while you're at it?"

"If you'd go, I would. But I know you won't. I'm thinking a little day out would do you good. If I wanted to pamper another woman, I'd send her to the spa, take her out for a night on the town. You're a tough nut. You don't work like other women do. You're . . . painfully practical."

I thought for a moment. "You don't need to cut your hair. I'd like you the same no matter what it looked like."

"Dreadlocks?"

"Well, maybe not."

"If I hate it, I'll grow it back. It grows like a weed. C'mon, Jana, we'll have a great day. You know you want to do this. If you weren't head over heels in love with me, you'd go in a heartbeat."

"Who said I'm . . ."

"A heartbeat. Shhh," He put his finger to my lips. "Stop thinking and grab your shoes. I'll get a phonebook."

* * *

Before I knew it, we were in Mukilteo, pulling up to a little gray house with a white puffball of a dog trying to leap the fence in greeting. I protested again. "I still say we should have called first. This could be any Hollander. We don't even know if they're related."

"You know, there's a great deal of spontaneity missing from your life. It's easy to just pop in."

"What do you know about spontaneity?" I scoffed. "I've been through your day planner. You schedule your showers. If we'd called first, we could have saved a lot of time. We might be driving around all day."

He smiled at me like I was missing something. Always the gentleman, Alex opened the chain-link gate to let me through. I clutched the ledger. He bravely stepped up to the door and rapped on it. He had a good missionary knock. I imagined us as a missionary couple out tracting. Even with his new haircut, he still didn't look the part. He'd only let me order a trim, leaving it roguishly long on top.

A heavy-set man with a white beard that was stained yellow around his mouth opened the door. He was wearing a tank top and pajama pants. I was stunned into silence. An odor emanated from the house, and he was standing in garbage.

Alex looked at me, gave up on me speaking, and gave his most good-natured smile to the man. "Are you Edward Hollander?"

"Yeah, who wants to know?" I tried not to stare at Mr. Hollander's hairy shoulders. When I looked down, I tried not to stare at the garbage or his long, yellowed toenails. I had expected a Hollander to be a genteel little old lady, the kind I would find in the Family History Center.

Alex seemed completely at ease. I cleared my throat. "Mr. Hollander, we found this ledger in our attic, and we were wondering if it belonged to your family." I held it out to him, sad to think of its new home.

He took it and flipped through some pages. "This is my great-grandfather." He put his chubby finger under the name of Howard Hollander. There was no death or marriage date listed in the ledger. A light rain started to fall. I cringed, thinking of the ancient pages getting wet.

"Come on in. Where'd you say you found this?"

We followed him into the house, keeping on a trail of cleared floor. Piles of clothes, old cereal boxes, and newspapers were all around us. The odor was much stronger inside, a mixture of urine, cigarettes, and decaying food. I candidly told him about hearing something sliding across the floor of the attic, thinking the house was haunted, and finding the chest.

He invited us to take a seat. Alex caught me by my elbow when I started to descend toward the crusty couch. He gave a nearly imperceptible shake of his head, glancing at the couch.

"I have a cousin who's nuts about this stuff. He's going to flip. What did you say your names were again?"

"Alex Steadman, and this is Jana." I liked that he left off my last name.

"Mr. Hollander, does your cousin do a lot of family history?" I asked.

"And then some. He's obsessed with it. He has charts, journals, pictures. It's interesting, you know, if you have time for that kind of thing."

I hoped I wasn't offending him by saying, "Maybe we can take the ledger out to him. Does he live in town?"

"He never comes out here. He's clear out in Bellingham."

"That's not too far. We're just out goofing off today. Why don't we take it up there for you?" Alex offered.

"Let me call him first. See if it's okay. I can't just give his information out. He's not listed, like me."

He left, and I looked at Alex. "Can you believe the rain just then?" I asked.

"In Washington, who would have thought?" I couldn't tell what Alex was thinking, but he definitely had mirth in his eyes. He was having more private enjoyment than I thought necessary.

We could hear the phone call in the kitchen. "Alex Steadman . . . That's right . . . found it in an attic . . . wants to bring it to you . . . Alex and Jana Steadman." Alex smiled at me and winked. I rolled my eyes but tinkered with the name *Jana Steadman* in my mind while we waited. Mr. Hollander peered around the doorway and asked, "You did say Alex Steadman, sir?"

"That's me."

"That's who he is, all right. Okay, I'll tell 'em."

I wondered how Mr. Hollander navigated the house day in and day out in bare feet. I noticed a chicken bone stuck in the olive-green carpet. Mr. Hollander hung up the phone and headed our way, down the trail. "He says he knows you and c'mon out. You know my cousin?"

"What's his name?" Alex asked.

"Harper Smith."

"The name doesn't ring a bell, but I'm sure we'll hash it out when we get there."

* * *

In the car, Alex admitted, "This is kind of fun. I can't wait to see his cousin."

"Be nice. I'm sure his cousin is a very good sort of person."

"I'm sure he is." Alex's crow's feet were straining from the smile.

I held the ledger possessively. I hoped beyond hope that Cousin Harper was worthy to receive it. I was planning to send him literature about the huge Family History Center in Salt Lake.

While we waited in traffic, Alex asked, "Will you tell me about your book?"

I looked down at the ledger in my hands. I opened to the first page. "It's a little worn out, over a hundred years old—"

"I don't mean that book. Tell me about your Book of Mormon."

"It's a little worn out, over a hundred years old . . ."

"I finally ask and you're making jokes? I would have thought you'd be more eager to talk about it."

"I am. You just surprised me a little. What do you want to know? I'm no expert, but I know my way around it pretty well."

"You read it every night?"

"I read a chapter a night. Sometimes I hit a long chapter and read half. Sometimes I'm too beat to focus my eyes, so I just let it fall open and read what I can."

"If you've read it once, why read it every night?"

"It's scripture study. I'm *studying*. It's not like a book that says the same things each time you read it. You change as you read it, and you learn different lessons from it all the time. Like last night, I came across this passage on faith that I'd never noticed before. I've read the book over ten times, but that passage only meant something to me last night, as though it magically appeared when I needed it or was ready to understand it."

"Tell me about faith."

I looked at him, wondering what he was up to. He must think he was giving me immense pleasure by talking religion. "Why?"

"Hmm?" He looked at me, surprised that I would ask. "Is it too private?"

"No." I took a deep breath and thought about faith. "Faith is like a little mustard seed . . ."

"If you plant it, it will grow. I hear you singing with Elise."

"Well, it *is* like a little seed, a mustard seed. You're familiar with how small a mustard seed is?" He rolled his eyes, reminding me he was a chef. I continued. "The point of faith is taking the first step to plant it, or letting it linger in your heart. Then it grows because you test it and find that it's true. So a first tentative step turns into a confident leap. After a while, it isn't faith anymore. It turns into knowledge, knowing that things are true. And you can't deny the things you know."

He quoted, "'I knew it, and I knew that God knew it, and I could not deny it, neither dared I do it.'"

"Joseph Smith." I was stunned and wondered when he'd read that.

He turned smoothly onto the freeway and merged into traffic. "When I read that, I thought, *So that's why she's so obstinate*. Hearing you explain it confirms. You *think* you know something. It was like you were saying it to me when I read it. It rang of something you'd say."

"I have a strong testimony. I still need faith sometimes, but I know a lot of things for myself. I guess I am like Joseph. I know these things, I know that God knows I know these things because He's told me Himself through the Holy Ghost, and I don't dare deny that I know them. I can't imagine thinking of denying that I know them. Exactly how much time have you been spending with Jeff?"

"What? I can't pick up a book on my own to try to puzzle out a woman?"

"That's not exactly why you're supposed to be reading the book. It shouldn't have anything to do with me."

"It has everything to do with you. Jeff made me see that."

"I'm glad you're listening to him." I hoped he wasn't dissuading Alex too much. A part of me was still happy that Alex was interested in me. "I *think* I'm glad," I added.

"It's good to see all the *brotherly* love you have for Jeff. I'm glad I saw it for myself. I was making myself sick. That you could fall for some kid like that and not me—it was driving me crazy."

"I like him," I said defensively.

"Oh, you like him fine. I can see that."

"I *really* like him. He's handsome."

Alex laughed. "And when he kisses you?"

Heat crept into my face. "I don't think that's any of your business."

"Because he hasn't. There's no *business* at all, is there? And if he tried, would you let him?"

"Did he *tell* you he hasn't?"

"I didn't have to ask. The two of you don't look remotely interested in each other. I think you've been thrown together by convenience and that's it. What does your religion say about chemistry?"

"If two people have the same eternal goals, it makes chemistry a lot easier."

"Is that all?"

"Well, you save most of that chemistry for after you're married." My face was hot.

"So you could marry Jeff tomorrow and be eternally happy? The subtly brewing chemistry will appear after you're married?"

I folded my arms and slumped down in my seat. "Apparently, yes."

"He wears garments too?"

The conversation was making me uncomfortable. My heart was beating in my ears, my palms felt clammy. He was just curious, just asking questions. I should answer them as professionally as possible. I couldn't pull myself to a sitting position without unfolding my arms, so I stayed put. "Yes."

"Why do you wear garments?"

"A symbol of covenants I've made with God, to remind me who I am and what I believe. Like a priest wears that white thing around his neck or a Jewish man wears the little round hat. Only I wear mine underneath my clothes because I'm reminding me, not everyone else."

"Covenants?"

"A covenant is a two-way promise between you and Heavenly Father," I repeated from memory. "We are a covenant people. We promise to keep the commandments and remember Christ. Heavenly Father promises to bless us when we do." I was glad we were off the topic of underwear.

"When you stand close to Jeff, do you feel the same feelings you feel when I stand close to you?"

Suddenly, talking about underwear didn't seem so bad. "No."

"If he asked you to marry him tomorrow, would you say yes?"

"No." I busied my eyes, looking at the majestic, lacy pines passing by.

"Because you love me?"

I reached over and turned his radio on, cranking up the volume. He laughed but stopped talking.

* * *

Harper Smith lived in a modest, two-story house on a large lot of land. I smiled when the door opened. A large picture of Christ hung on the wall in the entry. It was the standard LDS red-robed Christ, the one who looked pleased when you were good and disappointed when you were bad, the one with eyes that followed you wherever you moved around a room. I reached out my hand. "Brother Smith, I'm Jana Barrowman. This is my employer, Alex Steadman. We are renovating an old house to use as a store in Seattle. We found this in the attic with a box of memorabilia." I handed him the ledger.

"That's Alex Steadman, all right." Harper Smith was a handsome man in his fifties. His dark brown hair had a few shocks of gray running through it. He was trim and wore slacks and a golf shirt, with cordovan shoes. He showed us into a sitting room that looked like it doubled as an office. He introduced us to a good-looking woman, obviously his wife, of similar age, Tanya. She was shorter than him by a few inches and had short blonde hair. They sat across from us on a sofa.

Mr. Smith smiled kindly at Alex. "I was sorry to hear about your wife."

"Thank you." Alex said as though he'd heard it a thousand times and responded a thousand more. I bet he had.

"Where did you say you found this?" Tanya Smith asked as she leafed through the pages, holding the book like it was a treasure.

"We found it in the attic of a house Mr. Steadman owns." Alex blanched when I used his more formal name. He moved closer to me on the couch. "I have an apartment there. I'm renovating the downstairs into a shop. At night I could hear boxes sliding across the floor in the attic. Alex was kind enough to bring the box down for me. I think I was meant to find it because Heavenly Father knew I would bring it to you."

"Are you a Latter-day Saint?" Harper asked.

I smiled. "I am."

He looked at Alex and nodded as though he understood something.

"There is a whole trunk of memorabilia in the car," Alex offered.

"This is a surprise. Thank you for bringing it all the way out here. I'm glad you found Ed." Tanya looked as though she knew that finding Ed would be less than appealing.

"It was our pleasure," Alex insisted. After Alex unloaded the trunk, we exchanged quick good-byes because we had to pick up Elise from school. The Smiths waved as Alex pulled out. As he searched for a good radio station, he said, "That was oddly satisfying. I wonder if I have anything else that doesn't belong to me."

"It was wonderful. Thank you. I can't think of a better way to spend a day."

"They felt like you. The whole house felt like you."

"What do you mean?"

"There's something special about you, something so different it makes a person stop and wonder. It's there too."

"Oh, well, how could I be confused with an explanation like that? It's probably the Holy Ghost. He lingers in certain places or with some people."

We talked about the Holy Ghost the entire way home, who He was, what He did, and who He stayed with. I told him all of the stories I could think of. He told me of some times in his life when he'd felt guided.

"So it's the sixth sense, isn't it?" he asked.

"Sometimes I hear people talk about the sixth sense and I wonder. I don't really know. But you can listen to it. The more you listen to it, the more you hear it."

We were pulling up to Elise's school. Alex turned to me. "I have a get-together tomorrow. I just have to make an appearance. I don't suppose you'd consider?"

He'd just driven me all over Washington. I felt indebted. "I'll go."

"It's semiformal."

"Are you trying to change my mind?"

"You'll look like my date."

"I repeat: are you trying to change my mind?"

"I just don't want you to change your mind at the last minute."

"I know it's a date. I'll go this once." I waved at Elise. Alex got the door for her. I could see her little friends watch him dreamily. It made me laugh.

Elise chattered all the way home about Rosie Stevenson and her blue boots. After dinner, Alex walked me home. "I'll be gone tomorrow." He reached into his back pocket and handed me a key. "It comes with Gretchen's job. I'm not like you, so don't worry about privacy. Gretchen will pick Elise up from school and drop her off for a sleepover. I'll pick you up at seven for our date." He laughed. "You didn't even flinch when I said it."

I sighed.

"Maybe I'll see you in the morning." He kissed me on the forehead and left.

CHAPTER 14
Change of Scenery

At two in the morning I woke to a shrill, piercing alarm. I sat up in bed, trying to orient myself. When I realized it was the fire alarm, I leapt up and turned on the light. The landing was thick with smoke. I closed the door and leaned against the wall, eyes wide with fear. I tried to remember everything I'd ever learned about fires. I thought about going down the stairs to the front door but decided, since that's where the dancing light was coming from, I'd better try another way out. Looking down from my bedroom window didn't inspire hope either. I crossed the apartment and opened the front door again. The smoke was thicker and the light flickered brighter. A loud pop resonated downstairs. I swallowed hard. I shut the door and pushed a jacket against the bottom of it to stop a trickle of smoke. I grabbed my cell phone and returned to my bedroom window to look out on the dark yard. Alex's back door burst open, and he darted toward my house.

"Alex!" I waved, trying to call above the shriek of the alarm. "The ladder in the garage! I can't get down."

He swore and ran back into his house. He returned with the ladder and set it up against the windowsill. I tossed my phone to him and climbed out the window. As soon as my feet were on the ground, he took me by the shoulders and made me face him. "You okay?"

"I'm okay. The shop . . . It's on fire." The alarm pierced the night air. I shivered as he took my hand and led me into his house. He called the fire department. Within minutes, we were standing outside with Elise wrapped in a blanket. The firefighters said the houses were too close, and they made us evacuate Alex's too.

I held Elise, and we all watched, wide eyed, as flames licked the front shop window. The alarm sputtered out, and the night was silent, except for firefighters calling commands to each other. Neighbors were gathered around Alex, their faces lit up with the dancing lights of emergency vehicles. I shivered again.

The deft firemen had the fire out within fifteen minutes. We were allowed back into Alex's house again shortly after. I tucked in Elise, called April to ask if I could sleep at her house, then returned to find Alex in the yard. He shook hands with a fireman and walked over to me. "The good news is, it's out."

"What caused it?"

"A circuit overloaded. The bad news is the house isn't as up to code as the previous owners promised. The wiring is ancient, which I already knew, but I didn't think it was that bad. I should have hired an electrician to put in the track lighting and the alarm. I thought I could handle it."

I exhaled in exasperation. "I hope we don't have to tear out walls to get to the wiring. We were so close to finishing."

"I wish it were just that. The captain said he'd have to report the house. As of business hours tomorrow, this thing will be condemned."

"What? How can they do that? Don't we get time to repair it?"

"If I understand right, the repairs will be costly. An inspector will have to okay it, and the captain tells me once the inspector sees it, there are any number of other violations he'll find." He turned to the house and opened his arms wide. "I present to you, the money pit."

I balled my fists and closed my eyes. I took a deep breath and opened them again. April pulled up. "Good night, Alex." I walked toward the house.

"Whoa, where do you think you're going?"

"To get my pillow. I'll sleep at April's. I'm too tired to think about this. I'm exhausted." I walked through the open door. The smoky stench was heavy in the air. I thought of eBay listings advertising crafts made in a smoke-free house. All of the merchandise smelled: every last figurine, wreath, and doily. I'd have to start from scratch. But where? Not this house.

Alex followed me. "You can't go upstairs. The floor probably isn't safe."

I sat down on the couch, which was singed black on one end. "About this shop you don't even know if you want to finish . . ."

"It's covered by insurance. About the new job you're taking . . ."

"About my homeless in Seattle problem . . . This is God's way of telling me to go home to Utah."

"This is God's way of telling me the electrical wiring in old houses is scary." He leaned forward, resting his elbows on his knees and putting his head in his hands. "This is my fault. I had no business playing electrician. You could have died."

"But I didn't. I'm fine." I nodded my head to the side. "I'm homeless . . . but fine."

"We'll get you a new place in the morning." There was a light rap on the door. Gretchen poked her head in. Alex smiled at her. "Elise is in bed. Can you stay over a few hours?"

Gretchen looked around the charred shop and grunted, giving Alex an *I told you so* look before she clucked her tongue and disappeared outside.

"She's *still* mad at you?"

"I've got it handled." He yawned. "I know of a house in Bellevue. You can stay there for a few months until the country house is ready."

"I'm not moving to the country house, in case you weren't listening the first time I told you. You remember, the time before Elise said you told her I'd be living there but it would be a while because I'm slow. Isn't that mean to do to a little girl, Alex?"

"We just have a difference of opinion, that's all. I'm wearing you down."

He *was* wearing me down. There was no possible way I'd be leaving Washington. I cared about Alex and Elise too much. "At any rate, I'm beat. Good night." I left him sitting on the couch.

April was standing outside, gaping at the charred windows. She pointed to the shop, mouth open but speechless.

As soon as I was close, she covered the few steps between us and pulled me into a fierce hug.

"I'm okay. I'm okay," I said as she squeezed me so tight I worried about her cracking one of my ribs.

"You can sleep at my house."

In the car, after I told her what had happened and how Alex had helped me down the ladder, she drummed her fingers on the steering wheel. "I wish you could just stay with me. They'll cut off my housing assistance if they know I have someone staying with me though."

"Alex said he has someplace I can stay. Don't you think this is a sign that I should be going home?"

April tsked. "It's a sign that Alex shouldn't be an electrician. That's what it's a sign of."

When I woke, I found Alex dozing off on April's couch downstairs. I thought about letting him sleep. He was breathing evenly and looked like an angel. A smudge of ash was streaked across his chin. I sat down beside him. He stirred and rolled his head toward me. "I had you holed up in a firetrap. I didn't know." He sat up and wiped a hand over his face.

"Why aren't you home getting some more sleep? And why aren't you with Elise? She's probably scared."

"Gretchen showed up early. She's having a girl's day out with Elise. I couldn't see sending her to school this morning. She was shaken up by the fire. We have a lot to do today. Get dressed. I'll show you the house where you'll be staying."

* * *

When we pulled up to the house in Bellevue, I looked at him and said, "No."

"You haven't seen inside."

"It's bigger than yours. It has outbuildings. This isn't a house. It's a mansion."

"It has a security system—installed by a real electrician."

I coughed. "You can't be serious."

"Just for a few months." He guided me up the front walk and handed me the key.

I opened the door. The entryway was hardwood. A massive staircase dominated the front hall. I turned to him again. "No, Alex, it's too big. I'm just one person."

"Let's at least check it out. Maybe you'll change your mind."

"If it were you, would you choose it?" A strange look crossed his face. I thought about the country house. "Honestly. Do you already own this house?"

"Yes," he said sheepishly.

"What don't you own, Alex?"

"You."

I sighed and sat down on the bottom stair. "Tell me about the house."

"I bought it a few years ago from a friend."

"Why don't you live here?"

He laughed. "It *is* a little too big. But it's a safe place to keep you until we find something smaller. I don't mind if you just stay at my house."

"You know I can't do that."

"At any rate, this is a great house," he argued. I shook my head no. "It has a mother-in-law apartment off the garage."

That piqued my interest. "That should do."

"I wouldn't like having you out here alone." He sat down beside me. "Did you know that all the houses on my street were built by the same construction company in the 1940s?"

"I didn't realize they were all that old. They look so sturdy."

"Sturdy and probably not up to code. I have to think about that. My house has never had the electrical updated either. Elise and I can stay here, where we know it's safe. This was built in 1992. And Brad has never been stalking around out here. The alarm system is the best."

I should have known it was coming. There had to be something to make it all convenient. "I don't know if going from the house next door to the mother-in-law apartment is such a good idea."

"There's a whole garage between us. I won't bother you at all. I have to think about Elise. I want her close to where you are so you can help out. This isn't as close to work, but it's close enough, and there isn't an evil little wire in the wall waiting to torch us to death."

I gave up. "So if I had liked the house, were you going to let me stay in it and you and Elise would have taken the apartment?"

"I never thought you'd like the house." We both laughed.

I stopped. "No, seriously. I'm not cleaning *this* house."

"I'll get a service."

* * *

I only brought my original suitcases and bedding from my apartment. We put everything else in Alex's country house. The mother-in-law apartment and the whole Bellevue house were already furnished. The new apartment was twice as large as the last apartment, with hardwood floors, bay windows, a spacious living room, and a garden tub. The bed was an ornate four-post queen. The actual house proper was much nicer than where Alex had been living the last couple of years. I was confused about how his head worked. I couldn't imagine owning this house and living in the other one. He must have done it for Vanessa. I put the last of my new slacks in the closet. The phone rang. It was Alex. "We have a date in an hour. Did you forget?"

"No." I had forgotten. "I'll be ready."

"Do you have something to wear?"

"Of course I do. Are you micromanaging?"

"No." I heard the word in stereo. I turned to look at him and flipped my phone closed.

I sat down on the edge of the bed. "About boundaries . . ."

"You left the door open." He shrugged. "Are you all settled in?"

"Just about. How about you and Elise? Are you settled in?"

"She thinks it's Christmas. Gretchen will stay the night. I think you should be safe here. Maybe we'll get you a dog. What kind do you want?"

"What kind eats Brad?"

"Admit it. You're glad you're still in Washington."

I felt like a kept woman. The problem was, I didn't want to go home. I couldn't deny it anymore. I didn't want to be away from Alex. I studied the floorboards while I swallowed the truth.

"Don't look so sad. Think of the water pressure."

"I can't wait to take a bath." I looked at the clock. "Time for you to go. I've got to get ready."

He armed the alarm before he left.

I wasn't going to bring it, but my mother insisted a woman should never go anywhere without a little black dress. I called her to thank her. I had to tell her my new address anyway. She was horrified when she heard about the fire and wanted me to come home. I pointed out that a fire could happen anywhere. She liked the new arrangement, with me living closer to Alex. When she asked if I was going to drive to the shop every day to restore it, I explained my new duties.

"Has he talked about anything more permanent?"

"He sounds like he'll keep me working for him as long as I'm willing."

"That's not what I meant. Has he talked about marriage?"

I groaned. "Mom, he's not LDS."

"Maybe he'll ask anyway."

"I've got to go get ready for a date."

"Who with?"

"Alex," I said flatly.

I could *hear* her smile. "Have a good time, dear."

I walked into Alex's office and waited for him to get off the phone. He was wearing a black tux. He turned to look at me and let out a low whistle. "You know, I would have picked you up. How was the bath?"

I laughed. "Heaven."

"I feel bad, making you live in squalor for so long. You see the extra perks you get when you date your boss?"

"Let's go before I start thinking you're being serious."

We passed the Seattle temple on our way out of Bellevue. I felt a pinch of guilt about being on a date with Alex but still stared at the spire as long as I could.

"And you're closer to your temple. There are all sorts of perks."

"I'm sold." Looking at him with his dark hair and tuxedo was intoxicating, so I tried to look at everything else. I knew I wouldn't be able to hide my admiration, and he would gloat for months. "I have to admit, it does feel safer. It's back in a neighborhood, set away from the street. I have my own private parking in the garage."

"I'm closer."

"I don't really think you're that much closer. I have to walk through the garage, the mud room, the kitchen, the dining room, the family room, and past the library to get to your office. That's about as far as across the yard, farther even."

"Well, it feels closer to some of us, so don't pop our bubble."

"Enjoy your delusions."

"Oh, I am." He laughed wickedly.

"What are we going to?"

"Fund-raiser for a literacy program. I hope you like to dance."

I looked at him, frozen in fear. "Dance?"

"I'm sure I told you about the dancing. We can find a quiet corner."

My heart started to beat in painful thumps. *A quiet corner. A date with my boss holding me in a quiet corner.* I closed my eyes and tried to breathe. It was exactly everything I wanted and everything I didn't want at the same time. *It's just Alex . . . It's just Alex . . .* I kept repeating it until I calmed down.

"Don't think I'm not noticing you closing your eyes tight against the pain of the thought." There was humor in his voice.

"No. It's not painful," I squeaked.

"If I don't take a date, I get hit on all night."

"What an unenviable position to be in." I was trying not to think about him holding me.

"Not that I would mind dancing tonight." He lightly traced his fingers down my forearm. A jolt of electricity shot through me and made me gasp. I put my hand on top of his to make him stop.

"If you don't mind, I seem to be a little agitated just now."

"Are you always so nervous on your dates?"

"I'm not nervous."

"I don't bite."

"Of course not." I studied the ivy hanging over the edge of the freeway. If I were being honest with myself, I had to admit the only difference between this date and every other date that I'd been on for the last year was that I liked this man, possibly loved him, and had a certain level of chemistry for him that I had heretofore been lacking on any other date. I laughed quietly. That was a sad statement about my dating life.

"Are you going to tell me the joke?"

"Just saw a crazy squirrel."

He smiled at me and gave up on conversation. We were quiet until we sat down in the hotel. The banquet hall was dimly lit, and there was, indeed, a dance floor. Alex told the waiter I needed water instead of wine. He offered me a coke, but I didn't want to be conspicuous. "Are you still nervous?" he asked.

"I never was. It's just you, Alex. What's there to be nervous about?" I sat up a little taller and looked around. I noticed there were a lot of very nicely dressed people staring at us. They looked away when I looked at them, but there was no doubt we were drawing attention. "Okay, now I'm nervous."

"Feels good to be honest, eh? I don't want you to be nervous. It's nice having you here, on my arm. I want it to happen again . . . and again . . . and—"

"I get the picture."

"Do you think you'd say yes again?"

"Let's see how bad this is."

"It won't be bad at all."

Several women seemed to be shooting eye daggers in my general direction. I sat closer to Alex.

"We have a few minutes until dinner. Do you want to meet the mayor?" he asked.

I took a deep breath, determined to be a good sport. "Sure."

He introduced me to half a dozen interesting people before dinner began. I shook large hands, small hands, and limp hands, in the case of most of the females who weren't as thrilled to meet me as they said they were. I smiled my most charming smile and tried to pretend I was somewhere else. I laughed at the same time Alex did and tried to keep people talking about themselves instead of us. I was beginning to appreciate why he didn't like social functions. He would excuse us from one set of people, and another set would be ready to take their place. There was no end. It was a relief when dinner was announced because we could sit down. Our table had three other couples. While dessert was served, a keynote speaker presented a short speech about the literacy program, asking everyone to give themselves applause for their donations. Soft music played, and couples drifted toward the dance floor. I looked around the room and noticed a few people still watching us.

Alex led me to the dance floor. He slid his arm behind my back. It was hard to relax when he was so close, but it was preferable to the socializing. "When they try to cut in, you say no," he advised.

"No one's going to—"

He tilted my chin up so I was looking into his eyes. "When they try to cut in, you say no."

"I say no," I repeated obediently. Less than a minute later, a handsome man who looked only slightly older than Alex tapped him on the shoulder.

"May I cut in?"

"No, thank you," I said mechanically.

After another man and two women asked, I sighed and asked Alex if we could find a quieter corner to dance in. He chortled, pulling me between couples until we were trapped in a corner, where we were harder to see. We danced again, humming lightly to the music. I rested my head on his shoulder, and he kissed my hair. When the song ended, he asked if I wanted to sit down.

"No. Can't we just hide back here for a while?" Everyone in our vicinity seemed to have the same idea.

"Sure. It's your date." He grinned. "You look fabulous tonight, not as good as you do in the morning, in your pajamas, but it's a close second."

"Primping is wasted on you," I complained.

He pressed his cheek to mine. "How long do you want to dance?" he asked.

I looked around the room. Several people were still staring at us, though they had to crane their necks. "The rest of the time. It's better than talking to everyone."

"I *was* flattered. I didn't know you were just hiding from the crowd. I thought you were enjoying the way I was holding you." I blushed. He pressed his face to mine. "Your cheek is warm." He sighed. "It's only fair that I tell you if you monopolize all of my time dancing, it's going to be in the paper tomorrow. I'm enjoying it. I hope you continue to allow it. I only mention it because hell hath no fury like a woman scandalized."

"Oh." I pulled back from him a little to look at his face. "What will it say?"

"It could say any number of things. It will point out that we made a public appearance together and were so involved with each other that we avoided everyone else. There will be pictures."

"I expected pictures."

"Of us dancing, close."

"This could complicate things with Jeff. He's already under pressure."

"So do you want to stop dancing?"

"No, consider me warned."

He chuckled and tucked my hair behind my ear. "You smell good."

I closed my eyes. "Thanks." I looked at him. "We have awhile. Maybe you can tell me a story. Tell me about the day Elise was born. Better yet, start with the day you learned you were going to be a father."

"I was cooking marsala sauce at the restaurant. Vanessa walked up behind me and said, 'I'm pregnant.' Before I could faint, she handed me a white rose. I still have it in a drawer somewhere."

"What did it feel like, knowing you'd be a father?"

"I was excited. My dad was only so so. He was in the background of our lives. I needed him more than he was there. It lit me up to think that I was going to get the chance to be the kind of dad I always wanted to have. I thought we'd have a boy though. I couldn't imagine a girl. That was a surprise. I bought her baseballs and tractors, but it didn't work. She seemed to be born knowing what she liked."

"Tell me about the day she was born."

"Well, Vanessa, you know, she was beautiful." I nodded. "She was beautiful, but she didn't take the pregnancy very well. She had a lot of hormone issues, I think. I pulled the doctor aside one visit and asked when she'd be better. He said since it was a female baby, Vanessa had a lot of extra female hormones in her body. So I pretty much knew early on that I was in for a hard few trimesters. It was fall. That's when Vanessa usually shone, but that year she was ornery about missing so many things and not being able to do what she was used to. I had to pull double time at the restaurant. At home, I waited on her hand and foot. Not that she just sat around or anything like that. She was always busy. I only picked up the slack. We were decorating the Christmas tree early, and she was being really nice. I can remember how wrong that felt after eight months of her crabbiness. She was suddenly easygoing and happy. Luckily, I had an epiphany and talked her into going out to an ice cream shop near the hospital. She wasn't in labor yet, but I was sure it would start any moment. We pulled into the ice cream parlor, and she had the first contraction. Elise came fast. She's always been impatient. I raced Vanessa to the hospital, three buildings away, and her water broke as soon as they helped her onto the table. Within a half hour, I was holding Elise."

"How much did she weigh?"

Alex looked into my eyes for a moment. He rested his face against my cheek again. "Six pounds, ten ounces, eighteen inches long, blue eyes, dark, fuzzy brown hair. That lasted about a week. I was so proud she looked like me, then poof, she was bald."

"You're definitely fuzzy, and she does look like you."

"Within two weeks, Vanessa was back to normal. She was a new woman, crazy about Elise. She skipped postpartum depression. I think she used it all up during the pregnancy. Doesn't it bother you when I talk about my wife?"

"No, Vanessa is part of who you are. You can't just take her out of you. It doesn't happen. You wouldn't be you without her. When I think about Vanessa, I feel gratitude for you and Elise."

I rested my head on his shoulder. We danced the next song in silence. When it finished, Alex asked, "Are your feet tired yet?"

"Ha. Why would they be tired? You've been holding me up." I couldn't stifle a yawn. "But it must be getting late." The crowd hadn't thinned out.

He looked at his watch. He laughed. "We've been dancing a long time. We have to take a circuitous route home. It will take longer. I hate for it to end, but we can dance barefoot at home."

"Not a good idea."

"I thought it was." He looked around. "Okay, you have options. One, we head for the main doors and meet and greet our way out." I groaned. "Two, we sneak out those doors, get our picture taken on the other side, and then be followed to the car, which isn't a big deal because we switch cars."

"Very James Bond. Do we switch cars through the front entrance too?"

"You have to switch cars either way."

"You're a complicated fellow, aren't you?"

He tapped me on the nose. "Hey, I've been doing this a long time. I make it as uncomplicated as possible."

I opted for the side doors. We slid out, trying to be as inconspicuous as possible. Alex looked murderous when I stopped on the other side to talk to the photographer I met at the mall with Jeff. We posed for a few pictures. I admitted that this was an actual date, our first.

I was curious. "Did you read the Book of Mormon?"

"I'm reading it now. We're taking the lessons. There's something to it, I'll give you that."

We wished him a good night.

In the elevator, Alex asked, "Hasn't anyone ever taught you not to smile at crocodiles?"

"He's a friend. I like him. Jeff found him."

"So would you do that again?" Alex asked after we were in the car.

"Yes, but just out of pity. I can't stand the thought of you doing it alone. Those women look at you like you're fresh meat."

"The dancing wasn't worth it?"

"Was it to you?"

"Well, if you're not going to dance with me at home, I'd have to say the dancing was worth it."

We pulled into the garage at one in the morning. "I'll walk you to your door."

"How gallant."

We walked to the door, but when I reached for it, he pulled me to him like we were dancing again. He looked at me, then he leaned down and kissed my temple and my nose. He paused in front of my lips. "I'm waiting for you to say stop."

"So am I," I whispered.

He kissed me softly, and I closed my eyes, giving in to all the sensations I'd been forcing myself not to want for months. When he pulled away, I couldn't speak.

"Your face is warm," he commented.

My knees were weak. I had to blink to turn my brain on. "Oh," I touched my hot cheek and smiled shyly. "Well, thank you for dinner. Good night." I slipped into the apartment and quickly shut the door. I felt like I was floating. I could still smell his aftershave. As I took off my dress and got ready for bed, my practical side was listing off all the mistakes I'd just made, telling me how foolish I'd been. After I prayed, I lay in bed wide awake. I was still smiling. Being foolish felt so good.

CHAPTER 15
Boundaries

I woke up with a pounding headache at eight. I forced myself to stand up and walk around. The water on my face in the shower helped clear my head. By the time I finished my cereal, I was admitting that the first boundary for my relationship with Alex should be no idle alone time. The headache was beginning to ebb. As I buttoned my blouse, I admitted that the second boundary should be that he shouldn't be kissing me. I was his employee. He was my boss. He wasn't on my list of people to marry; hence, I shouldn't be dating him *at all*. He didn't align with my eternal goals.

I found him reading the paper in his kitchen. He pushed it toward me. The local section had a small article about us and a picture of us dancing. It didn't say anything that was untrue.

"Okay, let's talk about boundaries." I pushed the paper back to him. "First, no idle alone time. If we're together, we're working. Second, you'll have to stop kissing me. No good can come of that."

"Anything else?" he asked, looking unstunned.

"Not yet. Those were just the most obvious that leapt out at me."

"You're not going back to Utah?"

"No." I smiled, ashamed. "But I should. I'm working myself into it."

"Boundaries set. Let's get to work."

I had expected him to at least object to not kissing me.

We didn't talk on the way to Shallots. At the restaurant, we sat in a corner booth, quietly paying bills. The room was lit brighter than it ever was when the restaurant was open. He left to receive a delivery but was back in a few minutes. He helped me gather bills and papers into piles, and we took them back to the office. Alex sat on the edge of the desk, reading receipts for me to enter into the computer. He responsibly filed each one after he read it. Gretchen would have been proud. The whole time, the only words that passed between us were related somehow to the work we were doing. I rode with him to pick up Elise, and he dropped us off at home then left to open the restaurant.

I was putting the dinner dishes in the dishwasher when he walked in and set his tie on the table.

"I've been invited to dinner Thursday by Theodore Hansen. Would you like to come?"

"Is Channing going to be there?"

"Of course."

"I'll come just to save you. But don't let me forget to call Jeff."

"By all means, call Jeff," he said, laughing. "I can call him if you want."

I rinsed a cup and put it in the dishwasher. I turned to get the dish towel, but it was gone.

"Looking for this?"

I held my dripping hand out for it. He leaned down and kissed me. I tried not to drip on him. He backed away, kissed the tip of my nose, and tossed the towel to me. "Not kiss you?" He was laughing as he left the room.

"Yeah, right," I said to empty air. I sighed, wishing I was sorry about the kiss.

Since he was home, I figured I was excused. I grabbed my purse and walked through the garage. I locked the door behind me then threw some popcorn into the microwave and kicked off my shoes. Alex had a massive collection of movies. I had borrowed *Sleepless in Seattle*. Just as I was grabbing it to put it in, I heard a knock at the back door, and I cringed.

April was standing there with Alex behind her. Before April could say anything, Alex said, "You didn't say good-bye."

"Good-bye." I smiled politely, pulling April into the apartment and shutting the door behind her, making sure he heard the lock turn.

"Why is it," she asked, "that Alex is the one who calls me with the new address and not you?"

"I was getting to it. What do you think?"

"It looks more like some place he should live, that's for sure. It took me three minutes to get here. I love it."

"Wait until you see my tub; you're going to die." I pulled her to the bathroom.

"I want one of those. Do you think he'll get me one for my birthday?"

I shrugged. "We can ask."

"I take it things are going better, then?"

I bit my bottom lip. "I'm trying not to think about it. I was just going to start a movie. Do you want to watch?" I showed her the DVD.

"I've seen that three times; maybe another day."

"I've seen it three times too, but I need something to do for a few hours."

"I'm here under false pretenses," she confessed. "Your parents sent me to make sure you're settled in. I'm going to ascertain if you need to go home. They figure you must be pretty shaken up about the fire."

"Alex will take care of me." I made myself blink. "Is Dad very worried?"

"He's taking it harder than your mother."

"He hates that I'm gone. I'm sure this isn't helping. Make sure he knows I'm fine. I'll call him when you leave. Maybe if he hears it from two of us, he'll believe it."

"So," I said, waving my hand in a grand gesture, "does it pass? Are you going to tell them I'm safe and sound? It has an alarm system."

"I'm going to tell them he's spoiling you rotten."

Another rap on the back door interrupted us. I wasn't surprised to find Alex on the other side. "Why do you get to keep April all to yourself?"

"She's here checking up on me. Can you believe it? My parents sent her."

"I suspected as much. Tell her about your new job so she doesn't think you'll be sitting in ashes at the shop all day." He stepped through the door.

"New job?" April asked.

"I'm a gopher." I shrugged.

"Administrative assistant," Alex amended.

"Whatever." I waved it off.

"It's hard to impress Jana, isn't it?" April asked him.

"Most of the time." He winked at me.

"Tell them I'm not ready to come home yet. I'm working on it."

"Tell them I'm working on her not coming home, but she'll visit for the holidays," Alex added smugly.

April raised her eyebrows. "Anything else I should tell them?"

"Nothing they can't read about."

Alex picked up the DVD. "What are we watching?" he asked.

I sighed.

"I'll let you two get to your movie." April laughed. I showed her out the front door that exited to the side of the house.

I turned to Alex. "*We* are not watching anything because that would be idle downtime."

"I have an awesome theater room. Elise likes this movie."

"I guess if she sits between us, there's no harm."

"Don't you enjoy spending time with me just for the sake of it?"

"No. It's an exercise in futility. Come on. I already have the popcorn."

"You love me," he said matter-of-factly as he locked my door.

I didn't deny it. I just followed him into the house.

* * *

Jeff actually sounded jealous when I told him I couldn't make our date on Thursday. He wanted to know what I was doing. I was honest and said I was going to dinner with Alex. He wasn't too jealous to reschedule for the next Thursday. Alex came to my door promptly at six. He handed me a bouquet of yellow roses. "Rose petals for your bath."

"If you don't mind, I'll just let them bloom on my kitchen table." I buried my face in the them and inhaled. There must have been two dozen. "Oh, that's heavenly. Did you smell these?"

He smelled. "Smells like roses."

"It takes a lot to impress you, doesn't it?" I asked.

"Not as much as it takes to impress you."

"You impress me," I admitted.

He smiled. "I knew it."

We talked about the Hansens on the way to the restaurant. Alex wanted me to understand the business deal he'd been discussing with them. As we pulled into the parking lot, Alex surprised me by asking, "Are you going to church Sunday after next?"

"I haven't decided if I'm going to the Bellevue ward or the old ward. It would be kind of awkward to sit with Jeff when he knows I went out with you, but then again, it would be awkward in a new ward when everyone already knows my face from the papers."

"I'll go with you."

"Yes, that will make me feel much less conspicuous, thank you." I tried to keep my tone light.

"You don't want me to go?"

"I do. I'm just wondering why you really want to go."

"I'm curious. I want to see if it feels like you and if it feels like the Smith's house. I want to see if you're right about the Holy Ghost."

"Of course I'm right."

"I've never thought of Him as having a job before. I guess I've never thought of Him as anything separate either."

"Well, I'm right, and He'll tell you I'm right."

"You know, you've never really preached to me. You haven't shoved the religion down my throat or anything. Thank you."

"I figure if you want to know something, you'll ask."

"Let's talk about harder things than religion," he said.

"Politics?"

"The holidays, starting with Halloween. I'm going to be out of town. Do you want to take Elise trick-or-treating?" He turned the car off.

"Oh, it's too bad we're not in Utah. You can walk around at night on the trails in the gardens at the University of Utah or the dinosaur museum in Ogden. They're the best. The museum has spooky trails. Dinosaurs growl at you, and they decorate the dinosaurs so they're eating, with people parts hanging all over. I wish she could see that."

"I could fly you home."

"You have no budgeting skills. You can't keep flying me home."

"If you were home, I wouldn't have to worry about who was going to watch you."

"You make it sound like I'm a kid."

"I just want you safe."

I thought about my mother's homemade witches' brew root beer, the pumpkin cookies, and eating pixie sticks with Rachel. "Maybe. I'll think about it. I think Elise would have a blast."

"Okay, then there's the Barrowmans' Thanksgiving. I've been assigned the apple pie and potato salad."

"My mother's already giving you assignments?"

"She e-mailed."

"Two flights to Salt Lake and two flights home, three tickets each time . . ." I added.

"And Christmas. This is the worst."

"Why would Christmas be the worst?"

"Well, Vanessa's parents never did like me. I have to take Elise. Last year . . . I don't want to think about it. I thought you might go with me. Just a few days the week before Christmas."

"They'll be thrilled to see me." I let the sarcasm drip from my words.

"You're a big part of Elise's life. They should at least meet you."

"I'll think about it."

"And then there are my parents. My mother's sick of reading about you and wants to meet you. I've pushed it as far as Christmas, but much further and she'll show up on my doorstep."

"Okay, I'm really nervous about meeting your mother. What's her name?"

"Elise."

"That must get confusing. What if she doesn't like me?"

"She's just like me. Don't be nervous. She likes everyone."

"Promise?"

"I promise. Vanessa's parents will be the hardest. And then we can spend actual Christmas with your parents."

"We?"

"You'd spend the day without me?"

"Maybe we could just think about Halloween for now."

"And Thanksgiving?"

I thought about showing up for Thanksgiving without Alex. My mother would be impossible. "And Thanksgiving, but you should know I hate potato salad."

"So do I," he admitted.

"You're right. Holidays are harder than religion."

* * *

After dinner Alex and I walked through the dark parking lot. "Even if he paid me five times what he's offering, I'd never sell Shallots to that pig."

"Now, now, darling . . ." I imitated Channing fanning herself.

Before he opened the car door for me, he swept me up in a hug and kissed me. "I should give you a raise."

"It's a sin that I get paid for my job already; don't make it worse. Besides, this isn't work. It's a date."

"I really take you out on some tough dates, don't I?"

"I scrub up nice in public." When we were in the car, I asked him if Channing had ever pinched his behind.

"All the time. You know it really makes you feel for women and what they must go through. How can you stand it?"

"I can honestly say I've never had anyone treat me that poorly. I'd probably slap anyone who tried."

"I guess fishing in the right pond has some perks. I'd hate to see anyone treat you like that too."

I fastened the latch on my purse then unfastened it. "Doesn't it feel odd to you to suddenly be this close?"

"We always have been."

"I mean, just suddenly, things are different between us for no apparent reason."

"Things are only different for you. When you left the first day, after the interview, I knew what I wanted."

"That long ago?"

"If you had said no, I would have found something to do in Utah."

"You would have come for me after knowing me only a few hours? I don't believe it."

"You would have forgotten me so soon?"

"You were just going to be my boss. You're married."

"You still think of me as married?"

"We believe marriage can be eternal."

"When a Mormon loses his wife, can he remarry?"

"Sure." I pictured myself next to Alex, who was holding hands with Vanessa and me. I had to shake the vision off.

"But somewhere in your mind, you think I belong to Vanessa."

"Yes." I said it quietly. It was part of why he was off-limits. If I were Vanessa, I wouldn't want to share him.

"Vanessa's very real to you, like she still lives."

"She does."

"Do you feel guilty?"

"Tremendously." I swallowed hard.

"Don't." He reached for my hand. All the way home I tried not to think about loving Vanessa's husband.

CHAPTER 16
Zorro

My dad tweaked the end of Elise's wing. "I don't think I've ever seen more beautiful fairies."

Elise twirled and held her wand high. "Jana can make anything."

We had been in Utah for three days. It was unseasonably warm for October, but I wanted us to be polar bears so I could keep Elise warm while we were trick-or-treating. She was set on fairies. I imagined Alex trying to get her to play with tractors and laughed.

The doorbell started ringing at three in the afternoon, and my father had had a steady stream of patrons ever since then. I'm sure word had gotten around that he was handing out full-size candy bars this year. My mother was livid because of the cost, but my father wouldn't be reasoned with. "All right!" "Yeah!" and "This rocks!" were common exclamations shouted at our door.

"You sure you're okay driving that far?" my dad asked. "Ogden's a ways, and there will be drunks on the road tonight."

"If we leave now, we should get back right about sunset. I'll be careful."

"I still don't like it. Pray before you go."

"I will." I straightened Elise's wings, trying to figure out the best way to get a coat over them for later. The doorbell rang again.

I heard my father say, "Aren't you a bit big for a candy bar, sonny? Elise, you'd better hand this one out."

She ran to the door and squealed with delight. "Daddy! Daddy! Daddy!"

"Don't suppose you'd drive our daughters to Ogden?" my father asked a tall, handsome Zorro.

I suddenly felt ridiculous in my green tights and flower petal skirt. Alex spun Elise around, set her down, then spun me. He set me down and traced his finger over the glitter by my eyes. "Festive, aren't we?"

"A man in tight leather pants, a cape, and mask hardly has room to criticize."

"I didn't criticize. My girls look beautiful." He kissed me on the cheek. "You like the pants?"

My father smiled when Alex said "my girls" and seemed even more pleased with the kiss. The day before, I had tried to explain that, for the most part, my relationship with Alex was platonic, but I could tell he wasn't buying it. This didn't help my argument. Zorro left his arm around my waist, which accounted for the satisfied look on my mother's face when she came around the corner.

He hugged her with his other arm. "I thought I'd pop in."

"I hope you're staying for a few days," my mother cooed at him.

"I suppose we can fit in one more day. Let me ask the boss." He leaned down to Elise. "Do you want to stay another day?"

Elise jumped up and down. "Yes! Can we? Can we?" My mother had been spoiling her in fantastic grandma style. Elise wasn't used to having a traditional grandmother. She looked like an angel with her ringlets bouncing and a cloud of glitter floating off of her with every jump.

"And you can stay here, Alex. I won't have you driving clear out to Park City day in and day out."

Alex looked at me for permission. "Your choice."

I shrugged. I was pretty sure he'd be more comfortable in Park City, but with all the kids grown and gone, my parents had several unoccupied bedrooms.

"Okay, I'll camp here, then. Where am I driving you to?"

My dad checked his watch. "Ogden. You'd better get going if you want to get back early." He then bellowed, "Family prayer."

The doorbell rang, and he handed out a candy bar before joining us in the front room. I looked nervously at Alex, but he was already on his knees, ready to pray. My father asked that we be protected and asked that the trick-or-treaters would be protected too. It was a short prayer. We got up, and the doorbell rang again. "Take care of the girls, Zorro."

"Don't forget to get dinner," my mother admonished. She stood us against the wall for scrapbook-friendly mug shots, and then we headed out.

"I was going to be a polar bear, which would have been more practical," I told Alex in the car. "Had I known you were coming, I would have stuck to it. For all the money in the world, I wouldn't want you to catch me in this getup."

"I might have paid all the money in the world just to see it." He laughed.

I had made the same costume for Elise. Our hair was styled with the same crazy updo, curls escaping around glittering crowns. He pulled down one of my curls and let it bounce back into place. I held his mask in my hand, tracing the black silk knot. I noticed he was covered in glitter from holding us. I brushed some away. "So what brings you to Utah?"

"Negotiations broke off early."

"Let me guess, they weren't good enough for your employees?"

His dark hair caught the sunlight. "I toured some of their other restaurants. I didn't like what I saw."

"It's got to be hard to sell your baby like this."

Elise leaned forward. "Are we having a baby?"

"No, I was talking about the restaurant. Your dad created it, so it's kind of like his baby."

"Like he made me, and I'm his baby."

"That's right," I said.

Elise looked at me. "Will you give me a baby sister, Jana?"

I looked uncomfortably to Alex, who appeared to be waiting for the answer too.

Finally I said, "I truly don't know." With as much excitement as I could muster, I told Elise, "You are going to love this place. They have robot dinosaurs as big as real ones."

"Will they have candy?"

"Of course they'll have candy. We'll trick-or-treat in the forest. I brought flashlights. Yours is pink." I handed it to her. She seemed to be content to play with it, shining it out the windows at other cars. The sun was still up, so I was sure they'd forgive us. I should have told Elise I'd never give her a baby sister, but looking at Alex, too much of me hoped for unseen miracles.

Inside the museum, Alex hoisted Elise onto his shoulders as they watched the life-size dinosaur robots. We meandered through the museum until I told Alex, "My dad thinks you're bringing me home early, and we still have to trick-or-treat. The trails outside are long."

He finished reading the plaque below a trilobite fossil. "Okay, let's go get some candy!"

"And we didn't get dinner," I reminded him.

"Sugar for dinner!" He picked Elise up and grabbed my hand, marching toward the doors.

I had to run to keep up with him. "I hope you're not serious."

When we reached the trails, he pulled me close and kissed my forehead. "Ah, I love Halloween. I'm glad I made it home in time to see you. This really is great. I almost missed it."

"You could have helped my father hand out candy bars."

"I love Halloween because tonight I am Zorro! No cameras. No one cares about Zorro."

"I do." I realized I shouldn't have said it and was immediately sorry.

He hugged me and kissed my forehead again. He had glitter on his lips. Elise laughed at him.

We meandered down the wooded trails. I was embarrassed that I was more frightened by the roaring bushes than Elise. I held on tight to Alex's arm. Staff waited around the park with bags of candy. Finally, Elise's bucket was full. Alex was staring up at a tyrannosaurus with a torso hanging out of its mouth. Dismembered body parts were strewn haphazardly around the tree tops near its head.

"Okay, looking at this dino is making me hungry," he announced. "Let's go find some zombie stew."

"Ew, gross," Elise said.

We ordered hamburgers at a drive-through window. I called my dad to tell him we were on our way home. It was after sunset, and I didn't want him to worry. Elise ate quickly in the backseat so she could start eating candy. Twenty minutes later, she was asleep with a pile of empty wrappers on her lap.

"It's a long drive, but it's worth it, don't you think?" I asked Alex.

"It was great. Let's do it again next year."

I didn't say anything. I wasn't sure I was going to be around next year.

He cleared his throat. "I'm sorry about Elise asking about the baby. I didn't coach her to do that, I promise."

"I know."

"I *am* looking to something more . . . *permanent* in the future for us, but I swear I don't talk to her about it anymore."

"I believe you."

"She's just very perceptive. I would never lead her to—"

"I said I believe you. I know you wouldn't want to hurt her. Don't you want to talk about dinosaurs or something?"

"Have you thought about the future?"

"I try not to." I looked out the window at the oncoming traffic.

"So now would be a bad time to ask you about—"

"Yes." I cut him off.

"You don't even want to talk about it? Getting marr—"

"We've been on two dates. Do you usually bring up things like this after a second date? I'm surprised you don't scare more women away."

"Just so you know where my half of this caravan is headed."

"I think I know."

"I'm willing to spell it out for you," he offered.

"I think I can read it just fine, thank you."

He smiled and took my hand. Looking ahead he said, "You infuriate me." But his tone was soft.

I kissed his hand. "Ditto," I said sweetly.

We didn't speak the rest of the way home.

***

Alex carried Elise to the room she was sleeping in. A few stray children were still ringing the doorbell. My father was still in good spirits with ten candy bars to spare. He slipped one into Elise's bucket as Alex walked by.

"You spoil her, Dad."

He winked at me. "I think we'll take Prince Charming and the fairy princess to Temple Square tomorrow," he informed me.

"I don't think he wants to hear it."

"He'd be a fool not to expect it. I want my little girl to be happy."

I kissed his cheek, leaving glitter. "Good luck. He *has* been asking some questions, so I guess it's not totally far-fetched."

"Of course it isn't. I like Alex, and it isn't because he can cook."

"No," I laughed, "it's because he can fish."

"It looks like you like him too."

"I'm trying not to," I admitted.

"But she's failing." Alex's voice made me jump.

"You'd think I would have heard the creak of the leather pants."

"I've got to bring in my luggage and change. These pants look good, but comfortable they ain't."

When he left, I told my dad, "I never would have guessed that of all the guys I've dated you'd prefer the one with leather pants."

"I'd prefer the one who can take care of you the best."

"He's not a Latter-day Saint," I reminded him.

"He is, he—"

"—just doesn't know it yet," we said in unison.

* * *

I showed Alex to my brother's room. To my mother's credit, it didn't smell like my brother anymore. "My dad is taking us to Temple Square tomorrow, and I expect you to be a good sport."

"Always am."

I smiled. "Yes. You are."

"Good night."

"Good night."

He looked at me quizzically, probably because I didn't kiss him good night.

I found my dad downstairs with the ice cream and a bowl. I pulled another bowl out of the cupboard. We ate silently for a while.

"How serious is it?" he asked.

"The churning in my stomach because he's not what I expected, or the relationship I'm in denial about?"

"You answered my question."

"What would you have done if it were mom? What if you found her, but she wasn't what you'd been planning on?"

"Hard to imagine. I reared you to expect what you expect. It's my fault. It never occurred to me to educate you about plan B."

"And you shouldn't have. There's only *one* plan."

He pointed his spoon at me. "That there is. You'd do well to remember it's bigger than any plan we can conceive of. Things happen the way they do for a reason." Pointing down the hall, he continued. "That's God's son in there. He's come for him now. You're going to see him unfold into the man he's meant to be."

"He's not bad now," I objected.

"No, but he hasn't grown into what he will be either. I feel it, like if we don't turn right or left and just keep going where God expects us to go, we're going to find a treasure worth keeping."

"I wish I felt that way. I just feel confused. I scare myself. I think I love him. Not just love him. It's like, when he's gone, I don't want to breathe. I keep asking God to tell me what to do, which way to go. Either I'm too distracted to hear the answer or there isn't an answer to hear."

My dad put his big hand over mine on the table. "God won't choose for you. You're here to exercise your agency. You choose. After you make the commitment, you go to God and He'll tell you if it's right. Don't wait for Him to make your choices, honey. He won't do it."

My dad slid his chair back and patted his belly. "I've got to cut down. Your mother's been on me. Now I'll be in trouble for being late to bed."

"I'll rinse your bowl. Get to sleep. We don't want you in trouble." I hugged him, and he went to bed. I sat alone, listening to the clock tick. Pushing the ice cream around in my bowl to make it look appetizing wasn't working. I slid it away from me.

"Too much sugar in one night?" Alex asked.

I didn't turn around to look at him. "How much did you hear?"

"Enough. I was coming to see if you seriously thought I could go that many days without kissing you good night."

I leaned my head back to look at him. "Can't you?"

He stood over me and shook his head. "No."

I carried the bowls to the sink and rinsed them. He took my hand and turned out the lights. He kissed me at my bedroom door. "I don't need a commitment. It's enough to know you love me."

"I didn't say . . ."

"You did. You could be kind and say it to me though."

I tried. "I might . . . It's possible that . . . I can't say it." I gave up.

"I love *you*." He kissed me.

Once again I felt like I was swimming in deep water. "I love you too." I said it in a defeated whisper.

He held my face in his hands. "Loving me is not a bad thing."

"No," I admitted, giving way to the tingle in my toes, "it's not so bad."

"Tomorrow we'll work on your flattery skills. My poor ego." He kissed me on the forehead and went to bed.

* * *

As I sat at my parents' old table, eating my cold cereal, I couldn't help thinking how out of place Alex looked in our kitchen. I had to laugh.

"What?" he asked.

"Crazy squirrel."

"I'll show you crazy squirrel." He started tickling me.

"Get her, Daddy! Get her!" Elise shouted.

My mother cleared her throat. Alex straightened, looking innocent.

"Eat up," my dad said. "We'll hit the museum first. They have a children's exhibit upstairs."

Alex was being a very good sport about going to Temple Square. My mother was scheduled to sit with a woman from the ward who had recently had a stroke, so she couldn't go. Elise was excited for the field trip.

* * *

Alex walked through the museum with my father while I played upstairs with Elise. We colored a family tree for her, and she played house with me. I was sweeping with a toy broom and Elise was hanging clothes on a clothesline when the men found us.

"Daddy, Daddy, I made you pizza!" Alex sat in a child's chair next to my dad while Elise set the table and served them wooden pizza. She gave my father two pieces because he was the guest.

Alex bought Elise a handkerchief doll at the gift shop. She cradled it through lunch at the Joseph Smith Memorial Building. I showed Alex my favorite statue of Joseph Smith in his stocking feet, reading scriptures. Alex leaned over my shoulder while I looked to see if the bronze was actually engraved with James 1:5. It was. I leaned back. "You're making my dad a very happy man. Thank you for being so accommodating."

"It's interesting. I didn't know the doctrine was so complicated. I didn't know the history was so deep."

"I don't think the doctrine is complicated. My dad just knows a lot. If he gets talking your ear off, just tell him."

We left the building and walked over to the reflecting pool at the temple. Alex sat between me and my father on a bench while Elise ran around and around the pool. There were only a few people walking by.

Alex gazed up at the temple spires. "Why get married in the temple instead of a church? What's the difference?"

"Eternity," I offered. "It's, well . . ." I thought for a long moment. "I never wanted to put it this way to you because it sounds so insensitive. Please forgive me and know that I don't want to hurt you. I *do* love you." My father pretended not to listen as he waved at Elise across the pond. "You and Vanessa had a secular marriage. You were married until death do you part. And . . . you've parted. You aren't married." *But you will be as soon as you figure out what I'm saying is true*, I thought but didn't say aloud. "You've lived out your contract. In the temple, through the power of the sealing ordinance, you'd be sealed to your wife for time and all eternity."

"My wife you or my wife Vanessa?"

Exactly, I thought. What did it matter anyway? He'd always be Vanessa's first.

"Both," my father answered.

Thanks, I thought sarcastically. I shot my dad a dark look.

My dad continued. "You would be sealed to Vanessa and Elise for time and all eternity. The priesthood of Jesus Christ has been restored to the earth. We talked about the priesthood at the museum. Do you remember the baptismal font—baptisms for the dead? There are other ordinances. We work tirelessly in the temple to bring these ordinances to those who can no longer receive them themselves."

A strange look came over Alex's face. He was quiet for a while. When he looked up, a tear escaped his eye. "Time and all eternity? It doesn't end?"

"It doesn't have to," my father said.

I was suddenly struck with a stab of jealousy. I felt how Alex wanted Vanessa to be his forever. And she *should* be his forever; Elise should be theirs forever. I couldn't see how I belonged anywhere in the arrangement. "I'm going to find a restroom. I'll meet you back here."

I walked calmly to the Joseph Smith Building but ran as soon as they could no longer see me. Several people stared. I found a bathroom and entered a handicap stall. I leaned against the wall. My heart hurt. Every part of me that I never allowed to love him seared with pain. Of course he loved *her*. He should. He wouldn't be Alex if he didn't. He wanted *her* forever. I looked up at the ceiling. I knew God wanted them sealed together. *I've always known it.* Why was this hitting me so hard now? I was glad he loved her. I wanted him to be happy. This was exactly the best thing that could happen in his life. I could see it on his face—he understood. When he'd said, "It doesn't end," he'd known he'd see Vanessa again. And I was glad, oh, so glad.

My face burned under hot tears. *A forever family.* He was going to be part of a forever family. I realized I was hyperventilating and tried to breathe slowly. My lips were numb, and my nose was running like a faucet. *So happy for him . . . So happy for him . . . Loves his wife . . .* Little black spots obscured my vision, and I knew I hadn't contained the hyperventilating. I stepped out of the stall and staggered to the counter, gasping for air. A tall woman helped steady me. I reached for a faucet, and she turned it on. She stood behind me and rubbed my back as I splashed my face. God had even sent an angel to comfort me. I was a hideous, loathsome creature who couldn't rejoice in a moment of eternal triumph, and God still loved me. I laughed. When I stood up, she handed me paper towels then hugged me. "There, there, it isn't so bad. You're okay, sweetie." Then I leaned on a complete stranger and bawled like a baby.

When I had cried myself out, I stood back and laughed. "I don't know who you are, but someone has a really great mom. You got me breathing again. Thank you; you're an angel."

"I followed you when I saw you run in. I saw your face and thought you looked like you could use some help."

I hugged her again. "Now the trick is to go out there and look like I haven't been crying." I wiped my nose with a paper towel. "I'm being an incredibly bad sport about some very good news."

I looked in the mirror. The hair fringing my face was wet, my eyes were a florescent bloodshot color, and my face was pale. "I'm not going to fool anyone." I was trembling and stood against a wall. She walked me to a bench.

"Are they going to miss you soon?"

"Pretty soon."

She dug in her ample purse. "Here, take my sunglasses."

"I couldn't, but thank you."

"Take them. They were ninety-nine cents at a gas station in Phoenix."

"I like Phoenix."

"So do I." She smiled, and I took the glasses.

They were nondescript black. "What's your name?"

"Angela."

"Angela, like an angel; thank you."

I stood up, feeling sturdier. She kept her hand on my back as we walked out. Alex, Elise, and Dad were walking toward us. I slid the glasses onto my face. "I was coming back. You didn't have to come find me." Angela patted my back and said good-bye. Before she left, I hugged her again. "Dad, Alex, this is my friend Angela. I ran into her in the bathroom."

Angela shook their hands. "You look just like the Master Chef."

Alex held his hands out. "Guilty as charged. I'm parading as a tourist today."

Angela looked at me, then she dug in her purse again. Handing me a card, she said, "Here's my e-mail. I've got to hear about this one. It's good to meet you." She nodded at the men. "Take care."

"I'll e-mail soon." I held up the card. "Thanks for the address."

Alex walked behind me, shaking his head as he joked. "Can't take you anywhere without running into people you know. You're quite popular."

"It's a curse." I laughed, heading for the doors so I could be outside, where sunglasses wouldn't look so out of place. My eyes burned with dried tears. Alex matched my stride, and I threw out, "You wouldn't believe how annoying it is to be recognized everywhere I go." I laughed again, but it sounded forced.

* * *

I leaned my head against the cool window on the way home. My father wisely didn't speak to me, and Alex stayed busy in the backseat playing rock-paper-scissors with Elise. She was winning.

"Jana, I don't think lunch agreed with you. Why don't you lie down for a while?" my dad said when we got home.

"That sounds like a good idea; maybe you can have Mom show Elise some computer games." On the way to my room, I grabbed a washcloth and ran it under cold water. I made it to my room, collapsed on my bed, pulled off the glasses, and pressed the washcloth onto my swollen eyes, letting the cold seep into my eyelids. In the blackness, I let myself die a little. I prayed silently without getting up. *Thank you, Heavenly Father, for helping Alex come to a point where he is ready to hear the gospel. Thank you for blessing him and his family.* I waited for a choking sob, but it never came. *Thank you for Angela. I'm sorry I'm such a selfish, jealous woman. Please help me be a better person. Please help me to be really happy for Alex and Elise. Please help me to see things like You do so this won't hurt so much anymore. I'm sorry I fell in love with someone whose heart is already taken. I'll leave him alone.*

I ended my prayer and sighed. I cleared my mind and just lay there, feeling the numbness of my existence. The door opened. I couldn't think of who it might be. I lay still, not wanting to know, hoping I looked like I was asleep and they would go away.

My dad cleared his throat. "You okay?"

"Yep."

"Jana." He held my hand. I pulled the washcloth off my eyes. His chin quivered. "I don't like to see my baby hurt so much."

I hugged him and cried. My nose started running. "Can you tell him I died and send him home?"

"You've got to take him by the hand and show him the gospel at home." He rocked me back and forth.

"Dad, I can't take him by the hand anymore. Let someone else do it."

He pulled me back to look into my eyes. "Who's the best person to do it? Who did God position perfectly to help him get through this?"

I hugged my dad fiercely. "Who's going to get *me* through this?" I felt so sorry for myself. The tears came hot on my cheeks.

"I thought you loved him."

"I do, more than anything." I sniffed. "And I get to watch the man I love fall madly in love with his wife again while he thinks about being with her forever."

My dad sat away from me, clearly disappointed by my jealousy. "Do you want him to stop loving his wife?"

"Of course not. I'm happy for him. If I could go out and buy him any gift at all, this is the gift I would get for him."

"Then you do love him. Can you not comprehend that he could love you as much as he loves his wife?"

"She gave him Elise. They've . . . been together in married ways." I gulped. "Doesn't it make sense that he would love her more?"

"It doesn't have to be a contest. You can just let the man love. Of all my children, I never would have expected this from you, Jana." I started crying a fresh round of tears. He hugged me again. "I'm sorry. I'm no good at this. I should get your mother."

"No, please don't tell her. Can't I just be sick for a while?"

"You need to talk to a woman. I don't know how to help the pain you're in." He was trying to soothe me, holding me and patting me on the back. But knowing how disappointed he was in how I was feeling, how jealous I was of Vanessa, made his soothing ineffectual.

Feeling like a total disappointment, I pulled away and sniffed. "I'm fine." I faked a smile. "Look, I'm brave. You think I can help him with this. You think I should. I have no faith in myself. But . . . I believe you. You've never been wrong. If you think I should do this, I will do it. Maybe for a month, and then I'll come home."

"You can get him on the right path. Are you sure you can handle it? You're a basket of nerves."

"If you think I can handle it, I can handle it."

"You have great faith in your old Dad, eh? Why don't we put some in God? If anyone could use a priesthood blessing, I think it's you."

He stood up and locked the door. I sat down in the chair at my vanity. I looked in the mirror. My eyes were bloodshot with puffy circles. I sighed heavily, wishing I could die. I looked heavenward. *Whatever You want, whoever You want me to be. I'll do it. I'll be it. If You say I can do it, I can.* In the blessing, I was told I had a great work ahead of me in Washington, though it didn't sound like it had much to do with Alex. I was blessed with strength, fortitude, foresight, and courage. God seemed to know my thoughts more than my father. I was admonished not to grieve but to rejoice. He reassured me that things would work out in the end exactly as He had intended. He said I would be blessed for my diligence in adhering to gospel standards. He alluded to angels He'd sent—I thought of Angela—and angels

He would send. The last thing I was blessed with was peace. When my father ended the blessing, I felt a warmth fall upon me from some heavenly realm. It washed my head until I felt free of the headache, and the heartache was numbed. My father sat down on the edge of the bed. "I thought he'd bless you with some sense, make you think straight. I didn't hear that. Did you?"

"No, no sense, but probably more than I deserve after being such a boob." I lay down under my covers. "I think I could sleep for a week."

"I can only buy you tonight. They're getting suspicious."

"I knew you saw it. I knew I couldn't fool you."

"I heard your heart break like it was a pencil across my knee. I saw it on your face. You fell at his moment of triumph. I can say this, and I am just speaking as a man," he kissed me on the cheek, "a man *can* love twice. Have some faith. Eternity would be a long time to live without him. I don't think God intended for either of you to languish here alone." He pulled my blankets up around me and gently pulled one of my curls. "Are you going to be all right?"

I could barely keep my eyes open. A wave of fatigue pulled at me. "I am now. Thanks, Dad."

He turned my light off and left. I was asleep before the door shut.

Sometime later, a light tapping on my door woke me. The door opened, and I recognized Alex's silhouette as he slipped into my room. "Are you awake?"

It was a struggle to keep my eyes open. "I am now." I tried to sit up but quickly lay back from a surge of dizziness. Alex turned on the light. "Down, off, anything," I begged. He dimmed the light. "Lower," I commanded. He dimmed it to the lowest setting.

"Sorry. I should let you sleep. I'm so selfish. I kept waiting through dinner, thinking you'd come down."

"I haven't been feeling good."

He sat next to me on the bed. I was so tired that I just closed my eyes. I was nearly back to sleep when he said, "All of this, this bizarre rightness you brought along with you, it all fits together. There isn't a piece of it that doesn't fit with another piece or older pieces. It smacks of truth."

"Hmmm," I said, hoping he'd be quiet so I could drift off again.

"I mean, it's so simple and straightforward that it couldn't possibly be true. Yet, oh, I don't know, if I were God—not saying that I'd ever be that great—this is how I would have done it. It's easy, organized. It has a plan for everything. I probably sound foolish to you, after you've had it your whole life, but I don't know how else to explain it; I'm hungry for it. I want every detail. I've read two magazines while I've been waiting for you to come find me."

I sat up, slightly more alert. "You've been reading Church magazines?"

"I had to sneak downstairs to get scriptures so I could look up the references, just to see if the articles were true. And they lead everywhere. One scripture leads into another. Jana?"

"Hmmm?"

"If I were baptized next week, we'd have to wait a year to go to the temple. Could you wait a year?"

"Mmm." I bit my lip. He'd have to wait a year to be sealed to Vanessa too, I thought sleepily.

"Mmm, yes, or mmm, no?"

"Temple's nice." I slumped down farther into the bed.

"You could wait a year?"

"It does seem like a long time," I admitted, unwilling to have another conversation about us. I blinked, trying to wake myself up. I looked at him; his gaze was piercing, and I could tell he was serious about what he was saying. Suddenly, I couldn't keep the tears from my eyes. These tears weren't from feeling sorry for myself. Alex was spiritually awakening. My father was right. I remembered his words. *That's God's son . . . He's come for him now. You're going to see him unfold into the man he's meant to be . . . We're going to find a treasure worth keeping.* And I was going to be beside him. I was going to watch him become that man. I thought of Elise and how different her life was going to be in the gospel. I thought of them together forever. My heart swelled with gratitude.

I brightened. "I can't believe we're having this conversation." I smiled and took both of his hands. "I can't tell you how many times I've wanted to say something. How many times I just wanted to sit you down and bear my testimony."

"But you have. Maybe not all at once but by the way you live. And you've always been ready to share what you know." He squeezed my hand. "You've never pushed me, and I want you to know I appreciate that."

I studied my hands. Maybe I had already done my part in Alex's spiritual awakening. Maybe I didn't need to go back to Washington at all. I looked around the room, wondering if Vanessa would be able to come in spirit to watch her husband accept the gospel. Where would she be? Putting her invisible arms around his neck? Jumping for joy?

I suddenly felt very disconnected from him, like an invader. He felt more off-limits than ever before. I couldn't help the shadow that must have passed over my face.

"I have to take you home." Alex cut into my thoughts. "I want to leave tomorrow. I have a bad feeling about having you here right now, like you won't come home at all. It's hard to describe, just this incessant need to get you back to where you belong."

I was beginning to feel the fatigue again, and my eyes grew heavy. I wriggled deeper under the covers. *Alex loves Vanessa.* He brushed hair away from my forehead. *A man can love twice.*

He knelt down beside the bed. "Will you pray with me?"

I opened my eyes. "Now?"

"Yes."

"I don't know how coherent I am right now."

"I'll talk."

I slid out of bed and knelt beside him. He took my hand, and for a moment, I wondered if I was dreaming, if Alex Steadman was really in my bedroom praying with me. He asked Heavenly Father to bless me to feel better, asked that we would be safe on our trip, thanked Him for miracles, and asked a blessing upon my family while we were gone. It sounded like he'd prayed a lot before. I remembered Elise praying and wondered again if Alex had prayed in the early days after Vanessa had died. Something tugged at my heart, something about Vanessa, but I stuffed it deeper down so I didn't have to feel it.

Alex brushed his lips against mine and told me to get some sleep so we could leave early. He lifted me into bed and straightened my blankets as though I were Elise. It was easy to slip off to sleep again, though I had to admit I was having some strange dreams.

* * *

In the morning, I woke to my mother opening the door. She had a tray of food. "I could thump your dad. As if I don't know how to take care of my own daughter. *Please.* I had to wait for them to go golfing before I could sneak up. Been guarding your room like a bulldog."

I sat up in bed. "Dad has been a little weird."

"Worst timing in the world, but Alex thinks he's taking you home today. We've got to get you fit to travel. Just look at your eyes. I think they'll load up as soon as he gets back. Alex didn't even want to go golfing, but Stan insisted you sleep in. There's no reasoning with either one of them, and your father is just as set on you shipping out today as Alex." She left the room and came back with a wet washcloth. "Can you eat with your eyes closed? You'd think they'd have the good sense to let you stay down in bed a couple of days."

I lay back while she put the cloth on my face. She handed me a piece of toast. "I'll stay in bed when I get home, I promise. Really, all I have to do is sit on an airplane. It won't be so hard. I'll sleep." I was trying to remember what Alex had said last night about why it was so important to take me home today, but I couldn't. "We have to get home anyway. Alex wants to go to church on Sunday."

"He could go with us."

"I want him to see what his ward is like. He'll take good care of me."

"I know he will. Here." She replaced the cloth with a new one. "You're already looking better. We should have done this last night. I'll go draw a bath for you."

"I think I'll shower."

"You should bathe. I don't want you standing too long with the state you're in. I have half a mind to call and tell that restaurant what we think of their lunch."

"No. Don't. No one else got sick. It's just a fluke that it hit me so hard. Maybe I've been working too much."

* * *

I was playing a computer game with Elise when my father walked in with Alex. Alex looked subdued and depressed. My father wasn't as buoyant as he usually was after a good game, but he didn't look sad. I wondered what they'd talked about.

Alex hugged me. He kissed my lips in front of Elise, something he hadn't done before. Elise was beaming. He put a soft hand on my shoulder. "Let's get this show on the road."

Dad put my bags in the rental car's trunk. I kissed my parents and promised we'd come for Thanksgiving.

"You're doing the right thing. I'm proud of you," my father whispered in my ear.

"I know you are." I hugged him tightly.

"Think you should stay. You're still trembling," my mother complained.

"I'm fine. I'll be 100 percent by tomorrow. I'll call you."

"Abigail, you know I'll take care of her. She'll be fine. I'll keep her down for a few days," Alex promised.

I slid into the car, glad for the fog that seemed to hamper my thinking. I slept on the way to the airport.

"You've been through something more than I thought, to be knocked this hard," Alex observed on the plane. "When I told your mother I'm keeping you down for a few days, I was serious."

"I'll be fine tomorrow. You'll see."

"If you're better tomorrow, you're still staying down."

"Yes, Mister Steadman, if it makes you happy. I'll watch movies all day. But don't you dare pay me for lying around. Maybe we can stop by a bookstore on the way home and I can pick something up."

"I'll go get a book if you want one. *You* are going straight home and straight to bed."

I shrugged, already feeling the natural fatigue that I suspected was a gift from God. I tried to remember why I was going home with Alex when I knew he was going to start working toward building his forever family with Vanessa. He took my hand and pressed it to his lips. I looked at him with my heavy eyes. *A man can love twice.* I wondered if I'd known Vanessa, if I would have been friends with her. If I had known them, it never would have occurred to me to look twice at her husband.

"What are you thinking about?"

"Vanessa," I said honestly. "I hope everything works out just right. It would make me so happy to know you have your family for eternity." Deep beneath the fatigue, I felt a prick when I said "*your family.*" I hoped he hadn't seen me flinch.

"Your father and I had a long talk."

"I figured you would."

"He told me about the time you hunkered down in the doghouse with the bunny your brother was selling, how it took him two hours to talk you out."

"It pooped all over me, but I didn't want him to sell it."

"He told me I have a month."

"Oh, I wasn't going to tell you that."

"He knew you wouldn't."

"I'm glad you two can get together to conspire against me."

"We're conspiring *for* you. He just wanted to make sure I knew how completely obstinate and unbending you could be. I told him I'd already been dealing with some of it. A month isn't a lot of time. I have hope though."

"Why would you bother to hope?"

He shifted his body toward me so his back was to Elise. In a low voice he whispered, "Tell me to never kiss you again. Tell me we're done, you're moving on. Tell me you're not going to love me anymore."

I couldn't help the tears that welled in my eyes. I just stared at him, repulsed by the words he'd asked me to say.

He kissed me longer than he should have on a public plane. The fog that was protecting me dissipated, and my ears burned. "That's why." He leaned back in his chair, took out a conference *Ensign*, positioned it in one hand, and started to read. He took my hand with his free hand, and I shifted so I could fall asleep.

His hand was warm. I didn't doubt that he loved me. I knew that he loved Vanessa too though. I thought about what he'd asked me to say. Within a month, I'd have to find the strength to say those very words. A small point of reason started to swell within me. I could choose to share Alex with his other forever family or not have him at all. I shifted again, still not comfortable. I thought about life if I returned to Utah. How could I possibly fall in love with someone else when I loved him so completely? I looked at him. How could he possibly fall in love with someone else when he loved his wife so completely? But again, I had to admit that I didn't doubt he loved me. *A man can love twice.*

He slapped the magazine onto his thigh and looked at me. "You're not sleeping. You're too quiet. It's making me nervous. What are you thinking?"

"Love."

"What about it?"

"How it works, what it means." I shifted to face him, leaning my cheek against the headrest. "Love is a verb. It's a funny falling at first, something . . ."

"Electric?"

"Sure, electric. But then it's a verb. It's a choice to serve someone for the rest of your life, to put their happiness and comfort before your own. It's a doing word."

"Okay, I'll give you that." He was quiet for a while. "This whole . . . for lack of a better word, *snag* that we're going through—you're going through—it's all about trusting warranties."

"Really? Explain."

"Like my projector in the theater room. When I bought it, the salesman said it would last about five years. I could purchase an additional warranty for an extended time, so I did. Now we enjoy the projector, and

I don't worry about it breaking. I don't spend a lot of time thinking about the warranty, but I know it's there, that everything will work out when it finally flicks out after its last movie."

"I'm a little fuzzy on the electronic connection."

"The gospel is the warranty. Everything will work out in the eternities, but I'm not going to sit around now and worry about things over which I have no control. I'm going to enjoy the show. Sure, I'll secure the ordinances necessary to put things in order, but I'm not going to worry about the fine print. It's all taken care of; maybe I don't understand exactly how, but it's all taken care of."

I didn't say anything.

"How can you worry about sharing me with someone who isn't even here?"

Apparently, my father had been completely candid with him. "It all comes down to that, you know. I'm greedy. I don't want to share." I shook his hand lose and folded my arms. "I'm horrid. I know it." My eyes burned with tears. "I should be so excited. You're just not what I expected. This wasn't my plan. I was going to marry someone like Jeff, someone simple. Everything was going to be simple. Suddenly, I don't know where I stop and you begin. My basic instinct tells me to go find something simple, but . . . I can't . . . I can't imagine loving someone else. I've been trying, but I can't even see it."

"I'm flattered, but your greed had better not cost me the woman I love. You'll never be happy without me."

"That's what I'm afraid of."

He picked up the magazine again. "There *is* no space where I stop and you begin. It doesn't exist. It never has, since the moment I met you. Maybe you thought you had a space there, but it never existed." I thought about the crystal cats in my room, how amazed I was that he was so confident back then, when he barely knew me. He continued. "Have you thought about what we talked about in your room last night? The temple?"

"I thought that was a dream. Why don't you come to church and see if it's right for you before we start worrying about any of that."

"I'd rather secure my claims as soon as possible."

"It could be a passing fancy."

"It's no more a passing fancy than you are. Jana, I swear . . . you . . . No. I'm not going to let you ruin this for me. I'm going to enjoy loving you. I'm going to enjoy you loving me. You can go ahead and wallow in whatever imaginary grief you've drudged up to keep yourself from being happy, but I'm going to enjoy this. Every minute of it, even if it's just a month, which I highly doubt it will be. You can't hold out forever. I have eternity on my side. I have *your father* on my side. I understand they sent your father to get you out of the doghouse because you won't listen to anyone else. You can't stand against us long. Why don't you just come nice and quiet? No one has to get hurt."

"You make it sound like I'm a criminal." I folded my arms and spent the rest of the flight doing my best not to think.

CHAPTER 17
Cowbells

ALEX HELD THE DOOR OPEN for Elise and me. I insisted we arrive at church ten minutes early to get a seat up front. I figured it would be easier to be stared at if we couldn't see the people who were doing it. I chose a side pew behind where I guessed the deacons would be sitting. The chapel wasn't very crowded. I leaned over to Alex. "You shouldn't take the sacrament yet, not until you understand the covenant involved in taking it. Just pass it to me."

Alex looked around the pew and held up a hymnbook. "I sing like a frog."

"No one expects you to sing a cappella."

A tall man with silver hair approached us. "Mr. Steadman." He held out his hand. "I'm Bishop Larsen. It's good to see you. Sister Barrowman. I read you were LDS."

"This is Elise Steadman," Alex introduced.

She shook the bishop's hand.

He bent down. "It's good to meet you. Are you nervous?"

"Nope." She showed him her handkerchief doll.

"She's a beauty." A member handed Bishop Larsen a tithing envelope. The woman did a double take when she saw Alex's face. "Are you staying in the Bellevue house, then?" the bishop asked.

Alex smiled. "We are. We had to relocate due to a problem at the other houses. Jana lives in the apartment." I was grateful to Alex for clearing that up.

"I'd like to meet with you after sacrament meeting. My office is on the east side."

"I'll find Elise's Primary class, and we'll meet you there," I replied.

I sat down, resisting biting my nails. The bishop's counselors introduced themselves on their way to the stand. I felt eyes on us and purposely didn't look around. I felt most conspicuous when Alex put his arm around my shoulders during the talks. I hoped I wasn't blushing. After sacrament meeting, several members converged upon Alex. I told him I'd meet him at the bishop's office, and I took Elise to Primary. I looked over my shoulder as we were walking out, and Alex seemed to be in his element surrounded by rapturous women, especially since these women would never pinch his behind.

It didn't take long to get Elise settled. I found Alex already in the bishop's office and sat with him across from the bishop. I couldn't help feeling like I was eight years old in a baptismal interview. I wondered if meeting the bishop had any significance at all for Alex. The bishop pushed some papers toward me to fill out so they could transfer my records. He asked Alex a few light questions while I filled out the paperwork. I looked up when I heard Alex say, "I'd like to meet with the missionaries so they can teach me the lessons. I want to be baptized as soon as possible. I understand I can be sealed to my daughter in a year."

The bishop quickly scanned the look of shock on my face. "Sister Barrowman, may I speak with Brother Steadman alone for a few minutes?"

"Sure, I'll just . . ." I motioned to the door and took the paperwork with me. Once I was sitting in the hall, I sat back, wondering what exactly Alex was telling the bishop.

A lady nearly jogged down the hall to reach me. She bounced into the chair next to me. "I have to know, does he cook for you?"

I laughed. "Yes. I've gained ten pounds."

"Well, it doesn't look it. I'm Sherri Plunket." She shook my hand firmly. "Can you imagine that, just marching him into church? I've read your name, but I can't remember it."

"Jana Barrowman."

"So is he going to be in this ward? I've got the activities committee all over me." Her teased hair had pleasant blonde highlights, and she jingled with jewelry as she talked.

I laughed again. "I don't know if he'll do a Relief Society activity. You can ask him."

"I didn't even know he was a Mormon."

"He's actually new to the church." I shifted uncomfortably in my chair. "He's excited about being sealed to his wife and daughter in the temple. His wife died about a year ago, you know."

"Oh, that's right. That wasn't your daughter, then?"

I shook my head.

"You are dating him though?"

"I guess I am, but just recently. The papers jumped on it before it happened."

Sherri told me she lived on the street behind us. She said she could see our backyard from her patio. She had three kids, and her husband was the Sunday School president. She was inviting me to go walking with her in the mornings when the bishop stepped out of his office and exchanged me for Alex. He didn't want to go to class without me, so he decided to wait. I was sure Sherri would keep him company. I tried to conceal my smile as I thought about her asking him to teach a cooking class.

Bishop Larsen had me sit down, and we talked about my family. He was pleased to hear my father was a temple sealer. When he mentioned that Alex wanted to marry me, I tried to skirt around the subject, feeling awkward. The bishop was a good man. By the time he finished talking to me, I felt more excited about attending our new ward. When he shook my hand and opened the door, we found Alex listening good-naturedly as Sherri and a middle-aged brunette talked to him in excited, happy tones. The bishop said, "Gospel Essentials is in the cultural hall today. If you hurry, you can get him to the last of it." He handed me two manuals, and I tugged Alex away from his audience.

The way everyone stared at us when we entered class made me feel like we were wearing cowbells. I led Alex to the back of the room. The teacher stopped to have us introduce ourselves.

After the closing prayer, I left Alex in a crowd of back-slapping men. I introduced myself in Relief Society, making sure to mention that I *rented* an apartment from Alex Steadman. I sat by the exit so I could get Elise as soon as class let out. I knew I'd be a center of interest for the sisters. My plan worked flawlessly, but only because I left right before the closing prayer. Alex was waiting for us and swept us quickly out the door.

"Even church feels like a social function with you," I complained.

"After a while, they'll get used to me. It'll be nothing. They'll barely remember my name."

"Bishop thought you might reactivate some inactive sisters."

"That blonde lady wearing the jewelry store wants me to cook for the women."

I smiled.

"I don't know much about beans. Don't know beans about beans, ha ha. I tried to tell her, but she wouldn't hear it."

"Well, there's cooking and then there's Mormon cooking. Two different worlds. Maybe you can teach them to chop onions or something useful," I suggested.

Elise was wearing a CTR ring and a paper crown that said "Daughter of a Heavenly King."

"What did you think, kiddo? Could you do that every week?" Alex asked.

"I have a friend named Sarah Plunket. She wants me to come play."

"I just met her mother, Sherri. We could probably arrange something," I told her.

Elise started singing "Follow the Prophet" from a handout she'd received at church.

She was loud enough that I wasn't worried about her hearing when I leaned over to ask Alex, "What's the big idea, telling the bishop you intend to marry me?"

"Was it a secret?"

"Are you going to tell everyone? It will make life incredibly awkward."

"I told Sherri Plunket."

"Alex! You may as well have put a sign in the front yard."

"I can do that too. I made sure she knew you wouldn't have me."

"Don't tell her that either. Oh, you peeve me like no one can. I'm going to have to serve with these ladies, and they'll all think I'm crazy from the get-go."

"Why would they think you're crazy?"

"Not marry Alex Steadman? I mean, c'mon, who's dumb enough to turn that down?"

"You said it. I didn't." He pulled into the garage. I got out and headed for my apartment. Alex caught me at the door. I could still hear Elise singing in the car. I sighed heavily and leaned back against the door. "I'm sorry. I know I'm overreacting. I'm just finding myself in an awkward situation. I shouldn't blame it on you. It's my fault."

He leaned down to kiss me. I couldn't help myself; I put my arms around his neck and held him tight.

"Being rejected by you isn't as painful as I thought it would be," he said.

I hugged him. "You mean so much to me. You really do. After I picked my jaw up off the floor, I was really excited that you want to take lessons from the missionaries."

"But if I didn't want to, you'd still care about me?"

"Of course." I smiled. I knew I should be striving to distance myself, but I couldn't bring myself to be anything but honest with him.

* * *

To my chagrin, the Relief Society presidency rang Alex's doorbell when I didn't answer mine. They found me in his apron pulling cookies out of his oven. Of course, Alex walked them right back to the kitchen to see me. I was sure it was a quaint domestic scene.

After the presidency left, we spent the evening watching Godzilla movies. It was during one of the movies that I found a sales proposition on the coffee table. It was a thick booklet outlining the offer of a Wisconsin company, highlighting their holdings, and explaining their plans for the restaurant. As I flipped through the pages, tuning out Godzilla shrieking over Tokyo, I decided I'd show it to Scott. Perhaps he could put something like that together for Alex so he would take Scott's offer seriously. I'd spent a lot of time with Scott and Alex at the restaurant as I worked on the books and orders. I really thought Scott could handle owning the restaurant. He was very responsible. The more time that passed, the less it seemed likely that Alex would ever find anyone suitable to buy the restaurant. I was certain Scott could do it, and I knew he would be good to the employees. I asked Alex if I could take the offer home to look over it. He shrugged and said I could if I wanted to. Apparently he'd already looked at it and been unimpressed.

He leaned forward and piled a few jewelry catalogs on my lap to go with the offer.

"What's this?"

"I thought you could look . . . at rings," he said.

"Alex, I don't think I'm ready to. I have some things to reconcile before I make a choice like that."

"Well, okay, but," he took one of the catalogs and flipped to a page with a corner turned down. Pointing to a gaudy dowager ring with a black opal, he said, "That's the one I like. I can't imagine you'd like something like that, but if you trust me . . ."

I rolled the catalog and smacked his arm with it. "You do not like that. You searched the whole thing for the worst just to scare me."

"I'm deeply offended that you'd insult my favorite," he quipped.

Despite my conscience yelling that I should set it down and back away, I flipped it open. Alex handed me a suspiciously convenient pen and told me to circle what I liked. He watched over my shoulder as I picked out half a dozen. I found one I liked the most and made the circle extra dark. I handed him the catalog. "Don't you dare. Not one diamond, not until I'm ready."

"Sure." He leaned back, smiling. "Not until you're ready."

CHAPTER 18
Fish Bait

I SPREAD FILES OUT ON the round table in the corner of the restaurant. I could hear Scott clinking around in the kitchen. I didn't know how long it would be before I got him alone again. I opened the kitchen door and looked around for anyone else. "Are you alone?" I asked him.

Looking too pleased at the question, he told me he was. I showed him the purchase proposal Alex had let me take the night before. "I think if you do something like this, he might take you more seriously. You know, show him where you're getting the funding from and what you're going to do with it."

Scott let out a low whistle. "I can only afford half what these guys are offering."

"Maybe he'll settle for half. Who knows, maybe he'll sell half of it to you and have you run it. Would you be interested in something like that?"

"Sure, if I had a chance to buy the other half later. Maybe he would take payments. If I paid him the profits for a year, it would make up for a substantial portion of the amount I can't pay."

"Well, you won't know if you don't ask."

"I'll pull together some numbers. I'd need your help. I couldn't make anything like that. It looks like they paid a CPA or someone to put it together."

"I'm no CPA, but I can certainly copy this. Alex will be back in a half hour. Don't mention it to him yet. We'll show it to him tomorrow."

"You can work that fast?"

I had him write down the information I would need, then I had him explain his vision for Shallots. I was especially curious about the employees. Scott wanted to implement a bonus program, giving employees a percentage of profits. He said he thought it would inspire them to continue making the restaurant succeed. I liked it. I hoped Alex wouldn't be upset that I was meddling in his business.

After giving Scott my e-mail address, I spread more files across the round table and started sorting papers. Someone, I assumed Alex, slid into a chair across from me. I finished a few calculations and stopped breathing when I looked up. Brad was staring at me, looking less polished than usual.

"Hi," I said, looking around for Scott.

"I know you don't want to see me. I just came to apologize."

"Really?"

He was wearing a rumpled golf shirt and didn't have his usual expensive watch on. He still looked handsome, though there was something different in his eyes that I couldn't place.

"I went crazy when you left; I couldn't believe it. You didn't call, and then there was the chef. I turned into a monster. I don't know what got into me. You know your bishop called my bishop back home?"

Alex must have told the bishop the whole reason we'd moved. "Oh."

"It's no big deal. I deserved it."

I was quiet, my eyes continually darting to the kitchen door. Curiosity got the better of me when I didn't see anyone coming to my rescue, so I asked, "What were you going to do if I was in the house?" I had played out the scene a hundred times, in a hundred different ways, trying to decide what he was there to do.

"I was going to make you see you were making a mistake. I was going to make you understand." He looked up with tears in his eyes. I thought I saw self-loathing. "You weren't making the mistake. I was. I knew it was wrong to break in . . . You just never listened to me." A tear broke loose and made a track down his cheek. "It sounds stupid, but . . ." He leaned forward. "I've been a little . . . *unbalanced* lately. I've spent a lot of time repenting. I'm not done yet. I feel terrible about it. I'm going home tomorrow."

"Can you get your old job back after going to jail?" I wasn't sure I believed him, but this was outside what I considered to be his acting abilities.

"It's waiting for me. I plead down to trespassing. They couldn't prove that I was there to harm you or steal anything. I had a good attorney. But still, Jana, I'm sorry. I'm sick with sorry. You know, I've never been that good. I know you thought I was, but really, I've always been a bit of a jerk and this . . . It was so humiliating sitting in that cell. You're probably scared out of your wits. I can't even ask you to forgive me. It's that bad. I don't think you should. I came to apologize, but you weren't home. I probably would have scared you more anyway." He leaned forward. "I wasn't going to hurt you. I promise." He studied the table. "I'll go home and crawl under a rock for a while, get my life in order, but I swear I'll never bother you again."

I couldn't think of anything to say.

He continued. "I was so worried about being successful that I forgot everything that was important. And look at what I am now." He hung his head. "No, don't look. I'd rather you not see it."

I still really doubted he was this good of an actor. I used to easily spot his little white lies. I tried to sound bright. "That's what the Atonement's for. This will all work out, Brad. Have faith." I was torn between wanting to comfort him and wanting to scream and run. He was definitely different than I'd ever seen him. He was humble. Any hint that he'd ever been a cocky Jim Dandy was gone. He looked around. "I'd better get lost before Steadman shows up. I felt bad coming this last time, you know. I waited for him to leave, and I felt sneaky about it. I make myself sick. Jana, I'm so sorry about . . . about . . . me. What are my parents thinking? What will the ward say?"

"Maybe they don't know. It can just be between you and the bishop. I didn't tell my bishop, just so you know. It didn't occur to me. I think someone else must have told him. When he heard you were LDS, he probably searched out your name."

"Doesn't matter. This problem wouldn't even exist if I were a decent person." He rubbed the back of his neck. "Well, have a good life. I hope everything works out with the chef."

"I hope everything works out for you too."

"That's hard to see right now, but I'm sure it can't get worse. That's the great thing about hitting bottom. Good-bye." He turned and left. His always square shoulders were hunched forward in defeat.

I pushed papers around for a while, trying to process the conversation. I realized I wasn't going to be able to do any work. My brain wouldn't latch onto the calculations. I gathered the papers and files and headed to Alex's office. The door shut behind me, and I jumped.

"You're white as a ghost," Alex said. "Did Brad get in here, then? Where was Scott?"

"How did you know?"

"He was pulling out when I drove in."

"He came to apologize. I guess Scott's in the kitchen."

"You don't really think he came to apologize, do you?"

"He seemed sincere."

"You should have run or called the police. Screaming would have brought Scott." Alex was tense. He didn't shout, but his words were hard and commanding.

"I didn't need to scream; he just wanted to talk," I said defensively.

Alex laughed in a cynical tone. "Tell me you're not that gullible."

"I think he's repenting of everything. He was all broken up. He just came to say good-bye."

"He just came to get your guard down so he can take you." It was almost a growl.

"I think you're wrong. He was really disgusted with himself for breaking in."

Alex sighed and sat down on the edge of his desk. "And did he say what he was going to do to you when he broke in?"

"He told me he wasn't going to hurt me."

"Jana," he crossed the room and cradled my face in his hands so I was looking at him, "*he* is dangerous. He's shown us that, hasn't he? This doesn't change anything. I don't care if he's in Europe. We're going to act as though he's still here."

"But he's going home. We don't have to worry about it anymore."

"He wants you to think he's going home. You are so naive. It is hard enough watching out for you when you're scared. Don't let your guard down."

"I am not naive. I've known him for a long time. I'm telling you, he was different."

He crossed to sit on the couch and rested his elbows on his knees. He studied his hands for a few moments. "While I wish we could agree on everything, we obviously won't. I'm not saying who's more bullheaded right now. However, I'm going to ask you," he looked up so his eyes pierced mine, "concerning this one thing in particular, to pay heed to what I'm saying. I need you to promise you will continue to be as careful with your safety as you have been these last few weeks—hopefully more careful."

I just stared at him.

"Because you love me."

I groaned. "Because I love you, but I think you're wrong about him."

"And if he gets you alone again, you *will* scream, run, call the police, something besides sit down and chat with him?"

"He just wanted to talk."

"Jana?"

"I will scream, run, or call the police," I said dryly. "If you could have only seen him yourself . . ."

"For both of your sakes, I'm glad I didn't. He's not someone who would *want* to see me anytime soon."

"I'm going home."

"I'll follow you."

"Of course you will. I'll see you there." On the way home, I kept running the conversation with Brad through my head. He seemed really sick about what he had done. I wished there was a way to make Alex see that.

At home I asked to use Alex's computer. I closed the door to the office to send the signal that I wasn't up to company. The first thing I did was take out Angela's e-mail address. I hadn't forgotten how kind she'd been to me in the bathroom. I knew she was dying to know why I was bawling about the Master Chef. I sent a one-line e-mail, asking if she was LDS. Then I pulled up a spreadsheet and found Scott's e-mail. I started to figure the numbers. He was going to mortgage the house he owned outright and use up a savings of seventy thousand dollars. The house was worth eight hundred thousand, but he was only going to mortgage six hundred. I called him on my cell phone.

"How is it you live in an eight hundred thousand dollar home without a mortgage and you're twenty nothing." I could hear the dinnertime kitchen sounds of the restaurant.

"I'm twenty-six," he said defensively. "I *am* paid well. I dabble in the stock market. I guess Alex didn't tell you how much he pays me."

"You guessed right. I don't want to know, so don't tell me."

"I paid the house off a few years ago, after getting on at Shallots. Working here isn't like working at McDonalds, Jana."

"I wasn't inferring that you were flipping burgers. The numbers just surprised me, that's all. I wanted to verify them."

"I could probably pay more if I hawked my watches and sold my car, but I don't think Alex will make me do that."

"Sheesh, how much are your watches worth?"

"You probably don't want to know—more than my car anyway. I've got dinner rush here."

"Okay, good-bye." He hung up. His offer was almost a million shy of some of Alex's shabbier offers. However, I was certain Alex would at least consider Scott if I could format the offer in a serious package.

I checked my e-mail again. Angela had responded, saying she was LDS and wondering if I was feeling better. I spent twenty minutes typing out my life story, with a plea to keep it private at the end. I figured she deserved to know the whole story, especially what a twit I was, after everything she'd done to revive me.

Alex brought me a plate of linguine at six. I changed screens so he couldn't see what I was doing. "Thanks for letting me use your office. I hope I'm not in your way."

"No problem."

"I shouldn't be that much longer."

He left, and I printed a cover page and some spreadsheets. I checked my e-mail again. Angela had looked Alex up on the Internet after she'd met me and saw my picture everywhere. She promised to keep my private life private and pointed out that Alex would be mine for eternity when we were married in the temple and I shouldn't worry about where I would stand with his deceased wife. I deleted the e-mail. "Oh, sure. It sounds like a cinch when you put it like that. Why worry?" I said sarcastically to the screen.

I dismantled the offer Alex let me take and reused the binding and cover, being careful to position the window over Scott's name. I decided to take it to Scott to make sure it was right before I showed it to Alex.

Unfortunately, Alex snatched it out of my hands when I left the office. "Scott? You've been working with Scott?" He flipped through some of the pages. I leaned against the wall, watching him as I chewed my lip. He plucked a pen from my hand and began circling and underlining numbers and words. I cringed, lamenting how crisp the offer had looked only moments ago.

"I know it's low," I said.

"No, no, I'm thinking of something else. Maybe I don't have to sell it. Not all of it anyway. This, with the bonus incentive program, isn't bad. Did you put this together?"

"I thought if he formatted the offer better, you might take him seriously. Those are his numbers and his ideas. You weren't supposed to see it yet."

"He has more funding than I imagined. It shouldn't surprise me. He's always at work. I don't know when he'd have time to spend the money. Can you rework this with me? We'll give it back to him and see what he counters with."

"Okay, but it's only fair to tell you he hasn't seen his own offer yet."

"Oh, I've written all over it."

"I think he'll forgive you."

* * *

At four thirty in the morning I yawned deeply, looking at Alex. I tried to remember why I'd told him I would come with him to buy supplies. It was way too early. Alex drove over a bridge and down a back road to a dock. He had me lock myself in the car, and he bounded over to a boat. When he said the supplies were fresh, I didn't realize they were quite that fresh. He knocked on the side of a fishing schooner. A gruff-looking man looked over the side and waved at him excitedly. He rushed down a ladder and shook Alex's hand. As they started talking, I decided it was light enough to do my makeup. Alex had shaken me awake at four fifteen and commanded me to "get a move on."

I had barely enough time to apply my makeup before Alex had me pop the trunk. Two men were carrying bundles wrapped in white to the car. Alex tapped on the window and had me give him the keys. He leaned down to tell me, "No ice today. We've got to drop these off."

"He was happy to see you," I said.

"I pay up front. I make sure everyone knows where I get my fish. It's good business for him."

"Tell me again, why do you have to come so early?" I tried to stifle my next yawn.

"I've been so good for business that if I wait a few hours, his stock is depleted. I choose the *best* fish."

"Well, I should probably go home to take Elise to school. Gretchen might get testy if I'm not there to take over this morning."

"I have an appointment at the house at one, but I need your help putting together a counter to Scott's offer." He started the car and pulled onto the road.

I pulled the offer out of my bag and started looking at his notes. I couldn't make sense of them, so I closed it. I leaned back and let myself fall asleep.

After we took Elise to school, I told Alex to take a nap, but he wouldn't. He pulled me into the office and paced behind me, telling me what to type. His counteroffer was generous, considering how much he'd be losing by not selling to a higher bidder. He wanted to retain a say in how the restaurant was run, but he didn't want to run it. He would sell Scott 60 percent of the controlling interest with an option to buy 20 percent more in the coming year. Alex would retain a 20 percent interest indefinitely, taking that percent of the annual profits.

I printed Scott's original offer and stapled Alex's counter into a folder. Alex sat down behind his desk when I stood up. He held up the offer. "Thank you. I'm sure you made it a lot easier to understand than I would have on my own. I'll have to run it by my attorney before I give it to Scott."

His cell phone rang. He spoke a few affirmative words into it and snapped it closed. "Brad's in Utah; must have driven all night."

"You had Brad followed?"

"No. I had him confirmed. Now, go run to your wolves or whatever you had planned today. I'm going to hunt down my attorney."

"Did you have me come with you this morning so you could protect me from Brad?"

He closed his eyes and pinched the bridge of his nose. "I just wanted to know you were safe. You can't blame me for that, especially when you'd just as soon pull up a chair and chat with him instead of run screaming."

He lifted his offer again. "Thanks for the help." Then he walked out and left me sitting in the empty house.

I walked to the entryway window and watched him drive away. I decided to take the afternoon off. When I stopped in the kitchen to fill a mason jar with milk, I noticed the ring catalogs in his trash can and felt a sudden panic that he didn't want to marry me anymore. I knew it was an unreasonable feeling; after all, I had so many reasons not to marry Alex. I pictured his face when he realized he could be with Vanessa forever. The rapturous expression had been burned into my mind. The image didn't hurt as much as it usually did when I pulled it forward. I wasn't as jealous of Vanessa as I had been. I felt a genuine gratitude toward her. I just couldn't understand what my eternity would be like with her holding Alex's other hand. I went back to Alex's office and pulled up the pictures from the disk he'd let me use weeks ago. I tried to imagine things from Vanessa's point of view. She'd had to leave the people most dear to her before she was ready to go. I wondered what she was thinking now, what it was like in the spirit world. I was sure she watched over Alex and Elise. I knew she could see me. Looking at the pictures of the three of them together stirred feelings of gratitude once more. I knew Alex wouldn't be who he was now without her. And Elise . . . Elise was a precious gift to leave behind.

I sighed. Pulling up a full face shot of Vanessa, I spoke to her. "You're going to be sealed to your family for time and all eternity." Her eyes looked happy. "I'm in love with your husband." Her eyes still looked happy.

I pushed my chair farther away from the computer. "What do you want me to do? You should have a say in this. Eternity's a long time. I wish I could hear you." Just then a ray of sunlight highlighted the desk to my right. Alex had a pile of Church flyers and pamphlets. I thumbed through them. One had a picture of a temple on it. I held it up for Vanessa to see, as though she really lived inside the computer. "This is where you'll be going. I don't suppose you've met any missionaries over there yet?" She stared back at me blankly.

"I'm glad Alex has Elise. I'm glad he married you. I'm sorry you don't have your body anymore." I thought about that for a while. I summoned memories of dancing with Alex and holding Elise. These were things Vanessa couldn't do anymore. I propped the pamphlet up against the computer. She couldn't even go to the temple on her own. I raised my hands in front of my eyes, studying the slight blue lines that represented my circulating blood. "I can help you. Alex is getting baptized. You can be baptized too, and more. You can be ready when it's time to be sealed to him. I can do your temple work if you don't mind that it's me, that I love Alex." I studied her face, waiting for a response. "Well, I can ask him anyway. Maybe he wouldn't want me to be the one." I shut down the computer and laughed as I left the office. I'd just had an entire conversation with myself.

Alex called. "I might be a few minutes late to my appointment. Could you entertain them when they get there?"

I told him I would and snapped the phone shut. I decided to go upstairs and scope out Elise's new room so I could make a list of supplies to paint it. It had nondescript white walls and a white canopy bed. We could do a lot with ribbons and feather boas. I looked at one bare wall and contemplated painting a Tuscan mural. I dismissed the idea when I thought about the purple I knew would cover everything.

As I left the room, I decided now was as good a time as any to explore the upstairs parts of the house I hadn't seen yet. I passed Gretchen's room, spacious with a large bay window. It was decorated with a lilac motif. It had a private bathroom and a desk with a computer in the corner. It smelled like vanilla.

The next room was full of exercise equipment and had a mirrored wall. It smelled like old gym shoes. The next room was full of cardboard boxes and looked like it had never been occupied. I stepped in, too curious not to look inside the boxes. The lids were folded instead of taped, so I figured I could get away with peeking. The first box was full of baby toys. The next box was full of women's clothing I assumed were Vanessa's. The next box was full of scrapbooks and journals. I pulled them out and made myself comfortable in a corner. I was pretty sure I shouldn't be snooping, but I was curious. The first scrapbook was full of pictures of Elise, from her birth on. Alex and Vanessa looked like teenagers. I laughed to see how skinny he was. I wondered if he'd started working out after Vanessa died to get his mind off of his grief. He was skinny in all of the pictures I'd seen of him before her death. Now he was filled out in his chest and had a thicker neck. His eyes looked darker when he was younger. By the time Elise was about two, Vanessa had started journaling in the scrapbooks, so I was able to read about their vacations and various outings. My favorite was a trip to Maine. They looked so happy. Gretchen was in some of the pictures and was about twenty pounds lighter than her current weight. Vanessa wrote a story about spending the day at the beach and Alex's horrible sunburn. Alex wrote a story about a stream they found with a beaver dam. It was the only thing I'd seen that he had written about their lives together. His story talked about lying in the grass with Elise for an hour, watching silently, until a beaver had appeared. A three-year-old Elise was holding a plush beaver toy a few pages later.

I flopped onto my stomach and opened a journal. It was a newer journal, and Vanessa talked about the cancer and her concerns about Elise and Alex. She'd actually written out a speech for her own funeral services. One of the entries stopped my heart. It was a letter to Alex. She had written it on paper that had gold embossed designs around the corners. It was written in tidy, flowing cursive. She professed her deep love for him and told him she wouldn't be far away.

> *. . . I want you to find someone new. I don't want you to be alone. I'd love to leave someone behind who will love you the*

way I do. I wish I could choose her myself. It would break my heart to watch you bear life's burdens alone, to watch Elise miss out on a mother. Choose someone good, someone who will teach Elise good values and someone who can keep you in line when you get crabby.

Stay close to Elise for me. Don't let her forget me. I don't ever want her to doubt that I love her. I am so sorry I have to go. I never would have chosen to leave. I want you to know that. But it is right. I feel it now; somehow, I'm resigned to it, as though I don't belong here anymore. But I will leave my heart with you. You can bring it when you come.

I was crying when I finished reading it. I was crying for Vanessa and how hard it must have been to leave them. I was crying for Alex, thinking of how hard the last months of her life must have been. I was crying for Elise, who was missing exactly what Vanessa was afraid she'd be missing. I could read that Vanessa wanted him to find someone, but I couldn't reconcile it with the possibility that he could love me as much as he loved her. I knew I'd never ask him to stop loving her. I put my head in my hands and wished I were a better person. I wished I could swoop in, marry him, and make his and Elise's world right. But I was a selfish creature. I didn't want to share him forever.

The sound of Alex's car keys jingling in his hand startled me. He stood in the doorway for a while, looking thoughtfully at the unpacked boxes and photo albums before he sat down against the wall next to me and pulled the journal into his lap. It was only twelve thirty, and I hoped that the appointment with the attorney had gone well, since he was back earlier than he had planned. I didn't know if I should feel like an intruder. I wanted to ask about the attorney, but I didn't want to interrupt him while he read Vanessa's sacred letter. I didn't bother to wipe the tears from my eyes. I pulled another scrapbook to me and started flipping through it, acting as though I had every right.

He finished the letter then picked up another scrapbook. We didn't speak the entire time. I must not have been in trouble because he would hand me a new scrapbook or journal as soon as I set down an old one. We stayed in the room, occasionally opening a box, looking through journals and scrapbooks, until the doorbell rang at one o'clock. He left me to answer the door. I was surprised to hear the missionaries. I didn't leave the room. I knelt down and opened another box. Whatever was inside had been carefully wrapped in newspaper. I'd snooped this far; what was a little newspaper? I started digging. It was full of framed pictures of Vanessa, Elise, and Alex. I circumvented the sitting room and took a back route to the garage, where I found a toolbox.

Armed with a hammer, screwdriver, and box of small nails, I snuck back upstairs. An hour later, I stepped back to admire my work. Elise's wall was covered with pictures hung under a large floral arrangement I'd found in the boxes. Eventually I'd end up taking it all down to paint, but I knew Elise would appreciate having this to look at now, so it was worth it. I could still hear the missionaries, so I left Alex a note on the counter, telling him I was getting Elise, and I ran out to my car. I couldn't wait to show her the wall.

When we got home, I found Alex replacing my nails with anchors and screws. Elise gushed over the wall. She jumped wildly on her bed. "I love it! I love it! I love it!"

"I'll pick up some purple ribbon tomorrow for the swag, and we can put matching ribbon on your bed posts. I can work up a little lamp with purple silk flowers. We can work purple into a quilt. Maybe, if your dad will finance it, we can make a quilt with some pictures in the blocks." Elise leapt off of the bed and hugged me tightly.

Alex handed me the pictures to hold while he replaced the nails. When he was done, he showed Elise the scrapbooks. She had seen them all before, but it had been a long time. I left Alex and Elise in the box room so they could talk about Vanessa.

* * *

At home, I set my book down when the microwave beeped. I hopped off of the couch and bounded into the kitchen. I was starving. My nuked low-calorie meal tasted like cardboard after eating Alex's cooking, but I reminded myself it was for a good cause. I was still eating when Alex's familiar knock startled me. I carried my fork and cardboard food to the door and opened it. Alex was standing there with a plate of seared salmon and fresh asparagus. "I brought you dinner." He looked at the pasty noodles in my hand. "Yum, you beat me to it."

"Is salmon fattening?"

"It depends on where you get it."

"Is this one? Because it's making my dinner look very unappetizing."

"Nah, I'm sure it's fine," he replied. He walked past me and set it on the kitchen table. "This goes well with a really dry white wine." He put his hands in his pockets. "I'll never taste that again. It's funny to think about. I guess I'll donate my collection to Scott."

"I don't know what that's like, to drink something and then suddenly not be able to drink it anymore. It must be weird."

"There are a lot of new rules, commandments. It's almost overwhelming."

"The trick is not to feel confined by them but to search out how they liberate you. Every commandment has a reason, though some we don't fully understand." The fish flaked off when I touched it with my fork. "Oh, this is so good. Thank you. I think I'll go running in the morning."

"My attorney pointed out some major flaws with my offer. I was wondering if you could help me revise it a little so I can run it over to Scott."

"Sure." I took a few more bites and pushed the plate away. "Lead the way."

He sat down next to me at his desk while I edited the old files. Soon the printer whirred, and I pushed away from the computer. I yawned. "I don't think I got enough sleep last night."

"You woke up early. I didn't expect you to be such a good sport."

"Always am." I stood up and headed for the door.

"Jana?"

"Yeah?"

He looked like he was about to say something important but changed his mind. "Could you stay with Elise while I run this over? I don't know if Gretchen's staying tonight. She didn't call."

"I'll get Elise into bed; don't worry about it. I can't wait to hear how Scott takes it."

* * *

I read Vanessa's journals to Elise until she fell asleep. I could barely keep my own eyes open, so I grabbed a throw and headed downstairs to one of the fluffy leather couches. I ran back upstairs and stole a pillow off of Alex's bed. I tried not to look at his room, but it was impossible not to notice the masculine pieces of furniture. The bed was large, with great oak posts. It was outfitted with a dark paisley comforter and suede-looking pillows. I started down the hall but gave in and walked back to his room. I climbed into bed, justifying my actions as wanting to be close to Elise so I could hear if she needed me. I fell asleep as soon as I inhaled the slight scent of aftershave on the pillowcase.

I woke up when I heard the closet open. Alex was taking his shirt off. I sat up. "No. Don't yet." I rubbed my face and swung my legs out of bed.

"I'm sorry I'm so late." He sat on the end of the bed with his shirt open. "Scott and I ended up talking for a few hours. I think this is actually going to work out. I don't know why I didn't listen to you sooner."

I headed for the door, feeling drowsy. Alex picked up my shoes and followed me downstairs to the living room. "Are you upset?"

"No. I'm just a little beat."

"Scott was great. I think we came up with a better plan than either of us started with. We have to run it through the attorneys, but I know it will fly." I couldn't stand the way his chest lured my eyes anymore. I stepped forward and pulled his shirt closed. He laughed and fastened a few buttons.

I sat down on the couch, slipped my shoes on, then leaned back and closed my eyes.

"Do you need me to carry you home?"

"No. I can walk. I just need to talk myself into it. I'm surprised you're not tired."

"I was just going to crash down here. I didn't mean to wake you up. You can go back up to bed."

"I shouldn't sleep in your bed. I didn't want to use Gretchen's. Your bed looked so much more comfortable than the couch."

"It is." He sat down next to me. "You were crying when I got home this morning."

"It's all so sad. How can you stand it?"

"You learn to handle the cards you're dealt. Are you okay with everything you found today? It's not driving you away or anything? I still get the month?"

"Do you still want the month?"

"I ordered a ring today."

I suddenly felt more awake. I leaned over and hugged him, fighting happy tears. "I wish you hadn't."

He hugged me back. "You're gushing with disappointment. I can tell you're heartbroken. Could you hold me a little tighter?"

I let go, realizing my hug had been fierce with relief. He pulled me close and put his arm around me. I closed my eyes. "I was thinking, Vanessa doesn't have to wait a year to go through the temple."

"No?"

"I can take her name now. She can be baptized and ready for the sealing ordinance when the time comes."

"Would you *want* to do that?"

"Would you have a complete stranger do it?"

"I don't know if I want *you* to do it. Sometimes I feel like you're more loyal to her than you are to me. She's not even here anymore. I don't want the two of you getting any closer."

"I thought you might say something like that."

"Do you disagree?"

"Maybe it would be therapeutic for me to do it."

"I'll think about it."

We sat there too long, and I started to doze off again. Alex lifted me and carried me through the garage. I handed him the key. He kissed me good night, and I stumbled into the apartment. He armed the alarm and locked the door. I kicked my shoes off and fell asleep, thinking I wasn't ready for a ring.

CHAPTER 19
Two Nuts

A WEEK LATER, ALEX TOLD me to clear my schedule for Elise's birthday. It didn't take much to figure out he'd arranged his baptism. The missionaries had visited every day in the past week. I didn't want to feel like he was choosing the Church because of me. In my heart, I knew that wasn't the case. The greatest appeal of the gospel for him was the part that allowed families to be together forever. He was doing it for Vanessa and Elise.

I just about fainted when he walked me into the stake center and my parents, Rachel, and the baby were there. "Surprise!" they shouted.

"Wow. This is quite a surprise." I couldn't keep the excitement out of my voice.

Elise ran to my mother, her white dress flouncing. She hugged her and then hugged my father. My mother pulled some candy out of her purse.

My dad was already dressed in a white jumper. Alex leaned over to me. "You didn't think I'd have anyone else do it, did you?"

I hugged my family then claimed the baby. I sat on the couch, counting fingers and stroking baby Anna's face. Rachel sat beside me. "I should have made a quilt for your angel. I'll start one tomorrow" I said. "Oh, she's so perfect. How are the children adjusting?"

"They're adjusting fine. The flowers were gorgeous, by the way. Alex went overboard. The hospital room wasn't big enough to hold them. I had to send them home with Troy. Maybe we can start the quilt tomorrow."

"Tomorrow? How long are you staying?"

"Jana, I'm here on exile. They teamed up against me. They think it will help if I have a change of scenery for a few days."

I looked at my parents across the foyer. My mother was watching us with concern. "What's going on? Are you fighting with Troy?"

"No, nothing that bad. The kids are adjusting to the baby all right, but . . . I'm not. The doctor had to put me on antidepressants. I've never had anything like it. I just wanted to die. The medicine is working for the most part but . . ."

"They shipped you off anyway. I have a room for you. We'll have fun. I'm going to decorate Elise's bedroom this week. You can help. So you're staying here for the week and flying back with us for Thanksgiving? How long are Mom and Dad staying?"

"Yeah, I'll be here until then, and I think Mom and Dad are flying home tonight."

"That soon? I wish I could see them longer."

"Alex wanted them to stay longer too. They won't listen to him, which I find odd, considering they think he hung the moon. Did he?"

"Did he what?"

"Hang the moon?"

"Uh, yeah, pretty much," I admitted. "He's really that great."

"Didn't I see you holding hands when you walked in?" She had a teasing glint in her eyes. I nodded and rolled my eyes at her suggestive look. "And he's getting baptized. When are you getting married?"

"It's not like that." Alex was walking over to me. "I'll explain when we get home tonight."

I stood up, and he kissed me. "I need to get dressed. I'll see you on the other side."

*　*　*

We were the loudest table at Shallots. Scott brought out some sparkling nonalcoholic cider. He was beaming. Between acquiring the restaurant and inheriting Alex's wine collection, he'd made out like a bandit. The cider was terrible, but we smiled and drank it anyway. Alex ordered sodas for everyone. Elise held the baby most of the night. I wished I could have held her more. I could see the envy on my mother's face. At least I'd have Anna as a guest for a while.

"Are you sure you won't stay?" Alex asked my parents when the evening began to wind down.

"I'm working tomorrow afternoon," my dad reminded him.

"I guess you'd better go, then. But we could reschedule your flight for the morning," he offered.

"Best ship out tonight. We'll see you next week for the big turkey roast."

We still had some time before my parents had to be to the airport, so Alex showed my father around the restaurant. I was sure they'd just ducked into Alex's office to talk about me.

My mother demanded the baby and cooed to her while Elise balanced as much silverware as she could on an upside down goblet.

I turned to Rachel. "Even if you're only here because you're psycho, I'm glad. It's hard to see Mom and Dad go. And it'll be refreshing to see you. I feel a greedy joy having you all to myself for a while. I haven't really had that since you were married."

"I guess not. I'll tell you what though, I haven't had a vacation from dishes, laundry, and chauffeur duty for ten years. I'm going to milk this for all it's worth. I wish I didn't have to go crazy to get it, but I'll make it count. I already miss my kids. However, I have to admit, when I called to tell them that I landed safely and heard the chaos in the background, I looked around me at the airport and reveled in the peace and quiet."

"The airport is so crowded."

"It was peace and quiet compared to the other end of the phone." She smiled and changed the subject. "Alex and Dad are taking a long time." She twisted in her chair, looking for them.

"I'm sure they're talking about me. Dad's pretty sure I'm crazy too right now. I wonder why they decided to pair the nuts up."

"I don't know, but let's make the most of it. We'll make a quilt. We'll make five. We can spoil Elise rotten. I can't wait to see what you're doing to her room."

"Alex said I could decorate his room and the country house too."

"Oh, the country house, I see. The Bellevue house, the Seattle house, the Park City condo. Are there more?"

"Probably," I admitted. I told her about driving to the Bellevue house and realizing it was his.

"So was he just not going to tell you it was his? How many houses does he have hidden away?"

"I don't know. He's a little quirky about admitting how much he has. He doesn't share a lot of numbers with me. I see the books, but I've never seen his personal accounts. The restaurant is doing well. It's like he thinks the money will scare me away or something."

"Aaaah, run! Rich, handsome, famous guy. Help me! Help me!" Rachel waved her hands in the air.

Elise burst out laughing. I always forgot her little ears were nearby.

I jumped when Alex put his hands on my shoulders. "You called?"

We all laughed. I felt sorry for the customers who'd come for a quiet, romantic evening.

* * *

I got Rachel settled then headed over to the house to tuck Elise in. Alex was already in her room. "I like the way you just let yourself in, like you already live here."

"Oh, sorry."

"No. I really like it. I'm being serious," he assured me.

"I just wanted to talk to Elise before she went to sleep." I sat on the side of her bed, and Alex stood in the doorway. "I brought you this." I handed her a little wallet-sized frame with a picture of Jesus in the River Jordan. "I wanted you to have it to remind you that you'll receive the gift of the Holy Ghost when it's your turn to be baptized. When you listen to the Holy Ghost, God will always point you in the right direction, even if you can't see it's right at the time."

She set down the doll I'd given her earlier that day. "Like the Liahona?"

I suddenly felt guilty for not being more involved in their conversion. She knew so much already. I vowed to teach Elise something every day. "Exactly like that. Good night, sweetie." I kissed her forehead and headed downstairs.

Alex caught me in the kitchen. "Wait. Are you going to take time off this week? I need to teach Scott the books anyway."

"I might take some time off, but I won't go far."

"I'm a little jealous. Rachel's going to cut into the time I get with you."

"Like we don't spend enough time together already. That's what got us into this mess."

"I'd rather you didn't refer to the happiest part of my life as a mess." He lifted me onto the counter and kissed me.

"Okay, you're making me dizzy, and my brain's shutting down."

"You can't live without me."

Knowing that he needed to hear it, I gave in and admitted, "I can't live without you." He lifted me down and spun me around. "Okay, not helping with the dizzy euphoria. It's time to let the blonde fluffy lady wobble home."

He kissed me again. "I'd better hold you up."

"Suddenly the word *swooning* has more meaning in my life."

Alex laughed and carried me home. I protested the whole way. When he set me down on the couch, I thought Rachel's eyes were going to pop out of her head. ". . . totally unnecessary," I continued the argument we'd been having in the garage. He laughed, told Rachel good night, and left.

"Good to see you two getting along."

"I was a little dizzy. He was overreacting."

Rachel pulled a blanket to her and started nursing the baby. "I like the apartment. I love the tub. I'll come visit just for that. I can't wait to try it. The view is to die for. Are we a little spoiled?"

"He is good to me, but I'll have you know, the old apartment smelled like a coffin, had no water pressure, and sported yellow cupboards."

"How was the tub?"

"Claw foot, old fashioned, huge. But the water heater was small, and there was never enough hot water to fill it. I mostly showered."

"I've got all night; start spilling the beans," she invited.

"You're going to think I'm stupid. Just don't tell me that at the end. I don't want to hear it. I want to hear consoling words."

"I was watching Mister Beefsteak with you tonight, and I doubt there's much reason to console. He looks at you like you're his sun. He gravitates toward you in every movement. He—"

"I get the picture. Do you want to hear this or not?"

"Shoot."

I told her about realizing I was attracted to him, him moving the cat figurines in my room, fishing with Dad . . . I told her everything and relived every moment. I described how Brad had looked in the police car. I cried when I came to the happy moment at the temple when Alex had realized Vanessa would be his forever. I told her about Angela in the bathroom and showed her my new sunglasses. I told her about Brad at the restaurant. I ended by telling her about the pictures I'd hung in Elise's room last week and how Alex had said he'd ordered the ring. "That pretty much catches you up."

"You're right. I want to smack you."

"That was consoling. I knew you'd think of something to comfort me."

"What are sisters for?" She smiled brightly.

It was almost midnight when we finished talking. I lay back on the couch. "Wow, that was really cathartic. Thanks for listening. I bet you're sorry you asked."

"I'm glad I came. Maybe I can talk some sense into you."

"Tomorrow. Right now, I'm going to bed."

* * *

I was surprised to find April in my apartment when I got back from taking Elise to school. "I'm taking Rachel to the spa. She needs a break."

Rachel handed me the baby with a giddy expression. "I'm going to get the works. Apparently, Alex has some connections."

April hugged me. "I'm going to take a mud bath. I'll tell you what it's like." She giggled. I couldn't believe they were just going to leave me home. Of course, Rachel could use a break, and someone needed to watch the baby. April was a good dose of medicine for depression, but I still felt left out. Rachel pointed out all of the supplies I would need and left me with a car seat and a reminder that I had her phone number.

"If my family calls to check up on me, tell them I'm in therapy." She fluttered out the door after April.

I sat down on the couch and snuggled Anna. After twenty minutes of cooing at her, I'd nearly forgotten that I'd been slighted. Alex knocked on the back door. "Come in." When he walked into the front room, I told him, "You can just let yourself in; you don't have to knock."

"No. Don't give me that kind of power. We'll keep it formal until you give up and marry me. A man can only handle so much temptation." He sat down beside me and cooed at the baby.

"You sound pretty confident that I'll give in."

"It's just a matter of time. You'll come to your senses. You can't live without me."

"Not a doubt in your mind?"

"If there was competition or something, sure, but there isn't. And I know how you feel about me. You've said it yourself. I know you can't continue to deny the words coming out of your own mouth, the kisses coming from your own lips. Give me that baby." He held her up and rubbed noses with her.

I thought for a moment. It had been a while since I'd heard from him, but I decided Jeff still counted as competition even if we were a little behind on dating. "There's Jeff."

"I called him for you. There's no Jeff."

"Alex!"

"Were you going to go out with him again?" He kissed Anna's cheek. His charms were working on her, just like they did on every other woman. She smiled and clutched his fingers.

"No, but it wasn't your place."

"I didn't see you calling him. You can't just leave him hanging out there like that. We're golfing on Thursday after we stop at the mall."

I laughed, realizing that Jeff was going to stop by to see Melee. "Great, now *you* can date him."

"He was more attached to you than I thought. He didn't take it very well until I invited him golfing."

"I'm glad a few clubs and a little ball could soothe his sorrow."

"You know Jeff. He's not one to wallow in self-pity."

"He's not one to turn down a free game of golf either."

"Don't feel bad. He's not the only one. Scott was asking if you had any single sisters. I explained the whole abstinence before marriage thing, and he decided you weren't such a great catch after all."

"Oh." I shuddered. "I guess that's how the world at large feels about the issue." Anna was still holding his finger with her tiny hand. "It's another change you'll have to make." I shifted uncomfortably. I assumed he'd had many opportunities to play around.

He raised an eyebrow at me. "You're curious. I can tell you want to know."

"No. I'm sure I don't." My face blazed red.

"Since I know how backward your brain is lately, I'll just tell you. I didn't take my wedding ring off until I took your father fishing."

I tried to stifle my sigh of relief. I held my hands out for the baby, but he pulled her possessively close. "When do *I* get to go to the spa?" I pouted.

"That would be defeating the point. The point was to get you to myself."

"I'm so jealous. They're lying there getting back rubs and sipping sodas."

"I didn't know it was something you would like to do. You can go today."

"I would if you could go with me."

He smiled. "I'm not really a spa type of guy, but I'll give you a back rub."

"No." I held out my hands for the baby again, but he wouldn't hand her to me.

"What do you want to do today? We can take the baby," he offered.

"I was planning on holding the baby all day." He still didn't hand her to me.

"My mother's dying to meet you, and she loves babies. We could just show up with Anna. I'd love to see her face. You know what she'd think? We'd have to tell her the truth before she killed me, but all the same, I'd like to see her expression."

I bit my bottom lip. I wasn't sure I was ready to meet his mother.

"We can't sit around here all day, Jana. Let's go make a little old lady very happy. She could use a baby fix."

"I guess if you call her and warn her, it would be okay."

Alex called her on the way. I noticed he didn't tell her we were bringing Anna, so I made him call her back. He flipped the phone closed. "You ruin all my fun. She's going to cook us lunch. I will just qualify that statement with the fact that my mother's cooking is why I became a chef."

I suddenly felt intimidated by the fact that I couldn't break an egg without having to fish the shell out of the bowl.

When she opened the door, I gasped. Elise Steadman was where Alex got his good looks. She had honey brown hair styled into a perfect bob. She was my height, and her hazel eyes were lined with thick lashes. Her nose had the same lines as Alex's, but it was downsized to fit her delicate face. Her lips formed a perfect rose ribbon. She smiled a flawless smile. "Jana," she hugged me tightly, "it's so good to meet you."

"It's good to meet you too." My words were muffled in her freesia-scented hair. She invited us in, and I couldn't help but notice how beautiful her home was. "You have a lovely home. I like what you've done with it." I turned to Alex. "Did you grow up here?"

He was holding Anna, but when Elise held her hands out for her, he reluctantly handed her over. "No. We had this house built a few years ago. I did, however, grow up in the yellow hovel next door."

"That's the guesthouse now," Elise qualified. "Couldn't get him out of that old willow to save my life."

"This was Uncle Todd's cow pasture."

"How was your baptism, dear?"

"Good."

I studied the white carpet. She'd known about the baptism but hadn't come. All Alex had in the world for support was me and my family. I slipped my fingers into his hand and stood closer to him. Elise had the same talent for stories that Alex had. She asked me a few questions then started telling me stories about Alex. Like him, she seemed to sense what would most entertain the person with whom she was speaking. She was very energetic and animated when she talked.

She told us she'd made chicken soup with homemade noodles for lunch. We followed her into the dining room. When we sat down, Alex leaned over and whispered, "One, don't pray out loud. Two, my brother and I call this porcupine soup for a reason. Watch for bones."

I looked at him quizzically.

Alex dished some soup for me.

Elise gushed that Alex had finally found someone. She remarked several times that I was "cute as a button." I tried not to cringe at her copious use of the word *cute*. She was a very gleeful person.

The soup was greasy and bland. It did indeed have small bones floating around in it. The noodles were a fourth-inch thick, and they were very chewy. I wished she'd served something on a plate so I could have pushed it around to look like I'd touched it. The only way to be polite with the soup was to eat it. I carefully spooned the watery broth to my lips, avoiding anything that floated. I looked sideways at Alex, understanding for the first time what he really meant about his mother being the reason he'd become a chef.

Elise asked me about my family, quizzing me about my siblings and parents. Then she moved on to my education and the jobs I'd held. It started to feel like an interview. Alex tickled my side when he slid his arm around me. I tried not to squirm. I noticed he hadn't eaten much of his soup either. I set my spoon down, figuring if he wasn't finishing it, I didn't have to either.

He thanked her for lunch and said we had to get the baby back to her mother. Elise walked us to the door, not surprised by the short duration of the visit. She handed the baby to Alex and hugged me tightly. "You are a darling." She reached up and patted Alex's cheek like he was a little boy. "She's a good find. Good job."

I slipped into the car while Alex fastened Anna in the car seat. I couldn't help feeling I'd just come inside after a windstorm. Elise spoke so fast, with such a high level of energy, that I felt tired watching her lips move.

"That was a short visit," I noted.

"I can only take so much of my mother. I try to visit often and quickly," Alex admitted.

"She's very nice."

"She's hyper and flighty. Can you see why my father travels?"

"I think she's very beautiful. I'm sure it can't be all that bad. You did name Elise after her."

"It was actually Vanessa's idea. Mom never liked Vanessa. Vanessa didn't like her much either, but she liked the name and decided it would be a decent peace offering. It worked. My mother mellowed out a little after that."

"Did you pay for their new house?"

"I paid for half of it." He started on another tangent. "Your family, Jana, is amazing. I never knew exactly what I wanted my family to be like, but I always knew I didn't want it to be like the one I came from. Now I've seen your family, how it works, and I know what I want. We're going to build a family like yours. All of our children will know their worth. We'll vacation often, teach them to work, pray every day. They're going to turn out like you and Rachel."

I didn't respond. In my mind, I saw a heavenly backdrop with Alex in the middle. Vanessa was standing on one side of him, Elise holding her hand, and I was standing on the other side, flanked by several children. I took a little satisfaction that my side was bigger but immediately felt ashamed at the thought. I sank down in my seat, deciding I was really a horrible creature.

"Does it bother you when I talk about *you* being the mother of my children?"

I sighed. "How many children do you want?"

"All of them."

"That's a lot. I don't know if I can pull that one off."

"I mean, all of them that are supposed to come to us. I don't want to leave anyone out. Do you think about them waiting for us?"

I had a vision of children peeking down at us from celestial clouds. They were the same little Janas and Alexes I'd just imagined a moment before. Suddenly, a whole other dimension crowded my quandaries. I looked sideways at Alex, wondering if he was aware of the new pressure he was adding. He raised innocent eyebrows at me and looked back to the road. I sat up a little straighter, thinking of unseen children in the backseat beside Anna, watching me, their future mother.

Giving up on waiting for an answer, he asked if I wanted to go to lunch. I agreed, and we drove to a little dive of a Chinese restaurant. "Don't judge it by the cover. It's the best little secret in Seattle," Alex asserted.

He insisted on holding Anna while he ate. When she started working her mouth over her fists, he gave her a cloth napkin to suck on. I pulled out a bottle. Rachel had already measured the formula. I added the water. Deciding my chances of getting the baby away from Alex were slim, I handed him the bottle. She drank eagerly. I wondered if Jeff liked babies and children like Alex did but realized it didn't really matter since Alex had done me the service of dismissing Jeff. I tried to drudge up some frustration over his meddling but couldn't, especially when I thought of the way Jeff looked at Melee.

"I have another social function tomorrow night," Alex said. "I don't suppose you'd like to flank my arm again. It will be like the literacy dinner."

"I'd love to. I'll have to pick up a dress."

"After we eat, we'll have another hour before we pick up Elise. I'll buy whatever dress you want."

"*I'll* buy whatever dress I want. And we need to talk about rent."

"*Rent*? Jana, I thought we'd covered this already. I'm not charging you rent."

"How can we say I'm renting an apartment from you if there's no rent involved?" He stared at me with a complacent grin. The sounds of Anna suckling the bottle were suddenly amplified. I melted under his gaze. My neck grew warm. He was mine for the taking. All I had to do was stand up and make my bid. "Alex, I . . ." I couldn't do it. I had to think it out. Making a decision under the power of his gaze wasn't a prudent thing to do. "I think you're the most beautiful man I've ever seen." I lowered my eyes and smoothed the napkin on my lap.

"And you want to have my children."

I blushed and looked away with a giggle. "I *want* to pay you rent."

"I'll let you pay half the electricity, and I'll take ten bucks a month for rent."

"You call that rent?"

"Tell me how much you want to pay, and I'll increase your monthly salary by that much."

"You can't do that. I feel unethical already, getting all of these perks just because I'm dating my boss, which I shouldn't be doing."

"Okay, you're fired."

"And I'm supposed to live in the apartment for free now? Stay in Washington without a job?" I asked calmly. "Like I'm your pet?" I batted my eyelashes.

"And bear my children, mother Elise, help out with some light bookkeeping—you know, the basics." He leaned toward me over the table, suddenly seething with frustration. "How do you take something so simple, like falling in love, and make it this complicated? Look at it logically. Forget the world; just look at it logically. Can you live without me? Could you pick up and go, never seeing me again?"

My stomach knotted, and I couldn't help the way my face dropped like I'd eaten a sour grape.

"Could you?" he asked again.

"No." Anna started to fuss. "Give me the baby. I'll burp her." I put a napkin over my shoulder and started patting her back.

He pointed at me, still leaning forward. "Do you doubt that I love and adore you? Do you doubt that I will take care of you for the rest of your life?"

"No. I don't doubt it." Hearing him say it made me want to leap across the table and hug him.

He leaned back and lifted his hands. "Then *where* is the problem?"

"She won't burp." I laid Anna on her stomach across my lap and started rubbing her back. She let out a belch that practically rattled the ice cubes in my cup. I made a mental note to tell Rachel about that one.

Alex rounded the table and pulled a chair next to mine. He leaned over so I could feel his breath on my neck. "The problem, Jana? Where is it?"

"I can't think when you're this close to me." I set Anna in her car seat and wiped her face.

"Maybe you're thinking too much."

I put my hand on his chest and pushed him away softly. "Okay, you can buy me a dress."

"See, we can work this out. A little compromise here, a little compromise there. You can pay me ten dollars for rent."

"That would be hard without a job. Maybe I can keep working for Shallots with flexible hours so I can help you with Elise for free."

"I can arrange that."

Thankfully, that seemed to satisfy him, and he let me leave larger questions unanswered though it was obvious that he was growing impatient.

* * *

Alex dropped me off with the baby before he picked up Elise. Rachel was sprawled blissfully across the couch. "Do you think he'll get me a spa pass for my birthday every year?"

"I'd forgotten I was jealous until now."

"Doesn't he ever pay for you to go?"

"He said I could go today, but I didn't want to give up the baby."

"What did you do today?"

"He showed up right after you left. Apparently, he was getting you out of the house. He held the baby and wouldn't give her back. I met his mother. He took me to lunch. And then we went shopping for a dress for our date tomorrow night."

"I can't quite peg your relationship. I don't know who's quirkier, you or him. Let me see the dress."

I grabbed it from the kitchen, where I'd left it when I walked in. I pulled down the plastic, and she let out an excited, "Oh! Oh! Oh!"

"It's more than I would have spent, but Alex liked it." It was a burgundy velvet dress with little gems embroidered around a V-neck collar. The bodice was darted, and the skirt cascaded into fluted panels. When I tried it on, he liked it so much that he had me turn around so he could take the tag. He sent me to get dressed while he paid for it. I had to admit that it was flattering.

* * *

After school the next day, Elise and I set up a quilting frame in my living room. Alex and Rachel were gone. There was a note on the table, saying they went to order the pie for Thanksgiving. "That's likely," I muttered, wondering why the Master Chef would *order* a pie.

We had the quilt mostly tied by the time the phone rang. "Hello, gorgeous, did you miss us?"

"You can't just kidnap my sister. What are you doing? Bring her back."

"She wanted to see the country house."

"It's all good and fine to talk to her for a half hour while I pick up Elise, but three hours is a little excessive, isn't it?"

"We're bringing dinner home for Rachel and Elise. You'll need to be ready in twenty minutes if we're going to have time to drive to the banquet. I'll send Rachel in with the food, but I need to shave and get dressed. I'll pick you up at seven."

We hung up. I looked at Elise, trying to decide how safe it was to leave her with the nearly perfect quilt and a needle. Rachel walked into the living room with her arm draped in bags and set the car seat on the floor.

I glared at her.

"Okay, okay, don't be mad. I told him we had to get you some shoes to match the dress. You are *so* going to love these." She knelt down on the floor, and I knelt down beside her.

"Did Alex buy all of this?"

"Yes."

I opened a bag and pulled out several items of clothing meant for Anna. "And he had to spoil the baby? Did you even go to the country house?"

"We drove by it. Pretty out there." She handed me a pair of strappy burgundy heels. "I tried them on for you and picked the most comfortable pair. Don't you love them? Aren't they great?"

"I don't know if we should be encouraging his buying sprees," I lamented.

Rachel took Elise by the hand and had her sit down beside us. I gingerly lifted the needle out of her hand before she dropped it. "And this bag is for you. You are going to love it. I bought one like this for my daughter last month. Gorgeous. Just gorgeous."

Elise pulled out a dainty yellow dress and squealed with delight. "Can I try it on now?"

"Wait, don't forget the rest." Rachel pulled out a beautiful matching bow barrette.

"It feels a little like Christmas morning, doesn't it?" I admitted. "Go ahead; try it on."

"Does it ever! Good heavens, he's wonderful." Rachel fanned herself.

"He's won his way into your heart with money; remember that," I admonished.

"He's *so* romantic." She glanced at Elise, who had forgone changing in private and was stripping down in the living room. "The things I could tell you when you get home tonight would make your head spin." I suddenly wished we were alone. "Elise, why don't you stay with me and help with the baby while I finish the quilt? Jana, you have fifteen minutes. Go get dressed."

I ran to my room in a panic. I was fastening my earrings when I heard Alex in the living room. He knocked on the door and opened it. "Are you ready?"

"Almost. I just have to get my shoes. That was a pretty expensive pie you ordered."

"Don't worry. My friend is in Salt Lake, so it won't be stale. I can't see taking it on the plane."

"That's not what I meant."

"Are you referring to the gift Rachel has for spending my money? It made her happy. Isn't that the point? She is here to cheer up. I can buy cheer."

I turned to chastise him but couldn't speak. Once again, he was breathtaking in his tux. I sighed and looked up at him sappily. "You're hopeless." I tried to remember how I used to sit next to him day in and day out resisting his smile.

He pulled me up and spun me around, looking me over. "You really are a stunning woman."

I slipped into the shoes they'd just bought me and looked in the full-length mirror. They really did look better than the black ones I was going to wear.

We walked into the living room to say good-bye to Rachel and Elise.

Rachel sat down on the couch, resting her elbows on her knees and her chin in her hands. She sighed. "Watching you two is really making me miss Troy. I wish he were here. I wish we were going with you. I want to borrow that dress when I get home. Maybe he'll take me downtown for dinner." She sat up and surveyed us with a mischievous grin. "Oh, I wish I had a camera."

"It's not prom, Rachel." I said.

"Don't worry," Alex assured her, "I'm sure there will be plenty of cameras. We can download pictures later."

As we left, I looked over my shoulder at Rachel. She pointed at Alex and pantomimed fanning herself then fainting with delight on the couch. I rolled my eyes at her, though I had to admit she had a point. Elise was having snorting fits of laughter. I was sure they were going to get along fine while we were gone.

On the way out to the car, I held Alex's hand, and he helped me in before climbing into the driver's seat.

"I was thinking we should leave for Utah tomorrow," he commented. "We don't want to get stuck in the Thanksgiving crowd."

"Two days early? I guess it's worth it to beat some of the crowd. I don't think Rachel will want to go. It will be too soon for her; three days isn't a lot of time to get a grip on the depression she's dealing with. It will be hard to get a good flight if we're leaving tomorrow."

"It's not a problem. I'm going to stay in the condo though. Your mother will have enough to handle with your whole family there."

"Doesn't it bother your mother that she won't see you Thursday?"

"Thanksgiving with my mother. Think about that. It ceased to be a problem as soon as we were old enough to drive away. *Food* and *my house* aren't exactly words anyone should use in the same sentence."

I smiled. "She isn't very sentimental, is she?"

"She's sentimental about some things in her own little world. She has books full of pictures of grandkids, more than she ever had of us when we were little. Elise doesn't like visiting. She can't touch anything, and the white carpet doesn't lend itself to children playing. My mother is very concerned about children sullying her possessions." He drum rolled on the steering wheel. "I don't want to stay too long tonight. Do you want to watch a late movie or anything when we get home?"

"We shouldn't. I have to get ready to leave tomorrow, and truth be told, I've been dying to get home so I can pump Rachel for information."

"So that's how it works, is it? She's your spy and not mine."

"Unless she's playing double agent, in which case I'll have to pummel her."

"She didn't tell me anything I didn't already know. I tried all afternoon. She could be a politician, talking all the time but never really saying anything."

I laughed hard. I forgot how well Rachel could handle people. It seemed the great Alex Steadman had met his match.

* * *

Rachel was sewing something new and Elise was asleep on the couch when we got home. Alex gently lifted his daughter. I followed him across the garage to get the door for him. When I came back, Rachel was holding up a skirt.

"What do you think? I had extra fabric, but not a ton, so I made it for Elise. She can wear it to church after the novelty of the new dress wears off."

"I know she'll love it." I decided not to beat around the bush with our travel plans. "We're leaving tomorrow for Thanksgiving. Are you going to be okay with that? I know it's not as long a stay as you were planning on."

"I do miss the children. And watching you and Alex has made me homesick for Troy. I want to go home and thank him . . . I just"—her eyes watered—"I don't think he knows how much I appreciate him. It's time to get back to my own romance. I think I'm ready to go home. I miss them all so much."

"I thought you'd be less eager to go."

"It was a nice rest. I think it did the trick." She stood up and yawned. "That man looked like a Greek god in a tux. I can't wait to show Mom. You promise there are pictures?"

I sat down and started tugging my nylons off. "I promise. Speaking of *that man*, he said you weren't in the least bit enlightening today when you two went out. Thank you."

"I try."

"So dish," I commanded.

"I'll dish. First, I really want to smack you. He's so sweet. I don't know what your holdup is. He said he'd wait the year to marry you in the temple, but then he got silent and morose. He doesn't have a doubt in the world that you'll marry him. After seeing you together, I don't have a doubt either. You know, you finish each other's sentences, you move at the same time in the same way.

"I'm serious. And I'm not exaggerating. In fact, I'd say I was putting it mildly. I could see it a little when you came out for Dad's surgery, but it's grown to so much more than that. It's like you're already married."

I pulled her into the bedroom while I changed into pajamas. "So what was bothering him? No. Let me guess—waiting for children."

"He's worried you'll die before he can take you to the temple, and then you'll never be his forever." She sat down on the bed. "So romantic. Poor thing, especially after losing his wife. I guess the Brad thing really got to him. I never would have thought Brad could break down like that. He's too stiff, for one thing."

"So that's why Alex is so protective? He thinks I'm going to die?"

"Brad and fire aside, surely you can understand why he'd worry about something like that. I gather he holds tight to the people he loves, especially after Vanessa died. He took me to see her grave."

"No." My mouth gaped in disbelief. He'd never even done that with me.

"Yes. Why does that surprise you?"

"He's never even taken me there. Tell me about it."

"It was on a grassy hill with a beautifully engraved marker and a marble bench. He cleared the leaves off of it and sat down on the bench to tell me what I just told you."

"I don't believe it."

"Come here so I can smack you. I can already see you'd do anything to make him happy. You can't stand to see him the least bit uncomfortable. Marry him already and put him out of his misery. Then when you're hit by a car, he can still take you to the temple next November."

"With Vanessa. He could make a whole day of it. Two wives with one stone," I said more bitterly than I'd intended.

"You are so wrong about this. You *can* feel that you're wrong, can't you? You're usually levelheaded. You've got to have some sense of how wrong your thinking is here."

"I guess I've never come to terms with my polygamist ancestry, if that's what you're going on about."

"Polygamist? Jana, you'll be his only wife. The other one is dead."

"While we're here, I'll be the only one. Then what? I can't share him forever. I love him too much." I sat down on the bed as tears filled my eyes.

"Your only other alternative is to lose him," Rachel said disgustedly. "Both of you would only be half a person. You belong together. God has done this on purpose, Jana. Can't you see that? From Vanessa leaving your résumé out to this moment—this whole thing is destiny."

"I don't believe in destiny. We are governed by our choices."

Rachel shot eye daggers at me. "Polygamy was necessary at the time, wasn't it? Think about the tiny, budding army of God. Think of the opposition. How do you grow a large enough army in the beginning to withstand the blows of Satan? God needed to place as many of His children as He could under the covenant as quickly as He could, and polygamy helped aid in that effort."

"That's deep. I've never thought about it that way before."

"And it feels wrong to us because it *is* wrong now. We intuitively feel that polygamy is wrong. *Back then*, it was right. What you're talking about is eternity, not polygamy. God will work that out. It will be right, and you will feel it is right at the time because you will know His will. If you would just wake up for five minutes, you'd see it the way everyone else does. Wouldn't you rather share him than lose him?"

I had warm tears streaming down both cheeks. "Am I crazy?"

She took pity on me and put her arm around my shoulder. "Join the club, sister. Join the club." I cried a long time while she held me. "Jana, I love you. I hope I'm not too hard on you, but you need it this time. You're usually making my little brain see the right way. Maybe after all these years, I can do it for you." She sighed heavily. "Maybe you can come see the shrink with me. Did I tell you I get a shrink?"

"No, are you okay with that?"

"They take this postpartum thing seriously now. Don't want me to go too far off the deep end and take an ax to everyone."

"Nice. Rachel, I'm so selfish. I haven't even talked to you about your problems."

"Apparently my problems are only temporary, until my hormones settle down. I wouldn't wish it on anyone though. I mean, sometimes I can't see the use of staying on earth anymore. It's like I'm shouting in my head about what a horrible mom I am, how hideous my housekeeping is, how I'm not doing enough to make my husband happy. It makes me sick. I can't stand to look in the mirror some days. And every time I look at my family, I feel unworthy to have them."

"It's not true, Rachel. It's just Satan trying to get the best of you. He's just following you around until you realize it's not your voice at all. It's his. Those are things he wants you to believe. I've seen you with Troy and the kids. I know it isn't true. And I wouldn't feel bad eating off of your floor. You could stand to be messier. It would be healthy for you."

"I'll admit it's Satan putting these things in my head if you'll admit it's Satan tainting your thoughts. Can you trust your family? We all see it, what you can't. Isn't it possible you're in the wrong? Isn't it possible that God is over all and that He will work out the differences after you die so you'll be happy—the celestial kingdom is called *never-ending happiness* for a reason, you know?"

"I'll think about it. You've given me a lot to think about." I crawled onto the bed, fluffed pillows so I could lie down, and stared at the ceiling. Rachel did the same. We studied the white textured shadows. I reached down and held her hand like I used to when we were little. I squeezed her hand. "I bet it's like Shakespeare. All the world is a stage . . . Our minds are the stage, and if we give Satan an audience, he'll dance all over our stage. The trick is to look away so he doesn't have anyone to perform for. He'll be as much our constant companion as the Holy Ghost is if we let him."

Rachel squeezed my hand. "Okay, you win the deep thinking contest."

"When you look in the mirror, see what God sees, Rachel. I can't stand to think you'd hate yourself so much."

"It's not that bad anymore. I'm doing better. The pills help. This has helped." She lifted our hands. "I needed a vacation so I could look objectively at what I have at home." We were silent for a while. I wondered if she'd fallen asleep. Then she said, "Alex loves you."

"I know."

"You're supposed to marry him."

"I guess I know that too. I'm still trying to accept it, that's all. Aren't we a pair, making ourselves miserable over nothing?" We laughed and sniffed. Anna started crying.

"Time for the chow wagon. Usually, I wake up for this. It's nice to be already awake for once."

"I think I'm just going to go to sleep. I'll pack in the morning."

"I didn't bring much. It will be harder to pack for Anna than it will be to pack for me. I don't know how I'll fit all the stuff Alex bought her."

"You can use one of my suitcases. I still have most of my stuff at home."

I brushed my teeth. Rachel slept in my room instead of hers, like when we were children. I didn't want to be far away from her either. She was my sanity in any storm.

CHAPTER 20
Turkey Roast

"And that's the gist of it," Alex said at the end of the condo tour.

"When you said *condo*, I was thinking a little apartment."

"It's smaller than the house."

"Not by much."

"Why don't you stay awhile tonight? We can pop popcorn—"

"And watch Mechagodzilla!" Elise enthused.

"Are you sure you don't want to stay in the valley?" I asked him again.

"For your mother's sake, we need to stay here. The house is full enough already."

"She won't understand."

"Nonetheless, you can't deny I have a point."

"You do," I admitted.

"You can stay here," he offered. "I have plenty of rooms."

"My dad would have an aneurism. I'm still his little girl."

Alex looked at Elise. "I guess you are. Are you going to be okay driving the canyon?"

"Been doing it all my life. It's a pretty easy road."

"I want you to call me when you make it to the mouth of the canyon. Then when you make it off the freeway. Then when you get home."

"I'm pretty sure it would be more dangerous to drive while I'm on the phone. I'll call you when I get home. It will be thirty minutes, tops." I leaned in to hug him. "I love you. Don't worry. I'll see you tomorrow. I promise."

He didn't look like he believed me.

On the drive home, my eyes often darted to the side of the road, looking for deer waiting to ambush me. I drove more slowly than necessary and found an old Cadillac that looked safe to follow. Something about what Rachel had told me felt ominous. It was as though I could suddenly die and miss my eternity with Alex. I called him from the driveway of my parents' home. I could feel his relief through the phone.

*　*　*

On Thanksgiving morning, Alex and I ended up running to the grocery store for last-minute yams and other items that were sure to be sold out. I tore the list in half, and we agreed to meet at the register. I was placing cornmeal in the basket when I noticed Brad staring at me from the end of the aisle. He was with a beautiful black-haired woman. She was reading olive oil labels. I smiled. She looked like someone I'd be friends with. She had an angelic quality to her face and had kind, round eyes. He didn't look like his old self. His posture wasn't as straight. His hair wasn't as tidy. He was still handsome but nothing like the sleek panther he used to be. He had gained a little weight, so his face had a more boyish quality to it. They looked good together.

I smiled but didn't call out to him. He sunk his hands in his pockets—his jean pockets. I'd never seen him wear jeans before. He smiled back resignedly. I pointed at the woman and made a thumbs up sign. He smiled a little bigger and nodded. I got the idea that he wasn't necessarily eager for me to meet her. I made a motion with my thumb to warn him that Alex was in the store a few aisles over. He nodded and looked behind him nervously. I couldn't help laughing. He stifled a laugh when he looked back and saw me chuckling. I waved a small good-bye. He waved back. I turned the cart around, suddenly anxious to get Alex out of the store.

I found him, of all places, behind the meat counter, showing the butcher techniques to cut fillets. He was wearing an apron and looked intent on staying awhile.

"I hate to ruin your fun, but we're expected at home. Maybe you could come back tomorrow."

"I suppose you're right." He pulled the apron over his head and shook hands with the butcher.

I gathered the groceries he'd set on the counter and herded him to the register before we had a chance to run into Brad.

*　*　*

The Thanksgiving crowd filled every spare chair in the house. They were mostly interested in Alex. I didn't get to talk to him very much because he spent most of the time entertaining my siblings. As I sat at the table pushing corn around with my fork, I decided it wasn't much better than one of his social functions, though at least there was hope that my family would come to accept him as commonplace after a time. I blinked hard, realizing I was thinking of the future like it was real. The truth was, I couldn't imagine sitting at any future Thanksgiving without him. Rachel caught my eye and smiled reassuringly. I tried to return the same emotion in my smile to her.

Soon it was dark and everyone was piling into cars. My mother was beseeching Alex to stay the night. He wouldn't. Elise was asleep on the couch. He carried her to the car. I opened the door for him. He buckled her in then turned to hold me. His breath frosted into clouds. "Look at that. Do you live here? I hardly saw you all day. What was your name?" He kissed me. "You taste familiar. Why don't you come home with me?"

"Uh, no." I was laughing. He looked striking in his black wool overcoat and white scarf.

He leaned down to my ear and whispered, "What if I told you your mother was a really good cook."

"I'm sure if she heard that, *she'd* go home with you." I had only worn my sweater outside, and I shivered a little. He slid his coat off and draped it around my shoulders.

"Step into my office." He opened the car door.

"You're not kidnapping me, are you?"

"No, I just want to talk, and I don't want you to have blue lips." I sat down in the car, and he turned up the heater.

"What is it?" I asked.

"I just missed you. It's frustrating having you so close and not being able to spend time with you."

"It was irksome, wasn't it? Maybe next year you can fake a cold so you don't have to talk so much."

"So there is a next year? I'm only asking because my month is up next week."

I remained quiet. I couldn't lie and say there wasn't a next year, but I still needed to work out my reservations about sharing him forever with Vanessa. In the time since Rachel and I had talked, I'd felt my heart change slightly. I wanted to will myself to come around, but I knew I still needed to trust God a little more. I felt selfish again and wished I could hide under a rock.

He didn't press the question. He just sighed and took my hand. "Next year we'd better be driving away together."

"We probably will be," I admitted.

He smiled a tired smile, and I had to wonder exactly what I'd been putting him through. He walked me back to the door, where I gave him his coat. "Get some sleep," he ordered.

"Yes, sir," I replied. He kissed my forehead then walked away.

I meandered up to my room and lay down. My dad rapped on the door then opened it. He sat down on the end of my bed, stood up again, shut the door, and then sat down a second time. "How goes the month?"

"Good," I admitted.

"Are you making any headway?"

I thought about how I'd just realized I expected to be with Alex every Thanksgiving and said, "Yes, I think so."

"Keep it up. I've come to recruit. We're drowning in dishes. Can you dry?"

"You two have already done so much. You should leave it to me."

"It will be done in no time with three of us."

To my relief, they didn't talk to me at all about Alex. We worked in companionable silence. Within twenty minutes, there was no remaining proof that Thanksgiving had happened.

* * *

I thrashed in bed, struggling against the blankets. I woke up with tears running into my ears. The dream had been hideous. Alex had been on a boat. I'd been on a dock, but I'd waited too long and the boat had pulled away. I'd jumped into the harbor and swum, trying to catch up to him. Alex had watched me for a while, but then he'd lost interest and turned away.

Cheerful yellow light spilled into my room. I jumped out of bed. I had to talk to my father. I ran downstairs to the kitchen, where my mother was reading the paper. "Where's Dad?"

"Out back putting up lights." Every year since I could remember, my dad had decorated our backyard with Christmas lights. He insisted it cheered the few neighbors who saw it. I think he loved the lights so much that the front yard wasn't a big enough canvas, but I was careful to keep my opinions to myself. I slipped my mother's garden clogs on and grabbed the first coat I could find. I was halfway across the backyard when I heard, "Jana."

I spun around to see Alex following me. "Well, you're up early," I said.

"It's not that early." He walked to me but stopped several paces away. I could feel something wrong in the air. "I'm taking Elise home today."

I let the words roll around in my mind. *Elise, but not me?* "Oh, so soon?"

"It's time for us to go. I want you to stay here." I stumbled backward but managed to stay upright. He took a few more steps toward me. "It's a good place for you to *think*. You can come home when you're ready . . . for more."

It took me a moment to realize the full meaning behind his words. I wasn't welcome at home until I would make the commitment to marry him. He turned to leave. In a panic I asked, "Why are you going?"

"Jana," he was still facing away from me, "do you love me?"

"Yes, you know I do."

He turned and looked at me. "Then I'm going home to wait, because I've never met anyone as painfully honest as you, and it's only a matter of time until you start being honest with yourself. I hope I'll see you soon." He turned slightly to the large pine behind me. "Stan," he said in farewell.

The tree responded in kind. "Alex." Then he was gone.

Tears ran down my face. "Alex," I said too quietly for anyone to hear. When I regained some of my composure, I rounded the tree. My father was sitting on a cast-iron bench, pulling nets of lights out of a plastic tote. I sat beside him, too stunned to speak.

"You see these? Aren't they great? Look at that, all those lights on one net, no walking back and forth to string 'em up. I just drape them over like so. It's like wrapping a baby in a blanket. Here, take this." He handed me an edge of a square piece of netting. He plugged it into an extension cord, and the lights blinked on. My heart was growing tighter by the second. I was sure it would implode any moment. *Alex actually left me here.*

My father continued. "Genius thing, the net." I wondered if he was rambling to distract me. "You can catch things, fish, bears, you name it. But if your net has a hole, the fish is going to swim right through. Look at these intersections." I tried to humor him and focus my eyes. "A good net has strong links." He tugged on the net. "People come to me all the time asking, 'Stan, if these ancestors are divorced,' or 'This cousin remarried and had these children after being sealed to the first man,' or, well, they come up with all sorts of problems . . . It bothers people when things aren't tidy, aren't easy. It's a common concern, how things work out in the end. It's normal to be concerned. You have to give it over to faith." He ran his fingers along the lines of the net, stopping every now and then to twist a bulb. "The folly of their thoughts is they think they're sealing *their* families together. They want to do it right . . ." He looked at me, blue eyes piercing. "Jana, they're not sealing *their* families at all. They are sealing together the family of God. It's *His* family. The sealings, like these intersections, make strong connecting points until, in the end, it's like a net that catches everyone. You could see how that could catch everyone, couldn't you? You could see how God wants His family sealed together forever, just like we want our families sealed together forever. He loves His children." I nodded. "So it doesn't matter if Cousin Ted was divorced twice and married Aunt Frieda in the end anyway. What matters is . . . what's at issue is, was this son of God sealed by the priesthood to his father and mother and so on. Is he secure in the net? Alex's will be a stronger intersection, that's for sure, but it will catch everyone, won't it?"

Somehow my father had taken my very personalized central concern and turned it into something bigger than me, Alex, or Vanessa, for that matter. *Sealing together the family of God.* I had goose bumps that weren't from wearing silk pajama pants outside in November. My chest warmed, and I looked at the blue morning sky and thanked Heavenly Father. Months of worry evaporated in that one thought. I knew what I had to do. I stood up. "I'm going home." He smiled and stood to hug me. "Thank you, Dad."

"That's my girl."

When I walked into the kitchen, my mother didn't look up when she said, "I packed your bag. There's a change of clothes on the bed."

I pulled the newspaper down to the table and hugged her.

I kissed her on the cheek. "Thank you, Mom. I love you."

She picked the paper up like this happened every day and said, "I love you too. Don't forget to call."

* * *

I waved good-bye to my father and walked into the airport. I stopped in my tracks as soon as I was through the doors. The ticket counter had long lines. I wasn't sure I could just waltz up and buy a ticket. I'd never done it before. I looked around, pausing to watch people around me, then swept my eyes back to the ticket counters. In that one sweep, I caught the striking contrast of a white scarf on a black wool overcoat. Alex and Elise were sitting on a bench by the escalators. I ran to them. Alex watched me calmly. I stood over them for a moment then sat down beside him, dropping my carry-on to the floor.

"That didn't take as long as I thought it would." Alex sounded casual.

"Are you waiting for your flight?" I asked as though my being there didn't mean anything. I tried to hide my ragged breathing.

"We have an hour to kill."

"Three tickets?" I asked.

"Yes." He bent over and put his face in his hands for a moment. When he looked up, there were tears in his eyes. "Three tickets."

I hugged him as tightly as I could, then I pulled Elise to me and held them both for a long time.

* * *

Elise and I stood on the rocky shore, tossing pebbles into an uncaring ocean. She studied a pebble in her hand. "It's not as fun as a lake. You can't even see the ripples here," she complained. She sat down on a rock and started arranging stones around her in a circle.

The day was warm for November and promised that a storm would roll in later that night. Alex leaned against an outcropping of large boulders, watching us. He motioned with his finger for me to join him. I carefully navigated the rocks to stand by him. He caught me by the waist and lifted me onto one of the boulders so I was sitting, looking down at him. "Elise, psst, come here," he called.

She left her circle and danced over the rocks that had just threatened to trip me. Alex put an arm around her then pulled a small black box out of his pocket. I gasped and covered my mouth.

"Jana Barrowman, will you marry us?" they asked at the same time. They must have rehearsed it because the timing was perfect.

I leapt down into Alex's arms. "Yes!"

He laughed so loud I was sure anyone on the beach would have heard it.

Elise started running around us. His hand was shaking as he placed the simple ring I'd chosen on my finger. Then he kissed my hand and sighed in relief.

We walked back and forth along a stretch of beach while Elise built stone fairy houses. After a while, we sat on the boulders near her and watched the sunset. As the wind blew my hair, the sun kissed Elise's golden brown locks, and the orange sky lit Alex's face, I was sure I'd never had a more perfect moment in my life.

CHAPTER 21
About Time

THE PHOTOGRAPHER CLICKED THROUGH THE photos on her camera screen. She handed Alex her card and promised she'd contact us before the end of the week to show us the prints. We decided it would be better to give the press engagement pictures instead of having them hound us. Alex was smiling when she left.

I sat down on the sofa and peeled the itchy cardigan off. Alex sat down on the coffee table across from me. "How do you want to do this?"

"Do what?"

"Well, as I see it, we have several choices. We can wait the year to be married in the temple. I'm sorry I didn't find the gospel sooner, but that's just how things fell into place. We can have a secular ceremony and then be sealed in the temple in a year, a year after the ceremony."

I twisted the ring on my finger. "Before I say, tell me what you want."

"First, I want you to be happy. It would be easier on me if we were married sooner than later, but I'll understand if you want to wait for the temple. You've been counting on a temple marriage all your life. I'm willing to wait if you need to."

I rubbed my eyes. It would be a relief to be married and put all the hard choices behind us. "I don't know. A year is a long time, but it's hard for me to imagine a civil ceremony. We could have a civil ceremony and hold off on a reception until we're sealed."

"Because just getting married isn't something to celebrate?" He didn't sound bitter or angry.

"It's seems odd, throwing a party for something so temporary. I mean, compared to the eternal marriage thing, a regular ceremony . . ." I shrugged.

"Hmm." He studied the carpet. He sat down next to me and took my hand. "When we get married, it will be something to celebrate. I can wait a year to see you happy."

I didn't know if I was relieved or sad. *A year.* It seemed like forever. I scooted closer to him. So much could happen in a year. I thought about what Rachel had told me. He was afraid I'd die before we were married, and then he'd never have me forever. I studied his face. The crow's feet I loved were smooth. He looked resigned but not altogether unhappy. What was a year when it secured an eternity? I sighed heavily. "I guess we'll wait, then."

* * *

April carried a dustpan past me to the front porch. "You don't want to know what I found under the kitchen sink."

"Another dead mouse?" I asked. "I guess you'd get those out here more than in the city." I pushed the roller up the side of the paint can to catch the drips. We had lit a fire in the sitting room fireplace, and the room overflowed with the rich smell of camping.

"You missed a spot." April was wearing a bandana around her gray hair and was holding a broom. "Again, I ask, why are you doing this yourself when Money Bags was so willing to pay to have someone else do it?"

"It makes it feel more like it's mine." Alex said we could hire a painter, but I was being stubborn. "Painting is simple, and I have a lot of free time since Scott hired more help." The irony hit me as I pushed the roller against the wall of the house I'd promised I'd never live in. In a few weeks, we'd be married. The year had flown, working at Shallots. But now I found myself scrambling to fill my free time. We'd finished all the preparations for the reception weeks ago.

"Speak of the devil." April was looking through the naked front window.

Alex burst through the door and headed straight for me, wearing a large smile. October leaves floated in behind him. April frowned.

"Don't touch"—I tried to warn him, but it was too late. He was holding me close and cutting off my sentence in a kiss. I struggled away—"me. You'll get paint on your tie. Oh, Alex, that was my favorite one too."

He loosened it and pulled it over his head. "You can have it, then." He turned to April and gave her a hug. "Did you find anything fun? Trunks in the attic?"

April looked up at him. "And how are we short people supposed to reach the attic?"

Alex laughed. I headed for the kitchen, determined to wash the splotch of paint from the silk before it set in.

He called after me, "Let's pack up. I've come to gather my women so we can eat. I'm taking Scott to California tonight to meet some suppliers. If we hustle, I can make an earlier flight."

"Ugh, I'll have to rinse out the brushes. It's going to be awhile."

He appeared in the doorway with the brushes and a pan. "Not so. Where are the bags?"

"Alex, you're going to get paint all over your clothes."

"Give me some credit."

I held up the tie.

"It came out, didn't it? Now, find me some bags." I pulled out some garbage bags, and he began wrapping the brushes and roller in them. I was happy to see he'd at least rolled up his sleeves. He covered the paint pan. "Voilà, all wet and ready for the next job. I wouldn't wait too many days though. I used to do this all the time. Did I ever tell you about the stint I did texturing ceilings in high school?"

"No, but you're sure I can just leave them?"

"If you come back and they're rock hard, you can buy more."

* * *

At lunch April folded her napkin and laid it across her plate. "So how does this sealing work with Vanessa?"

Alex and I looked awkwardly at one another. I thought we should seal him and Elise to Vanessa before we were sealed. I even wanted it on the same day. He disagreed. It was really his choice, so I was giving him his way. He wanted our marriage to be special and separate. We'd plowed through more than one bucket of burnt almond fudge ice cream agreeing to disagree about it.

Alex dabbed his lips and set down his napkin. "I'll be sealed to Jana first; then on Elise's next birthday, Elise and I will be sealed to Vanessa."

April pointed a finger with a chunky ring on it at me. "You should have married him months ago. The worst day married is—"

"Better than the best day single." We recited together.

Alex put his hand over mine. "But some things are worth waiting for."

April shrugged then turned to Alex. "Then it's your own fault for not being baptized the moment you saw her."

Alex and I laughed long and hard. Tiny crow's feet stretched near his eyes when he smiled at April. "That it is. That it is." He sounded just like my father.

CHAPTER 22
Thornless Roses

Elise giggled as she rubbed her hair with white balloons. "I'm Electro Head!" Her static hair reached out to tickle the ceiling. The minivan smelled like latex. We'd bought as many balloons as we could fit in the van and still see out some windows.

"Sweetie, if I have to do your hair one more time today, I'm going to have a fit. Don't pop the balloons on the barrette." She looked like a fuzzy haired angel in her white dress. Sequins sparkled on the bodice.

Alex pulled over near the hill. He opened the doors for us, and I handed balloons out to him. Elise was impatient, but I was determined not to pop any. My simple, white, calf-length dress made it necessary to take small steps. My extended stomach made balancing on my heels tricky. I kicked them off near the bottom of the hill. The bench overlooked a meadow below. It was full of various statues and markers. Alex wore a suit, and when I looked over at him, he was checking each balloon to make sure it had a little note card attached to it. We'd spent all morning writing notes to Vanessa before going to the temple. Elise went a little crazy with the hole punch, so several cards had numerous holes. She was careful not to punch over the words.

Alex carried a white rose.

"I'm not sure a balloon is going to be able to lift the rose," I said.

"Who said anything about using just one balloon?" He handed me seven balloons, and he kept five. He tied them together and started fastening the rose to them.

"Give me the rose." I held out my hand. He didn't move. "Trust me." He handed it over. I peeled the thorns off of it and handed it back.

"Good thinking."

"Now?" Elise asked.

"Why don't we pray first?" Alex looked around. We were alone. He had us sit down on the bench. A balloon began to float away. Alex caught it in his free hand and handed it back to Elise. He sat beside us and prayed, the rustle of balloons in the background. "Our Father which art in heaven, we come before Thee, grateful this day for the abundant blessings that Thou hast given us. We ask Thy blessing to be upon this, our eternal family," he laid a hand softly on my stomach, "that we will be able to rear our children in peace and happiness. We thank Thee for Vanessa and thank Thee that we have, all of us, been sealed up unto Thee. Please help her get these messages." He ended the prayer, and we stood.

"Now?" Elise asked impatiently.

"Now," Alex confirmed.

Elise let her balloons go one by one. Alex let his go. They easily carried the rose skyward. I handed Elise six of mine, and she continued to let them go one at a time. Finally, I let my single balloon fly. The note simply said, "Thank you." Vanessa had given me the two most important people in the world, and I wanted her to know I was grateful. Alex pulled me into his arms and kissed me while Elise stood on the bench, watching the balloons float higher.

He stroked my cheek. "My abundant blessing."

"I'm abundant, all right," I said, patting my stomach.

He put his hand on my stomach again, something he did several times an hour, and said, "Born in the covenant, the first one in my family to be born into the covenant."

I nuzzled into his embrace. "I love you, Mr. Steadman."

"I love you, Mrs. Steadman."

A breeze carried the balloons higher and scattered them. Elise watched until she couldn't discern the white dots in the sky. "Let's go eat. Grandma Abby said she had a gift for me. I want to see it."

Alex ruffled her hair. We held hands as we walked down the hill. I looked back one last time and whispered, "Thank you."

A breeze scented with pine needles answered, and I smiled.

ABOUT THE AUTHOR

SHERYL C. S. JOHNSON HAILS from West Jordan, Utah, where she loved sleeping in the backyard with her mother and counting stars. She graduated from Westminster College with a degree in finance, during which time she converted to the Church. She owns the digital scrapbook website GrannyEnchanted.com and loves writing fiction. She now lives with her favorite people in a wind tunnel, where she is blown back and forth between Ute and Cougar fans.